Applause for Herman W

A HOLE IN TEXAS

"It is refreshing and salutary to encounter a novel by a writer who wants to remind us that one of the features that characterizes a great nation and ensures its continuing greatness is its commitment to big projects, in this case, scientific research. *A Hole in Texas* is an entertaining, eminently readable novel that sheds light on what happens when politicians vote to scrap projects in basic science. . . . Although this novel broaches some fairly disturbing matters, a certain lightness of tone — a kind of coziness — prevails."

— Merle Rubin, *Los Angeles Times Book Review*

"Wouk spins a crackling yarn and writes with an enduring vigor that whippersnappers might envy." — Janet Maslin, *New York Times*

"A quick read that serves double duty as an entertaining contemporary romp and a gently compelling argument for taking the Superconducting Super Collider out of mothballs."

— Mike Shea, *Texas Monthly*

"An engaging novel. . . . *A Hole in Texas* offers a refreshing contrast with the treatments of mad scientists that are so abundant in literature and popular culture. . . . Wouk accurately depicts science as an often interactive and collegial enterprise."

— Jay M. Pasachoff, *Science*

"Ingenious. Absolutely ingenious." — *Kirkus Reviews* (starred review)

"A light, sprightly story about lost love, high-energy physics, and the machinations of Washington. . . . Playful, thoughtful, and passionate, *A Hole in Texas* will charm fans with its companionable warmth and wry humor." — *Publishers Weekly*

"Mr. Wouk is known for the thoroughness of his research and the old-fashioned skill with which he spins a yarn. *A Hole in Texas* is no exception. Even readers with the haziest sense of recent developments in subatomic physics or the workings of congressional subcommittees will be enlightened as well as entertained." — *Economist*

"Enjoyable. . . . A lively and entertaining novel."

— Stuart Shiffman, Bookreporter.com

Books by Herman Wouk

Novels

Aurora Dawn

City Boy

The Caine Mutiny

Marjorie Morningstar

Youngblood Hawke

Don't Stop the Carnival

The Winds of War

War and Remembrance

Inside, Outside

The Hope

The Glory

A Hole in Texas

Plays

The Traitor

The Caine Mutiny Court-Martial

Nature's Way

Nonfiction

This Is My God

The Will to Live On

A HOLE IN TEXAS

A NOVEL

HERMAN WOUK

BACK BAY BOOKS
Little, Brown and Company
New York Boston

Back Bay Books / Little, Brown and Company
Time Warner Book Group
1271 Avenue of the Americas, New York, NY 10020
Visit our Web site at www.twbookmark.com

Originally published in hardcover by Little, Brown and Company, April 2004
First Back Bay paperback edition, June 2005

Library of Congress Cataloging-in-Publication Data

Wouk, Herman.
A hole in Texas : a novel / Herman Wouk. — 1st ed.
p. cm.
ISBN 0-316-52590-1 (hc) / 0-316-01085-5 (pb)
I. Title.
PS3545.O98H65 2004
813'.54 — dc22 2003020148

10 9 8 7 6 5 4 3 2 1

Q-FF

Designed by Meryl Sussman Levavi/Digitext

Printed in the United States of America

To my brother

Victor Wouk, PhD,

California Institute of Technology '42

with admiration and love

A HOLE IN TEXAS

❦

It could probably be shown by facts and figures that there is no distinctly native American criminal class except Congress.

— Mark Twain

AUTHOR'S NOTE

At a rough guess, 99.9999 percent of all Americans don't know what the hell a Higgs boson is. Nevertheless, when Congress voted several billion dollars to fund a search for the thing, American taxpayers footed the bill. Then, when this gargantuan project, the Superconducting Super Collider — the largest basic science project in world history — was well under way, Congress abruptly pulled the plug, killed the project, and voted another billion dollars just to close it down. That left some two thousand particle physicists high, dry, and unemployed on a forlorn plain outside Dallas, and these scientists were not used to such career jolts, or in blunter language, such jerking around. Ever since coming up with the atomic and hydrogen bombs, they had been the pampered darlings of Congress. But all that suddenly and rudely ended. The sole residue of their miscarried quest for the Higgs boson was a hole in Texas, an enormous abandoned Hole.

It's still there.

1. THE PARTICLE PHYSICIST

We all have bad days, and Dr. Guy Carpenter awoke to rain drumming on gray windows, with a qualm in his gut about what this drab day might bring. Late at night an e-mail had come in, summoning him to an urgent morning meeting at the Jet Propulsion Lab with no reason given, an ill omen indeed to a survivor of the abort on the Texas plain. He was in pajamas at the desk in his den, gnawing at a slice of Swiss cheese on sourdough bread as he marked up a gloomy cost estimate of new space telescopes, when his wife burst in, her long black hair hanging in wet tangled ringlets, her soaked nightgown clinging transparently to her slim body. "Sweeney got out," she barked.

"No! How, this time?"

"I took out the trash, *that's* how. They collect it Wednesday at seven, or have you forgotten? It's raining buckets, I hurried, I left the screen door unlatched, and the bastard slipped out. I tried to catch him and got drenched."

"I'll find him."

"Don't you have that meeting at seven-thirty? I'm wet through and stark naked, as you see, or I'd look for him."

"No problem. Sorry about the trash."

Dr. Carpenter threw on a raincoat and plodded out barefoot on slippery grass. The downpour was helpful. Sweeney hated the wet, so he would be holed up in some dry spot of the backyard instead of hightailing it over the fence for a major chase, and if that failed, a general neighborhood alarm. Penny's obsession for keeping her cat indoors was a given of their marriage. Wonderful wife, Penny, with a human weakness or two such as a slight streak of jealousy and an unarguable dogma that outside cats were short-lived. Sweeney, a resourceful Siamese, ignored her for a doting fool, he knew he would never die, and he lay in wait for any chance to get out.

Poking here and there, Carpenter spied the bedraggled creature under a padded lounge chair. *Okay, Sweeney!* He crouched to grab the beast. Sweeney inched rearward just beyond his grasp, blinking at him. Standard cat maneuver, but this was no time for such foolery, so Carpenter kicked the chair aside and pounced on the cat. With an electric stab of pain, his back went out. Three weeks of slow healing, shot in an instant! He had pulled a muscle playing tennis, with an overhand smash at set point plunk into the net; and now this, no tennis for at least another three weeks. Standard Carpenter performance, he thought, clutching at his throbbing back. Guy's colleagues regarded him as a top man in high-energy physics, his wife Penny adored him when he remembered to take out the trash, but he had a downbeat opinion of Dr. Guy Carpenter, due to a perfectionist bent always nagging at his self-esteem.

"Bad cat," Penny said as he brought Sweeney in, meowing in outrage. Muffled in a bathrobe, she was drying her hair. "Good Lord, you're drowned. I hope you didn't catch your death. The Project Scientist phoned in a huge tizzy —"

"Call her back, say I'm on my way."

Wincing at each move, he dressed, limped out to the garage, and eased himself into his car. When he pressed the garage-door opener, nothing happened. What now? Low battery? He lurched to Penny's car and tried her remote. It did not work, either. The wall button goosed the door to rattle upward a foot, then it halted. He had never before tried using the manual lift. How did it work, exactly? He grasped the thick rough cord in both hands and with excruciating pain hauled the screeching door halfway up, where it stuck. His lower back aflame, pulsating, he called the Project Scientist on his cell phone to beg off from the meeting.

She was unsympathetic. “Guy, take a couple of Aleves. Peter’s on his way. Why don’t I alert him to pick you up? You’ve *got* to be here.”

“Why me, Ottoline? I’m crippled, I tell you —”

“You know more about the Superconducting Super Collider than anyone here.”

“The Super Collider? So what? It was killed back in ’93. It’s dead and forgotten.”

“Not anymore.”

“How’s that? For crying out loud, Ottoline, *what’s up?*”

“Not over the phone. I’ll page Peter and see you in a bit.”

Penny said, “Aleve, my foot,” and gave him two of her migraine capsules. “These will do the trick.”

“Codeine? I’ll be a zombie,” he protested, downing them.

“All the better. Don’t commit yourself to anything involving colliders.”

“Not with a knife at my throat.”

Soft soothing warmth gradually suffused his back as he waited for Peter Braunstein. Memories flooded him, memories long suppressed, released and made dreamily vivid by the opiate. Those years in alien Texas, years of working his heart out on that stupendous machine; years of the greatest fun and challenge in his life, and the worst frustration! He knew too much, that was the trouble. The monster might well have worked, but then again, every one of those ten thousand supermagnets had to function flawlessly, and they were his responsibility. He had fought in vain for more time, more careful designing, more testing. Hurry, hurry, national prestige at stake, get the thing going, then see! That was the word from on high, with unsubtle slurs about his foot-dragging —

"Guy?" Peter Braunstein on the cell phone. "I'm calling from my car. You okay?"

"I'll live. What the devil's going on, Peter?"

"I just asked Ottoline when she called me about you. She said, '*Budget,*' and hung up. Be right there."

Budget . . . The haunt of modern science . . . The delayed-action bomb that had sunk the SSC! The NASA budget review in Congress happened every year around this time. NASA supported the Jet Propulsion Lab, JPL supported the Terrestrial Planet Finder, and that project was Ottoline's baby, so no doubt that was why she was on edge. Still, why the urgency? Their project had never yet run into a money problem. The Terrestrial Planet Finder was part of NASA's Origins Program, which was exploring two grand questions about human existence:

(1) Are we alone? (2) Where did we come from?

A tall order, a noble endeavor, and their part of it was to search for signs of life on planets circling remote stars. The new space telescopes, if they could get the budget for them, would go a long way toward solving these riddles . . .

Honk, honk outside the garage. Stooping to pass under the half-raised door was pleasantly painless. Guy's burly bearded tennis partner, a Cornell classmate and now an eminent astrophysicist, helped him into the high front seat of a battered camper. It was Peter Braunstein who, after the Texas debacle, had recruited Guy for the Jet Propulsion Laboratory. He said as he drove, "Well, let's hope it's NASA that's getting the heat, not our project."

"Peter, we're small potatoes."

"We're *NASA* small potatoes, Guy. NASA's been in trouble ever since the last Americans flew off the moon, you know that. No one big mission, a grab bag of dicey missions like ours, the media just yawn at the marvelous leaps ahead in space science, and every now and then a disaster throws the whole nervous bureaucracy into shock —"

"Go ahead, cheer me up," said Carpenter. He was happy at JPL, proud of his work on the Planet Finder, and he tried not to think beyond his day-to-day work. For a high-energy physicist, relocating yet again at his age would be murder.

"Oh, Ottoline's the worrier. I think we'll be okay. It's just that Congress is muttering more and more every year about money for NASA. Martian landscapes and floating astronauts are getting to be old stuff, Guy. Where's the payoff?"

"A new more powerful bomb, you mean?" said Guy Carpenter. "Contact with aliens, maybe?"

"Something," said Braunstein, swinging the car into the JPL parking lot.

2. THE CRISIS

Here we go," said the Project Scientist as Guy Carpenter shuffled into her bleak windowless office, its gray-painted walls lined with discouraged greenery in long boxes. Peter Braunstein came in behind him. "Feeling better, Guy?"

"Passable." His back was quite numb now, his brain thickly fogged by codeine.

"Okay, then. Tell them, Rafe."

Lounging on a hard chair, his feet up on another chair, was the System Engineer, a short broad-shouldered Englishman in jeans and an old sweater. "Right. Gentlemen, the Chinese have got the Higgs boson."

"What?" Braunstein all but yelled. Carpenter simply stared.

"You heard me."

"The *CHINESE?*" said Carpenter.

Rafe chuckled, glancing at the Project Scientist. "The Chinese."

"Ah, jokes." Carpenter sounded relieved.

"You wish!" Ottoline's face hardened. "That's how I reacted at first. It's very serious."

"Ottoline, it's inconceivable."

"You're here to tell us why," she said, "and you'd better be convincing."

"Oh, look, they haven't got the machines, they don't begin to have the technology — why, even the Europeans at CERN, when they shut down for an upgrade, admitted they were five years away from getting the Higgs." He shook his head in disbelief. "The *Chinese?*"

"Stop saying that," snarled the Project Scientist. "Yes, the Chinese!" Dr. Ottoline Porson was a big blonde in her fifties, with a huge behind, and gray streaks in her hair. She was one of America's great astronomers. "Raphael knows what he's talking about. Go on, Rafe."

"I'm expecting a fax from London any minute," said the System Engineer. "I got a call last night — late morning over there — and I phoned Ottoline straight off —"

"I took that call in the bathtub," she put in. "I slipped in my hurry to get out and e-mail you fellows, darn near broke my neck —"

Carpenter demanded of the System Engineer, "Who called you?"

"Staff writer at *Nature,* to tell me that something bloody hot was in the wind."

"Come on, Rafe." A leak from the leading science journal in the world was a sobering surprise. "Are you saying that you have a mole at *Nature?*"

Raphael's grin was a shade smug. "Female mole. Former girlfriend, truth to tell. Good science writer. We're still on excellent terms. She's the editor's girlfriend now."

"And she reported *what?*"

"An article has come in from the Chinese, so sensational that *Nature* is still debating whether to run it."

Slumped in his chair, Guy Carpenter said slowly, "Is there coffee around? I'm not up to speed here —"

Peter Braunstein jumped up. "Coming, Guy."

"Thanks, Pete . . . Ottoline, where shall I begin? They have no industrial infrastructure for such an effort. Not by miles. No scientists of outstanding calibre. Technicians by the horde, yes, but —"

"They've made ICBMs," interrupted Ottoline. "They've exploded H-bombs."

"Political stunts," said Guy, "jump-started by the Soviets, when they were still friendly."

"Wait, wait," said Rafe. "You worked on an accelerator in China yourself, didn't you?"

"Years ago. Primitive cyclotron. Department of Energy sent me over after Mao died, part of a detente that didn't last. Fascinating country, beguiling people, but *backward?* Beijing was a city on bicycles."

"That's changed," said Ottoline. "A lot has changed."

Braunstein returned with the coffee. "Rafe, the fax in your office is chattering."

"Here we go." The Englishman hurried out.

Ottoline said, "Peter, Guy claims they don't have the physicists to do the job."

"I wouldn't say that." Braunstein scratched his beard. "Just offhand, Guy, how about Liu Layu?"

"We know where Liu Layu is," said Guy. "He's heading their nuclear-weapons program."

"You *think* we know where he is," said Ottoline. "You're talking about China, remember."

"Then there's Wendy," said Braunstein.

"We know where she is too," said Guy.

The Project Scientist shifted in her chair to look at Guy. "Wendy?"

"Wen Mei Li. She's been kicked upstairs from high-energy physics to some big job in their Science and Energy Ministry. Or whatever they call it. She was in our physics program at Cornell."

"Absolutely brilliant," said Peter, looking to Carpenter. "Queen of the campus in those Chinese dresses of hers, with physics majors trailing her like baby ducks — why, even Professor Rocovsky had a case on her — but argumentative, prudish, never drank anything but water. She worked on the Stanford accelerator for a while, then went back to China —"

"Was she really that pretty?" asked the Project Scientist.

The hot strong coffee was clearing Guy's head. "Look, Ottoline, are you regarding this as an emergency?"

"If *Nature* prints the article, yes indeed."

"For our project?"

"Obviously."

"Nothing's obvious to me this morning. Explain why."

"Guy, you worked on the Super Collider —"

"Yes, five and a half years of my life down the drain. So?"

"Could it be revived?"

Sipping coffee, Guy Carpenter took a long pause before answering. "Now listen, Ottoline, anything can be done, given the budget. The tunnel is still there in Texas, if that's what you're asking. About eighteen miles of it, and huge deserted buildings, and thousands of computers, and untold miles and *miles* of pipes and wires and magnets. If they haven't been cannibalized or looted, that is. I've never been back. It was a tragedy, a catastrophe, a scientific *Titanic*. The Superconducting Super Collider is killed, murdered by Congress, gone forever. To get it going again might take eight to ten billion dollars, and even then —"

"*'Anything can be done, given the budget,'*" she broke in. "Suppose it's true? Suppose the Chinese have brought off an underground Sputnik? You weren't here when I had to go before Congress on the Space Telescope because the mirror failed —"

"You did? But the astronauts fixed it, it's a glorious success, it's opening up the universe —"

"Fixing it took two years, Guy. The media staged a circus over the fuzzy mirror, and Congress had fits. You can't predict *what* Congress will do when something like this surfaces and the media get hold of it. There's only so much money for science every year, and —"

"Here you are, Ottoline." Rafe strode in with a thick sheaf of paper. "The whole article. There's a letter coming through too." He darted out again.

She peered at the top page. *"Evidence of Higgs Field Particle Detection —"*

"Authors?" Guy asked.

She held the sheaf up to her eyes, removed her glasses, and squinted. "*Wen Mei Li* — aha, there's your Wendy, gentlemen, leading off — *Wu Kwang, Zhao Dapeng, Liu Layu* —"

"Liu Layu also!" exclaimed Peter Braunstein.

Ottoline said, "This is a very poor fax. Blotchy. *V. Abramovitch, I. Gorin.* Goodness me, two Russians. That's the lot."

"How about it, Guy?" said Braunstein. "Wendy *and* Layu, plus a couple of Russkis. Interesting, would you say?"

Carpenter cleared his throat and spoke hoarsely. "Okay, the Russians have been ahead on titanium and niobium, we know that —"

The Englishman came back, waving a paper. "Well, it's a cliff-hanger. They're holding up the first August issue, and the editorial board is in special session right now, six in the evening in London. My lass will ring me when she hears something —"

"Whatever they decide," Ottoline said, "I can see we're already in trouble. This article" — she rattled the papers — "must have substance, and let's even say they reject it. *Nature* once rejected an article by Fermi, you know. Someone here will grab it. *American Scientist, Physics Today* —"

"That's for sure," said Braunstein, "or *Science* —"

Ottoline's voice went higher. "Someone! A stampede could start in Congress to revive the Super Collider, and *that* could gulp half of all science funding. In which case —"

"You've lost me, Ottoline," interrupted the Englishman. "If the Chinese have already done it, where's the sense?"

"I'm not talking sense, Rafe, I'm talking American politicians, press, and above all television," said the Project Scientist. "And I'm talking budget. We're not high on NASA's mission chart, and —"

"As far as that goes," interposed Braunstein, "we're sucking hind tit."

Ottoline gave him an arid smile. "Thank you, Peter, for defining the parameters —"

"Whatever happens," said Guy, "we must have the orbiting telescopes, Ottoline, or the whole thing folds up —"

"No argument," said Ottoline. "Therefore I'd like a memo from each of you on a possible long stretch-out of funding —"

The telephone rang. Rafe reached to snatch it. "Right, puss, what's the word?" He nodded several times, glancing around somberly at the others, and hung up. "*Nature* is pulling two articles from the first August issue and featuring the Chinese bombshell on the cover."

"Fat's in the fire," said Braunstein.

"This meeting is over," said the Project Scientist. "Let me have those stretch-out memos, gentlemen, pronto."

"One thing, Ottoline, about that fax," said Guy, using his arms to push himself out of his chair. "Fax a copy right away to Rocovsky."

"Rocovsky? His eyes aren't that good. It's hardly legible."

"He'll decipher it."

Braunstein and Carpenter walked back to the camper in a light drizzle. "So, you're really limping," the astrophysicist said. "No tennis again for a while."

"Guess not, Peter, and no volleyball tonight, that's for sure."

"Bummer. Caltech will cream us, then." A team of faculty members played Jet Propulsion scientists once a year, at the birthday barbecue of a Caltech trustee on the lawn of his mansion. "Climb in, I'll take you home."

"Just to the mall, Saks entrance, Peter. I'll get a cab from there."

Braunstein glanced at him. "Saks?"

"Bit of shopping."

When Braunstein's camper left the mall, Guy Carpenter walked straight through Saks to a small dark post-office branch at the other entrance. There he filled out a form for relinquishing a PO box, and checked the box one last time. To his great surprise there was a letter, the first in half a year or more. Flimsy bluish paper, Chinese stamps. He took the letter to a window, read it slowly over and over, then tore it up into a trash basket. At a wooden stand-up desk he scrawled a long reply, mailed it, and turned in the form with the key.

When he got into the taxi, his back gave him a nasty twinge. Bad day. Bad, bad day. And far from over.

3. THE GAME

Bellows of laughter, shouted insults, and sporadic cheers rose from the guests crowding around the raucous moonlight volleyball game. Guy Carpenter looked on a bit apart, sidelined and silent amid drifting smells of fresh-cut grass and barbecued meat. In other years he had starred among these aging academics, a newcomer taller and faster than the rest, bounding around with white hair flying, making kills even from the baseline. Whacking at a ball — handball, tennis ball, volleyball, any ball, even a shuttlecock — did him good. He was an outstanding physicist, and he knew it; he also knew that physics was a game as well as a science, a blood sport played for the Nobel, in which he rated himself a clear cut or two below a Gell-Mann or a Rubbia. He blew off a fierce unreconciled head of competitive steam by slamming balls.

Piano music was starting up in the house. Penny already? Things must be dull in there. He went through open patio doors to the living room, where some guests chattered over plates of food and others clustered at the piano. Penny rippled a finish to "I Got Rhythm," and with a private little grin at him began to play and sing in a husky contralto.

Busted flat in Baton Rouge
Waiting for a train —

She seldom played nowadays, since Dinah had erupted into their lives. For a woman of her age with a grown son, a new baby was a harassing handful. The older guests at the piano sang along, and Guy joined in, smiling back at her.

But I'd trade all my tomorrows, Lord, for just one yesterday
Of holding Bobby's body close to mine. . . .
Da da da da da da da
Me and Bobby McGee . . .

⚛

Small summertime party at somebody's house in a fancy part of Ithaca . . .

Collegiate crowd. Girl in a blue-and-white halter dress at the piano, singing and playing "Bobbie McGee" with more than a touch of Janis Joplin. Afterward Guy approaches her at the punch bowl. An undergraduate, by the look of her, and he is prematurely gray, but what the hell . . .

"That was nice, that 'Bobbie McGee.'"

"Thanks."

"You're a student?"

Mischievous bright look. "Going for my master's in microbiology. You?"

"Physics department."

"Professor?"

Ouch. The gray hair. "Associate. Mainly I do research."

Pause.

"My name is Guy."

"I'm Penny."

They sip punch, looking into each other's eyes. On impulse he says, "Penny for the Guy."

Her eyes boldly flash. "Mistah Kurtz, he dead."

"Wow," he says. "You read Eliot?"

"I read anything, randomly. Butterfly reader." Off she goes into the party, leaving him surprised and impressed. Only weeks later does she confess that "The Hollow Men" is the only Eliot poem she's ever read. Came on it in an anthology. Sharp cookie.

Was it cradle snatching? She was so much younger . . . eleven years . . . still, going for a master's already — "Mistah Kurtz, he dead" — *Lord, Lord, of all the vain musings! These thoughts recur whenever Penny sings "Bobbie McGee." These thoughts, and others too . . .*

Party breaking up. There she stands, looking around.

"Hi, can I take you home?"

"You sure can, thanks!" The tart smile that still enchants him. "My date ran into a girl he broke up with. They talked it over and left together. I guess he forgot me."

"You're not forgettable. He's an idiot. Where do you live?"

And that was it . . .

⚛

A hand on his shoulder. "We miss you out there, Guy. It's close." Peter Braunstein held a large stein of beer in the other hand.

"I miss the game."

"Go, Penny, go!" Peter bawled. Peter stayed out of the annual game to tank up on beer. "Say, Guy, wasn't Ottoline a tad paranoid this morning about that *Nature* article?"

"Just responsible, Pete."

"Well, maybe. And how about Wendy surfacing? Surprise, surprise."

Penny was now pounding out a deafening "Pine Top's Boogie." Guy shook his head slightly at Braunstein, who rolled his eyes and barely muttered, "Oops." At loose ends, Guy wandered back outside, feeling low, *low,* out of the game, his back giving him the devil, his livelihood once more hanging in the balance, if Ottoline was right. He fixed himself a boilermaker at the dim-lit movable bar, having learned in his worst Texas days that booze could be a friend in need, albeit a risky one. The game was tied at 12–12, when a Jet Lab player went down on the grass, groaning over a sprained ankle.

"Hey, look, there's Guy!" someone yelled as the injured man was helped away.

"Guy, come on!"

"Guy, Guy!"

Chasing down the bourbon with a last swallow of beer, he plunged into the game, making one fast point and another, disregarding the electric stings in his spine. *"Guy! Guy! Do it, Guy!"* With a leaping net shot he clinched a win, shrugged off the cheers, backslaps, and handshakes, and limped back to the bar to swallow two Aleves with more bourbon. Unwise, but it worked. His agonized back calmed down, he ate another hamburger sizzling off the grill, and his mood turned quite rosy.

As they drove home Penny too was in cheery spirits, rattling on about the people at the party, and about the letter that had come in that day from their son in Australia. John was pursuing a PhD in anthropology, studying the art of the aborigines. Now he wrote that he might take a year off in Samoa, to dig into the quiescent controversy over Margaret Mead's stuff on sex among the adolescents. Guy said that John's way of hopping from area to area of research was worrisome. It reminded him uncomfortably of himself.

"If he does as well in his field as you've in yours," Penny remarked, "I won't mind."

The repaired garage door was working smoothly again. As she drove in and it closed behind them, she inquired, "Where and how did Wendy surface?"

Penny, all over! Sixth sense, eyes in back of her head, ears like a wildcat. He explained baldly about the *Nature* article. She nodded and said nothing more.

"Hi, everything's okay," the babysitter said over her shoulder, watching television. "Not a peep out of Dinah, she's a little angel." On the screen, corpses were rising out of a graveyard to ghastly music.

"What about Sweeney?" Penny opened her purse.

"Oh, you can still hear him." She gestured toward the bathroom. "He's never stopped."

Their regular sitter was down with a virus, and this girl, on seeing Sweeney, had squealed that she wasn't staying. "I *loathe* cats, and they all love *me!*" Penny had doubled her fee and locked Sweeney in the bathroom. Four hours later, he was still scrabbling and yowling. When Penny released him he stalked out, tail up, swearing at her in blue cat language.

On Guy's answering machine in the den, a tense high-pitched voice: *"Hi, Professor Carpenter. Quentin Rossiter here,* Washington Post. *Please ring me at this number, my home, no matter what time you come in. It's urgent."*

Now what? Could the news be out already? Guy pulled up the *Nature* website on the computer. Nothing about the Chinese. This Rossiter was a young investigative journalist, Guy recalled, who had gained early laurels by exposing a Bible-thumping Senator as a transvestite . . . Guy telephoned the reporter.

"Oh, hi, Professor. Thanks a lot for returning my call. It's about this forthcoming article in Nature.*"*

"What about it?"

"These Chinese scientists, what can you tell me about them?"

"Sorry, I haven't read the article, just heard talk about it."

"Why do you suppose the Russians are involved?"

"I can't say."

"In your opinion, should America revive the Super Collider?"

"I can't speculate on that. It's pretty late here, Mr. Quentin, and —"

"That's Rossiter, Professor. Quentin Rossiter. It's nearly 4 A.M. here, sir. You woke me up, but I'm much obliged. This is a breaking story. That woman scientist, Wen Mei Li, did you know her at Cornell?"

This was a stupid mistake, thought Guy. Why on earth did I call the man? "Mr. Rossiter, I'm bone tired. Try me at the Jet Propulsion Lab in the morning. Good night."

"I'll call you there, absolutely. Sleep well."

In a housecoat and minus makeup, a pallid Penny looked into the den. "Hi. Sweeney unrolled the toilet paper down to the cardboard, yards and yards of it, and ripped it up all over the bathroom. Annoyed about something. Who was that? Not John?"

"Hardly. Someone from the *Washington Post,* about the Chinese boson."

"Good Lord. So soon? Why did he call you?"

"Those fellows know how to dig."

Penny pursed her lips. "Stay as far from this thing as you can."

"No fear."

"Now tell me again. You're going to Boston when, and for how long?"

"Sunday, back Wednesday."

"Long way for a short trip."

"That's where our telescope designers are."

"Take a hot bath for that back. I've cleaned up Sweeney's revenge."

"Thanks."

Guy stopped by the maid's room fixed up as a nursery to peek at Dinah, asleep in an orange night-light glow under a pink blanket. All Penny had ever said was, "I want a little girl to dress up." After their trying and trying for years, here was this small demanding beauty of high voltage and contrary willpower.

In water hot as he could stand it, he soaked for half an hour, his thoughts roaming idly over the day, the sound track of the evening running on and on in his mind —

Da da da da da

Me and Bobby McGee

— shifting now and again to the rowdy bachelor party at Cornell, the night before his wedding, and Peter Braunstein drunkenly twitting him by leading the others with a splashing beer mug,

Da da da da da

Me and Wen Mei Li . . .

Penny and Dinah were still asleep when he hobbled to the front door the next morning, picked up the *Los Angeles Times,* and took it to his den with a cup of coffee. Nothing much on the front page, real lull in the news for weeks — no, here was something, a small piece low on the page:

**CHINESE DISCOVER
ELUSIVE HIGGS BOSON**

He called up on the computer the front page of the *Washington Post* . . . holy cow! Quentin Rossiter's byline story below the fold spanned two columns:

**CHINESE SCIENTISTS FIND HIGGS BOSON
"ULTIMATE SECRET OF THE UNIVERSE"**

The science in the article was an ignorant mishmash, but Rossiter had the newsy points right: the female Chinese physicist, the Russians, the debate inside the *Nature* staff. At the end, a note: *See Sharon McAllister, p. 2.* Sharon McAllister was the dragon lady of the *Washington Post,* terror of Congressmen and Presidents. Anxiously Guy clicked the link to her column.

SUNSET OF A SUPERPOWER?
BY SHARON MCALLISTER

In 1993, when the House of Representatives in its collective wisdom killed the Superconducting Super Collider, Senator Bennett Johnston spoke its epitaph, saying that the decision to abandon the SSC marked the sunset of American world leadership. A mere ten years later, a global thunderclap bursts on a shamed America. The United States Congress stands convicted of lacking the moral fibre to cross a scientific threshold, the final step to understanding the universe, or to quote Stephen Hawking, to *"knowing the mind of God."* Instead China, the one coming world power on the horizon, supposedly far behind us in technology, has crossed that threshold! This fateful turn in human affairs raises questions of the highest national urgency. Who was responsible for killing the SSC? What were the motives? Was it mere blind penny-pinching folly? Was it purposeful political back-stabbing? And has Chinese espionage been at work? Most important, is a belated effort to regain our rudely shattered world preeminence — in Chinese parlance, our *face* — still conceivable?

The telephone rang on the desk and Guy grabbed it. "Ottoline? For crying out loud, it's the crack of dawn —"

"It's almost ten o'clock in Washington, D.C. You know who Myra Kadane is?"

"Myra Kadane?" He thought for a moment. "Congresswoman. Her husband got drowned scuba diving in the Virgin Islands."

"That's another one. Kadane fell off a horse in Rock Creek Park. She's on the Science, Space, and Technology Committee."

"What about her?"

"You're going to see her."

"The hell I am. When? How? Why?"

4. THE CONGRESSWOMAN

Congresswoman Kadane, a small figure in a baggy gray sweat suit, was jogging along the towpath through hot sun and leafy shade, amid a straggle of morning runners. At the two-mile marker she turned, trotted back to the footbridge over the canal, and ran through Georgetown traffic all the way to her rented side-street house. Her Guatemalan maid met her at the door with a glass of fresh-squeezed orange juice. Sitting in the living room, a briefcase on his lap, a lean dark bespectacled man said, "Morning, Myra."

"Oh, morning, Earle, what's up? Want some juice? Or coffee?"

"I'm fine." He waited until the maid went out, then zipped open the briefcase and handed her a manila envelope stamped TOP SECRET in heavy red letters. "This came in from the Armed Services Committee. I thought I'd better rush it over here. Chairman Hurtle wants you to read it at once."

"The Chinese thing again?"

"I have no clue."

She slit open the envelope and glanced through the memorandum. Vertical worry lines appeared on her forehead. "When is that professor from Pasadena due?"

"Pam should be picking him up right about now."

"Oh, wow. I have to shower and throw on clothes. See you at the office."

"Any reply for Hurtle?"

The Congresswoman hesitated. Earle Carkin's inquiry was just a shade too casual. He had been Walter's Chief of Staff for years, and thanks to him she had eased smoothly into her husband's House seat, but she did not like him, as a cat does not like a dog, and could not trust him as Walter had. Pushy nosy fellow, she thought, something of a Uriah Heep. Still, for guidance about the House and its ways, he was an encyclopedia.

"Just let the Chairman know that I'll be there."

"You'll be there. That's it?"

"That's it."

Carkin left. Myra Kadane asked the maid for coffee and reread the document with care, the vertical lines deepening in her forehead. Flourishing the papers at a painting over the fireplace, she said aloud, "This is your speed, honey. I can't handle it." It was her husband's portrait, one of the few things she had brought from Bel-Air to give the dowdy little rental a feel of home. Sometimes the portrait did answer her; all in her mind, of course, but it was Walter's voice, and it could be helpful. Not today, not a word.

The red-eye flight bumped downward, waking Guy Carpenter out of a wretched doze. The sunlit picture-book panorama sliding by below — the sparkling Potomac, the Capitol, the White House, the spiky obelisk of the Monument — gave him no patriotic thrill. He had sweated through too many Washington hearings as backup adviser to three successive SSC Project Managers, summoned to explain overruns on time and budget. Of all things, he wanted no part of the present commotion on Capitol Hill. He had argued in vain with Ottoline against this stopover.

"Why can't you break your Boston trip for a few hours?" Ottoline had put it to him. "It's all at NASA's expense, on the same ticket. The Science Committee is important. She's a freshman, but she's a vote."

"What's my mission? To update the dumb-bunny widow of a Congressman on the SSC debacle?"

"We don't know what she wants. Nor that she's a dumb bunny." Ottoline took a heavy jocose tone. "Turning sexist on us, Guy?"

Ottoline provided his paycheck. It was not an argument he could win. So he had told Penny, who was not at all pleased. "Ottoline enjoys yanking your chain. Peter's too, and Rafe's. Talk about sexist! Once you're into this mess, you'll never shake free." Then she had simmered down, Penny fashion. "Well, maybe it'll be interesting, at that. She was in the movies before she married Walter Kadane."

"I wasn't aware of that. You know everything."

"You're just out of it. He was a heavyweight Democrat, big-time Los Angeles film lawyer, before he went to Congress. She wasn't a bad actress. Too short to be a real star. Her movie name was Moira, Moira Strong. She gave all that up when she married Kadane, and got to be quite the Bel-Air hostess. I doubt she's a dumb bunny. Maybe you can strike a blow for Ottoline's budget, who knows?"

"Obviously that's the idea."

"Well, just don't go falling for the merry widow."

"Ha."

Soon Carpenter sat on a leather settee in the Congresswoman's outer office, reading a *New York Times* editorial about the Chinese find, which led off by quoting Napoleon: *"Let China sleep. When she wakes, the world will be sorry."* It urged the President to call for an immediate International Higgs Boson Conference, preferably under the UN. Carpenter recalled from a college history course that Napoleon had actually said, *"Europe* will be sorry." The august *Times* seemed to be in somewhat of a dither.

"You must be Dr. Carpenter." Small slight woman, classy dark suit, large brown eyes, engaging smile, swift stride. "Thank you so much for coming in."

"My pleasure, Congresswoman." Very tall man, white hair ill suited to an ascetic face and wiry build, trouble getting to his feet. Such were their first impressions of each other, as they shook hands and exchanged pleasantries. In her office she sat down in an armchair, motioning him to a sofa, but he took a straight-backed chair. Short silence. Congresswoman Kadane said, "Okay, how did they do it?"

One minute into their encounter, Carpenter dropped the dumb-bunny idea. "May I ask you something first?"

"By all means."

"What am I doing here?"

"To enlighten me on this Chinese news and the Super Collider story. I'll be most enormously obliged —"

"Why me?"

"You've heard of Quentin Rossiter?"

"He's been telephoning me, and to be blunt, I've dodged him."

"Understandable, he's a pestiferous ferret. That's his job. Old friend of my Chief of Staff. You'll meet Earle in a moment. Rossiter told us you're the right man for the lowdown on the Higgs boson, and the truth about what happened to the Super Collider."

"Generous, but undeserved."

"He also told us you weren't answering calls, so I phoned Dr. Porson myself. I simply wanted to talk to you, but she mentioned that you were coming east and would stop by. It's most cordial of you, Professor."

Aha, one puzzlement cleared up, Ottoline volunteered me. It figures. What nerve!

"Not at all. Now about the Chinese —"

The Congresswoman held up a hand. "Mind if Earle joins us?"

"As you wish."

Earle Carkin appeared and sat off in a corner. Guy Carpenter started by asking her what she knew of physics. All she remembered from one high school course, she told him, was making dimes slick with mercury and getting knocked silly by a static-electricity machine. "Just assume I'm a total ignoramus, Professor. Start from

ABC. I have an unexpected urgent meeting in half an hour, and I know you've got to fly on to Boston. Please tell me what you can, in the time we have. Is this Chinese discovery for real?"

The possibility could not be ruled out, Carpenter replied. Leaked faxes of the *Nature* article, which had yet to appear in print, were already being intensely studied all around the world, but he had not yet read it. As for the collapse of the Super Collider, that was a tangled tragic saga, and he could recommend various articles and books. He was explaining some elementary facts about the physics of the Super Collider, when Carkin spoke up. "Professor, pardon me, isn't this Chinese report an obvious hoax? Wouldn't our spy satellites have detected a huge construction in China like a Super Collider?"

Guy's experience was that in such meetings, staff spoke when spoken to, not otherwise. He turned to look at Carkin. "Not necessarily. It could be far underground."

"The Fermilab and Stanford accelerators are both underground, yet quite visible in satellite pictures. I've checked that out."

"When those were built," Guy said drily, "secrecy was not an element. The whole world knew about them."

Myra Kadane glanced at her watch. "Thanks, Earle," she said, and Carkin departed. "My meeting is right now, Dr. Carpenter, I'm truly sorry. Look, let me be frank. I've consulted several physicists here in Washington about the Higgs boson, but they only make my head spin —"

He pushed himself to his feet as she stood up. "Well, this stuff isn't easy."

"It sure isn't. You're a find. When you talk, I understand you. Quentin Rossiter is a nuisance, but he has a nose. Dr. Porson said you're returning to Pasadena on Wednesday. You couldn't possibly stop in Washington again on your way back, could you?" The request went with a winning little smile.

Guy rapidly calculated that Ottoline would be ecstatic, Penny irritated. "Why, thank you. If I've inadvertently said something useful to you, I'm glad. Seems to me I've been bumbling at random."

"Hardly."

"Well, I'd have to check with Dr. Porson."

"I understand."

"And of course, with my wife. We have a fairly new baby."

She smiled at him. "How marvelous."

"Let me call you from Boston, one way or the other."

"Terrific."

Leaving the office, Guy passed a stooped man with tousled grayish hair and a much-wrinkled face, who gave him an apprais-ing look through half-closed eyes.

"Good morning, Myra." The Chairman of the Science, Space, and Technology Committee, Congressman Horace Wesley of Ver-mont, dropped heavily into the armchair. "Who was that white-haired chap?"

"Physicist who worked on the Super Collider."

"Hmmm!" Wesley's thick grizzled eyebrows rose high, his voice dropped low. "Well, as you live, don't bring up this *Omega* memo of Bob Hurtle's with him, or with anyone else."

"Heavens, no. Isn't Hurtle waiting? He's a tartar about starting on time."

"You and I have to talk first." Wesley's deep sigh was half a groan. "Myra, Bob Hurtle led the fight against the Super Collider in the House."

"Ye gods, I didn't know that."

"Well, pet, it's the truth. If any one man sank the Super Collider, it was Bob Hurtle. Bear that in mind, and whatever you do, don't mention Sharon McAllister to Bob Hurtle. Right now, Bob's as touchy as a bear with a sore nose."

"Got it, Horace. Thanks."

Myra liked the Chairman. He was inclined to baby her, but that was quite all right, sometimes even helpful. She had gradually discerned that this tough-talking pol, a ten-term Republican, at bot-tom felt passed over. Chairing the Science Committee was a post of prestige, but the power was elsewhere. Walter had been different, putting up cheerily for many years with any committee assignment he got, and he had been gaining ground among House Democrats when a stupid horse had ended all his worldly concerns in an instant.

"Now listen, Myra, about that *Omega* memo, what did you do with your copy?"

"Tore it up and flushed it."

"Well done. Bob should never have put such things on paper. Where could he have possibly gotten that information? What we *don't* need right now, Myra, is a national panic over the Higgs boson, whatever the Sam Hill it is. My view is that Bob's trying to cover his rear end with heroics."

"Horace, he sort of panicked me."

"So I figured. Well, stay cool. Say nothing at this meeting. If there's any talking to be done, I'll do it."

"Yes, Mr. Chairman."

"Good girl." Horace smiled his fatherly smile, with teeth a shade too white to be real. "Ready to go?"

"Be along in a minute." She darted into her tiny bathroom for a hard scrutiny in the mirror. On her way out of the office, she said to her secretary, "When's my hair appointment, Pam?"

"Friday, ma'am."

"Change it to tomorrow, and tell Lucien to get me in, no matter what."

5. THE OMELET

Shoes off, Guy Carpenter lounged in shirtsleeves on a hotel bed, studying the updated telescope designs with mingled excitement and concern. These four radically new infrared instruments, if and when they were actually built and flying in formation a million miles or more from Earth, would far excel anything on the ground or orbiting in space, for probing the remaining unknowns in the universe. Trouble was, the cost estimates were orbiting way out in space too. More budget battles . . . Myra Kadane was someone to know, Ottoline had a point . . .

Winsome lady, that Congresswoman, petite slight thing, oddly bringing to mind Wen Mei Li. *"Okay, how did they do it?"* Mei would start a meeting with just such a hard incisive slash. And that beguiling smile when she invited him back to elucidate the Higgs boson! Was it a middle-aged fantasy that this former movie star really seemed to be taken with him? Like many a happily married man, Guy Carpenter had his errant dreams and his fugitive attractions. Nice to think that a drudging particle physicist could, even for a flash, interest a powerhouse woman like Myra Kadane . . .

His cell phone chirped. Penny sounded rushed and excited. "Hi, I just got your voice mail. What's up? How's it going? Where are you?"

"I'm in Boston, taking it easy in a Marriott. All's well. Telescope meeting was good. Dinah all right?"

"Fine. Fed herself a bowl of corn mush, and only half of it hit the floor. She's fast asleep. What happened with Myra Kadane?"

"She asked me to stop again in Washington on the way home."

"Oh?" Measurable pause.

"I didn't agree to do it. I'm checking with you before I talk to Ottoline."

"Is Kadane a dumb bunny?"

"Not at all. She's ignorant and she knows it. I liked that. She has a creepy Chief of Staff."

"Look, Guy, you have no choice, you must let Ottoline know about the Congresswoman's request. She'll turn a hippo handspring."

"I won't get home until Thursday, then."

"What's Myra Kadane like? She was quite pretty in the movies. Somewhat elfin."

"Businesslike. Very much the brisk officeholder now. Nothing Hollywood about her."

"Well, so, I guess Dinah and I will see you Thursday. Have fun."

"How's Sweeney?"

"Since you ask, he ate your dental floss."

"Hell! Again?"

"When will you learn? He checks the bathroom every morning."

"Another blasted vet bill —"

"No, no, I saw the end in his silly mouth and pulled it all out in time. He called me a vile name. The telescopes look good, do they?"

"World-class breakthrough. If we can get the budget, we'll be seeing the freeways on planets in Andromeda."

"Be real nice to that Congresswoman. Not too nice. Bye."

❁

Guy never remembered how terrible the weather could be on the East Coast until work dragged him back there. The shuttle from Boston to Washington was rising and plunging through black clouds like huge shaking fists, with lightning zigzagging all around. Customary end-of-life thoughts: *Why the hell did the moronic pilot take off in this? — well, John can always come home and look after Penny and Dinah — kee-RIST, we're dropping — should have listened to Penny and upped the insurance when Dinah was born — oh, it's a quick death — I swear to Christ, if I live through this, only Amtrak hereafter in the East* . . . With the thud of wheels on the tarmac, thoughts of death, insurance, and Amtrak evanesced. Across the aisle a pleasant-faced young man with a bushy mustache said, "Made it."

"Just lucky," Guy said.

Earle Carkin greeted him in the terminal with a wave of a cell phone. "Hi, Professor. Myra would like a word with you — why, hello there, Quentin!" He was addressing the pleasant-faced young man with the mustache.

Myra Kadane's voice was warm and lively on the phone. "Dr. Carpenter, it's late for the office, and I owe you a dinner, at least. Suppose you come by my house for a drink? Then we'll pick some good restaurant to talk —"

"Whatever you say, Congresswoman. Dinner's not necessary —"

"Well, let me speak to Earle. See you shortly."

While Carkin murmured into the phone, Rossiter beamed at the physicist with an innocent open countenance. Carkin shut the phone, saying, "Right. We're on our way. Professor Carpenter, Quentin Rossiter. Would you mind, Professor, if we give Quent a lift?"

"I can grab a cab," said Rossiter. "I'm just going to the Chinese embassy."

"No problem," said Carkin. "I'm taking the professor to her house, and the embassy's another five minutes."

"I don't mind," said Guy.

Rossiter said as they walked out of the terminal into drizzly gloom, "Professor, I hope you know you're sitting on a humungous story. Nobody has the whole picture like yourself."

"Whole picture of what?"

"The Super Collider, and what happened to it. You had few peers on the project, if any, isn't that right? Top physicists were reluctant to work there."

"Top physicists didn't care to uproot themselves, true enough, and live on a godforsaken plain in Texas for five, eight years."

"You did it."

"So I did."

Guy Carpenter's response was like the drop of a guillotine. A long silence ensued, a bloody head in a basket. Not another word was spoken as the car drove over the Memorial Bridge, under the Kennedy Center overhang, and up the black glistening Rock Creek Parkway. At the K Street turn into Georgetown, the reporter remarked from the backseat, "Professor, somebody at MIT told me today that Dr. Wen Mei Li is coming to the United States."

Guy was startled into responding, "Most unlikely."

"Well, it's not confirmed as yet. The embassy may have something on it. I know the CIA is checking on everyone who was in the physics department at Cornell when she was there. That includes you, I believe."

"It does."

"I thought you'd be interested."

The Congresswoman said, closing her front door, "What the devil is Quentin Rossiter doing in Earle's car?" The inside of her house surprised Carpenter: cramped, old-fashioned, run-down, what Penny would call tacky, except for a skillful full-length portrait of an American businessman over the mantel of the brick fireplace. Guy described his run-in with the journalist. She shook her head, frowning. "I'll give Earle what for. In Hollywood we call that a setup."

"It happens in academia."

"How about a dry sherry?"

"Please. I guess Rossiter thought it was worthwhile, flying up to Boston and back on the chance of cornering me."

Pouring the wine, she gave him a sidelong glance. "I would guess it wasn't."

"No, it wasn't." He sat down stiffly on a straight-backed chair.

"Forgive me, Dr. Carpenter, but you strike me as an athletic sort, yet you're moving like an ancient gent. Are you okay?"

"I will be. It's a story." He told her about Sweeney and the garage door. Myra Kadane began to laugh, head thrown back. "Sorry about your back, Professor, but Lord, that's funny."

"It didn't seem funny at the time." He was laughing too. "And Ottoline Porson's alarm wasn't funny at all."

The Congresswoman sobered. "She does take the news seriously?"

"We all do. *Nature* isn't the *National Enquirer.*"

"Now look, Professor, it's my maid's night out. I know good restaurants where we can talk in peace, no music, or we can keep it real simple. What say I make us an omelet, Guatemalan style, hot as blazes? Not a lot to eat, but —"

"I'm for it."

"Fine. It'll save time, that's for sure." She went into an open kitchen, and came back tying a large pink apron over her short-skirted black suit.

"Is this your late husband?" He was regarding the painting close up.

She nodded, with a sad affectionate glance at the picture. "He had it done when we got married. He was much better looking than that. I miss Walter." She gestured at a glass-front case jammed with books. "Reading matter in a rented house. Old bestsellers, Anita Loos, Warwick Deeping, Michael Arlen, Fanny Hurst, and such. Kind of quaint and sad, like mossy tombstones. Have a look, I won't be long."

The portrait of Walter Kadane was the work of an expert at painting well-heeled clients, Guy thought, a facile job which nevertheless captured something lifelike in the man. On the standard blue-suited fleshy body, the artist had affixed an astute Jewish face, with keen eyes and a touch of humor about the mouth. Kadane's sharp painted gaze made Guy Carpenter feel almost an intruder. At random he took from the bookcase *The Four Horsemen of the Apocalypse*. "Blasco Ibáñez, eh?" he muttered. "Who he?" As he leafed through the thick moldy volume, spicy south-of-the-border smells drifted from the kitchen. Soon Myra Kadane looked out, brushing hair from her face and removing the apron. "Dinner's on. You get to open the beer. Lots in the fridge."

The Guatemalan dish was blistering hot and quite tasty, insofar as he could taste it. She shrugged at his compliment. "Saturnina does it better." He poured beer for both, and they ate and drank. Abruptly she said, "Walter voted to kill the Super Collider, you know."

"Did he? Well, a lot of Democrats did. It was the Democrats who sank the project."

"So I'm finding out, and that truly puzzles me, Dr. Carpenter. This was pioneering science, cutting-edge physics, perhaps affecting the future of all mankind. Just the thing for liberal intellectuals like Walter. Right? The Republicans were supposed to be the benighted hidebound penny-pinchers, yet they were all for it. Why the role reversal? What happened?"

"You're jumping to the end of the story."

"Where does it begin?"

Guy Carpenter hesitated, gulping beer to cool his scorched tongue. "He didn't discuss it with you?"

"We hadn't been married that long. I was redecorating his glorious Bel-Air house, rolling in money and loving it. Till then I'd had a hard life. Wonderful guy, Walter. If he mentioned the Super Collider to me, I don't remember it." Carpenter went on eating and quaffing beer. "Well, the story?"

"Not till I finish this omelet. Or it finishes me."

What a charming laugh she had!

"You have a new baby, you say."

"Newish. Going on two. And a son of twenty-two, off in Australia working on his PhD."

"From your first marriage."

"Nope, same marriage." She arched her eyebrows at him. He added, "Well, that's how it's gone."

"Why, that's absolutely beautiful. I've missed out on kids. Too involved with acting. Also, truth to tell, with actors." She talked about Kadane's son and two daughters, all grown-up and married. They weren't like a family of her own, she said, though she got on well with them. She had one step-grandson, a destructive roly-poly three-year-old, for whom she did feel real affection. "What does your wife do, Dr. Carpenter?" She pushed away her emptied plate.

"Penny's a microbiologist, a good one. When we lived back east she taught and did research at Boston U. She gave it up to keep house and raise John. When he grew up and went off to Columbia, she returned to research. She'd kept up with the literature and did right well, until Dinah came along. No regrets, she says, but I know it's hard on her. She's very well regarded."

"Microbiology. Something real . . . well!" She reached for the apron. "I'm sort of obsessive about cleaning up, do you mind? Years of sharing an apartment with other out-of-work actresses —"

"Go ahead. Take your time. I'll get on with *The Four Horsemen of the Apocalypse.*"

He let himself down carefully on a sofa, legs stretched out, and was skimming the book with some interest when she returned to the living room. "Say, Congresswoman, this could make a movie," he said.

"Oh, look, call me Myra. That novel made a big movie in the silent days, what we'd call a blockbuster, with Rudolph Valentino. Valentino! Talk about your megastars! Compared to Valentino, Tom Cruise is a body double. Who knows that? Who cares? Who reads all these books? *Sic transit!*" Carpenter started to sit up. "Stay as you are, you look comfortable."

She faced him in an armchair, sitting forward with hands clasped around slim knees, wide eyes sparkling at him. "Now! What's a

Super Collider, exactly? How and why was it killed? Is that what the Chinese have built? Should we revive that thing in Texas? And once and for all, Guy, *what's a Higgs boson?* Can you explain it to someone like me? Can anybody?" The rattle of questions made him laugh. She shrugged and smiled. "No hurry. Start at the beginning."

"So! I sing for my supper."

"Exactly."

Guy Carpenter wanted to sing well for Myra Kadane. A thousand times he had explained the Super Collider to visiting politicians, journalists, foreign dignitaries, and assorted busybodies. Justifying the mounting cost of the Hole had been part of his job, because he had a knack for vivid simple science talk. He had delivered the Higgs boson pitch in a format as shallow as TV interviews, as dense as an endowed lecture at Berkeley, and in long or short versions calibrated to the varying brains of Washington bigwigs with budget clout. Run that worn tape for Myra Kadane? A bore, and not good enough for her. How tell it in a fresh way? How live up to her eager expectant look? *All right, here goes, courtesy Blasco Ibáñez. Apocalypse! And keep it simple, true but simple. This is an actress.*

"Very well, Myra. The story begins with the bomb that fell on Hiroshima." She stared, transfixed. *Good, that got her attention.* "And let's take this step-by-step. To make an atom bomb you need atoms, right?"

"So far I'm with you." Still staring.

"Well, but how do you acquire these atoms? *A-tomos* in Greek means noncuttable, indivisible, the smallest thing that exists. Now exactly what is an atom, that smallest thing? The ancient Greeks wondered about that first, Myra. Wondering about the right question is half of science. The other half's doing the thinking and the work to get the right answer, which may take years, or centuries, or millenia. Okay?"

She mutely nodded, eyes big and round.

"So, find the answer to that old Greek question, get yourself a supply of these atoms, and — with a lot of trial and error and expense, of course — it turns out that, guess what? You can make yourself one hell of a Guatemalan omelet of a bomb." Responding to the glow in those admiring eyes, Carpenter was spreading his feathers a little. "Well, you do just that. You beat Hitler to it. You shock the Japanese into surrendering. You win World War Two. Right?"

"Right. Right! Right as rain."

"Therefore, Madame Congresswoman, answering a far-out, seemingly abstract question can turn out to be a very smart thing to do. Are you still with me?"

"I sure am. Got it! The Super Collider would have answered my number-one question, *'What's a Higgs boson?'* That's a far-out abstract inquiry too, just like that old Greek question, and maybe just as important. Therefore killing the Super Collider was a bad mistake. Maybe even a crime."

"Not so fast."

"I'm jumping ahead again?"

"A wee bit. Give me five minutes."

"For what?"

"To cover two thousand years."

That lovely laugh again. "Shoot."

"Well, let me amend that. Five minutes to the cosmic rays."

"*Cosmic* rays?"

6. THE APOCALYPSE

All the way down the long dig into Nature for the atom, Carpenter felt he riveted the Congresswoman. Jumping from the Greeks to give Newton a whole minute, he fast-forwarded to the 19th century, to Faraday and Maxwell, to the discoveries that cascaded from the experiments of the early 20th — down inside the molecule, down inside the very small thing prematurely called the atom, farther down inside it to the electron and to the nucleus, down inside the nucleus of the atom to the proton and the neutron. And *there,* he told Myra Kadane, you arrived at your bomb stuff.

Shoot a neutron into a uranium nucleus, he said — not too hard to do, with present technology — and by a fearsome stroke of fate, one rare form of uranium turned out to be so unstable that it would blow apart, losing some mass as energy and sparking out more neutrons; whereupon from a few pounds of it, inferno on Earth could erupt in an eyeblink! Uranium atoms splitting by the billions, by the trillions, all dissolving into radiant fire with the titanic energy locked in their mass since Creation —

Myra Kadane struck in like the smartest kid in class, "E equals mc squared! That much I do know. Einstein wrote a letter to Franklin Roosevelt, warning him that it was possible. Mass into energy. Roosevelt put our scientists on it, we got the bomb first, and so —" She peered at him. "What? Totally wrong? You're making a horrible face, as though my omelet is disagreeing with you."

He waved a reassuring hand. "Let it pass, let it pass —"

"No, I won't. What's the matter?"

"Not your omelet, it was fine. You said *our* scientists. Several key scientists were foreigners, Myra, mainly Jews driven out by Hitler, Einstein included —"

"Well, I know that —"

"Then don't overlook it, because that was the ball game! Hitler handed us the chance to get the bomb first, on a silver platter. If Nazi Germany had gotten it first" — he looked her in the eye and tapped the worn book beside him — "apocalypse! The Four Horsemen galloping out over the earth! The darkness of barbarism descending for a thousand years! You and I wouldn't be having this cosy chat, and we probably wouldn't be alive." Silent moment, then his tone brightened. "Well, Der Fuehrer idiotically blew it, as we all know. Now at this point the story does get more complex. If you're still game for me to go on —"

"Game? So help me, I'm following every word. You're absolutely great at this. Other physicists have left me flummoxed. Their books, too. How come?"

"Because I'm an arrant oversimplifier, and I'm trying just to zero in on the Super Collider, leaving out all but the greatest names, all the revolutionary ideas that created modern times, sliding past special relativity, quantum mechanics — we could be up all night and I wouldn't begin to get all that in —"

"Just keep going, I beg you. More beer?"

"There wouldn't be bourbon in the house, would there?"

"Walter's favorite! Ice and a splash?"

"Perfect."

Alone with Congresswoman Myra Kadane in this rundown Georgetown house, recumbent on a dingy old sofa, Guy Carpenter realized that he was feeling exceedingly pleased with himself. For him, this was an unheard-of state of mind. All that beer? Her shiny-eyed interest in his words? Those fetching legs displayed by a very short skirt?

"Okay, Myra," he went on, sipping the tinkling drink she handed him. "That was it. Digging down to those four particles — atom, electron, proton, neutron — ended a global war and opened a new age. What heroes the physicists were when I was growing up, and was I ever hooked on the field in college! Physics! The ultimate truth about the world, the unleasher of ultimate energy! The sexy science with the blue-sky budgets!" He smiled at her. "You're a good listener, Congresswoman. Here we are at the cosmic rays."

"Really?" She checked her watch, laughed, and reached out a small hand to pat his arm. "Good going. Almost spot-on! Now what on earth are they?"

"Patience. Back to the Collider. We can't see these subatomic particles, you understand, we detect them with various contraptions — cloud chambers, bubble chambers, spark chambers, we call them. The early ones were small, the improved ones are colossal and costly as sin — and we tape those tracks and study them.

"*And,* big surprise! As we improved these devices, mysterious brand-new particles started to show up. Not electrons, not neutrons, not protons, nothing familiar, a truly puzzling development. Physicists went checking on mountaintops, and sent up instruments in balloons, and found out that these new particles — very short-lived, but real — were being spawned up there by the cosmic rays. Cosmic rays, Myra, consist of particles that come smashing into our atmosphere out of deep space at almost the speed of light. Their power is unearthly, their origin we don't quite know. We do know that they collide with the atoms of our upper air, and that these new particles spray out as debris. All a collider really does is simulate such collisions —"

She said brightly, "Artificial cosmic rays, then."

"Not bad." He smiled and nodded. "A-plus! Cosmic rays to order, you might say. How else could we study those strange new particles? Wait for random events caused by real cosmic rays? Hardly.

Colliders are machines that accelerate beams of particles up to near cosmic-ray power and speed, and bang them into a target or into each other. The greater the energy we can pump into the beams, the more new particles we can detect, and the more we find out about Nature. In the past forty years, by building ever bigger and more powerful colliders, we've made startling discoveries —"

"I know, like the quarks — *good grief, Professor Carpenter!* You do make the most hideous faces! Just tell me I'm being stupid. Don't turn into Mr. Hyde on me."

"Sorry, sorry. You hit a nerve." He ruefully shook his head. "*Quark* grates on me, that's all. A great physicist took it from a James Joyce book and stuck a patch of whimsy on an awesome truth of nature. You're right, *quarks* showed up inside the proton and neutron. Nobel Prizes rained down, yet the search for rock bottom in physics is far from over, in fact it's stymied. Down in that subworld of reality, Myra, when we penetrate deep enough — and we've been doing it — the mathematics tend to dissolve into absurdities, infinities, blank walls. The Higgs boson in theory can pierce those walls, and that's where the Chinese seem to have leapfrogged us —"

"How, leapfrogged?"

"Myra, if we had finished our project in Texas — and we were well on our way, I promise you, it really was going to be a *Super* Collider, more than fifty miles around, more than twenty times the power of any collider that then existed — if we had gone ahead with it, I say, we and not the Chinese would have found the Higgs boson. We'd have found it five or six years ago." Guy Carpenter shrugged. "But somebody had to pick up the tab, and your husband voted against."

She contemplated him in a pause that became uncomfortable. Had he offended her with the remark about Kadane? Was he showing off too much? Silence. Long silence. She held out a hand. "I see. Well, how about a refill?"

"Sure. Thanks."

"I'll join you."

She brought two tumblers and handed him one. He said, "Is

bourbon really your drink? You don't have to choke it down just to keep me company." A failed embarrassed attempt at banter, he thought as he uttered it.

"Not feminine, you mean. Walter used to joke about that. Puts hair on your chest, he would warn me. Well, when I drink, I don't drink pink ladies." She took a deep gulp. "Now, Professor, what about" — she hesitated, groping for words and pronouncing them wrong — "leptons, mesons, muons, gluons, oh, I don't know what all, hadrons, pions . . . they're in all the books. You haven't even mentioned them."

It was his turn to stare at her. "Bravo, Myra, for doing your homework."

"Don't patronize me. I'm on the Science Committee. I've been trying to inform myself."

"What books are we talking about?"

As she ticked off titles, he nodded and smiled or frowned. At one name he groaned. She exclaimed, "Hell's *bells,* Mr. Hyde, forget it. I'm sorry I brought up the books —"

"You really read those books? I'm staggered."

"Of course not. What do you think? Skimmed through them, riffled to the end, where the Higgs boson usually shows up. That's where they lapse into total gobbledygook, one and all."

"I won't do any better, Myra. I'm already putting you to sleep."

The Congresswoman was yawning like a cat, incompletely covering it with a manicured little hand. "Not at all! Oh, dear, forgive me. If you must know, when you called from Boston I chased Earle out to get me some books. I was up most of the night, boning up as though for a final, or an audition for a big part. I'm not in the least sleepy, and — what are you doing?"

He was at the windows, pushing aside drapes. "How far is the Georgetown Inn?"

"Why? Because I yawned once?"

"Enough particle physics for one night."

"You're copping out on me, Dr. Carpenter. Is it because we're up to the Higgs boson? Come on, give me a chance at it." She stood at the window beside him, peering out, so close that he could smell her delicate perfume. "It isn't far, but you can't walk anywhere in this rain."

Carpenter, however, was determined to leave, overwhelmed by a sudden sense that he had been listening to his own voice too long, that he was overstaying his welcome and mouthing off, that what he took for Myra Kadane's admiration was merely her adroit coaxing out of him the information she wanted. The bourbon had gone to his head, and her charm too. The thing was to get the hell out with his dignity intact, and perhaps her good opinion as well.

"Myra, the Higgs is a brute, that's all. I've got a long flight tomorrow. I'll plug in my computer on the plane, bat off something, and e-mail it to you. Then we can talk on the phone all you want, maybe even tomorrow night —"

"Not the same thing —"

"Probably better. I'm not a bad writer on physics, I've had offers from publishers to expand some of my articles into books, but I hate writing. For you, I won't mind."

"Very well. I'm grateful, of course. I'll call a cab." As she picked up the phone, she gestured at the painting. "Just tell me this. Why do you think Walter voted to kill the Super Collider? Especially since, as you say, it was so far along?"

"Your husband was a party man, wasn't he?"

"True blue."

"Then he voted the party line, that's all."

Myra Kadane wrinkled up her face, and for a moment looked much older. She ordered a cab and hung up. "Too obvious. On a thing this important, he'd have voted his convictions."

"You knew him. I didn't. Possibly he felt Texas didn't deserve the Super Collider."

"What do you mean by that?"

"Myra, I sometimes think the Super Collider was done in by politics masquerading as a budget cut. Bare-knuckles politics. Raw regional politics. We academic innocents should have seen it coming. We didn't. We'd been toiling away for years, heads down, when Congress up and fired us all overnight. Shock of our lives. A colleague of mine said, *'Well, our fifty-year ride on the Bomb is over.'* "

"It wasn't that simple, surely."

Guy Carpenter threw up his hands. "Look, I can't account for the killing of the SSC! Try asking four physicists and three politicians what happened, and you'll get seven explanations. The Rock has the best answer I know, and even he —"

"The Rock?"

"Herman Rocovsky. Obscure genius behind the entire project. He's emeritus now out at Stanford, influential as ever, you should talk to him —"

A horn honked outside. "There's your cab. Send him away, Guy. Truly, I'm wide awake."

Wry smile and headshake. "Thanks, Myra, for the omelet, the bourbon, *The Four Horsemen of the Apocalypse,* everything. Very nice evening." He got into an old blue taxi and waved good-bye.

In an upstairs bedroom Myra Kadane took off her earrings and her suit, and sat down at the dressing table in her slip to wipe away makeup. Interesting man, that Guy Carpenter! Brilliant, but remote. Why that melancholy air? Did he have some gnawing worry? That telescope budget, perhaps . . . ? *Damn!* She hit the dressing table with her fist. Bemused by all the science talk, she had failed to ask him the one question that mattered most! Too late now.

She was drawing water for a bath when the door knocker sounded below . . . *rap, rap, rap.* Throwing on a terry robe, she ran downstairs and peeked out through the chained door. The physicist stood there in the rain beside the same taxi. "We give up," he called, "where's the Georgetown Inn, exactly?"

"I don't believe this. Come inside."

"The driver's an Ethiopian," he said, brushing rain from his face. "Couldn't be pleasanter. Plaited black hair down to his shoulders, very cheerful and religious. He just doesn't quite know where the Georgetown Inn is."

"Good Lord, it's a landmark! Three blocks up and four blocks to the right. These D.C. cabdrivers! Think he could find the Washington Monument?"

"Well, he does seem somewhat new here, but a truly gentle soul.

Sorry I disturbed you. Three blocks up and turn right. Good night again —"

"Oh no you don't, Guy Carpenter. Now that you're back, you'll have a nightcap with me. No particle physics, I promise, just send him away."

"I couldn't do that, he's too friendly and sweet natured. I'll take that nightcap, though." Carpenter was relieved by her welcoming manner. Maybe he had not made quite such an ass of himself as he feared.

"I won't be a minute," she said and dashed up the stairs. She fussed among her housecoats and put on an old print silk robe that Walter had brought back from a business trip to Shanghai. The physicist was on the sofa, leafing through *The Four Horsemen of the Apocalypse* again. "Hooked on that book, eh?" She laughed. "Well, what now? Why the wild look?"

"Nothing, you startled me." He sat up. "I was engrossed in figuring out which character was Rudy Valentino. Pretty robe."

"Thanks."

Myra Kadane was a little shorter than Wen Mei Li. Just as thin, eyes just as dark, just as keen. No steel-rimmed glasses. Probably a standard Shanghai pattern, that dragon robe. With one thing and another Mei Li was much on his mind. He was looking at an apparition from a weekend in Shanghai, years and years ago, though the Congresswoman's skin without makeup was smooth and pale pink, nothing like Mei's exquisite ivory tint.

"Now see here," she said, pouring the drinks, "I'm glad you've come back, there's something I certainly should have asked you. Does the Chinese discovery have any possible military application?"

Guy Carpenter blinked and hesitated. "That very question came up at a hearing about the Super Collider, shortly before it was killed."

"Well?"

He shrugged, and tossed down the bourbon. After a pause she held out her hand. "Okay. By the bye, Dr. Porson mentioned your budget problem with the telescopes. I'm bearing it in mind." Her handclasp was cool, dry, and strong.

What do you know, this woman's a politician, at that. Mission accomplished! "I'll tell her. She'll be pleased."

"It's been an experience, Professor. A one-year physics course in one night."

"Well, Myra, maybe those books will make a bit more sense now. The ones that didn't turn me into Mr. Hyde."

With the laugh he liked so much, she opened the door. "Wow. Will it ever stop raining in this town?"

As the taxi drove off with Dr. Carpenter, she closed the door and said to the painting, "Nice man, Walter, eh?"

The rich warm voice replied, "Very nice. Watch out."

"What, dear? Don't be silly. Two kids, twenty years apart, with the same wife?" She brushed a hand on the painted face. "That's one uxorious physicist, sweetie. Good night."

7. THE BOSON

"Lunch, sir?" The flight attendant had to tap Carpenter's shoulder, so intent was he on his laptop screen.

Glad of the break, Guy Carpenter fell to on a pasta dish, declining wine. Two hours of piling words on the screen, and he had yet to get to the Higgs boson! The computer was running away with him, or rather his memory was. A bitter screed was pouring out, full of buried anger and regret at the five years of his life *"trashed by Washington troglodytes,"* as he had just written.

Very vivid, Professor, very clever, but off the subject, all that stuff. Try again.

⚛

Aloft, en route L.A. via Dallas.

My dear Congresswoman —

I've been batting at my laptop too long about bygone Super Collider horrors. No reason to impose such stuff on you, when all you asked for was some light on the Higgs boson. I'll probably delete the whole sour outpouring. Now I begin afresh, minus the personal vitriol.

Way back in 1983, the Super Collider idea was born when two elusive particles, long predicted by theory, were discovered at CERN, the big European collider outside Geneva. The Italian director got a Nobel Prize, and we American physicists had egg on our faces. Why, nobody beats the good old Red, White, and Blue in science! The home team was galvanized to plan the biggest goddamned collider of all time, which would without fail produce the next major predicted particle, *the Higgs boson.*

Well, designing the SSC took four years. Then our big guns in physics, the High Energy Physics Advisory Panel in the Department of Energy, marched into the Oval Office in a body and pitched the thing to President Reagan. He sat there behind his desk, so I've been told, fingering his inevitable three-by-five cards as he heard them out, then he grinned that beguiling grin and just said, "Throw deep." That's how it happened, Myra. That's how America got committed to build the Superconducting Super Collider. *Win one for the Gipper.* There was even some talk of calling it the Reagan High Energy National Laboratory, though that faded off.

How I got into the SSC and how it got aborted is all in my previous diatribe, and if by some remote chance you're interested, and we ever have another omelet evening, I can give you quite an earful about that complicated adventure.

(Here Carpenter halted, mulling over the reference to the omelet. Too cute? Beside the point? God save us, flirtatious? Decision: *Delete that sentence.* He did.)

So, about the Higgs. You recall that Greek question, *"What's the smallest thing that exists?"* By seeking and finding an answer we got the Bomb, we got nuclear power plants and submarines, we learned how the sun and the stars shine, and there were huge benefits in medical fallout. Pretty good gain in understanding and manipulating Nature! Well, the question that points to the Higgs boson may turn out as richly productive. Or it may not. We don't know. The question may strike you at first as trivial, or what is much worse, philosophical: *"How come anything at all exists?"* I can just hear you saying, "Professor, in what way does that question differ from *"How many angels can dance on the head of a pin?"* Well, Myra, nobody knows whether angels exist or dance, whereas we know that the big bang happened and that we exist. That's the difference.

We have clues to the bang that add up to a near certainty. There's no doubt — I say this as an astrophysicist now — that the universe is expanding, the galaxies racing away into the void. Calculating their distance and speed and reversing the numbers, we can run the film backward and arrive at the Beginning. That gives us a time frame. *Clue one.* Next clue. The big bang had to occur with an eruption of radiant HEAT beyond anything the human mind can conceive. Again, calculation shows that within such a time frame, there should still be a cool residue of that primal radiation, out there in the universe. Well, in 1965, Myra, in the observations of a couple of guys working for Bell Telephone, *that radiation showed up.* Serious scientists, mind you, not line repairmen. They nabbed a Nobel for it. World scientists have tested and retested for that background radiation ever since. It's there, all right. *Clue two.*

Therefore we're not dealing with dancing angels but with reality, with substance, with matter, with the stuff of all things. In short, with MASS, and *the Higgs boson has to do with mass.*

So let's rephrase the question more precisely: "How does mass come to exist?" Because what came boiling out of the bang, Myra, was not mass but a "plasma" — not even a gas, nothing as definable or stable even as hydrogen or helium, nothing but an unimaginable swirl of pure radiant energy and evanescent particles. How did that fiery stuff ever simmer down to *mass,* to familiar substances and things? *That's* the mystery. How come everything about us here on our little earth is so stable that you and I just get up in the morning and go about our business? How did we get to such a reliable comfortable state from that wildfire Genesis, ten to fifteen billion years ago? How account for tigers, trees, skyscrapers, sitcoms, and Myra Kadane?

Here again Guy Carpenter paused, wondering how to proceed and savoring the line about tigers and Myra Kadane. Rather nifty, that. He could picture her smiling over it in the dumpy house, lounging on the sofa that faced the portrait, maybe even wearing the Shanghai robe. But the next part could well lose her. Conveying this stuff was a lot tougher in e-mail than face-to-face.

Okay, let's go to the idea of "force fields," specifically the Higgs field, and look, Myra, *don't* let your eyes glaze over, what comes now really isn't that hard. In your high school physics class, remember, you got knocked across the room by an electric shock. Right there you encountered a "force field," a bit too close up, the electromagnetic field. It pervades the universe, runs your hair dryer, conveys the starlight, and also, unfortunately, the sitcoms. So you're familiar with one force field. There's another you know just as well, the gravitational field. Let go the hair dryer, and it drops to the floor. Step on the bathroom scale, and a pointer moves. Gravitational force field. It governs the moon swinging around the earth, and indeed every single thing in the universe, from dust motes to rotating galaxies. So that's two force fields.

Still with me? We plunge into yet a third one, the Higgs field. It differs from the other fields in a right simple way, to wit, *there's no evidence that it exists.* Peter Higgs, a Brit physicist, came up with his theoretical field some years ago to account for mass. Assuming that (a) the Higgs field is there, a force field with very odd quantum characteristics, and (b) all particles interact with that field, then (c) *the tiger and Myra exist because your molecules have acquired* mass *through the famous Higgs boson, interacting with the particles that make up your molecules.*

I'll try to clarify that and we'll be done. Don't despair, Myra, and allow me a bow because I haven't drowned you in an off-putting jumble of nomenclature. Fermi once said about pions, muons, and the rest, "If my brain could retain all those names, I'd have been a botanist."

So what are bosons, exactly, and what do they do? Here we go. Up here in "real life," where we spend our days, gravity acts by keeping the moon in place and breaking your elbow if you fall downstairs. You know all too well how electricity acts, it shocked you out of any interest in physics. Now way down there in subatomic reality, a weird underworld with weird laws, a force acts *by means of certain interacting particles, "messenger particles"* — BOSONS — *that convey the force.* There! Hold on to that, and you've just about got it. You can't picture it, you just have to believe it.

What the Higgs boson does is TRANSMIT *the force of the Higgs force field to give each particle its mass as that particle interacts — via the boson — with the field.* Mass exists, substance exists, you and I exist, because as the horrendous plasma cloud cooled down, the Higgs field kicked in, the swirl of particles slowed and clumped, and the matter of everyday reality gradually came to exist, the ninety-two elements in Nature from hydrogen to uranium, endowed with mass by the star-making process throughout the universe. One of those elements was carbon, and with carbon you're into the life sciences, the other frame of mystery that produced you and me.

That's about the best I can do, in a crude dash at the Higgs for a Congresswoman with an inquiring mind. Just as well. I have to close the computer. I'm landing in Dallas for a two-hour stopover.

Carpenter had not been back to Dallas since the collapse of the SSC. The airport now seemed twice as big and five times as crowded and rackety, otherwise the same, haunted by mournful recollections and ten-gallon hats. To blank out the recollections, he bought a paperback thriller and took it to the waiting lounge, but hardly followed the plot as he turned the pages, thinking back on the e-mail to Myra. He decided that he had to write more, and once settled in his seat on the plane to Los Angeles, he got straight at the laptop again.

❈

Hi, I'm on my way home.

Last night I left unanswered your question, *Is there any military application of the Chinese discovery?* I suspect, Madame Congresswoman, that that was the whole point of your arranging to meet me. I don't blame you one bit. As I told you, that very question was asked in Congress about the Super Collider. No serious scientist could then have answered that yes, in a sense there was a military aspect. If I now tell you nevertheless *that yes, there was and is,* you have to understand that it's utterly theoretical, years if not centuries down the road, and may never materialize.

Myra, when James Chadwick, another Brit, discovered the neutron in 1932, no reputable scientist would have connected it with Sunday-supplement piffle about driving the *Queen Mary* around the world with the atomic energy locked in a glass of water. Lord Rutherford himself, Chadwick's mentor and perhaps the greatest of particle scientists, declared around that time, "Any talk of harnessing the energy in the atom is moonshine." Yet in 1945, only thirteen years after Chadwick's discovery, we set off the first atomic bomb on a mesa in New Mexico!

It's the essence of basic research, you see, Madame Congresswoman, that its outcome is unknowable. Should you, as a Science Committee member, ask me at a hearing, "What benefit to the American people can we expect if we revive the Super Collider?" you're asking for targeted research. Chadwick didn't know what to expect when he smoked out the neutron. If he and scientists like him had been assigned to do only targeted research, Hiroshima might not have happened. Not in 1945, for sure. Better for the world? Who knows? What you're asking, what you're probing for, is the possible threat of yet more powerful weaponry.

Well, once the Higgs boson is discovered (if it exists!), defined, *and controlled to the point of manipulating mass* — and I'm not saying it's possible, I don't even believe in the Higgs field as yet, it remains for me a beguiling conjecture (one of several) to explain a lot of anomalies — but if the Chinese have really done what they claim, then it's more than a conjecture, we're in the postnuclear world, the Higgs world, and *in the very very long run,* it could be Katie bar the door. Because mass, remember, is only (as you yourself quoted) "$E=mc^2$," energy compressed by an unbelievably gargantuan factor, the square of the speed of light. *Manipulating and controlling the awesome energy in mass verges on the conceptual field of weaponry.* I'll say no more. I've already said more than I would among my fellow scientists. Speaking seriously, it's moonshine. The narrow sliver of doubt, excitement, and worry consists of this, it may be Lord Rutherford's brand of moonshine.

Having written all that down, Carpenter now wondered about including it. There was nothing secret about any of it, but it was not quite common knowledge and could be given an alarmist spin. Well, a Science Committee member was entitled to the information and would be sensible about the use of it. He signed and sent the e-mail.

Drying Dinah after a bath, Penny heard knocking at the door from the garage. That had to be Guy, at last. *Knock, knock, knock!* "Coming, *coming!*" She hurried to open it, the naked infant on her arm. "Well, hi there! Welcome home, where's your key?"

"Packed it, very stupidly." Penny and the baby were smiling at him, both with the same-shaped mouth, same smile, the endearing resemblance only getting stronger. He put down his bags. "Give me that baby." He hugged the smooth little creature to him, she put damp hands to his bristly cheeks, and he felt that, come what might, his life had not been an utter waste. "Everything okay? Heard from John?"

"Oh, yes, a long e-mail from Samoa about Margaret Mead and

Polynesian sex. He's becoming convinced she really was hoodwinked by prankish Samoan teenagers. How was your flight?"

"Endless."

"A fax just came in from that Congresswoman. Lots of pages."

"Already? I sent her an e-mail from the plane to L.A., stuff and nonsense about the Higgs boson that she asked for. I guess she's baffled and wants more. Why don't you read it?"

"You're sure I should?"

This interplay went fast, her side-glance, his offhand answer, her sharp query. She might be dying of curiosity, but unless he told her to, she would not touch it, not Penny. Myra Kadane couldn't have written anything indiscreet, so what was the harm? "Go ahead, I have to shower, I'm all sweat and grime. You'll get a notion of what she's like. Uninformed, but far from dumb. She volunteered that she'll bear our telescope budget in mind. Her very words."

"Well, well. Ottoline's the clever one, sending you to work on her. Want something to eat? I can make you an omelet."

"Sounds great." No point in mentioning Myra's Guatemalan version. Take too long to explain.

Later he sat at the kitchen table in a bathrobe, reading the fax as he ate Penny's familiar cheese omelet with chives.

> Dear Dr. Carpenter,
>
> Many, many thanks! Let me apologize straight off for scribbling this response. My cursed computer has crashed again, and I'm in a desperate hurry to get this off to you —

"Strange handwriting, isn't it?" said Penny, drinking coffee opposite him.

"How, strange?" he asked.

"Well, sort of like a man's, straight up and down, no frills. That party invitation is preposterous. I can't possibly go."

"Party, eh?"

> Your e-mail explanation is a tour de force. Thank you! I truly understood it while I read it, though it's hard to hang on to. As

you said, "the Higgs is a brute." For obvious reasons, I tore up the last two pages, and I'd suggest you delete that passage from your computer. I'll be going over and over what you wrote, but meantime, instead of nagging you with queries, I have a suggestion. I suspect your wife makes social decisions, so please give this scrawl to her, with my earnest plea that she accept my invitation.

Guy looked up from the omelet. "Do I project a henpecked image, old thing?"

"Read on."

I can't ask that you come to Washington for another consultation, but there happens to be a handy alternative. Bel-Air is only an hour's drive from Pasadena, and that's a lot better than flying cross-country! On Sunday Walter's family is having a do at what they call "the old house," where I live. They all have their own houses, all very well-off. The oldest, Sean, is a film lawyer and packager. He took over the firm when Walter opted for Congress. Walter never expected a skittery horse to snuff him out in his prime, but as a careful lawyer he had an up-to-date will, with an unusual proviso.

On the anniversary of a Jewish parent's death, the children are supposed to say a memorial prayer called "Yorsite." I remember Walter going to do Yorsite for his father at his temple. His will directs that for his Yorsite they invite a few friends to the old house, show some great film he had a hand in, and give them a gourmet dinner with wines from his prime cellar. That's how he wanted to be remembered, not with Hebrew prayers they don't understand. Since Walter died there have been three of these Yorsite parties. They're nice. If you and Penny could come early — scheduled for three-thirty, usually starts about four — you and I could quickly review what you wrote. I do have a few questions, and I would be so *immensely* grateful! While we talk Sean can take your wife in hand, show her around, introduce her to guests. Please call my office in the morning. Earle will give you details. I'll be in committee all day. Sean knows about this and is interested to meet you. Again, *please* tell Penny, Myra Kadane begs you both to come.

"Me at a Bel-Air bash? Wild horses!" said Penny. "Forget it. If you think it matters for Ottoline's budget, you go, that's our bread and butter."

"We both go."

"Oh, yes? For starters, what do I wear?"

"Hollywood wears grunge these days. Wear anything."

"Spoken like a man from Mars. They're back to putting on the dog, with emeralds."

"Buy a new dress. Whatever you need."

"Right. I tool over to Rodeo Drive tomorrow, pick up a pretty little nothing, and we take a second mortgage on the house."

Guy could distinguish between the words and the music of his wife's reactions. Penny was intrigued. "Why not, if it comes to that?"

"Anyway, it's *Yahrtzeit,* not *Yorsite.* She's got it wrong. I once had a Jewish boyfriend who was religious."

"First I hear of him. Or of this observance."

"No need for you to hear of him, until now. It's *Yahrtzeit.* What about Dinah?"

"Stephanie's a perfectly reliable babysitter."

"What does *'obvious reasons'* mean?"

"Come again?" His mind went racing back over the fax. Ah, yes. Awkward words, those.

"She suggests you delete something from your computer *for obvious reasons.* Says she tore up her pages."

He picked up the fax and glanced through it. "Hm, you're right. More physics stuff. Not relevant to the party."

Penny's expression was quizzical. "Physics stuff."

"Physics stuff." She was looking him in the eye. There was no help for it, and no point going into it. Not with Penny. "Okay, it's the Congresswoman's notion of national security."

A heartbeat or two. "You're kidding."

"I'm not."

Penny hesitated, then laughed. "Our pokey life is getting interesting, by God! National security, eh? And a Bel-Air party! Hot dog. There's a printout of John's e-mail on your desk."

8. THE PARTY

The thick freeway traffic was slowing to a dead stop. Far ahead in a dirty haze of exhaust fumes, an 18-wheeler was jackknifed across all but one lane, and cars were trickling through that lane like sand through an hourglass. "This does it," said Penny. "We're late already. You won't get to talk to your Congresswoman about the boson."

"I don't know. Maybe she'll decide to skip *Tootsie*."

"Think so? I wouldn't dream of it. I love Dustin Hoffman."

Penny sat smiling, arms folded, with no trace of her wonted snappishness in freeway stop-and-go traffic. How come? Born in New England, Easterner to the bone, Penny had spent years in Stanford, years in Dallas, now years in Pasadena, ever yearning for Guy to get summoned back to do physics in civilization, that is, anywhere from Chicago eastward. Meantime she endured, not without sporadic grumbling. Why no snarls today? The clothes, Guy thought, the clothes; new navy-blue silk suit, pale-gray shirtwaist, spiffy hairdo; Penny in her "Bobby McGee" mode, a seductive female with class, and cheerily aware of it, those great legs handsomely on view in the skimpy skirt.

"You're in good spirits," he remarked.

"Dear, how often does one get to go to a Bel-Air Yahrtzeit?"

For her part, Penny was looking forward to sizing up Congresswoman Kadane. Guy was a faithful old dog, no doubt, but she never forgot the talk she had heard at Cornell about Guy and Wen Mei Li, nor the shock of the handwritten poem she had come upon, poking into a book of Ernest Dowson's verses in his bachelor flat. Clipped to the page of Dowson's famed plaint, *"I have been faithful to thee, Cynara! in my fashion,"* was Guy's rhymed, piercingly earnest lament that he could never again love a woman as he had loved Wen Mei Li. Penny had replaced the book, and had said nothing about the poem then or since. But she had endured agonies, and had put Guy through a wringer of devious torment before agreeing to marry him. She seldom thought about it, it was all so long, long ago! Yet there it was . . .

When they turned off Sunset Boulevard into Bel-Air Canyon, it was half past three. The old Pontiac wound slowly along the crowded road, a Rolls-Royce Silver Cloud ahead and a gunmetal Lexus on their tail, passing mansion after mansion in varied grandiose styles from Bauhaus modern to Tudor half-timber, each one set in hilly flowery acreage and barbered green lawns, "Ye gods, the money, Guy, the *money,* the sheer MONEY here!" Penny exclaimed. "I didn't know there was this much money in the whole wide world."

"Sheltered life," said Guy.

A line of cars waited at a jammed driveway curving uphill to a weathered yellow edifice, Spanish mission style, with a giant satellite dish on the bell tower. Young men in red jackets were running up and down the line. A freckled lad peered through Guy's open window. "Kadane party, sir? Valet parking, if you care to walk up. It's faster."

They got out and strolled along the road and up the driveway, past a numbing display of spanking new German and Japanese cars, with a few interspersed Italian and British machines. Coming upon a lone Lincoln LS, Penny gave its hood a little pat. "Dr. Livingstone, I presume," she said.

In the high-ceilinged entrance hall, Myra Kadane and a tall bearded pudgy man of thirty or so were welcoming guests. Penny hissed as she and Guy fell in line, "Christ, that's an elegant lady!" This puzzled Guy. Myra's jewelry, pearls and gold, had no flash at all, and her short white dress looked quite plain to him, though showing fashionable dollops of bosom. "Hello, there!" She held out both hands to them with glad relief. "At last! Sean, meet Penny and Guy. Or maybe I should say, Dr. Carpenter and Dr. Carpenter."

"Ah, intellect!" Sean laughed and shook hands. Except for the close-trimmed reddish beard, he looked a lot like the portrait of his father. "Raises the party's tone. Much needed! Welcome."

"Fearful traffic," Penny said to Myra. "I was afraid we'd miss half of *Tootsie.*"

"No way," said Sean, eyeing the good-looking microbiologist. "Dustin's here. Come and meet him."

"Dustin *Hoffman?* Whee."

Myra said as Sean took Penny off, "We don't have much time, Guy. Follow me." She threaded through noisy guests to a wood-paneled billiard room and closed the door. Sudden quiet. They sat down in two overstuffed red leather armchairs. "Peaceful in here, eh? Your Penny's mighty attractive."

"Thanks. Main thing is, she's smart."

"I'll bet she is. Listen, Guy, your e-mail was a godsend, and I want to read that sour diatribe too. Did you save it? I have a notion that that's the real story of the Super Collider."

"A worm's-eye view," said Guy. "I saved it. I'll send it on."

"Good." She glanced at her watch. "They won't start the film without me." She took a clipboard and pencil from a low side table. "Now, what does *superconducting* mean? You've never explained."

"Myra, you said we haven't much time —"

"Too complicated?"

"Oh, maybe not. Real quick, it takes thousands of giant electro-magnets to keep bunches of protons racing around a fifty-four-mile oval track. The cost of power to those magnets would be astronomical, out of sight, if not for this new superconducting technology. Fermilab developed it. You cool the conducting wires, see, wires of very special alloys, way down — I mean, way, *way* down near absolute zero, with liquid helium — and their electrical resistance vanishes. Absolutely vanishes! *No* resistance! Therefore, *super*-conducting. Got it?"

"Sure. Amazing. Power cost plummets like mad."

"Exactly so."

"Well, that wasn't so complicated."

"You don't know what I left out."

She laughed with that endearing toss of her head and penciled a check on the pad. "Next, at what point after the big bang were the elements formed?"

"Come off it, Myra, for crying out loud! What on earth has that got to do with your Science Committee, or the Higgs boson?"

"I'll tell you what. As we sit here, my Chairman and the Chairman of Armed Services are meeting in Washington, and they may well launch an urgent inquiry into this business. The media are getting out of hand, most of all cable TV, recycling Chinese boson, Chinese boson on the half hour, when nothing much else is happening. There isn't a single scientist on my committee, we're all ignoramuses, and you're my chance to sponge up what background I can. You've helped me a lot. Please keep talking —"

"Not today, not on that giant topic —"

"Today, yes. I've got you today, Guy."

"Well, if it'll help you at all," Guy said with a skeptical head shake, "in a nutshell, here's how the whole thing goes, Myra. Big bang! *Plasma!* Plasma cools first into hydrogen and helium atoms, plus a bit of lithium, the lightest elements. Mostly hydrogen. Gravity coalesces those light elements to form stars. Stars burn the hydrogen — that's how they shine. Old stars burn out and explode, and the ashes, the heavy elements, scatter out all over the place — the universe, that is. Gravity pulls *them* back together, and you get planets and people out of the heavier elements. How's that, since you insist?"

She looked oddly at him. "You believe any of that?"

"Believe it? I believe it all. It's true."

She made a face and scribbled rapidly, then quizzed him some more about the Higgs boson, noting his answers. Another glance at her watch. "Showtime. Thanks! I gather from what you say, and what I've read, that this so-called Standard Model of the Universe, this 'theory of everything,' is all hooey."

"Interesting, Madame Curie. Why do you say that?"

"Professor, you just told me that in the equations, particles are treated as points without mass. Put in the masses and the structure goes haywire, unless and until the Higgs boson — *if* it exists — fixes the mathematics. That's what you said, isn't it?"

"Don't call me up before your committee."

"Why not?"

"I'd have to tell you you're talking through your hat."

She put aside the clipboard with a grin. "Let's watch *Tootsie*."

In the two-story library walled with volumes floor to ceiling, guests were ranged around on settees, couches, and armchairs. As soon as Myra Kadane came in, a section of books slid noiselessly aside to disclose a full-size movie screen, and Sean walked before the screen to talk about his father's Yorsite. Penny, sitting beside a small man on a love seat, slyly twiddled fingers at Guy, her lips forming "YAHR-TZEIT." The film began, and after a while, having seen it more than once, Guy dozed off. Loud applause startled him. The wall of books was sliding back into place, Dustin Hoffman was smiling and bowing, and Guy saw Penny beckoning insistently, so he pushed through to her.

"Dustin, this is Guy, my husband, the physicist."

Though the actor looked older and smaller than Guy had pictured him, his presence was princely. "Your wife's a real savant about the human genome," he said.

"It's her trade," said Guy, "when she's not raising kids."

Shaking hands with a megastar was strange, and as he looked around, this whole Yorsite party was even stranger. He was still half awake and somewhat disoriented. The women all seemed to be glossy young beauties, and the men made him feel utterly out of place. He alone wore a tie, while they to a man sported modish jackets and open shirt collars. More than that, if he wasn't crazy, they all *looked* alike. They were uniformly quite young, and they all had beards. It was as though he had fallen in with a clutch of youthful clones of Yasser Arafat. They tended to be plumpish like Arafat, the beards were all short and on the scraggly side, like Arafat's, and unless he was hallucinating, they all uncannily *resembled* Arafat. Perhaps this was because at a Yorsite party they would be mostly Jews, and Arabs sort of looked like Jews, or vice versa.

A large man in a brown tweed suit, with a heavily lined pink face, appeared and led Dustin Hoffman away by an elbow. "It's been a pleasure," the actor said to Penny over his shoulder as he left.

There at last, Guy thought, went another outsider like himself, that big fellow in brown: red woolen tie, smooth shaven, probably in his sixties. "Who was that?" he asked Penny.

"Guy, he was on the cover of *Time* last week. That's Sinclair Holloway. Did you just wake up?"

"How can you tell?"

"Bloodshot eyes, dear, bleary manner."

"Holloway . . . Oh, yes, Chairman of the Board of something. AOL? Bertelsmann? Something in the octopus line." They were strolling into an enormous long living room, its walls lined with pop art like a dealer's gallery, where waitresses were passing trays of champagne and hors d'oeuvres.

"TransUniverse," said Penny. "The new very big one. It just merged General Foods with Bertelsmann, and bought up Fox and Boeing."

Guy said, "Still dickering for Antarctica, no doubt."

Guy scrutinized the paintings they walked past — a huge torn-open Cracker Jack box, a zebra-striped toilet seat, Clark Gable as Rhett Butler in colored dots — and halted at the biggest artwork in the room, an immense square canvas painted a solid dead black. "I give up on this one," he said. "What is it?"

"Minimalism," said Penny. She was peering at the dinner seating plan on a side table. "Well, well. I rate table number three, with Sean. You're with the Congresswoman at number two."

Guy took two glasses of champagne from a passing tray. "Who's at number one?"

"Dustin, of course, with Holloway."

"Dustin, eh?"

"Yes, Dustin. Nice man, Dustin. Really interested in the human genome. Say, Guy, this is great champagne. Great Yahrtzeit! Bless Ottoline."

Sean came shouldering through the guests in a great rush. "Back into the library, folks, if you're interested in a breaking news story," he called out. "ABC News is interrupting the tennis matches, something about the Chinese and national security —"

Most of the guests went on drinking and chatting, others drifted into the library, where the wall of books was sliding away again. Penny and Guy sat down on a couch beside a baby-faced person with a notably sparse beard, just a few straggling curly blond hairs, which he kept scratching. "I guarantee this will be a big nothing," he said, feeding himself fried shrimp from a plate. "Just more of this boson crap that CNN has been carrying on about. Now ABC's jumping aboard, that's all. Sean's an alarmist. I'm Tim Warshaw." Guy recognized the name. He liked disaster movies, the more disastrous the better, and Timothy Warshaw was the big new disaster producer. His *Meltdown of the Eiffel Tower,* about French high school geeks bringing down the Tower with superlasers, damming the Seine with molten iron and flooding all Paris, had won an Oscar for special effects. "I'm a fan of yours," Guy said.

"Well, thanks —"

The tennis game on the screen was blotted out by three words, EXCLUSIVE BREAKING STORY, with a blast of ominous music. The words faded, and there was Peter Jennings.

Good evening. ABC News has just learned that urgent hearings by the Armed Services Committee and the Science, Space, and Technology Committee of the House will commence at once in Congress to deal with the Chinese boson discovery. ABC has obtained possession of a top-secret document, circulating among selected members of Congress even as I speak. The content is so sensitive and so startling that ABC News has consulted with military leaders and the National Security Adviser before breaking the story. Viewers are cautioned that, while what they will now hear is confirmed by the highest scientific and political sources, key details are withheld.

Guy saw Myra Kadane slip into the library and drop into an armchair nearby, looking grave. Tim Warshaw said to him, "Pretty good buildup to a lot of nothing." Jennings's face now took on a solemnity, and his voice a sonority, that brought forcibly to Guy Carpenter's mind his election night announcement that Al Gore had won Florida.

The title of the document is . . . OMEGA. Omega *is a code word for a new weapon of inconceivable magnitude.* (Long pause.) *A Boson Bomb.*

Long, long pause to let that sink in to a stunned America.

It is not yet known, according to the Omega *document, whether the Chinese have yet succeeded in making the Boson Bomb, or are preparing to do so, or have the technology to create such a bomb. What is known is this: The principle of the Bomb involves the manipulation of mass, the ultimate source of energy in the universe, through the agency of the Higgs force field. It is also known that, if and when such a bomb is built, it will exceed the destructive power of the H-bomb, as the H-bomb exceeds gunpowder. The Chinese have the Higgs boson, and the United States does not. That is what is at stake. I'm Peter Jennings.*

9. THE FALCON

Timothy Warshaw leaped to his feet, exclaiming, "Holy shit, this thing has legs now," and hurried away as a hubbub arose in the library. Guests were noisily streaming in from other rooms, everyone talking at once. *"What was it? EXACTLY WHAT did Jennings really say? A bombing attack? Where? A Boson Bomb? What's that? Is the President coming on? What the fuck is a* boson? *Special session of Congress? Are the Chinese mobilizing? Do we still eat dinner here?"*

Penny nudged Guy. "Look at your Congresswoman." Myra was slumped in her armchair, her head down on her hand. "Did you know about this *Omega* business?"

"Me? How could I possibly know?"

For Guy Carpenter, this party was now taking on the aspect of a fever dream. There went Myra Kadane, striding out of the library in a distracted manner. Jennings's reference to "manipulating mass," echoing his own e-mail to Myra, was eerie. Years ago, Herman Rocovsky had enjoyed fantasizing in that vein late at night over brandy. That was where Guy himself had picked it up. A lightning flash — *it could even be that Jennings had gotten that language from Rocovsky!* What the devil did Peter Jennings, or anybody else at ABC, know about the Higgs field, or manipulating mass? The media people ate out of the Rock's hand, the more so as he was content to educate them as an anonymous "source."

"Penny, let me have the cell phone." She carried it in her purse whenever they both left Dinah. "I'm calling the Rock."

Dustin Hoffman was approaching them, his smile tentative, his eyes worried. "Dr. Carpenter! What do you make of all this?"

With an apologetic shrug and a head shake, Guy hastened off. "He'll be back, Dustin," Penny said. "It's his field. He worked on the Super Collider —"

"That thing down in Texas? He *did?* Thanks, Penny." Hoffman turned on his heel. "Sinclair should know about that right away."

In the billiard room Myra Kadane gave Carpenter a harried look as she closed a cell phone, gnawing her lips. "Well, the hearings will happen all right, Horace Wesley says. Score one for Peter Jennings."

"Were you aware of this *Omega* document, Myra?"

"In fact, I was. Why?"

"I'm trying to call the man who'll know more about it all than anyone alive."

"I want to talk to that man."

"Let me try to arrange it," Carpenter said. Rocovsky's office did not reply, and he was not at home, either.

"Guy, how real is this Boson Bomb?"

"Scientific rot."

She sighed. "Good! I'm sure you're right. But you yourself wrote me — in that e-mail from Dallas, you know — about 'manipulating mass.'"

"So I did. And I described it as moonshine, with a long string of *ifs,* generations away."

"I smell Quentin Rossiter in here somewhere," said Myra. "No secret in Congress is safe from Quentin. Not for long. Come, life goes on, let's eat."

The dinner tables were set on a glassed-in patio overlooking a garden lush with banana fronds, flowering hibiscus, and blooming lemon trees. Some guests were already seated; others were looking at place cards. "Here we are, Guy, and you're on my right — *wait* a minute!" Myra picked up a card. "Timothy Warshaw? I *told* Sean to put Tim at table number one —"

"He rates that?"

"Professor, *Eiffel Tower* did a hundred sixty million domestic, and in Japan it topped *Godzilla.* Damn, who's fooled with the place cards?"

"This Warshaw looks like such a kid."

"The audience is kids nowadays, dear man, so kids make the movies. If you're over thirty in this business, you're expected to use a walker and develop Alzheimer's. As I got to know only too bloody well, before Walter rescued me — Sean!" She brandished the card at her stepson.

"Right, right." He came bustling up. "Sorry, Myra. Guy, you're at table number one. Sinclair wants to meet you."

"Go, Guy," Myra said. "Follow the money."

Sinclair Holloway and Dustin Hoffman sat with three beards and four women, three of them doll beauties, one about Penny's age, not pretty but chic in a tailored yellow suit. Holloway offered his hand and said in a slow harsh voice with a trace of an accent, "Dr. Carpenter, sit down here, by my good ear. Dustin, move." The actor affably took the vacant chair on Holloway's left. "Dustin says you worked on the Super Collider."

The phantasmagoric aspect of this party, the physicist thought, was really getting to him. Holloway's profile was hawkish, his pouchy eyes had the veiled brightness of a raptor's, and his bony handshake offered only half his fingers. Guy could have sworn he diffused a real chill, like a figure of dry ice. It seemed odd that Holloway was not giving off wisps of vapor. Still, his smile was warm, like winter sunlight on snow. "Tell us about it."

"Long story," Guy ventured through a constricted throat.

"Well, what about this Boson Bomb, now? How serious is it?"

"I wouldn't take off for Tasmania just yet."

Holloway grunted. "My opinion exactly. I've done a lot of business in China. Nice people, smart but slow, all tangled up in red tape, not efficient. Now, you realize that Illinois should have had that Super Collider, don't you? I was on the Illinois site committee. Bad business! The Department of Energy could have saved a bundle just by upgrading Fermilab outside Chicago. Then the thing would have been done, not canceled and wasting billions —"

Dustin Hoffman, a thumb to his lips, was observing the physicist and the Chairman with a detached half smile. The beards and the ladies were paying puzzled attention. "Could be," Guy said. "There was a problem of underground water at the site, as I recall —"

"There was a problem of underground Texas dollars," retorted Holloway. "Texas offered a billion up front, on the quiet. Money up front was supposed to be irrelevant to the site decision. Ha!" The laugh came out a squawk.

"Sinclair," the lady in yellow broke in, "I haven't the foggiest notion of what you two are talking about."

Hoffman said, "Neither have I. What's a collider?"

"Yes, and what's all this," said the lady in yellow, "about Texas and Illinois?"

Holloway turned to the physicist. "Shayna Daniels, great producer, Steven Spielberg in a skirt. She's right. Tell them about the Super Collider."

Could disorientation go further? Now he had to reel off his Waxahachie spiel to a table of beards, beauties, a billionaire, and Dustin Hoffman at a Bel-Air Yorsite party! No help for it, and he talked through the caviar, the vichyssoise, and on into the roast duck, fueling himself with glass after glass of the best wine he had ever drunk. At one point, Holloway brusquely interjected. "You know something, Dr. Carpenter? I never got the SSC picture this clearly before. In fact I didn't have the picture at all, the Governor of Illinois just wanted the damn thing, so we did our best to get it —"

"Dr. Carpenter?" The maître d', a tall handsome black lady, came to the table.

"That's me."

"You have a call on your wife's cell phone, a Professor Rocoxy?"

Holloway turned falcon eyes full on Guy Carpenter as he got up. "Rocovsky? You know Herman Rocovsky?"

"Worked with him for years."

"We have to talk more," said the Chairman.

"By all means."

Sean said, as Guy came to Penny's table and took the phone, "Sorry, Dr. Carpenter, I couldn't say no to Sinclair Holloway."

"Why, he's a barrel of laughs — Rock, hello. Hang on while I find a quiet place to talk."

"Give him my love," said Penny. "I miss the old crocodile."

Penny watched Guy go out through a sliding door into the garden and off among the banana fronds. Time passed, the dinner began to break up, and he did not return. Away from her baby and without the phone, Penny was restless. Well, he had much to discuss with Rocovsky, no doubt, after that broadcast! She went to the glass wall and peered into the darkening garden. "Looking for hubby?" Dustin Hoffman was beside her, smiling. "He's talking to Timothy Warshaw out there. Tim's producing the movie I'm making now. Your husband blew Sinclair Holloway away."

"Blew him away? How so?"

"Brilliant and understandable, Sinclair called him. Rare combination in a scientist. He had Sinclair almost purring. How about an after-dinner drink? They're making stingers."

"Stingers! Dustin, I haven't had a stinger since Cornell days. Oh, why not?"

"Great. Come with me. Tell me, what's your opinion of stem cells?"

In an open ironwork pavilion among the lemon trees, Timothy Warshaw and Shayna Daniels were enthusing to Guy Carpenter about a Boson Bomb movie. It was the greatest disaster concept, Warshaw roundly asserted, since King Kong. Just the alliteration in the title was box-office magic. He intended to start development immediately and he wanted Dr. Carpenter as scientific consultant.

"I guarantee you," said Warshaw, "that right this minute, ten quickie producers are talking Boson Bomb to ignorant hack writers. So what? Movies and TV shows about aliens were as common in this town as dog shit in Manhattan, before *Star Wars* came along. I'll make the *Star Wars* of the Boson Bomb, Guy, starting the day *Save the Moose* goes into the can, and —"

"He'll do it too," Shayna Daniels broke in, "and I'll produce it. I'm producing the moose movie."

In sheer bewilderment, Guy stalled. "Mr. Warshaw —"

"Tim, Tim!"

"Tim, did you say *Save the Moose?* Hardly your sort of movie, is it? Where's the disaster?"

Warshaw and Shayna Daniels looked at each other and laughed. "Try ten thousand moose all falling into a crater that opens in an earthquake," said Warshaw. "And why? Because the oil barons have pumped out all the oil under their habitat, that's why, leaving a vast hollow space in the earth beneath. I've checked this out with geologists. It's gold."

"You're an environmentalist? That's admirable."

"Let's be frank," Shayna Daniels said. "Tim would eat barbecued moose with pleasure. This moose thing is Sinclair Holloway's baby. He has it in for the oil interests something frightening, ever since he failed to take over Texaco. He doesn't care diddly-squat about moose."

Warshaw said, "Look, I fly to Saskatchewan tonight to do location footage. My writer is there with the unit. Cy Finkle, a genius. *Eiffel Tower* was his brainstorm. Can I get you to come to Saskatchewan for a few days so the three of us can kick this around?"

"We can put a plane at your disposal," said the producer, "a nice plane."

Guy blurted, "I'm not a pilot," and felt like an idiot when Warshaw and Daniels exchanged indulgent smiles.

"Dr. Carpenter," said the producer, "a company plane comes with a pilot."

"Oh, of course." Guy was wishing he had drunk less wine. This Yahrtzeit party was spinning down into lunacy. Could they be serious? If so, what about Penny? His work at the laboratory? He stared at them, bereft of speech.

"Why don't we talk money?" Shayna Daniels went on. "No pressure intended, Dr. Carpenter, but speed is imperative. This concept has a green light from Sinclair Holloway, and I can't tell you how important that is, or how fast it can change."

"Well, I can listen," Guy Carpenter managed to say.

When he came in from the garden, the dinner guests were making their farewells in a great racket of departing BMWs, Lamborghinis, and stretch limousines. Sean was at the bell-tower door, seeing them out. "Hi, Guy. Looking for your wife? She's in the library with Myra."

The two women were alone in the enormous room, curled up on a sofa, drinks in hand. "*There* he is, Myra!" Penny waved a brandy glass. Myra Kadane had joined her to chat over stingers when Hoffman left, and Penny was as cordial as she could be to the Congresswoman, who did not register on her supersensitive radar as a threat; attractive, sure, but of another world than Guy, and not at all a man-eating flirt. Moreover, she was an ally in securing the telescopes, Guy's present life and his whole long-range future. "You get to drive home, honey," she called, laughing. "This is my third stinger. I haven't been this happy since John gave up hang gliding. Splendid custom, Yahrtzeits! Call Stephanie."

"I called Stephanie. Everything's fine. I can use some black coffee."

"Done, be right back," said the Congresswoman, jumping up.

"Why were you out there so long?" Penny wanted to know.

"You're not going to believe this. Penny —"

"Believe *what?* How's the Rock?"

"Huh, the Rock? Oh yes, the Rock's fine, sends you his best —"

"You were talking to that creep Warshaw, weren't you?" Penny narrowed her eyes at him. "Dustin told me."

"Dustin called him a creep? Bully for Dustin —"

"Dustin called him 'my director.' *Creep* is my emendation."

"Coffee coming." Myra Kadane returned, swirling a brandy glass. "One more for the road, Penny?"

"Hold everything!" Guy raised both hands. "No more for her. Penny and I both need your advice, Myra, need it badly."

"Bless my soul, you do?"

"It's about this Timothy Warshaw. Him and that Daniels woman. They've buttonholed me with an insane proposition involving fifty thousand dollars."

"What?" Penny sat up as at a crack of thunder.

"Go on! I'm all ears," said Myra Kadane, eager and amused.

He was describing Warshaw's approach when the maître d' brought a silver coffee service and poured it for him. "Thanks — Myra, they say they'll put a plane and pilot at my disposal, to take me to Saskatchewan and back and anywhere else, all mine for a week, and I give the orders. Things don't happen that way —"

"In this business? Nothing unusual." Myra was brisk and matter-of-fact. "Timothy and Shayna want to pick your brain. What do they know about bosons? They need you, or at the moment they think they do, so the wooing is on. With those two it can be cyclonic. Just bear one thing in mind and you'll be all right. If they decide they *don't* need you — and it can happen in an eyeblink, Guy — you're gone, a wad of snotty Kleenex dropping into a wastebasket."

"How reassuring," said Penny.

Guy said, "She gave me this card."

Myra took large round glasses from her purse to read it. "Ray Luntz, eh? Good pilot, Ray. Walter used him quite a bit. Hm, Falcon 900 EX! Snazzy French jet, top-of-the-line —"

"Tell me again," said Penny, "about the fifty thousand dollars."

"Well, that's for development, I think they said, something like that —"

"Right," Myra Kadane said. "Preproduction cost. For a consultant of your standing, cheap at the price. And if the movie is ever made, you get more money. Did they mention that?"

"I'm not sure, I was too staggered — look, Myra, here's something important, not like this nonsense. I told Professor Rocovsky that you want to talk to him. He invites you to come to Stanford anytime."

"Ah, now you're talking." She pulled a PalmPilot from her purse, *click, click, click,* and squinted at the little screen. "Actually, I could work it in tomorrow afternoon. How do I let him know?"

"I'll organize that for you." Guy rubbed his face with both hands. "Myra, what about this offer? I'm utterly out of my depth —"

"Up to you and Penny. I don't know your commitments —"

Penny said, "First of all, dear, let's find out if it's for real."

"Oh, yes? Tell me how."

"I say phone this moose fellow. Tell him you want to fly to Stanford tomorrow with Congresswoman Kadane, since Rocovsky invited her. Boson research. You should talk to the Rock anyway, if this thing is serious. See what Mr. Moose says. If you've really got the plane, you'll get the money. If he fudges in any way, just forget it. Party talk."

Myra gave her a surprised smile. "Good thinking, Penny, but Guy needn't call Tim, he's still here, playing billiards with Sean. They're a pair of sharks. Let me get him."

She returned in a moment with Warshaw, in shirtsleeves and suspenders, chalking a cue. "So you want to fly up to Stanford with Myra? Terrific. Call Ray Luntz and he'll be at your service. Just show up in Saskatchewan on Tuesday or Wednesday. Better Wednesday, okay? Because — you're shaking your head."

"I'm trying to clear it. Me, in a private jet —"

Warshaw nervously chalked the cue. "Dr. Carpenter, this is Sinclair Holloway business. TransUniverse has planes and pilots ready to go, like racehorses eating oats in the barn, just burning up money. Cost of doing business. Look, now that I think of it, why don't I talk to Sean right now, have him draw up a simple consultant contract tomorrow? You'll get it in a few days. A check will come with it." He held out a hairy manicured hand. Guy glanced at Penny, she barely shrugged, and he took the hand.

"Fantastic. Delighted. Shayna and Sinclair will be too." Brandishing his cue at Myra as he left, the director chortled, "I'm cleaning Sean's clock."

"Does tomorrow work for you, Guy?" Myra said. "I'm used to this drill, I can call Ray and set it up."

"What have I done?" he said to Penny, looking at his sweaty palm streaked with blue chalk. "My name as consultant on an idiocy about a Boson Bomb? It's unthinkable."

"Well, you're in it now," said the Congresswoman. "A handshake in this town is sacred. It means a deal, on one's honor. Unless one backs out, which is the usual thing. But you shouldn't."

"Why not? I feel doped, or something," said Guy Carpenter.

"Because out of twenty films in development, maybe one eventually gets produced. This thing will probably go *poof!* Meantime make hay while the sun shines, that's my advice. Suppose I call you after I talk to Ray?"

"Let's go home, dear." Penny stood up. "You have to pack, in case."

They found nothing to say to each other as they drove out of Bel-Air. After running along Sunset Boulevard for a while in sparse traffic, he spoke first. "Sweetie pie, you were thinking pretty fast back there."

"Guy, fifty thousand dollars cuts our mortgage by two-thirds."

"Not after taxes."

"In half, then. Or it goes into the college fund for Dinah. She'll cost four times what John did, you know."

He was silent until a red light stopped them. "They threw money around like this on the Collider," he burst out, "for bringing in high-powered technical specialists from abroad. It caused trouble, but at least it was rational. This is abysmal foolishness."

"What are most movies?"

"What do you think of Myra Kadane? You seemed real chummy there."

"She's no dumb bunny, that's for sure. No snob, either. Kicked off her shoes and talked a lot about her husband. Maybe because it was his Yahrtzeit, but I think she's still in love with a dead man. I like her."

Another silence.

"This damned consultant job, Penny! I feel as though I'm leaping off a ski jump at night, into a black void."

"Enjoy the soaring sensation," said Penny, "while it lasts."

10. THE JET

Guy and Penny stood peering up at the yellow smog hanging low over the hills west of Pasadena. "There it comes, I bet," she said. A black dot was sinking out of the murk toward the small airport, where private jets and piston planes, from lordly Gulfstreams to mosquito-like Pipers, were parked here and there all around them.

"I see it. I never knew this airport existed," Guy said. "Did you?"

"We didn't have to," said Penny. "Millionaire's Row. Quiet, Dinah."

In her arms, Dinah was insisting, loud but unclear, that she was bored, or wanted lunch, or was deliriously happy, or something. A mechanic working on a plane nearby waved a wrench at her and yelled, "Pretty baby!" The dot swelled to a stubby silvery jet that swooped in to land, turned around, and came howling to within a few feet of them. The engines muttered and died. A door opened, a small staircase unfolded, and Myra Kadane, in a pants suit and a baseball cap, trotted down.

"Oh, *Penny,* you brought Dinah, bless you. Please —!" Penny handed the baby into Myra's open arms. "All set, Guy? This is Ray Luntz."

The pilot, a lean grizzled man in chino pants, a Hawaiian shirt, and dark glasses, gripped Guy's hand hard and picked up his luggage. "Yes, sir, Dr. Carpenter. Weather at Stanford looks good."

"Helloo-oo, Dinah," the Congresswoman was cooing. "My God, you're glorious."

"Honorable Congress lady far too kind," Penny said with a head bob, "to our miserably ugly daughter."

Myra laughed. "Like to have a look at the plane, Penny? Go ahead, Guy, show her how the other half lives."

"The other one-thousandth of one percent," Guy said.

"Start up with a physicist! It's all right, Penny. See, Dinah likes me." Indeed, the baby was hugging the sweet-smelling stranger's neck hard, possibly so as not to be dropped.

Penny and Guy clambered aboard. Plumping down in one of the big soft armchairs, she swiveled to and fro, taking in the fancy fittings, the gleaming redwood tables folded by each seat, the oversize windows. "Nice. You've got this thing for a whole week? Unbelievable. Let's do a second honeymoon in Alaska, dear. I feel a strange yen for wild salmon."

"You're on," said Guy. "If you're fooling, I'm not. *'Make hay while the sun shines,'* Myra said. Quick trip to Alaska. Wild salmon." He leaned over and kissed her. "We'll do it, by God."

"We'll see," said Penny. "Come say good-bye to Dinah."

He hugged and kissed the baby, and managed an awkward hug with Penny, saying, "I'll call from SLAC, honey. The Rock will want to talk to you, I know."

"That'll be nice. Bye, Myra. Happy landings." She walked off into the terminal, not looking back. The baby returned Guy's wave as they disappeared inside.

The plane leaped into the air. Thrust hard against the back of his armchair, Guy exclaimed, "Wow, well named, this Falcon."

"It's a Mirage Fighter, actually" — Myra hardly had to raise her voice over motor roars soundproofed to a discreet moan — "just gussied up with plush and swanky woodwork for rich softies. What does *SLAC* mean?"

"Stanford Linear Accelerator Center. That's where those cute little quarks — which you know all about — were first detected. Three friends of mine, three Nobel Prizes."

"Why don't you have one?"

"Thanks, Myra. I'm not in their class."

"Doesn't luck play a part in it?"

Guy Carpenter exhaled a deep breath before answering. "Direct lady, aren't you? Well, it's a lottery, true enough. The line of theory you get into is chancy, and the price of a ticket is your life's work. Most tickets don't win, of course."

"What's the difference between a collider and an accelerator? Or is there one?"

"Oh, yes. By and large, an accelerator slams a stream of particles into a stationary target, while a collider whips two streams around in opposite directions and smashes them into each other. Advantages and drawbacks to both designs, which we can go into if you want —"

The copilot, Jerry, a slight man with sandy curly hair and a boyish grin, handed Guy Carpenter a mug of coffee. "How about lunch, sir? We have bagels and lox, or a fruit-and-cheese plate. Or for a hot dish, sir, lamb chops with Spanish rice."

"I had the bagel and lox on the way here," Myra said. "It's good."

"That's for me, Jerry, thanks." Guy sipped the coffee. "And what is this marvelous stuff?"

"Jamaica Blue Mountain, sir."

"Best in the world," said Myra Kadane. "Only coffee Sinclair Holloway drinks."

"Well, I never," said Guy. "I'm telling Dinah to marry anyone she likes, providing he has at least three billion dollars." He handed Myra Kadane papers from his dispatch case. "You wanted to read my whine about the Super Collider. Here it is, six pages of it. Then we'll talk some more about accelerators and colliders."

Myra Kadane put on glasses. Vertical wrinkles appeared on her forehead as she read the printout, page by slow page, now and then glancing at the physicist. He finished the coffee and reclined in the armchair, long legs stretched out, arms crossed, blatantly suffused with well-being. "I believe you could get used to a private jet," she remarked.

"Myra, I expect this thing to turn into a pumpkin anytime. Meanwhile, as my son might say, it's a hoot —"

"Bagel and lox, sir."

The copilot unfolded a polished wood table at Carpenter's chair, laid down a plastic mat, and served the bagel on a pale-blue china plate, pouring fresh hot coffee. The physicist had trouble biting into it, the bagel was piled so thick with cream cheese, onion, and tomato, but he managed to wolf it all down. "Never tasted such exquisite smoked salmon," he said at the last bite.

"From Finland, Sinclair's favorite." Myra Kadane tapped the document. "A sorry tale, Guy. I didn't realize Clinton broke a campaign promise to support the SSC —"

"Politics, Madame Congresswoman, politics. He also promised to cut the budget, and once he got in, the SSC — a Reagan project, anyway — was a nice juicy cut. Or so I've gathered since. At the time it was all too Byzantine for my academic head. I was fired, it was over, and I shut it from my mind. If Bush senior had beaten Clinton, the Super Collider would now be up and running — anyway, that's my guess — and we'd have found the Higgs boson, or we'd have proved it *didn't* exist. Either way the Chinese would be eating our dust, instead of the other way around."

"What about this last line of yours? It puzzles me."

"What line is that?"

"*'So endeth my long misadventure in pyramid building.'*" She took off her glasses and peered at him. "Pyramid building?"

"Oh, that. Parting shot of a long jaundiced gripe."

"Guy, those words are a summing up."

"Look, when we survivors of the Super meet and reminisce, and get drunk, and compare scars, there's one question we still rake over. Was the Super Collider truly hard science? Or was it a pyramid to aggrandize a few insider physicists at taxpayer expense, maybe copping them a Nobel or two? Tough call, to this day."

"And you come down on the pyramid side —"

"Wait, wait, leave me out of it. Rocovsky will give you the wisest judgment you're likely to get." He shrugged. "Then again, he's the insider of insiders. So there you are."

"You're stalling, Guy." She handed the papers back. "You have an opinion. Let's hear it!"

"You're compelling me to pontificate." He stared out at white clouds billowing past. "I hate it."

"Understood. Come on."

"Very well then, here's my opinion. I'd say that despite its origin — mainly a stung response, as I told you, to the CERN coup with the W and Z particles — and despite all that went wrong, and oh, Christ, did things go wrong, the Super in its concept was pure outsize American. The real thing. And the execution, as far as it got, was pure outsize Texan. Okay, maybe it was a pyramid of sorts, but maybe not, and now how can we ever know? Once started, it should have been finished. Nobody can say we *wouldn't* have penetrated to fresh interesting physics! Not to the Mind of God, of course not, but —"

He paused, gazing out at thinning mist as the Falcon began bumping downward. The ground was coming in sight far below. "At the least, Madame Congresswoman, wasn't it the old star-spangled college try, after all? Wasn't it the human spirit versus the unknown, the mind of Man versus Einstein's Old One — that's what he called God — or versus the universe, or whatever you choose to call what's out there? Wasn't it Don Quixote sallying forth to glory once more, this time with Uncle Sam as Sancho Panza?"

The physicist's voice hoarsened and failed him. He turned his face to the window, and Myra Kadane felt her eyes moisten. After a moment he cleared his throat and looked back at her soberly.

"To my worm's-eye view, Myra, the Superconducting Super Collider was aborted for complicated political reasons by myopic ignoramuses, who rationalized what they did on a grubby budgetary basis — to wit, all it could do was try to find out more and more about less and less for fewer and fewer people to understand. Perfectly true. There you have my opinion. How's that?"

"Pretty good." Her eyes were glistening at him. "I'm ready for the Rock."

The stretched white Lincoln waiting outside the link fence of the airfield looked to Guy Carpenter as long as a train. "Oh, no, Ray," Myra Kadane groaned to the pilot, who carried their suitcases. "You know I detest these things. They make me seasick."

"Ma'am, this was what I could get. There's a national conference of bird watchers on at Stanford today. No limos left but these. Sorry."

"Ever ridden in one?" she asked the physicist when they were inside. Far up ahead, the driver was visible only by his black cap. "They pitch and roll like a destroyer."

A shout in a thick Russian accent from the front, "Peetch? Rrrroll? Missus, try taking de veel, try turning a corner! Dese tings dey rotten. You dunt know! SLAC, mister?"

"Right, SLAC," Guy called. As they drove off he said to Myra Kadane, "What the devil do bird watchers want with limousines?"

"Mister, you be saprise," yelled the driver. "Dose bord vatchers, dey all on big expense accounts. Bord vatchers! Ha! I drive dem, I know. Nightclubs! Strip joints! America! Everyting a big bluff."

"I forgot to mention," murmured Myra Kadane, "that these things are also echo chambers."

A fast nauseous ride brought them to the SLAC administration building. The gilt lettering on the door of Rocovsky's office read DIRECTOR EMERITUS. "That's new," Guy Carpenter remarked, "and absolutely meaningless. The Rock will never be emeritus of anything."

In a wide chamber looking out on green trees and a rolling lawn, a diminutive figure in an old gray sweater got to his feet behind an enormous desk flanked by two large computer screens. "Hello, Guy. Welcome, Madame Congresswoman."

11. THE ROCK

Face-to-face, the Rock had a forbidding air, not at all like the genial old professor Myra Kadane had anticipated from the smiling photograph on his website. The wisdom and craft in that aged mottled countenance, in those wrinkled blue eyes, quite matched the long printouts of his publications, achievements, and honors, and the thousands of links to HERMAN ROCOVSKY.

"I knew your husband well." He motioned them to two chairs placed before the desk. "He came here now and then for a private talk, just as you're doing now. A responsible politician, an able mind. A real loss to Congress, to the country, and to you. I mean every word of this."

"Thank you, Professor Rocovsky."

"Horace Wesley reports that you're serving admirably in Walter's place."

"That's generous of Horace."

"Now then. How can I help you?"

Like a shot she came back, "Is there such a thing as a Boson Bomb, Dr. Rocovsky? Or can there be?"

Rocovsky blinked, stared at her, and turned on Carpenter. "Well, what does our distinguished friend here say?"

"We watched the Jennings broadcast at her house," said Guy. "I told her it was scientific rot."

Rocovsky suddenly laughed a dry old man's laugh, almost a cough, his shoulders shaking. "Harsh words, Guy."

"Dr. Carpenter also told me," said Myra Kadane, "that the *Omega* memorandum was probably your doing."

Rocovsky's face froze. "Chairman Hurtle had better track down the culprit who leaked that information to Peter Jennings. A gross breach of security! Of course, once Peter telephoned me, the cat was out of the bag."

"Worst person to get hold of it," said Carpenter.

"Not really, Guy. Peter did a fair job. Overdramatic, but that's his style. He got Hurtle's memo more or less right —"

"Professor Rocovsky, Bob Hurtle knows no more physics than I do," Myra Kadane rapped out. "Maybe less, since I've met Dr. Carpenter. Yet he went and wrote that memo on the basis of what you told him. Now all hell is breaking loose."

"Congresswoman," said the Rock stiffly, "when the Chairman of the Armed Services Committee calls me for advice, I'm duty bound to respond. I did not say there was such a thing as a Boson Bomb. I chose my words with care."

"Whatever you said to Bob Hurtle," she retorted, "you've touched off a national panic."

"Pardon me. The Chinese did that." Dr. Rocovsky stood up. "Please come with me. I want to show you something. Both of you."

They followed him down a corridor of open offices, where staff people clicked away at computers, to a small windowless anteroom. The light-green map that took up one entire wall was dotted with place-names and webbed with red-and-blue road lines. The legend in a lower corner read:

SUPERCONDUCTING SUPER COLLIDER
ELLIS COUNTY, TEXAS

A thick black oval line enclosed most of the county, centering on a town starred in boldface, ***Waxahachie.** The other walls had pictures of half-finished buildings, politicians cutting ribbons or digging with shovels, President Bush smiling in a hard hat, and a color blowup of a tunnel entrance, with workmen in it looking small as dolls. A large architect's model stood in the middle of the room, several plasterboard buildings clustered around what looked like a narrow blue lake.

"This is it, Madame Congresswoman, Moshe Safdie's vision," said Rocovsky. "The great Israeli architect, you know."

"I know Safdie." She was contemplating the model with awe. "He designed a cultural center that Walter headed."

"I saw this mock-up eons ago," Carpenter said. "So this is where it landed —"

"It's monumental," Myra Kadane murmured.

"My dear," said the Rock, with a new note of warm melancholy pride, and the smile of his Internet photograph, "it would have been the capstone of a great century of physics, the scientific mecca of the human race." In a caressing gesture, Rocovsky's hand passed over the honey-colored buildings, divided by the blue water and connected by a Venetian-like bridge. "Safdie conceived the entire complex around the cooling pond, you see. The liquefying of the helium throws off enormous heat, requiring tons and tons of this cooling water. Here to the west are the Collider structures, and across the pond are the public buildings — laboratories, lecture halls, libraries, every facility for the inquiring mind. When this wondrous vision was twenty percent realized — on time and on budget, Madame Congresswoman — your husband voted to kill it."

"Why, Dr. Rocovsky? *Why?* Do you know?"

"I do, and that opens a whole box of horrors. He agonized over his vote, I assure you. Well, now that you've seen it, let's talk some more."

As they walked up the corridor, Myra Kadane fell behind. Guy heard her click her cell phone and say sotto voce, "Ray? Do you know Waxahachie, Texas?" When he glanced back at her, she wagged a warning finger and put away the phone.

Back in the office, they sat down on sofas facing out to the lawn. "Guy, what do you make of the Chinese article?" Rocovsky asked.

"I've been on the run ever since it came out, Rock. Looks like difficult stuff."

"Yes, the math is quite subtle. If the Chinese really have the results they claim, it's a huge advance. *'A great leap forward.'* " He quoted Mao with a cold grin. "Very Chinese, that! I'll be a while working it all out. Beyond a doubt it's interesting physics —"

Myra Kadane interrupted, "It couldn't possibly be a hoax?"

"Physics isn't sociology, Congresswoman," the Rock said in a razor tone of dismissal. "It's no hoax. By the way, Guy" — his expression turned puckish — "you do know that Wendy's coming to the United States."

"No! Is she?"

"Indeed she is, to that Sun Valley world conference on particle physics."

"But her name's not on the Chinese roster."

"No matter, she'll be there."

"I'm amazed. I'd heard rumors —"

Myra Kadane could not refrain from putting in, "Who's Wendy?"

Rocovsky and Carpenter looked at each other. Carpenter said, "Dr. Wen Mei Li. Leading author of the *Nature* article."

Rocovsky nodded. "Outstanding physicist. Had a terrible time in the Cultural Revolution. Riding high again these days. Now, about Walter's vote — how much time have you got, Madame Congresswoman?"

"Dr. Rocovsky, my husband was Walter to you. I'm Myra, and I have as much time as you can spare."

"Guy, what does she know?" The aged face settled in severe lines. "Where do I begin?"

"She knows a lot. She does her homework, and she's a quick study. Tell her what happened. She'll get it, or she'll ask questions — as you may have noticed."

"I've noticed," Rocovsky said.

"He's being kind," said Myra Kadane. "I started out ignorant as a cat about all this. He's a superb teacher."

The old physicist glanced from one to the other. "Speaking of a quick study," he said to Carpenter, "how's Penny? And that brand-new baby of yours?"

"Not so brand-new anymore. They're both fine. Penny said she misses you."

"I'll call her after this."

A gray-headed woman in a green smock came in, put a bowl of dried apricots on the coffee table, and left. "Help yourselves," said Rocovsky. "Quick jolt of energy." He ate one and settled back on the couch, fingertips pressed together under his chin. "Have you talked to her, Guy, about the Space Station?"

"Some."

"It was in the same Appropriations Bill as the Collider, I know that much," Myra said. "It passed by one vote, and the very next day the Collider was killed."

"Just so, Myra." In Rocovsky's side-glance at Carpenter, there was a faint twinkle. "And do you know why the Collider was killed?"

"I've heard at least six different reasons."

"Let's hear them all."

Myra Kadane looked inquiringly at Dr. Carpenter. "Go ahead, Myra," he said.

"I'll give it a try." As she ran through the explanations, Rocovsky nodded with weary familiarity, making laconic comments on each one; but he peered in surprise at Carpenter when she mentioned the aperture problem. "You told her about that?"

"Absolutely not. Where did you get it, Myra?"

"Department of Energy. Some people who messed with the Collider are still there."

"*Messed* is well put," Rocovsky said. "Walter would be proud of you. Now about Walter's vote — have an apricot."

"Thanks, I will."

Rocovsky bent a stern look at Guy Carpenter. "You'll overhear a story that you're to forget."

"Shall I step outside?"

Myra said, "Don't be ridiculous."

"Not necessary," said the Rock. "It does Kadane proud. Myra, he was all for the Collider. He was thrilled by its grandeur. He understood that America had to recapture the lead in science. He thought, as I did, that the Space Station was in essence a tag to the great Apollo mission, a formidable engineering challenge, a nice foreign-policy move, but not hard science. He meant to vote against it, and he had decided to vote for the Super Collider, which he knew would get him in very hot water with the Democrats. He came here to discuss that decision. We sat right here in this office, talking far into the night. Myra, I turned him completely around. Walter went back to Washington and voted *for* the Space Station and *against* the Collider." Rocovsky took an apricot and chewed it down. "By changing his mind on the Station, he saved it. His one vote made the difference. That thing is floating around up there, and foreign astronauts are doing their photogenic space walks, because your husband listened to me. As for the SSC, I told him to toe the line as a party man, and save his political capital to fight another day on a science issue we could win. The Collider was doomed."

"But why support the Space Station" — Myra's brow was knit in puzzlement — "when you both agreed it wasn't hard science?"

"Because the Space Station was sexy enough for the House illiterates to vote for it. Barely! If the United States Congress had killed two major science initiatives in one fiscal year, America's world standing would have sunk below that of Europe, maybe even of Japan. The Space Station saved our face in 1993."

"May I speak to that?" asked Carpenter.

Rocovsky said slowly and icily, "To what effect?"

"I don't quite buy the reasoning, Rock —"

"You don't have to," said Rocovsky. "You're a fine physicist. I'm talking politics to a Congresswoman. Tabletop science is a memory, Guy. Science today needs huge funding, and we're funded by a scientifically illiterate society. It's a haunting problem, and on the SSC it was fatal. One man, and one man only, had the opportunity and the political clout to make the Superconducting Super Collider happen. He failed to do it, and to my dying day I'll hold him accountable."

Myra blurted straight out, after what Carpenter had told her, "President Clinton, of course."

The Rock shook his head. "Herman Rocovsky."

12. THE WARNING

Martini time in the Falcon at 35,000 feet, en route to Dallas. Myra Kadane had told Carpenter, on leaving Rocovsky's office, that, one way or another, she had to go to Waxahachie to see the ruin of the SSC for herself, so how about flying there in TransUniverse's Falcon? The physicist and the Congresswoman, bathed in the sunset glow through the large windows, were nibbling at hot hors d'oeuvres set out on a table between them. "I never thought I'd see Waxahachie ever again," Guy Carpenter was saying, "except in my bad dreams, yet in an hour or two I'll really be back in that Texas purgatory. If it's only another dream, it's a good dream this time because you're in it. Cheers." He raised his glass to her and drank.

"Cheers." Myra Kadane laughed, head thrown back. "Tell me, what was Penny's reaction when you phoned her?"

"Oh, Penny to the life. *'Ye gods, Waxahachie? Well, if she's hell-bent on seeing where it all happened, which for a committeewoman makes sense, and if you can face those memories, why not?'* Then she added, *'Just don't let her forget about the telescopes.'* "

Myra Kadane laughed harder. "I'm only one committee member, but I'm not forgetting the telescopes, and as I told her, I've got a pretty good in with the Chairman. That's a keen wife you've got."

"Myra, what are these delicious things?"

"Rumaki, chicken livers. Help yourself, Jerry's bringing more."

He downed a couple, sipping the martini. "Know what's really strange? I find myself looking forward to Waxahachie, and why on earth is that? The euphoria of this whole demented broomstick ride?"

"I think I know why."

"Tell me."

"Because despite the horrors, you were there with Penny and your son, and you were working on something grand, at the leading edge of physics. That's what turns you on, Professor. That's why this far-out Planet Finder project, with telescopes a million miles out in space, suits you. Now you're bitter about the SSC, but then you were happy."

"Happy?" The sunset light was fading on his lean somber face, and Myra Kadane could almost see memories, good and bad, flickering through his mind. "All right. Tidbit from my freshman philosophy course. Schopenhauer defines 'happiness' as the absence of pain. Waxahachie was a five-year pain in the ass, I assure you, so Schopenhauer must have overlooked something, because you're right, I was happy."

"Was Schopenhauer a bachelor?"

"Bachelor, pessimist, sex fiend."

"Maybe what he overlooked was love."

"Bingo." Carpenter brightened as the copilot brought a tinkling jug and a plateful of the bacon-wrapped chicken livers. "Ah, rumaki. Good-o. Mr. Holloway's favorite, no doubt."

Jerry refilled their glasses, smiling. "With his drinks Mr. Holloway prefers salted peanuts. Like some, sir?"

"No thanks — speaking of memories, Myra, I'll retain the memory of this Falcon ride, and this perfect martini and the rumaki, and the sunset through these big windows, and a movie-star Congresswoman to drink with, for the rest of my natural life." He raised his glass, and they clinked.

"*Ex*–movie star, Guy. *Ex.* Nicely put, but your abiding memory of riding this Falcon will be the Alaska trip with Penny to eat wild salmon. Ray did say it was feasible, didn't he?"

"Piece of cake, he put it."

The Congresswoman's cell phone beeped. "Yes?" She glanced at Carpenter. "Okay . . . *okay,* I said, not now. I'll call you back. Bye . . ."

Ray Luntz came out of the cockpit, removing his dark glasses. "Folks, there's some clear turbulence up ahead. How about delaying dinner for half an hour or so?"

"No problem," said Guy. "Where's the facility on this high-flying executive suite?"

The pilot smiled. "That panel aft slides, sir."

The physicist found himself in something like a lady's boudoir when he closed the panel — large mirror bordered by bright lights, porcelain washbowl with gold fittings, soap, towels, hairbrush and comb, boxed Kleenex, plush chair. No sign, however, of a facility. Another door led aft. Ah, facility in there, no doubt, for modest rich softies. But behind the door he saw only a dim tumble of life belts, luggage, golf clubs, and a rubber raft. Obviously he was a blind fool. Where could it be? He pushed and probed at one fitting and another as the plane bumped and wobbled. A gold-trimmed little square of wood looked movable, so he moved it. Well, well, a pink roll of tissue. Getting warm. Could the seat of this plush chair possibly conceal — eureka!

When he staggered back to his armchair, Myra Kadane was saying, "Okay, got it, Earle, thanks," and she closed the cell phone. The turbulence quieted, the plane resumed its calm gliding flight, and Jerry served lamb chops and rice with a salad and hot rolls, pouring red wine into thin-stemmed glasses. Guy tasted the wine and inspected the bottle. "SILVERADO GULCH, NAPA VALLEY. Superb stuff."

"Little vineyard Sinclair Holloway owns," said Myra.

"Really? I'll say this for Sinclair Holloway, he puts up a fine wine. These lamb chops smell marvelous too. Does Sinclair Holloway raise lambs?" He lifted his glass. "To memories."

"Selected memories," she said. They drank, and for a while ate in silence.

"Guy, who is Chien-Shiung Wu?"

He looked up from his food. "Chien-Shiung Wu? Why?"

"Tell me about her."

"Illustrious physicist. Worked on the atomic bomb during the war. Renowned for her breakthrough on violation of parity. Screwed out of a Nobel Prize, like Rosalind Franklin on the discovery of DNA. Sort of retro about women scientists, the Swedes. She died in '97. Why bring her up?"

"I had Earle Carkin check Wen Mei Li on the Internet. Most links compare her to this Chien-Shiung Wu."

"Rubbish. Both female Chinese physicists, end of comparison. Wu was a world figure. Wendy's an able scientist, not a great mind. Competitive as a racehorse, relentless attention to detail, yet not a fussy perfectionist, which is my shortcoming, or at least one of them. She's a born project manager, all in all, and God knows we could have used her on the Super —"

"What did you call her? Mei? Wendy?"

"Nobody called Mei Li *Wendy* to her face. Not more than once."

"I get the feeling that she was very attractive."

Guy Carpenter put down his knife and fork, drank wine, and looked her in the eye. "What's all this about, Myra?"

"Oh, when you and the Rock talked about her, something was going on. None of my business, of course."

"No mystery, the Rock was gaga about her back at Cornell, that's all. Campus joke, he even joined in the kidding about it. Mei was the Great Wall of China, stony and unconquerable —"

"And you?"

"Me? Just one of the many swains languishing after her in vain. Not a chance. Strictly a grind, Wen Mei Li, straight A-plus on all her papers. And Chinese to the bone, she might have had a career here almost like Chien-Shiung Wu's, yet with her eyes open, she went back to Mao's China. She paid a harsh price for being Chinese."

"Well, she'll be coming back into a media circus, a huge celebrity."

"I know, and she'll abhor it. It can't be her doing. She wasn't scheduled for this conference." He drank up his wine and refilled the glass. "Obviously the Politburo means to rub America's nose in her success, and her visit will be one huge photo op about how we've lost face. Lord, will TV and the press fall all over her! They can't help themselves, the lemmings."

The copilot looked in. "Dessert, folks?"

"Not for me," she said.

"We have chocolate cake, Dr. Carpenter, or a cheese plate. The Stilton is quite good."

"Mr. Holloway's favorite, no doubt. Or does he prefer peanuts?"

"His favorite, sir."

"I'll have it anyway."

Myra Kadane watched Guy Carpenter demolish a chunk of mottled cheese, then lean back in the armchair with his wine. "Guy, it seems Dr. Wen Mei Li has been corresponding for a long time, on and off, with an American physicist, so Earle Carkin just told me —"

"What of it? Our physicists have been working there for years. Some are there now. Correspondence is routine."

"This has been a personal handwritten correspondence, carried on through a PO box." He merely nodded, sipping wine. The Congresswoman went on, "Quentin Rossiter's writing a major story about Dr. Wen Mei Li. He's down to checking details. A bit of a swine, but he's good at what he does. He'll win a Pulitzer one day, perhaps even for this story."

A fixed look of cool unruffled attention was settling on Dr. Carpenter's face. It was a look born of many career crises, turf battles, showdowns, firings, failures of yearlong experiments — a look he had worn for months in the chaotic collapse of the SSC. "Well, let's see. I worked with Mei Li in China two or three months, back in '89, on a simple accelerator. I went on a State Department grant, so all my correspondence with her was copied to State files. No problem."

"Then you did see her after Cornell."

"As I say, briefly, on a detente mission."

"What was she like? Still attractive?"

"Well, older. She'd tended pigs, dug irrigation ditches, hauled stones in a quarry, and so on, for six years. The Red Guards were hard on intellectuals. She didn't talk much about that. She was making a fast comeback, she picked up the cyclotron technology in a flash and took complete charge. She had the machine up and running when I left."

"And that was it?"

"That was it."

"I'm relieved."

"Relieved? Why? There's nothing in the least secret about particle physics, Myra. It's an open scientific field all over the world."

Ray Luntz's voice on the intercom: "Starting our descent to Dallas."

"Ah, good." Myra's tone lightened. "Earle called to confirm the arrangements for Waxahachie. We're booked into an old hotel right in town, and tomorrow the judge who assembled the real estate for the SSC will take us on a tour of the ruin."

"Sounds good," said the physicist.

Control-tower gabble from the open cockpit. Otherwise silence, while they both looked out at the starry night, a rising full moon, and the lights of Dallas ahead and far below. Abruptly he swiveled his armchair to face her. "Myra, what on earth made you say you were *relieved?*"

"Quentin Rossiter can't use everything he gets from the CIA, Guy, but he knows a lot more than he writes. That post-office-box correspondence has a big red flag on it."

13. THE SPILL

The moment Myra Kadane came into the somewhat musty Governor's Suite, so-called, of the old hotel, she plugged in her laptop at the living-room desk and began clicking away, not even stopping to unpack.

Walter dearest:

I have tons to tell you, mainly about my meeting at Stanford today with your friend the great Herman Rocovsky. Dr. Carpenter brought me there —

She paused, fingers on the keys. *So much to write to Walter! Such a jumble!*

— and at last, my love, I've got a handle on the SSC crash.

I'm now here at the actual scene of the crime with Dr. Carpenter, in a Waxahachie hotel deep in the heart of Texas, as the song goes. And lower those raised bushy eyebrows, honey, the man is in a room on another floor, and anyway, I can hear his territorial tigress of a wife snarling from two thousand miles away. She and I had a nice chat over stingers at the Yorsite party, and she's smart and sweet and a mite scary.

Okay. Now I'll try to put down all Rocovsky said about Congress's four-billion-dollar fiasco while it's fresh in my mind, and I'll take this letter with me into the hearings as a memorandum . . .

Myra Kadane had been writing these quirky letters to her departed husband for years. At first mere incoherent outpourings of grief and love, they had so eased her anguish that she had gone on writing them, and gradually they had become a recourse in low moods, and a sporadic quasi-diary of her changed existence. Her fifteen-year marriage to Walter Kadane had whisked by, leaving her in enviable financial shape. As for finding another man, no thanks, it was not on her agenda. Other men had loused up too many of her years. She had found one good true man, he was no more, and she had survived him. Going to Congress in his place seemed much the best way to get on with a half-lived life.

So she had accepted the nomination, made the run, and won the seat. The fresh milieu had wholly absorbed her. She had file drawers full of these dashed-off letters, computer pages in the hundreds, all about her political experiences. Maybe, she sometimes thought, she might even one day publish a book, *Letters to Walter!* In that case, the Super Collider affair and the whole Higgs boson uproar might prove quite a chapter, thanks no little to this oddly attractive Dr. Guy Carpenter, the obscure white-haired scientist she had unearthed, who had a tart sense of humor, a formidable wife, and a murky link to a Chinese woman physicist.

Well, to begin with, Rocovsky blames himself for the death of the Super Collider!

Amazing, but he's dead serious. As he puts it, when the Navy sets out to build a nuclear carrier costing billions, it doesn't rely on annual appropriations, it gets a special Autho-

> rization Bill for the entire budget, over as many years as the job requires. The SSC should have had one overall Authorization Bill like that, and at the outset, when President Bush was for it, and California, Illinois, and Texas were all red-hot after it, *Rocovsky says he could have gotten such a bill passed.* He was the political tactician among those top physicists, they trusted his leadership, and he thought the heavy lifting needed to put such a special bill through Congress was unnecessary . . .

But it had been a long day, flying here and there since early morning, and what with martinis plus a meal with wine, she was feeling stupid. She unpacked, took a steaming shower and a long cold douse, then hurried back to the laptop.

> Well, Rocovsky calls it the worst misjudgment of his life. Once Texas won the site, the support for the Collider kept weakening in each annual budget debate, and the project bled to death. The other reasons I'd heard for its demise were all secondary, so he said in reviewing them with me.
>
> He also told me about your meeting with him that led you to reverse your votes on the Space Station and the SSC. It was a revelation, and I now can see —

The hotel phone rang on the desk. "Myra, it's Guy. I hope you haven't retired yet —"

"No, what's up?"

"How about coming out for a nightcap?"

A peculiar invitation! What now? She stalled. "Guy, isn't this a dry county? There's no bar in the hotel —"

"Leave that to me. The thing is, that judge will be here for breakfast, we'll go trudging around the ruins, and then you'll be off to Washington. I have to talk to you."

There was nothing casual or flirtatious in Dr. Carpenter's tone, the man was really pleading. She would have to dress and put on a face of sorts. "Sure. Twenty minutes."

* * *

A short taxi run past the outskirts of town, through moonlit fields where cows grazed or stared, brought them to an area of restaurants evidently built to bypass the dry laws. "Well, Verne's Club hasn't changed much," Carpenter said, seeing on the walls the same buffalo heads and longhorns as of yore, and a few middle-aged couples sedately dancing as usual to the music of a foursome in cowboy garb.

"It's a nice place," said Myra Kadane.

They sat down in a booth. She ordered a pink lady, and the waiter went off scratching his head. "How come?" said Guy, who asked for bourbon. "That's what you don't drink, you said."

"Right. Just a prop. I have some work to do yet tonight. Isn't that the 'Missouri Waltz'?" The musicians were starting a new set. "Harry Truman was Walter's idol. Do you waltz? Let's waltz."

"Anything you say."

She closed her eyes as they swung around and around the small dance floor, which crowded up for the waltzing. "I never dance anymore. Walter was a great dancer. Once we got married he forgot about it." Opening her eyes, she saw a heavyset man in jeans and an oversize Texan hat goggling at her as he waltzed past with an equally hefty woman in an equally big hat. She twined her fingers in Carpenter's and led him off the dance floor. The drinks were on their table. He tossed off half his bourbon at a gulp.

"Myra, about that correspondence with a red flag on it —" He paused, looking sheepish. "Well, to make a long story short, Mei and I *have* been writing to each other for years. Ever since I worked with her in China on the cyclotron. And the thing is" — the physicist paused, seeming to drag the words out of himself — "the truth is, Myra, that for those letters I've been using a post-office box." He emptied his glass and went on. "I'm confiding in you because you've been kind enough to warn me about Rossiter and the CIA, so —"

"Pardon me, ma'am." The heavyset man was at their booth, touching his big hat. "Aren't you Congresswoman Myra Kadane?"

"I am."

"Ma'am, I just want to tell you that Moira Strong was my favorite movie star. I have every video of your films that's still around."

"Why, thank you."

He touched his hat again. "It's all over town that you're here, you know. We sure hope you're looking into reviving the Super Collider." He touched his hat to Guy Carpenter. "Evening, sir. Hope I'm not intruding. Fact is, that confounded Super Collider near ruined my life."

"Really? Mine too," said Guy. The interruption was a relief from tension. "How come? Sit down."

"Well, just for a minute, thank you kindly." He handed Guy a card, *Benton J. Harvey, Harvey Roads and Earth Moving, Inc.,* and he poured out his tale of woe, raising his voice over the music. With firm SSC contracts in hand for building roads and hauling tunnel dirt, he had invested in new heavy equipment. The sudden shutdown had caught him short with huge debts. The markdown in the used market for such machines was murderous, the vultures had swarmed to Waxahachie offering ten cents on the dollar, and he had been unable to hold out. "State of Texas came along and helped fellows like me with a special fund, otherwise most of Ellis County would have been bankrupt, pretty near. And what happened to you, sir?"

"Well, I was a physicist —"

"A *physicist?* Oh, boy, say no more." Harvey stood up, shaking his head. "You guys *really* bought the farm. Well, life goes on, don't it? Been nice visiting with you all. Ma'am, you should still be in the movies, you don't look no different in person than in the videos, just better."

As he walked off, Myra said, "I like Texans. I've always liked them."

"They're beguiling," said Carpenter, "sort of like the Chinese, in a very different style. You just have to resist the charm when substance is involved."

"Guy, you were telling me you used a post-office box to correspond with Dr. Wen Mei Li. Why? For instance, why not e-mail?"

"Oh, she wouldn't hear of e-mail. Not for this, handwriting and snail mail as in our old days, she wanted —" His heavy sigh came out almost a groan. "It's very complicated. It all goes back to Cornell, when Mei and I first met, and —"

"Great balls of fire," boomed a hoarse voice. "If it isn't Guy Carpenter! I'll be damned. All Ben Harvey said was that you were a physicist." The speaker was fat, bald, and red bearded, approaching them with drink in hand. "*Some* physicist! Dr. Guy Carpenter, boss man of the Magnet Division! I'm Ernie Milson, Guy. Surely you remember me? You damn near fired me. Twice."

"Hello, Ernie." Guy recognized only the curly beard. The Milson he remembered had been bushy haired and thin.

"And here you are, back in Waxahachie! Excuse me, Congresswoman. I won't intrude, I've just got to visit with my old boss for a minute." Milson sat down without being asked.

"So, Ernie, you've stayed on in Waxahachie?"

"Guy, physicists are vegetating all over Texas, you know that. My card." It read *E. Milson, PhD, Super C Electric Supplier, Wholesale & Retail.* "After the closedown I got myself a job in the Liquidation Section. Guy, the thievery was unbelievable! Did you know that the trustees spent a quarter of a million dollars a month on security alone" — he turned to Myra, gesturing with his drink — "quarter of a million *a month,* Congresswoman, just to keep off the looters, the jackals, the hyenas? Utterly futile, and I'll tell you, Guy, I survived by joining the hyenas. I knew where the best stuff was, get it?" He broadly winked. "I did just fine. I had four kids, you know. Two are in college now." He finished his drink, clearly not his first. "Congresswoman, out of respect to you I'll not say what I think of the United States Congress. I just came over to shake the hand of my old boss, who damn near fired me, twice. No hard feelings, Guy, right?" He swept an arm across the table and knocked the pink lady into Myra Kadane's lap.

"Oh Christ on a crutch, I'm sorry, sorry. Oh, Jesus, I apologize," Dr. Milson stammered, whipping out a handkerchief and dabbing hard at Myra Kadane's lap until she knocked his hand away. A waiter rushed up with a towel, and two women swooped in to help. One was Mrs. Harvey in the big hat, the other Mrs. Milson, identified by her remarking, "Ernie, you clumsy drunken bastard, just wait till we get home!" The ladies led Myra off, and they soon returned, Myra with an irregular pink circle on her blue skirt where her lap had been. "It'll wash out," she said to Carpenter with a good-sport laugh for the benefit of the women. "Thanks, my dears. Let's go, Dr. Carpenter, shall we?"

Mrs. Milson put a hand on Guy's arm. "I'm so sorry, Dr. Carpenter. Ernie's not a happy man. He loved working on the magnets. He admires you. Oh, that chickenshit Congress! Pardon me, Myra."

"I quite understand, dear."

"Guy, was that the truth?" Myra asked as they taxied back to town. "Physicists like Milson, vegetating all over Texas? How awful."

"There were two thousand of us, Myra, out of a total SSC payroll of ten thousand. We physicists just got canned like the rest. Relocating wasn't easy, and —"

"Y'all really a physicist, mister?" the driver spoke up. "Well, listen, my daddy, he worked on that dang Super Collider. Master plumber, did right well." He went on to say, or seemed to say — his Texas twang was heavy — that his father had bought seventy miles (possibly seventeen) of chrome-lined pipe dirt cheap, and had them warehoused in Louisiana. He had also done well in washbowls, thousands of washbowls, picked up for the cost of trucking them away from the Super Collider buildings, and sold off in job lots at a profit. "Good sellin' item, washbowls. Pap's holdin' on to them dang pipes, though. Pap's gonna be rich someday, or us kids will be, when they rebuild that dang thang."

In the gloomy hotel lobby, a place of old carpets, heavy sofas, and potted palms, Guy Carpenter said, "Well, this is good night, I guess. We'll talk some other time. Thanks, anyway —"

"Oh, listen, Guy, if it's important, why don't you drop in to my suite in say, half an hour?" She brushed her hand at the pink splotch.

"Great! Bless you, Myra."

14. THE EXPLANATION

Guy Carpenter was up a tree, and he was hoping Myra Kadane could talk him down out of it.

The CIA after him, because of his correspondence with Wen Mei Li! Their letters red flagged! Had they also been read? To the eyes of an ignorant spook, the occasional equations might well have looked like a code rampant with high treason. And how would his actual reason for using a post-office box register with a CIA interrogator, or with a bloodhound like Quentin Rossiter? How would it sound — nightmare of nightmares — at a televised Congressional hearing?

Penny had a way of slicing through such quandaries with her razor-honed common sense. No consulting *her!* He desperately needed friendly feminine advice. The Congresswoman liked him, he knew that now, and far from being a dumb bunny, she had a good level head. Verne's Club had been a bad idea, and he was trying again.

* * *

"Come in, the door's not locked." She was at the computer, flicking furiously away. "Five minutes, and I'll be with you."

He sat down on an overstuffed old sofa. "May I ask what you're working on, this time of night?"

"A letter to Walter." She paused in her rapid clicks to glance over her shoulder. He was peering at her with a shocked expression. "What's the matter, Guy? That's what I'm doing. Call it therapy, or morbid sentiment, or whatever you like. I still love him, and I write these letters to him. Do you think I'm kidding, or crazy?"

"No, actually it's that robe, Myra. Weren't you wearing it in Georgetown?"

"That's right, it's silk, takes no room, so I packed it. What about it?"

"You really write letters to your husband?"

"Now and then. I've never told a soul about it before. Confidence for confidence, or something —"

"I haven't confided anything to you yet —"

"Oh, no? A surreptitious correspondence with a gorgeous Chinese physicist? Have you told *that* to anyone else?"

"Mei isn't gorgeous, never was. And it wasn't surreptitious exactly —"

Myra Kadane closed the computer lid and sat down in a dusty gray armchair opposite him. "Then why a post-office box?"

"What on earth is that letter about, Myra? What can you write to a dead man?"

"Anything and everything. At the moment, what Rocovsky told us today." She folded her arms and looked hard at him. "You wanted to talk to me? Well, talk, or go away and let me finish my letter."

"I do want to talk to you. I haven't been frank with you about Wen Mei Li. The truth is, she was my first love, and I was hers." He searched her face for a reaction. No surprise, not even a raised eyebrow, the same straight hard look. "Here's the whole story, Myra. It'll require some telling, it's not simple —"

"Take your time."

And so Guy Carpenter launched into his pent-up confession.

Of all the fellows who had dangled after Wen Mei Li, she had fixed on him, and he never knew quite why. Once it happened, the romance had blazed up into incandescence. All the other men in the seminar, including Rocovsky himself, had envied him when it became obvious that he and Mei Li were mad for each other. But their beautiful passion had gone nowhere, doomed by her adamant "Chineseness," as she called it. She had always held back, and infatuated as he was, he had been happy with things as they were. In the end she had transferred to Stanford, he had remained at Cornell, and they had exchanged many amorous and wistful letters. After returning to China she had written less often. With the Cultural Revolution the letters had stopped. For many years he had not known whether Mei was alive or dead. Meantime he had met and married Penny, and was living happily ever after. "Penny's a darling, she's almost perfect, and she's given up a lot for me. Bear in mind one thing, and don't judge me too harshly, Myra. When Mei and I were at Cornell, Penny was a gawky schoolkid, and I didn't know she existed, okay?"

"Okay, I'll bear it in mind."

Irony? Skepticism? He couldn't be sure. "I'm serious, Myra. From the start Penny has had a jealous thing about Wen Mei Li that I've never figured out. Why give a hoot about a romance that came and went years and *years* before I met her? But on this one subject my otherwise rational darling tends to see red. Will you take my word for it?"

"Go on."

"Okay. And now for that post-office box."

Back in the eighties, he went on, the State Department sent him to China on a brief mission as an adviser, and not until he got there had he found out that the head of the project was Dr. Wen Mei Li! She too was married, to an army general, but she said little about him. Working with her was a pleasure, she had quite recovered her old brilliance, and the work went quickly. Soon, his time came to leave. It was then that she suggested, with a sudden flood of tears, that they resume corresponding, just now and then. Taken by surprise, he promised he would, and when he got back home he rented the box —

"Hold it right there," the Congresswoman broke in. "*Why?* Why the stealth?"

"Give me a chance. As you can imagine, when Penny and I started dating at Cornell all her friends disapproved, and couldn't wait to tell her about that white-headed old Dr. Carpenter's romance with the glamorous, the legendary Wen Mei Li. They really piled it on, damn their souls, but at first she ignored them. Then somehow it got to her, she seemed to snap overnight. We had a fearful scene about *'that Chinese girl,'* and it nearly broke us up. Penny can be a terror, Myra —"

Myra Kadane said, "We all can be. Don't elaborate."

"All right. Now, when we married, I had to store some stuff to make room for her in my flat. When she got pregnant with John, we rented a house with a cellar workroom for me. In the packing case of books and files that came out of storage, I found a tied bunch of Mei's old letters. Very old, you understand. From Stanford and China, from before the Cultural Revolution. I'd forgotten all about them. I tucked them behind some tools on a shelf —"

"Say no more!" Myra exclaimed. "Penny came on the letters."

"You've got it —"

"No, I haven't. Why the hell did you keep them? Why didn't you tear them up?"

"Have you never done anything incredibly dumb in your life, Madame Congresswoman?"

"More times than you have hairs on your head. So?"

"I just thought I'd look them over sometime, it was a casual idiocy. Now one thing you must know. Penny *didn't* snoop. It's not her nature. You could write me a torrid love letter — forgive me, just an instance — and I could leave it out on my desk without a second thought."

"Forgiven." Myra tartly smiled. "Then what did happen?"

"It was the cat."

"The *cat?*"

"When we moved she had this huge malevolent orange tabby, Mehitabel. From the Don Marquis poems, of course. That cat hated me. I never knew why, but I got clawed more than once, and I mean she drew blood. Well, shortly after we moved into the house I had to go to a meeting in New York, and Mehitabel picked that day to disappear. Penny looked everywhere for the beast, upstairs and downstairs for hours. Finally she heard faint mewing from the cellar. She tracked the sounds to that shelf, to behind those tools. And there, like a cat in Edgar Allan Poe, was that blasted Mehitabel. She had led Penny to my gruesome crime of keeping those letters."

Myra Kadane burst out in a guffaw, then sobered. Carpenter hurried on. "It was just too much for Penny, don't you see? This bunch of old letters, some on flimsy Chinese paper with exotic stamps! WEN MEI LI! *Grrrr!* I tell you, when I got back from New York I ran into a buzz saw that damn near cut me in half. I *had* to rent a box, Myra, if I wanted to correspond with Mei Li. And I did want to. I felt sorry for her, and I had once loved her. Now I ask you — what would the CIA make of all this? And what do I do now?"

She gave him a long silent stare, head aslant. "A likely tale, Dr. Carpenter, I must say."

"That's what happened, Myra. That's the story."

"And you're asking for my opinion and my advice."

"I am."

"My opinion is that your story is ludicrous but somehow convincing. My advice is that you do nothing."

"But the CIA —"

"You're seeing CIA agents under the bed. What's your exposure? Suppose they've read your letters? They can't possibly disclose that they've done it, that's against the law. And after all, what's happened? You've exchanged letters with an old flame, who's now a big shot in Chinese physics. So what? Did Wendy ever mention the Higgs boson in her letters?"

"Not a word. Not a hint."

"Good! Prudent lady, your Dr. Butterfly. Look here, Guy, Quentin Rossiter obviously got Earle Carkin to scare you through me, that's all. You can expect Quentin to pester you from now on by fax, phone, e-mail, he'll promise not to write about you if you'll just talk, he may even fly out and waylay you at the lab. Just don't say anything. You're pretty good at that."

He was looking at her face intently. "Lord, you're reassuring me, Myra." He started to get up. "I couldn't be more grateful, and I'll leave you to your letter writing —"

"Wait, now. Sit down." He obeyed. "One part of your story is still very unclear. Just what did go on between you and Wendy at Cornell?"

"What's unclear? Are you asking whether we slept together?"

"You needn't answer, of course —"

"I'll answer, all right. The answer is no, not once, not ever."

Myra nodded, looking him in the eye. "You're being discreet. Good for you. I approve. Good night, then —"

"For crying out loud, Myra, it wasn't like that, believe me. I'm telling the truth! You have to understand. Mei is Chinese, and —"

"Oh, come on, Guy," she snapped, "the Chinese screw! That's how come there are so many of them."

He winced, then smiled. "What can I say, Madame Congresswoman? Have you ever seen the trees in New England in the fall?"

"Of course. Breathtaking colors, so?"

"Well, around Cornell in October it's the Garden of Eden. So long as I live, the color of autumn leaves, and their smell piled up and wet — or dry and burning — will bring back Wen Mei Li to me. Forever, till I die. And I don't care whether you believe me or not, it was first love, it was glorious, it was doomed, and we didn't screw."

"When you were with Wendy in China, did she own a robe like the one I'm wearing?" Carpenter's face went blank at this abrupt probe. "You reacted oddly to the robe in Georgetown, and you did again tonight. Why?" A taut silence. "Well, did she have one?"

"Okay, this is truth or consequences night, so here's the story on *that.*" He took an audible breath. "The weekend before I left China, her husband went off on maneuvers, and Mei and I spent that weekend in Shanghai. She suggested it. We did it just the way you and I are doing here, Myra — different rooms, different floors. It was nice until we ate at a French restaurant for foreigners on the waterfront. She spent the whole last day in her room in exactly such a robe, trying to drink tea and puking up her guts. She barely pulled herself together to come back to Beijing and see me off. That was when she cried, at the airport."

"Does she have any children?"

"Two boys. Why?"

"What does she look like?"

"Well, by now she'd be over sixty, she's two years older than I am. About your height, thin as ever, very pretty face still, but she's blind as a bat, so she always wears these steel-rimmed glasses that give her a schoolteacherish look."

Myra Kadane went to her computer and opened it. "I should talk to you about things Rocovsky told us, but I'd better just bat out what I remember. It's getting late. Maybe we'll talk tomorrow."

"You've been a friend." He walked to the door. "Good night. A thousand thanks —"

"Tell me one thing, Guy. Did you and Dr. Butterfly ever kiss, at least?"

"Oh, cut it out, Myra."

"I'm asking you. Not even kiss? For instance, good night?"

"Yes, Madame Congresswoman, we sure as hell kissed good night."

Myra Kadane came to him, the Shanghai robe close wrapped around her, and gave him a warm sweet kiss. "Good night. Sleep well. Don't worry about the CIA or Penny, and don't be late for breakfast."

15. THE RUIN

The telephone jerked Guy Carpenter awake, and he groped to answer it. Girlish voice: "Six-thirty, suh, foggy morning, you-all have a nice day."

He lay back on the pillow, trying to pick up the threads of his life. What was he doing in a narrow bed in this strange small greenish room? Ah, yes. Breakfast with Myra Kadane and a Texas judge, a helicopter flight around Ellis County, then a visit to the old SSC buildings; dismal prospect, except for a last few hours with that oddball widow who wrote letters to her dead husband, the Congresswoman with the inveigling laugh and ironic sparkle in her eye. He showered and shaved, humming "Bobby McGee" and wondering at his panic attack last night about the CIA and the post-office box. Gone, all gone. What sensible advice! What a surprise, that stirring kiss at the door . . .

He was thinking too about his late-night phone talk with Penny. A rush of news: Tim Warshaw desperate to talk to him, Quentin

Rossiter phoning four times, Peter Jennings breaking the story that Wen Mei Li was coming to America — Penny had been quite offhand about that, no trace of buzz saw, a real relief. And during an hour-long Boson Bomb special on *Frontline,* he himself had showed up in a clip from an old Super Collider documentary. *"Gad, you really look a lot better today, darling, than you did then! How harassed you were in those days!"*

In the coffee shop, Myra and the judge were already at a table, looking at newspapers. Not a head-turner like some actresses, Guy thought, yet striking in her poise and chic. Real class. The judge, a portly man in a black suit, stood up to shake hands. "I'm Elton Milius, and say! My wife and I caught you on TV last night, sir. I told my wife, I said, 'I declare, I'm having breakfast with that Dr. Carpenter tomorrow —' "

Myra looked up, smiling. "*You?* On TV?"

"Just an excerpt from a 1992 broadcast —"

"Pretty frightening *Frontline* show," Judge Milius said to her, "all about the Chinese and the Boson Bomb. And there's this gentleman here, standing at a huge magnet — why, maybe thirty feet long — and he's explaining the Higgs boson to some Senators. One of them asks whether the Super Collider will lead to a new superweapon, and he growls like J. Edgar Hoover, *'That's classified, sir.'* "

"Actually, I added under my breath, *'classified as a prime imbecility.'* "

Myra chuckled. The judge uncertainly smiled. "Well now, Dr. Carpenter, what about this Boson Bomb? Anything to it? Could our Super Collider have produced it? Or pointed the way?"

"Judge, don't lose sleep over the Boson Bomb."

"Coming from you, that's good to hear."

The silver-haired judge talked through breakfast about his troubles assembling land for the Collider. "Take old Ira Coulter, now, Ira owns the big filling station plumb in the center of the site, and plenty of acreage around it. Ira was typical. He says to me, 'Judge Milius, are you telling me, with a straight face, that a tunnel fifty miles long going nowhere, just running all around my property and a lot of Ellis County, is a good thing?' I told him, 'Ira, it's a great thing for you, for Ellis County, and for Texas.' 'I'm blessed if I believe you,' he says, but he signed over the property."

"What's become of all that land?" Myra Kadane asked.

"Why, ma'am, most of the folks have gotten theirs back, and have done pretty well." He smiled at Dr. Carpenter. "Better than you physicists, I daresay."

As they were leaving the coffee shop, Myra Kadane said to Carpenter, "The feeding frenzy goes on," and she showed him an Associated Press story splashed with a large photograph on the front page of the *Dallas Morning News:*

CHINESE WOMAN SCIENTIST COMING TO U.S.A.
DR. WEN MEI LI DISCOVERED "HIGGS BOSON"

The picture gave Guy Carpenter a turn. Almost, he could smell wet autumn leaves.

"She looks so young," said Myra. "Asians do stay young looking, don't they?"

"It's the only picture the AP could find, I guess. It's from the Cornell yearbook," Carpenter said. "Cheer up, Myra."

"Oh, go to hell," said the Congresswoman.

Fog drifted in the street, dank and thick. Judge Milius raised the helicopter pilot on his cell phone. "Folks, he says we may not see much, but he'll fly."

"Let's go," Myra said.

On the field where the helicopter waited, grass grew in long jagged cracks along the tarmac. "This was going to be the Super Collider's international airport," the judge said. "Now it's all going back to the brush and the rabbits." And indeed a rabbit streaked by them as the pilot was handing out heavy earmuffs with attached mikes.

The helicopter lurched aloft, thrashing through white mist. "The main idea, Congresswoman," bellowed the judge into his mike, pointing to a passing glimpse of green earth below, "is to show you the scope of the thing. It was big."

She shrieked, "I'm glad we're doing this."

"Well, you're a game lady, and the Super Collider sure can use friends in Congress." He turned to Carpenter and bawled, "Say, Professor, any chance the Chinese boson is a phony?"

"Haven't yet worked the problem, Judge," Carpenter howled.

"Because if it is, you mark my word, the Super Collider will rise again, and that old Higgs boson will be found right here in Waxahachie, after all."

The helicopter settled down in a sandy area, and the judge led them past several huge bleak windowless buildings to a sizable sunken circle of grassy rubble. "The main entrance was right here, Congresswoman," he said. "There were access shafts all along the tunnel, but the magnets came out of this Prototype Building we'll visit, and were lowered through here, so the shaft had to be extra big —"

"Don't we get to go down into the hole?" exclaimed Myra Kadane. "Good Lord, that's mostly why I came here —"

"Ma'am, even if it weren't full of water — which it is — you wouldn't have wanted to do that. Not safe."

"How disappointing!" She turned to the physicist. "Eighteen miles of tunnel, and we can't even take a look! Did you ever go down there?"

"Just once, with your friend Congressman Hurtle."

"What was it like?"

"Too cold to be Hell, otherwise a fair semblance. Graveyard smell of fresh-turned earth, banging and clanging of enormous fiery machinery, grimy workmen scurrying about like devils, not for claustrophobics. Hurtle stayed ten minutes and asked up and out rather urgently."

"Now for the Prototype Building," said Judge Milius. "Not usually open, but I've arranged it." He brought them inside a low long structure stretching off into the fog. On the ceiling, brightly lit globes hung in a single line, all the way out of sight.

Carpenter said wryly, "This brings back memories, Judge."

The judge chuckled. "I should imagine so."

"Is this building straight?" Myra asked. "Or is it an optical illusion? Doesn't that line of lights *curve?*"

"Aha!" The judge was delighted. "Right you are, Congresswoman. You're looking at the actual curve of the Superconducting Super Collider —"

Carpenter said, "We tested the magnets here, so the building was designed that way."

As far as the eye could see, the structure was stacked with immense cardboard containers. "What are these?" she asked the judge.

"Styrofoam cups."

"You're joking."

"Ma'am, they're Styrofoam cups. Inventory of a local factory that rents the space."

"Styrofoam cups, Myra," Carpenter said. "Wouldn't Congressman Hurtle be pleased? Nothing damfool like protons colliding at almost the speed of light."

Computer bag on her shoulder, suitcase in hand, the Congresswoman emerged from the hotel elevator. "Well, the fog did it," she said blithely to Carpenter, "two-hour delay on my flight. Now what?"

"I'll tell you what. There's a quaint old tearoom in this town, and I mean quaint, it smells of lavender and cinnamon, and you can buy souvenirs and gewgaws, from Chinese vases to Kewpie dolls. We'll have tea, maybe eat something, and go over your Rocovsky notes —"

"Good thought, you're on."

There were no other customers in the shop when they came in. "Lavender and cinnamon," she said, sniffing. "How could you remember, after so many years?"

"Smells linger in memory."

"Ah. Like wet autumn leaves."

"Just so. The dining alcove is upstairs." As they were passing through displays of whimsical merchandise, he halted. "What do you know! There's Mehitabel."

"Mehitabel? Where?"

He picked up a porcelain figurine and handed it to her, a fat little orange cat, humped and glaring, with tail erect and puffed out. "That's Mehitabel. Even the ears are right, Myra, the way she flattened them before she'd claw me."

"Mean, mean kitty," Myra Kadane said to the figurine.

He said to a hovering gray-haired lady, "Wrap her up good."

"Yes, sir, she's Royal Copenhagen. Very special."

"Why do you want the little monster?" said Myra.

"It's for you."

Myra Kadane laughed. "Oh, no, bring it home to Penny. It's her cat."

"Think again, Congresswoman. Remind Penny of Mehitabel?"

"Oh, Lord!" She laughed harder, throwing her head back. "Well, then, thank you, Guy. I'll treasure that cat as a reminder that scientists have weaknesses. It'll help me on the Science Committee."

They drank tea and ate dainty little sandwiches while she summarized what she had written about Rocovsky's comments. Carpenter heard her out, nodding and nodding. "Well done, Myra. You picked up most of it. I especially agree with the Rock that the end of the Cold War didn't affect the Collider project. That's a red herring; the race in basic science was still hot. And the hubris business, the idea that we physicists took on more than we could handle, doesn't convince me any more than it does Rocovsky. I was down there in the snake pit, you know, not feeling hubris at all, just sweating it out. The whole thing was a leap in the dark, no precedent, no sure future, everyone on edge, worried about their jobs. I'd emphasize personality clashes more —"

She took a small notebook and pencil from her purse and made notes. "What about the aperture change?" she asked. "Rocovsky lost me on that."

"Well, he's right again. He and I were the only two who were against it. Changing the diameter of the Collider magnet, just by one centimeter, cost a lot more than a 'mere' hundred million dollars, as the others argued. The ripple effect went through the whole project, spiked up the costs, and convinced some Congressmen that we physicists didn't know what the hell we were doing."

"And the foreign money?"

"Oh, yes. Well, he and I don't agree on that one. Congress wanted to fund it all with our dollars and keep the new secrets to ourselves, then when costs ran way up and political support got shaky, the opposition yelled to bring in the Japanese. At that point, of course, Tokyo just told us to get lost. A humiliation and a body blow, in my view, though he pooh-poohs it."

She penciled a quick scrawl. "About the political fiasco, here's what I took away," she said. "As long as there was competition for the site, support in Congress was solid, but once Texas was picked, the northern liberals dug in to kill it. They just loved sticking it to the Texans, who'd been voting en masse against their social programs. Have I got that right?"

"You have, and the crowning irony of the budget angle is that the Collider couldn't have cost more than fifteen billion at the craziest outside, whereas the Space Station is up to eighty billion and climbing. Congress killed the wrong science project —"

"That wouldn't be sour grapes, Professor?"

"Conceivably. As Mehitabel will remind you, scientists are human. And, Myra, before we part, I want you to know how grateful I am for your willing ear last night. You're a friend in need. Shouldn't I level with Penny about that post-office box and get it off my mind once and for all?"

She gave him a long sober stare. "You're asking my advice again?"

"I guess I am."

"All right, *then listen!* I did believe the business about Mehitabel and the letters. Bizarre, yet somehow it rang true. I didn't believe your story about Shanghai. Not for a minute."

Dismay showed on his face. "And if it happens to be true too?"

"Now look, you can be real plausible, Guy, and your tale of chaste first love and wet autumn leaves — well, I even believed that, sort of. But that platonic weekend in Shanghai, *uh-uh.* I tell you this as a friend and a woman. If you try it on that keen wife of yours, she'll gut you like a trout, mind my words." She picked up her purse. "Time to go." At the shop entrance he paid for the figurine and handed it to her. "Thanks, Guy." She took a deep breath. "Lavender and cinnamon, and Mehitabel. Quite a memory, at that."

It was a glum silent ride in the taxicab until they were out of Waxahachie and speeding to the airport. "Well, the sun's breaking through," she said. "I guess my flight will go. So now tell me about the telescopes."

He sat up, jolted out of his thoughts. "Are you serious?"

"To what else, Professor, have I owed the pleasure of your company? Dr. Porson sent you to lobby me about the telescopes. Well, lobby away, sir, the time is getting short."

"Why, thank you for the opportunity." He picked up her antic mood and adopted a mock formal tone. "The Terrestrial Planet Finder, Madame Congresswoman, requires four large infrared space instruments, flying in formation about a mile apart, in an orbit yet to be determined. At least a million miles from Earth, perhaps drifting away in its own orbit around the sun. Infrared, to pierce through the cosmic dust that obscures visual astronomy; far apart in formation, to get as long a baseline as possible for observing planets around the nearest stars —"

"What will the project cost, Dr. Carpenter, how long will it take, and what's the point of it?"

"Ten years in stages, ma'am, about a billion dollars, and the point of it is to make a start on finding out whether we're alone in the universe."

"I see. A worthy endeavor. Send me your literature, Dr. Carpenter. I'm not uninterested, though I can't promise anything, of course."

"Ye gods, you do sound like a Congresswoman."

"I'm an actress." They both laughed. "The thing is, Guy, I'm also a freshman, and on appropriations I just vote as I'm told. The telescopes are in the NASA budget, no doubt —"

"Yes, a very minor item —"

"Well, Ottoline Porson is a big name. That should help. Didn't she discover a bunch of planets out in deep space, or something like that?"

"Not bad, Myra! I'm impressed —"

"Guy, it's one click on the Internet. Not that I understand it —"

"Well, you have the main idea. She detected the wobble in nearby parent stars caused by planet systems, it made her name and got her the leadership of our program."

The taxi was stopping behind a long line of cars at a booth outside the airport. "What time's your flight, lady?" the driver called. "This will take a while."

"I'm okay." She turned to face Carpenter. "One final question. It's personal."

"Shoot." The last minutes of their brief accidental intimacy were melting away. Did she feel as he did, fleeting regret, however futile?

"There's a lot I've been meaning to ask you, Guy, and now it's too late. Just tell me this. What are you, anyway? A physicist, an astronomer, an astrophysicist? How did you jump from the Super Collider to space telescopes?"

"Very large and cogent question." Not what he expected, nothing sentimental, her way of saying he interested her. Good enough! He glanced out at the line of cars. The taxi was inching up on the tollbooth. "Very short answer, I started out as a philosophy major, Myra, then decided I didn't really care what Thales or Plato thought about truth, when hard demonstrable truth was there to be learned in science. So I went into physics. Physics digs deeper and deeper down into what's small, you see, astronomy reaches farther and farther out into what's vast, the math is the same, the thinking is much the same, and the quest is the same. Physics and astronomy both seek ultimate truth, out among the stars and down inside the atom, and they merge in astrophysics. That's what I do."

Her eyes shone at him. "A seeker after truth, then."

"That's a generous way to put it. It's how I pass the time and try to make a buck."

"Don't jeer, and don't belittle yourself. I've squandered most of my life in nonsense. Your quest is noble."

"Well, Myra, I like to hope so. The nobility, if any, gets somewhat fuzzed by the backstabbing for prestige and the lobbying for funds."

The taxi lurched past the booth toward the terminal. "Here we go," she said. "You've been an astonishing encounter, all too human, well worth knowing." When the taxi stopped at the check-in curb, she gripped his hand. "Good-bye, Guy Carpenter. My last word to you, don't you start up with Penny about Shanghai."

Unthinking, in a move as natural as breathing, Carpenter took the small Congresswoman into his arms and kissed her. She said, low and hoarse, "Oh, and one more thing. Mum's the word about my letters to Walter." A hasty kiss on his hand lifted to her lips, and she slipped out of the cab.

16. THE SCENARIO

He was glad to see Penny waving, in fact jumping up and down and laughing, as the Falcon taxied to the terminal. A reassuring sight! He descended the few unfolding steps, and there she waited, holding out her arms. "Hi! Long time no see."

"Where's Dinah?" he asked as they hugged and kissed.

"Sleeping like a stone, so I left her with Mrs. Green." This was the cleaning woman. "I didn't expect you back so soon. I'd just started the laundry when you called, so I'm not fit to be seen, but here I am —" She wore jeans and a baggy old gray sweatshirt, her hair was hastily combed, her lipstick fresh and careless — she had probably put it on as she drove, glancing in the rearview mirror — and as always, she charmed him, rattling on cheerily in that husky voice with the loving undertones, while they walked to the old Pontiac parked outside the link fence. "Guess what? You have a FedEx from that Sean Kadane. D'you suppose it's a contract and a *check?* We could sure use some money in the account — oh, and that pest

Rossiter actually wanted to fly out here and interview me. Ha! I squashed *him* good and proper. What else? Oh yes, message from Warshaw's office, you're to meet him at Cedars-Sinai in the morning. Suite P3. I got quite a surprise myself today, and —"

"Hold on, hold on. Cedars-Sinai? You're sure?"

"Right, the hospital. An airhead named Heather called. I asked her, what is it about? But it was all she knew." Penny drove off with a jackrabbit start. It struck Carpenter that his wife was acting a trifle manic. "Honestly, Guy, the flash on *Frontline* brought back those horrible times so vividly! You look ten years younger today, old dear. What's Waxahachie like now?"

"A ghost town full of live people. You had a surprise, you said?"

"Ah, yes, my surprise." She threw him a sprightly glance. "Remember Reba Wasserman?"

"Do I ever? Your Cornell roommate, who kept urging you to dump that white-headed old stick Dr. Carpenter."

Penny gave him an affectionate poke. "Come on, all my friends did that —"

"Well, what about Reba?"

"She's been named head of microbiology at the University of Vermont, that's what, and she offered me a job —"

"A job in *Vermont?*"

"Well, maybe she was just showing off, but she seemed serious —"

"Did she suggest what I was supposed to do? Tag along and take up snowboarding?"

"Well, what she *said* was, what with John off in Australia and you busy doing your thing at JPL, why not? I told her thanks, but forget it, I have a two-year-old baby. Kind of took the wind out of old Reba's sails, she never married, you know —"

"Department head, eh? I guess Vermont's too cold for top people. Reba's a milk-wagon horse in microbiology compared to you."

Penny caressed the back of his neck, looking very pleased. "That's unkind, and don't snarl so, dear. I did decline."

* * *

As soon as they were inside the house, he opened the FedEx.

Dear Professor Carpenter:

Tim and Shayna say welcome aboard the *Boson Bomb* production. Standard consultant remuneration, for an expert of your distinction, is half the fee on signing, other half on first photography. I've seen Cy Finkle's two-page outline. The movie is high-concept and will be fabulous. He's a genius. You sign the contract in three places, see the arrow tabs.

Cheers,
Sean

Attached to a three-page contract was a check for $25,000, signed with a great flourish by Shayna Daniels.

"Half a loaf, hey?" said Penny. "Well, a lot better than none. We get the hot-water heater, pay the overdue mortgage installment, and order the roof repairs. What's left will go to Dinah's college fund, and —"

"And," interrupted Guy, an arm circling her waist and pulling her close, "tonight, champagne dinner at the Athenaeum."

"The Athenaeum? Champagne? Wow. Impossible. I have chops ready to broil." It was Penny's way of agreeing. "We can't get the sitter on such short notice."

"It's seafood night, Pen. Alaskan crabs, Maine lobsters, Puget Sound oysters, and Veuve Clicquot. Figure something out."

"Hm. Maybe I'll ask Mrs. Green."

Penny wore her new suit to the Athenaeum. They ate oysters and broiled lobsters in the high-ceilinged dining room of the faculty club, and Guy reminisced about the meeting with Rocovsky, the Falcon ride, and the visit to the picked skeleton of the Superconducting Super Collider. When they finished the bottle of champagne, he ordered another. "My, you *are* going it! Well, once in a lifetime." Penny was all aglow. "The Rock called me after you and Myra left, you know. He was quite taken with her. The way he put it, I blush to say, was that she reminded him of me, only not quite as smart."

"I concur, but the lady's okay. She'll make a difference on the telescopes. She said so."

"Well, that's how we eat, so good for her."

"She's quick on the pickup, Penny, and she's thoughtful. The whole SSC scene got to her — the physicists stranded in Texas, the locals ruined by the shutdown, the abandoned buildings, the eighteen-mile tunnel we couldn't visit because it's full of water. She was really moved and saddened. She said these budget fights on the Hill can get to be a sort of Monopoly game, the Congressmen lose sight of how their votes affect real people out in the country."

Penny put her hand on his, her fingers cool from the champagne glass. "Ottoline was pretty cute, sending you to work on her. For a certain type of woman you'll do, white hair and all. Reba Wasserman missed the point. They all did."

The conversation was edging into difficult terrain for Guy Carpenter, and Penny's next words sent a small shock down his spine and out to his fingers and toes. "How about Wen Mei Li coming here? Reba brought that up right away, couldn't wait. Maybe that's why she called —"

"Oh, I'd guess the Chinese are sending her here as a propaganda stunt. I doubt she had any choice."

"Interesting, that's what Jennings said, she objected but was overruled, according to a Hong Kong source — well, well, if that isn't Peter Braunstein, and without Caroline! Who's that man with him, do you know?"

Guy looked around at Braunstein, walking to a far-off table, and his heart misgave him. The other man had a discernible bushy mustache. "I have no idea," he said.

The waiter popped the cork and poured more champagne. Penny merrily raised her glass. "Well, here's to the stupid Higgs boson, since it seems to be paying for all this." Guy clinked with her, hoping he was not seeing Quentin Rossiter under the bed.

Carpenter's mood next morning was exalted, after a high old connubial night enlivened by unplanned slapstick, his tumble out of Penny's bed. She was a restless thrasher, hence twin beds, and the loud thump had got them laughing and had sweetened the fond carryings-on. A breakfast steak had further lifted his spirits. But hospital odors are not cheering, and all this buoyancy was fading into unease by the time he came on Tim Warshaw, who was reading the *Hollywood Reporter* on a couch outside a private suite. "Hi there, Professor. We'll see him right away, the nurses are fixing him up. He has to use a bedpan, and —"

"*Who* does?"

"Why, Cy Finkle, the screenwriter. Didn't Heather tell you? He's lucky he's alive." Carpenter sat down, staring at him. "Cy's a wildlife freak, you see, he's got a warehouse full of animal footage — *Save the Moose* was his own original idea — and he was up there with the location unit, filming with his camcorder. The way he tells it, he was focusing with a long-distance lens on this beautiful baby moose when out of nowhere came the mother moose, or I guess you say cow moose, and trampled the fucking shit out of him. Maybe she thought the camcorder was a gun. Anyway —"

A slim dark nurse looked out of the room and said in a heavy foreign accent, "Any minute, Mr. Warshaw. We do sponge bath now."

"It's just as well," Warshaw went on. "Cy's got the most fertile brain I know. Before he got trampled, he e-mailed me a two-page synopsis of a Boson Bomb screenplay he dreamed up the night before, and it's incredible. I talked to Julia Roberts, swore her to secrecy, and she's crazed to play the woman astronaut — oh shit, I shouldn't have mentioned that, Cy wanted you to hear the story cold — anyway, Julia is definitely interested, she's my neighbor out in Trancas, she wouldn't shit me. Shayna's preparing a draft budget, and Sinclair Holloway, sight unseen, says, 'Go for it.' Which is great, because the buzz is that DreamWorks has got Günter Grass working up a Boson Bomb scenario. Günter Grass for the world market is smart, *smart,* and we have to move fast. So *Save the Moose* goes on hold, and —"

"Please to come in," said the nurse.

* * *

Returning home, Guy Carpenter found his wife guffawing at Sweeney and the baby, who were facing each other on the floor. "Hi, watch this, it's beyond belief. I've been laughing myself sick. Dinah has figured out how to mew, and this crazy animal is answering her."

And so it was: a squeaky *mew* from Dinah, a drawling *meoww* by the cat, looking straight at her and lashing his tail. *Mew!... Meoww!... Mew!... Meoww!* Both little creatures were hugely enjoying themselves.

"Penny, you haven't deposited that check yet, have you?"

"Are you kidding? I've been down to the bank, paid last month's mortgage and the one that's due tomorrow. The bank manager was real impressed. And I've ordered the heater —" She peered at his somber face and got up. "Problems?"

"How about some coffee?"

She lifted Dinah into her playpen and went to the kitchen. "Let's hear."

Dropping on a kitchen chair, he told her about Cy Finkle's accident. "They flew him back in a medical plane, Penny, he has a broken leg, head injuries, a dislocated shoulder — he's a mess, lying there all bandaged up, with one leg suspended on a pulley, yet the fellow's just full of energy. The way he ad-libbed his Boson Bomb scenario from his bed actually got me interested —"

"Is it any good?"

"It's insanely ridiculous. I was hoping you hadn't deposited that check. I may want out of this thing, Penny. The moose movie is postponed, the plane is canceled, no reason for me to have it now, Warshaw says —"

"Aha. No wild salmon, alas."

"Just so, in that regard, I'm a wad of snotty Kleenex. Amazing how quickly I got used to that plane, Pen —"

"I never took it seriously, dear. A freak impulse, a way to get you to sign up, who knows? Let's hear the scenario." She handed him coffee.

"Thanks." He took a gulp. "Ah, good. Okay, this happens sometime in the future, you understand. A sort of Hindu Saddam Hussein has gotten control of India, he's developed H-bombs and intercontinental missiles, and he's out to rule the world, threatening China, threatening us, and it looks like nothing can stop him, except a weapon powerful enough to wipe out all of India — the entire subcontinent, that is, nearly a billion people — in one shot. That should give him pause, and we do have this Boson Bomb, but we can't test fire it to scare him, because there's no waste area in the world big enough for such a test. What we do — I mean America and its allies — is shoot two astronauts to the moon with a Boson Bomb. They set it to go off on a timer, and they get the hell off the moon. It blows up, sure enough, makes a huge new crater visible to the naked eye, and that frightens the Hindus like anything, and they overthrow this bad dictator and kill him, which is fine, but meantime it turns out that the bomb has blown the moon out of its orbit. Scientists figure out that in a month or so the moon's going to come curving down and splash into the Pacific —"

"I like it," said Penny. "In what way is it ridiculous?"

"Lay off, I'm trying to tell this straight. It'll now take *two* Boson Bombs to blow the moon back into orbit, see, because of the acceleration from the first one, and there's only one more ready. There's still another improved one all assembled, and there's this female astronaut who's been training with it, and she alone knows how to fire it off, so up to the moon she goes with the top available astronaut, a dark handsome apple-pie American, only in fact he's a Hindu militant who infiltrated the program years ago. So on the voyage to the moon, which as you know takes three days, he makes advances to her, and things get kind of raunchy in that space capsule, because she really is attracted to him, till she finds out he's a militant and is repelled. Finkle hasn't worked out all those details, but there's your romance angle —"

"I'm dying to know how it comes out," said Penny.

"Oh, happy ending. The moon's blasted back into orbit, all right, and Julia Roberts — Finkle constantly calls the lady astronaut Julia Roberts — Julia Roberts cleverly ditches the Hindu at the last second, leaving him there on the moon repenting his evil ways while she rockets off to Earth. Humorous angle — the Man in the Moon now has three new visible warts on his chin because of the three Boson Bomb craters. There's another astronaut, the Mission Control chap, a Tom Hanks type, who's been in love with Julia Roberts right along, and they get together. The ending seemed a bit fuzzy, but remember, all this is only on two pages, and Finkle batted it off in one night, before he got trampled. You have to admire his fecundity. Well, what do you think?"

"The cow moose should have trampled him sooner."

Guy reluctantly laughed. "That's not generous. The fellow's not a fool. He told the story sort of tongue in cheek. 'Remember, it's only a movie,' he said more than once. What he wants from me is scientific double-talk — that's what he frankly called it — on a fairly high level. 'Not like that play *Copenhagen,*' he said. 'Too cerebral, but not like comic strips or *Star Trek* either. Borderline plausible. Things Julia Roberts can say and sound realistic.' None of that bothers me, Penny, but putting my name on the screen does. If you look at the contract, that's what they're paying me for. No name, no fee. It's there in the fine print, and —"

The telephone rang. Penny answered and handed it to him. "It's Peter."

"Hey, Guy! I thought you'd be here by now. Aren't you coming to the lab?"

"Peter, who was that gent with you at the Athenaeum last night?"

"Look, fella, we'd better talk. I saw you and Penny. So did he."

"Be right over." He hung up. "Penny, that man with Peter last night was Quentin Rossiter."

"Jeepers! Did Peter say so?"

"Didn't have to. It's him." Guy Carpenter leaned his head in both hands. "Penny, you know what Macbeth says, when he gets the bad news that he's had Banquo murdered in vain, because Banquo's son escaped?"

"Yes, dear, *'Then comes my fit again.'* You've quoted that often. Why now?"

"Quentin Rossiter seems to want my blood."

Penny shrugged, laughed, and patted his shoulder. "So what? You know the legend. The vampire has to be invited in or he can't hurt you. If he comes after you, stiff-arm him! That's what I did. Just don't talk to the monster, then he's helpless."

Carpenter brightened, and managed a smile. "Well said! That's the policy. That's what I'll do. Just get out the garlic, and keep a crucifix handy. I'm off."

17. THE VAMPIRE

Peter Braunstein was drinking beer, stocking feet up on his desk, but he looked neither relaxed nor cheerful. "Ah, there you are." He raised the beer can. "Your health! Bad form in the office, worse before lunch, sorry. Hair of the dog —"

"So you and Quentin Rossiter tied one on?"

The swivel chair squeaked as Braunstein sat up. "Oh, you know it was Rossiter?"

"I've met that mustache before."

"I see." With a heavy sigh, Braunstein nodded. "Look, Guy, get this straight, NASA set Rossiter on me. The word came down from Public Relations, *'Red carpet for Quentin Rossiter!'* Ottoline was out of town so it was up to me, and Guy, that man has a hollow leg. I *had* to drink along with him, just to be sociable. He started with a martini, after that he insisted on Guinness with the oysters, and with the petrale sole he wanted the club chardonnay, so to be quite honest I was soon feeling little pain. We talked for a while about our project, then came a barrage of questions about you, and our Cornell days, and of course a lot about Wendy. You know, about her coming here and all. I told him nothing out of line, Guy, nothing he couldn't get from people like Reba Wasserman, I promise you —"

"I'm sure of that, Peter," said Carpenter, very unsure of it. "Go on —"

Braunstein tossed the can into a wastebasket, clinking with another empty. "He seemed especially interested in Penny."

"Penny?" Guy put on his blank face. "Why Penny?"

"Search me. I told him how she'd been a star in microbiology at Cornell, then quit to raise John, and how when John went off to Columbia she returned to teaching here at Occidental College, and published those articles with Simon Duane, and how highly she's thought of in the field —"

"He wanted to know all that?"

"I couldn't tell him enough, it seemed. And of course, how she almost broke up with you at Cornell when she first found out about you and Wendy. Truly I skirted the Wendy subject, Guy. I really tried. Not a word about your work in China with her. This morning I woke up with a mean hangover, and I realized that the project talk was probably my eye, that he's writing about Wendy and just conned Public Relations. So I thought I'd better bring you up to speed on all this, and if I was a bit loose tongued I'm sorry, but there's no way I spilled the beans, Guy, to my best recollection."

"No sweat, Peter. No beans to spill, really. Where's Rossiter now? Gone back to Washington?"

"He's down the hall, talking to Ottoline."

Then comes my fit again . . .

Strapped for funding like all Project Scientists, Ottoline would turn herself inside out for the *Washington Post* reporter. And yet — Guy Carpenter was starting to think like a hunted man — what could she disclose that Rossiter didn't know? Peter's discretion about China had been futile. A simple search on Wen Mei Li in the State Department records would have turned up all the cyclotron correspondence. Rossiter couldn't have overlooked such an obvious source. The immediate question was, what to do about the vampire down the hall? Stiff-arm him, as Penny advised? More prudently, dodge him? Driving a stake though his heart was the answer, but a shade impractical.

Guy yawned, not out of boredom but stress, a signal from his sympathetic nervous system that he was getting into a nasty corner. "How long has he been with Ottoline, Peter, do you know?"

"Half an hour or so. I was there when he arrived, all bright-eyed and bushy-tailed. I got out fast, leaving Ottoline to deal with him. I'm too busy hating myself —"

"Don't take on, Peter, and thanks for the fill-in."

Decision: *Dodge him. Get out of this building. He'll surely barge into my office, but Ottoline can hold him for an hour.* Carpenter stepped into the hall, glancing both ways. Coast clear. Next he would have to pass by Ottoline's office, just inside the main entrance. *Go, Carpenter!* He strode down the corridor, rounded the corner, and darted out past her door into bright sunshine. The Pontiac was parked up the street. He made for it, feeling for the keys in his pocket.

"Dr. Carpenter! How fortunate." Rossiter materialized out of thin air. Or had he popped up from a manhole? He was not there, and suddenly he was. "Dr. Porson said you were the one man to explain the Planet Finder, better than anybody. Can we talk a bit?"

"I'm rather busy" were the words Carpenter managed to bring out of his threatened throat.

"Look, it's lunchtime. Everybody eats lunch," said Rossiter with an easy grin. "Let me buy you lunch at that charming Athenaeum club —"

"It's a faculty club, Mr. Rossiter."

"Oh, so it is. Well, Dr. Braunstein got me in, so I guess you can, only I insist on buying the lunch." Quentin Rossiter took his arm. "You have to tell me all about *'nulling interference.'* Have I got that right? Dr. Porson couldn't explain it. What's 'nulling interference'?"

"That's nulling *interferometry,*" Guy blurted, and at once regretted the irked reflex. Saying *anything* to Quentin Rossiter was inviting the vampire in.

"Ah, right, interferometry. Thanks. I'm a humanist dodo about science, Dr. Carpenter, but Congressmen do read what I write, you know. Do we walk to the Athenaeum, or is it far?"

Here was the moment of truth, *la ultima suerte* of the bullfights . . .

An aficionado friend in Mexico had once expounded to Carpenter *la ultima suerte* as they watched the gaudy matador sidle up to the befuddled bleeding beast, plunge the sword into its bowed neck, and as the creature crumpled, doff his hat to the cheering crowd. Carpenter had never gone to another bullfight. Why on earth was he thinking of that pitiful sight now? Vampire, matador, whatever the image, stiff-arming this tormentor was no longer an option. Ottoline herself had referred Rossiter to him. Ottoline controlled his bread and butter, and Penny's and Dinah's.

"Well, it's a few miles. Here's my car."

"Why, thank you. I've been getting around the town in cabs. Your Dr. Porson is quite a gal."

Actually Rossiter was no dodo about science. Ottoline had confused him with details on interferometry, but he had caught on fast to the concept of *nulling* — cutting out — a star's glare so as to study its planet's very faint light. He even grasped the reason for observing in the infrared, or said he did. "You know, I sat up late last night reading that fat press package your Public Relations gave me," he chattered as Carpenter drove in dour silence. "*'Are we alone?'* Fascinating! Our science editor, Fenton Parks, mainly snoops *Nature* and *Science* week in, week out for something new and hot. I bet Fenton's never written up this story. Dr. Porson will soon be hearing from Fenton, or from me —"

Carpenter hardly listened, recalling how utterly he had squelched this relentless nuisance in Washington, that rainy night in Earle Carkin's car. What was so different now? Only the perplexity of his correspondence with Mei. Why not face the music, tell Penny, take the blistering edge of her tongue, and get it over with?

"Earle Carkin told me that Myra Kadane is all for your project," the reporter went on blithely, "and that's great, because the Appropriations Bill is coming up in the House, you know. The Science Committee will hold hearings on the SSC fiasco, and the Armed Services Committee wants to dig into the threat of the Chinese boson. Illinois, California, and of course Texas are all caucusing about amendments to revive the Collider, a free-for-all of finger-pointing like you never saw is about to break out, and right now the House is like an overturned anthill."

As soon as they were seated in the faculty dining room, Rossiter ordered a double martini. Carpenter brusquely declined a drink. "Okay, Professor." The journalist laughed. "But lighten up, I'm not about to pump you. Not necessary. My story about Dr. Wen Mei Li is ready to go. I'm excited about it. Cutting-edge science, international scope, national-security issues, and at the heart of it an exotic woman nuclear physicist! It's got everything. You're not all that important in it, but you're there, and you know you are. Will you agree to that much? You're there."

Guy only looked at him mutely.

The waiter handed Rossiter a huge brimming martini. "No comment? Right." He raised the glass. "To Wendy, then, as Dr. Braunstein kept calling her. Wendy, your first love, the world-class physicist. Mmmn! Perfect martini, this club makes. Now look, I'm writing about her, not about you. Wen Mei Li's achievements, her ordeals, and yes, her love life too, but only incidentally, and that goes for her army-general husband. My take on your Wendy is that the key to her character, to her career, to her whole life, is her *Chineseness,* and that's the way you figure in this. The only way! The American physicist she loved when she was young, and gave up because she's Chinese."

He drank most of the martini, and setting down the glass hard, he took a new cold tone. "Now about the CIA, let me lay it on the line, Dr. Carpenter. I'm stymied because of the media backlash over that Los Alamos scientist, Wen Ho Lee, who got such a hard time from Intelligence. Whether he was a spy or not, wrongly treated or not, isn't the issue. The Agency is walking on eggs where a Chinese scientist is concerned, and therefore I know a lot more than I can use. Is that frank enough? I can't risk my in with the CIA, it means more to me than your minor role in this story. So if you want to talk about the post-office box and all the rest, that's one thing. Otherwise, I'll have to pussyfoot and hint, which will be a lot worse from your standpoint." He finished his drink and ran a knuckle across his mustache. "How do I write your part in this story, Dr. Carpenter? Your call."

The food arrived at this point, a Caesar salad for Carpenter, a Salisbury steak for Rossiter, who fell to with an appetite. "Say, this is superb," he said after a few mouthfuls. "You feed well, here at Caltech. You're not talking, Dr. Carpenter, and you're not eating."

"I'm thinking."

Rossiter burst out laughing. "Well, so you're human! You've been doing a great mime of a clam. Come on, I've spoken my piece. That salad looks good. Enjoy it."

They both ate without more words for a while. "Here's something that'll interest you," said Rossiter, chewing down the last bite of his steak. "I got an e-mail from Earle Carkin this morning. Dr. Wen Mei Li will be invited to testify by the Science Committee. And what's more —"

Carpenter was jolted into interrupting him. "Is that *possible?*"

"Is what possible?"

"A Chinese scientist, a witness at a Congressional hearing?"

"Why not? She can't be subpoenaed, but she can graciously agree. Think of the PR coup for the People's Republic of China! She probably won't be allowed to decline. What's more, Earle says the Armed Services Committee is also all hot for the idea. Her government may not like that so much, in which case she'll simply say no." The waiter was clearing their plates. As Carpenter signed the bill, Rossiter exclaimed, "Look here, I invited you to lunch, let me pay —"

Carpenter shook his head. "All signed for."

"Well, thank you most kindly, Dr. Carpenter. I'm booked to fly home today. I haven't checked out of my hotel yet. You say you're 'thinking,' and that's quite understandable. No doubt you'll want to talk to Penny. Why don't I stay on, and I'll phone you in the morning at your lab. How's that?"

Guy Carpenter measured the journalist with a long silent look. Rossiter broadly smiled, showing no fangs.

"Go fuck yourself," said Carpenter.

* * *

Driving back to the lab from the Athenaeum, Guy Carpenter did a lot of mulling over his new predicament. The glorious glow that he had felt when he told Quentin Rossiter to make love to himself — so to say — still buoyed him. *La ultima suerte!* His Mexican friend had insisted that bullfighting was not mere brutal baiting of a wounded maddened animal for sport, but a tragedy of death and grace under pressure, since the matador could get gored or even killed. It was rare, but it happened. Well, it had just happened at lunch. Carpenter felt he would never regret goring his tormentor, never forget Rossiter's astounded expression as the horn went in, never forget the smile fading off under the mustache, and the incisor teeth seeming to elongate in Rossiter's alternate image as Dracula with a press card. Without comment he had turned on his heel and walked off, and as Carpenter watched him go, a favorite line from Robert Burns had sprung to mind, his mantra of triumph as the *Macbeth* quote was his mantra of despair, *"a man's a man for a'that."*

But now what? The heat was on. How tell Penny, and when, and how much? By the time he got home in the evening, she would have fed and bathed Dinah, and put her to bed with a bottle. After that a martini with Peter Jennings was their routine, then dinner in the kitchen. Tell her over the martini? No, the TV news would be a bother. Over dinner? Maybe, but again, she would be putting plates on and off, interrupting the smooth-flowing narrative he was cooking up in his mind. For he was deciding, as he walked and pondered, that it was all a question of *tone,* and the tone to strike was a light one.

What was so very terrible after all in what he was now compelled to disclose to Penny? Nothing about Shanghai, of course. Only the stupid PO box, and his even stupider failure to let her know that the head of the cyclotron project had been Mei Li. No more. *That* was the trip wire, that one unspeakable mistake, and it would require some breast-beating. Fortunately, he and Penny had a marital shorthand that worked well in such sticky situations. One morning a long time ago, baby John had come toddling into their bedroom saying, "I done a bad ting." The bad thing, it turned out, was trying to flush his teddy bear down the toilet, causing a flood. Ever since, they had used that as the prelude to confessing a dumb mistake. *"I done a bad thing, I backed the car into a tree,"* or *"I done a bad thing, I paid three hundred bucks for a dress."* It was an apt beginning for an awkward disclosure, forgiveness humorously requested and bound to be forthcoming.

Yes, that was the way to go. *"I done a bad thing."* Of course no hint of the CIA — Rossiter could not mention it, so why alarm her? On Shanghai, blackout. Keep this light and keep it fast. Beyond this problem loomed tougher ones, such as Rossiter's swiftly oncoming and inexorably nasty story. One problem at a time! So thinking, Guy went to work in reasonably good spirits, and all but finished up his overdue report for Ottoline on the new telescope designs before he left the lab.

18. THE MUSIC

Like a clear running brook, a happy marriage generally has some bottom sediment, and the sediment in the Carpenters' marriage had been stirred into a muddy cloud by the national Boson Bomb tumult. As Penny sat in a veterinarian's waiting room, with Sweeney grousing in the case on her lap, she was thinking of Wen Mei Li, and of Congresswoman Kadane as well. Beside her a stout old lady's caged white cockatoo was uttering vicious screeches that matched the tenor of Penny's thoughts.

About the Congresswoman, Penny could do nothing. Ottoline had thrown Guy in with the woman, and no doubt he had enjoyed junketing around with a former movie star; but if the thought of it was irksome, that was mere fallout of a nasty jealous spell about the return from the past of Wen Mei Li. At some cost in willpower, Penny had been taking a casual tone with Guy about the celebrated Chinese physicist. What other option had she? Her overreacting long ago about the Mehitabel letters had left her wrung out and ashamed and — alone, in saner moments — even amused at poor

Guy, caught out by a cat. Even her wild rage back in the Cornell days seemed excessive at this distance in years. How could he help a romance that had come and gone ten years before she had met him, a romance in which, so he swore up and down, "nothing had happened"? That was as it might be, she would never know, yet he might at least have been open about it from the start, instead of giving Reba Wasserman and the others the malicious pleasure of rushing to tell her all about him and "Wendy."

What had pushed her over the edge was that handwritten poem, about which she had never said a word and never would. The shadowy Chinese woman had preempted her in the arms of Guy. He had loved that Wen Mei Li to distraction, declaring in mushy verse, written in heart's blood, that he could never love another as he had loved her. *"I have been faithful to thee, Cynara! . . ."* It had crazed Penny at the time, and decades later that elemental sting could still ache, like an old war wound in damp weather . . .

Dr. Melanie was leaning out of the examination room. "Penny? Come on in." The agile bony veterinarian and Sweeney knew each other well. As soon as she opened one clasp of the case, he squirmed out and rocketed around the room before submitting, flat eared and doleful, to his annual shots and an inspection of his fur. "Scratching a lot, you say?"

"Like mad."

"No wonder. Feel these crusty spots." Dr. Melanie took from a drawer a bottle of purple medicine. "Paint those spots every night for three days. That'll do it."

"Something smells wonderful," Guy Carpenter said as he came into the house.

"Sweetbreads," said Penny, doffing an apron.

"Sweetbreads! Hey, how do I rate that? No birthday, no anniversary, no nothing —"

"Payback for a champagne dinner, sweetie. Just pampering your suicidal taste for high-octane cholesterol."

"Thanks, love of my life. Once a year won't kill me."

"You're welcome. What happened with Rossiter?"

"Oh, long story. Let's have those martinis."

The first news item was a train wreck in Idaho, a passenger train plunging off a hairpin turn, pictures of piled-up cars and frantic rescue workers, close-ups of stunned bloody passengers with microphones pushed into their faces. Next an airliner swooping low over sea and palm trees.

Peter Jennings: *"Dr. Wen Mei Li arrived today in Honolulu to lecture at the University of Hawaii, but ABC can report that she will* NOT *lecture on the Higgs boson, her discovery that has created a world furor."*

Picture of an airport ramp, dignitaries clustered at the foot.

"Meeting her are the Governor of Hawaii, the President of the University, the Chinese Consul General, and the Commander of the Pacific Fleet."

The plane door opened, and out came a small figure in a tailored dark suit. In a close-up of Mei, Guy noticed much gray in her hair. Otherwise she looked the same, steel-rimmed glasses and all. "So that's your Wendy," said Penny.

"Wendy at sixty-three." (Don't tense up at *"your"*! Let it pass . . .)

Penny peered closely at the woman as she descended the ramp. "She could be forty. Asians age well, don't they?" At this echo of Myra Kadane's remark, Guy had the misfortune to smile. "What the hell's so funny about that?" Penny snapped. "She looks like a lady on a lacquer screen. She should be in a flowered robe, not that suit. Anyway, the skirt is too short."

Jennings: *"Washington is agog over still-unconfirmed reports that Dr. Wen Mei Li may appear before a Congressional committee."*

"What?" Penny exclaimed. "Can a foreign national testify in Congress?"

"Apparently." (Keep it terse, Carpenter.)

Next, Dr. Wen Mei Li in the terminal, ringed by TV cameramen, photographers popping flashbulbs, and reporters thrusting microphones at her.

> *"Dr. Wen Mei Li, in a few words, what is the Higgs boson?"*
>
> *"Dr. Wen Mei Li, are you considering defecting to the United States?"*
>
> *"Doctor, does China have the Boson Bomb yet?"*

> Jennings, with serious mien: *"The Boson Bomb, despite all the furor, is of course wholly theoretical — at present."*

Change of scene: the Capitol steps in Washington, a sedate white-haired ruddy man coming down into a crowd of waiting reporters.

> Jennings: *"National Security Adviser Dr. Homer Aptor, after testifying in closed session to key Senators about the Boson Bomb, again denies allegations of fathering a stripteaser's child."*
>
> National Security Adviser: *"It was a useful meeting. The Senators are properly concerned, and I reassured them that the administration is taking all prudent measures."*
>
> Shouted question: *"Sir, did you promise marriage to Bambi MacFadden?"*
>
> *"Sir, is it true, as Bambi claims, that you blacked out on an overdose of Viagra?"*
>
> *"Dr. Aptor, will you agree to a DNA paternity test?"*
>
> Aptor: *"I briefed the Senators with the most sensitive scientific information available from Nobel laureates. There is no present cause for concern. Thank you very much."*
>
> Several voices: *"What about Bambi MacFadden?* WHAT ABOUT BAMBI MACFADDEN?"

"All poppycock. Thank you very much."

Jennings: *"But according to her attorney, MacFadden stands by her story."*

Picture: a sallow man at a desk beside a pretty blonde in horn-rimmed glasses and a high-neckline black dress, touching a handkerchief to her eyes.

"My name is J. Gerald Reilly. I represent Mrs. Ernestine MacFadden, and we are preparing to compel Professor Homer Aptor by law to —"

"Enough!" Guy clicked it off.

"Oh, shoot, Guy, I wanted to hear all about Ernestine and Homer. You're cruel."

"You said something about sweetbreads?"

"Come along."

Their usual banter at dinner about the TV news sputtered, with Wen Mei Li a large difficult presence at the table, like a glowering silent mother-in-law. Penny broke the unaccustomed lull. "By the way, Reba called me again. Occidental finally came through with a report praising me to the skies. A bit late."

"Nice. These are the best sweetbreads you've ever cooked."

"You always say that. It started me thinking about going back to Occidental again. Why not? Something to do."

Guy paused in his wolfish devouring of the sweetbreads, glad of any topic but Rossiter or Mei. "Why *not?* Because you loved the research but hated the lecturing and the academic politics, that's why not. You quit long before Dinah came."

"I was determined to get pregnant. It's true, I've never enjoyed talking to vacant bored faces in a freshman science survey. That was all I got to do then at Occidental. Simon Duane's the department head now, I might do better —"

"And Dinah?"

"Dinah's a problem."

Dinner over, Guy said, "Just marvelous. Thanks, darling. I can use a *digestif*" — a jocular family word for brandy, introduced by John — "while I tell you about Rossiter. You too?"

"None for me. Be right with you." In the living room he poured and sipped a large cognac while she cleared dishes. "Okay, just let me get Sweeney," she said, passing through the room.

"Sweeney? Does he have to hear this?"

Penny laughed. "I won't be a minute." She returned, carrying the cat relaxed in her arms. Settling down in an armchair with him, she dipped a Q-Tip in a purple bottle and painted a spot on his fur, then another. "He's got some cat crud. Melanie gave me this stuff. Pay no mind. So, what did Peter want, and did you actually see Rossiter?"

"Did I ever! I told him to go fuck himself."

The purple Q-Tip froze in midair. "You didn't."

"In so many words."

"Bravo."

"Thank you. Best moment in my life since Dinah was born."

She gave him a whole-souled smile, with the love light in her eyes that was most of his happiness. "My hero! Start from the beginning. Tell me everything."

Guy started on a comic note, recounting Peter Braunstein's beery contrition. "He'll wear a hair shirt for a month, poor Peter. It'll ruin his tennis game, and it's pointless. Rossiter's hell-bent on writing the story about Wendy, and Peter couldn't have helped him much. The fellow waylaid me outside the lab, Penny, hooked onto my arm, and started dragging me to have lunch with him. Simplest thing was to take him to the Athenaeum and have it out. So I did."

Maneuvering quickly and lightly through Rossiter's cajoling and threats, Guy said that the reporter had obviously researched the Cornell days, probably talked to people like Reba Wasserman, and already had the whole picture. What Rossiter wanted from him was a first-person version of his early romance with the Chinese physicist. He pressed hard to get it. Very hard. Too hard. As she listened, Penny kept feeling the cat's fur and painting him here and there. It was a distraction Guy had not foreseen.

"And what did he say, when you told him to go bleep himself?"

"Not a word. He turned around and slunk out. He'll have his revenge in the article, no doubt. Let him do his worst."

"Right. Absolutely! And that was it? Was that all?"

"Not exactly." He hesitated and took a deep breath. "Penny, I done a bad thing."

She looked up at him. "How bad?" She dabbed another purple spot on the cat.

"Bad enough."

"Tell me."

"You remember when I went to China, on a State Department grant?"

"Why, sure." Dab, dab. "You were sent to upgrade a rudimentary cyclotron." Dab.

"That's right, that was when — Penny, do you have to doctor that confounded cat right now?"

"Does it bother you? Why didn't you say so?" Two quick last purple spots on the cat. "No more, go on. What was the bad thing you did?"

"The head of that cyclotron project was Wen Mei Li."

Penny's eyes rounded into circles of clear blue ice. "Really!"

"I didn't know about it till I got there."

"I see."

"I should have let you know, and I didn't."

"And why not?" Penny shoved the cat out of her lap. Sweeney stalked away with a low-spirited meow, and Carpenter sensed that this was not going to be a matter of backing a car into a tree.

"Oh, Penny, what can I say? Memories of Mehitabel, maybe. It was supposed to be a two-week mission, it kept stretching out into a whole month, and I somehow didn't get to tell you. It was an idiotic, incomprehensible lapse. I'm sorry."

"I bet you are, now that you've been forced to disclose it." She was regarding him now through narrowed blue ice. "Well, is that all?"

He could not readily proceed. The vexing cat business had thrown him all off stride. "No, no, that isn't all, but that was the start of it. That's how I happened to rent a post-office box, so as to correspond with Mei." Penny's face contorted in an ugly way. The eyes went veiled and slatey. "Penny, she asked me to write, and I agreed — again, an idiocy. I've since given up the box, but I had it for quite a while. That's the bad thing I did." He essayed a guilty half smile.

"When did you give it up?" Unsmiling response.

"Last week."

"Ah. When you found out that her name led off the article on the Higgs boson."

"Well, yes."

Long silence, while she just looked at him. "How often did you write?"

"Oh, not often."

"Once a year? Once a month? Once a week? Come on, spit it all out, now that you're spitting."

"Penny, it wasn't a *correspondence.* One or two letters a year, maybe."

"Never three?"

"God, how do I know? Possibly three, off and on."

"Love letters?" He made a despairing gesture with both hands. "Well, just what *did* you write about? Movies you saw?"

"Look, I know I deserve this, okay? Mostly about our work, and about our families. She's not a happy woman, that's really why I agreed to write —"

"Oh. Now I understand, unhappy woman, needed comforting. That makes sense. Did you comfort her while you were there too? Say, evenings?"

Guy fell silent, shaking his head. This was not working out as planned. Not at all. He groped for a way out of the deepening quagmire. "I've told you what I have to tell, Penny. It's *all* I have to tell. What we did in China was work on the cyclotron. *Nothing else.* It was bizarre, encountering her again, after all those years, bizarre and sad. The Cultural Revolution had all but burned her out, but her mind still worked, and —"

"Did she write you about the Higgs boson?"

"Not a word. I was totally amazed by the *Nature* article."

"And that's it, Guy? That's all?"

"That's the story, Penny."

"As you say, nothing else?"

"Nothing."

"What about Shanghai?"

"Huh?" The wind was knocked out of Guy Carpenter, as by a mule kick in the stomach.

"I asked you a simple question. *What about Shanghai?*"

A plaintive wail, louder than usual, came from the nursery.

"Christ!" Penny leaped up, glaring at her husband. "How absentminded can you get? You DIDN'T leave Dinah's door open, did you, when you got home and looked in on her?"

"I don't know," Guy babbled. "I may have —"

"If that wretched cat has jumped in with her again," Penny said through her teeth, striding out, "I'll chop his bloody head off."

My bloody head, thought Guy. It's my head, clearly, that she's inclined to chop off. Why the devil did she bring up Shanghai? What does she know? How can she possibly know *anything?* What can I tell her about Shanghai? Myra Kadane's admonition came strongly to mind. *Don't try that Shanghai story on that keen wife of yours, she'll gut you like a trout.*

19. THE TROUT

There, there, honey," Penny cooed, returning with the sobbing baby in her arms. "Bad kitty frighten poor Dinah darling? Shush shush, no more kitty."

"Sorry, guess I'm the culprit."

"All bad daddy's fault, bad daddy so sorry, shush shush. No more bad kitty." Penny sat down with the infant on her knees. The sobs quieted. Dinah regarded her father with a stolid unblinking baby gaze. It had never before occurred to Carpenter that his daughter had rather icy blue eyes. She was certainly not holding out her arms for a hug. Were the women in the house ganging up on him? Preposterous. He was seeing things again and had to take hold of himself.

"About Shanghai, Pen —"

"Yes, what about Shanghai?"

"What makes you ask?"

"Quentin Rossiter called me this afternoon, that's what makes me ask. He called right after I got back from the vet, and before I could slam down the phone, he managed to say, *'Don't hang up, I'm at the airport, just ask your husband about Shanghai. That's all. Goodbye.'* It made no sense to me at the time, I shrugged it off, but now I wonder. Does it make sense to you? What *about* Shanghai?"

His glass was empty, he craved another cognac, but it was no time for such a stalling move. He had to talk fast, and as a drowning man sees his whole life pass before his eyes — or so they say — he had to review the whole Wendy tangle in a twinkling. Guy Carpenter had a nimble mind in calculus, a lightning knack for perceiving the flaw in a failed experiment or in faulty apparatus, but creative narrative at short notice was not his forte. *What could Rossiter conceivably know about Shanghai?* That was the question. Had the man interviewed Mei? Unthinkable. Had there been anything about Shanghai in the letters that the CIA had snooped? Not that he could recall. Mei was as prudish in writing as she was in person, that had not changed. Nor had he referred to the weekend, ever. Or had he, by inadvertence? Penny was looking hard at him. So was the baby, winsome in her little yellow sleep suit, but disturbing with those round eyes of chilly purity.

A clutch at a straw — he did NOT have to account for the robe! That part was what Myra Kadane had found so hard to swallow. Rossiter didn't know about the robe, nobody in the world could know about it but Mei and himself, and of course the Congresswoman. This hugely simplified the calculation. Under those four searching blue eyes, under killing time pressure, Carpenter improvised quite a passable mix of fact and fudge. Mei's husband had gone off on maneuvers, he began. She had suggested that they go to Shanghai to visit her influential relatives who had escaped the Cultural Revolution, and afterward returned to Shanghai to resume their importing business. That had been the purpose, that and a tour of the remarkable recent changes in the ancient port city. Next day they had returned to Beijing, and he had flown back to the States. As he unfolded this version, which took some time — especially his entirely true description of the elaborate Chinese dinner at her relatives' home — Dinah's eyes began to blink, and by the time he finished she was dozing off. The monotonous matter-of-fact account had lulled her, which was fine, but what about Penny? Her eyes remained wide and keenly alert.

"How can Quentin Rossiter know any of that?" she asked.

"Honey, I have no idea. Fellows like Rossiter just ferret things out. Maybe he managed to talk to her family in Shanghai. Frankly, I'm baffled."

"And why would he call me with such a weird message? *'Ask your husband about Shanghai'*?"

"Pure malevolence, maybe. Who can say?"

"Who indeed?" Penny got up with the baby. "She's sound asleep. I'll put her back in."

Carpenter leaped to the bar when she was gone and poured a large cognac. Taking a long deep gulp, he sank into his old brown leather armchair, which had gone with him everywhere since Cornell days. Warm reassurance ran down his throat and out into his system. Ah, wise Omar Khayyám had said it all, hadn't he?

The subtle Alchemist, that in a Trice
Life's leaden Metal into Gold transmute . . .

Relax, Carpenter! The infected tooth was out at last. He slumped full-length in the old armchair, drink in hand, long legs outstretched on the old ottoman. It was his lotus position. Whew, that Shanghai bombshell had all but unmanned him, yet he had weathered it, and he could handle whatever came next. Penny was talking on the telephone in the bedroom and actually laughing. Encouraging sign. It crossed his mind that he had not yet checked his e-mail. He went to his den and turned on the computer. Right, mail from Myra Kadane, no less.

Dear Dr. Carpenter:

I feel a million miles from Waxahachie! Things are humming here, and counting on your discretion, I'll write freely.

The big news, which hasn't yet surfaced in the media, is that Dr. Wen Mei Li has agreed to appear before our Science Committee and has declined to testify for the Armed Services Committee. So Bob Hurtle's nose is out of joint right now, and Horace Wesley is riding high. There's a heavy tug-of-war going on between Wesley and Hurtle, since they scheduled separate hearings on the Collider and the Boson, citing different legislative interests. I've about persuaded Horace to leave you entirely out of this. He agrees that there are bigger fish than you to subpoena about the defunct Super Collider. However, I gather from Earle Carkin that Rossiter has gotten to Bob Hurtle, picturing you as some kind of key player with an obscure connection to Dr. Wen Mei Li. I don't yet know what will come of that. Just be warned.

If I can help you in any way as this devil dance unfolds, call on me. I'm greatly obliged to you for my visit to that Hole in Texas. I may be the only person walking these halls of Congress, aside from Texas Congressmen and Senators, who knows beans about the Superconducting Super Collider. It's all frantic talk in a vacuum of information. The media firestorm is on, legislative assistants are boning up on bosons and colliders with might and main, and there will be plenty of high jinks here next week. Just incidentally, Horace is personally looking into the status of the telescopes in the NASA budget. He's a good man to have on your side. Don't tell this to Dr. Porson until I know more.

What's happening with Tim Warshaw's Boson Bomb movie? He couldn't have a hotter subject for a blockbuster.

Kindest regards to Penny,

Myra K.

Guy returned to the living room, refilled his glass, and fell back in the armchair, putting up his legs. A cheering message, that. All might yet be well! Penny was still on the telephone, rattling away in calm pleasant tones. With the telescope funding confirmed, their future would be assured for ten years, and why look beyond that? This was the crucial budget year. Once the designs were approved and the contracts let, the project would *go.* It wasn't a monster like the Super Collider, provoking and tempting the annual axe wielders. It was too small. A billion dollars over ten years, in a time when the national budget was crowding two trillion! With the Chairman of the Science Committee behind it, a mere bagatelle —

"All set." Penny came in from the kitchen. "You're still tanking up, I see. I'll join you now. Not cognac, though."

He sat up. "What'll you have?"

"Oh, stay where you are."

As she mixed herself a scotch and soda, he ventured, "Long phone conversation."

"Two conversations, most of it with Geraldine. Mom's never liked talking on the phone. She sounds great —"

Geraldine was their travel agent. With a qualm, Guy said, "Wait a minute. You talked to your mom?"

"Right, and she's beside herself with joy, of course." Penny sat down and drank. "She's still got all the baby stuff, she says, from that summer we spent there ages ago with John — playpen, crib, pram, toys, the lot." Penny's manner was bristly, her voice overcontrolled. Messing with her in such a mood was perilous. "Geraldine's trying to book me on an early flight, she'll be calling right back. I don't want to get home in the wee hours, or stay in an airport hotel overnight. Either way would be lousy for Dinah." She looked at her drink and thumped it down on a side table so it splashed. "I don't really want this. I have packing to do." She wiped the splash with a tissue. "Now. Who sleeps in the nursery tonight? I would, but I thrash around so, and the baby needs her sleep before the trip. So you will."

Though rocked back on his heels, Guy was not about to submit to such foolishness. Going home to Mother! Absolutely ludicrous. As usual, Penny had been miles ahead of him, playing it cool while initiating a crazed revenge in blind rage. If she thought it was a fait accompli, she would find out otherwise. *A man's a man for a'that!*

"Let's back up a bit, Pen, and now you listen to me. You have a history of overreacting, you know you do. This time you're involving Dinah, which is a different story entirely, and —"

"Guy!" Clang of steel on stone. "I very strongly advise you not to argue with me, it's all set except for the flight time, and we'll know that in a few minutes —"

"What on earth did you tell your mother?"

"That Dinah and I are coming, nothing more. She flew up on cloud nine, asked no questions, just burbled about John's baby stuff, and my old clothes that are still there, and about shopping for Dinah's food. I won't have to pack much, I haven't gained weight in years —"

"Penny, if you're serious, which I refuse to believe, Dinah's my child too, and —"

"Oh, she is, is she? Know that for sure, do we? Fact of nature, hey? Ever heard *'It's a wise child that knows its own father'*?" Her eyes took on an evil glitter. "Let's have a little chat about reversed roles here, shall we? Shifty two-timing mother, complacent deceived father, and see how —"

"Okay, you're seething. I don't blame you, but such frenzied talk doesn't help —"

The telephone rang. "That'll be Geraldine. Don't, *don't* you crowd me now," Penny exclaimed, hurrying away. "I don't want to say things that can't be unsaid, and I'm close to it, I warn you."

As on a robot arm, his glass went to his lips. Empty. Just as well. No more of Omar's subtle alchemist, not now. He shouldn't have drunk anything at all after dinner. He hadn't begun to grasp his predicament. This was Operation Mehitabel to the fourth power. Did Penny have a case for such a draconic act, walking out with their baby? What had he done, so far as she could possibly know? He had felt sorry for Mei, so he had agreed to write to her, and he hadn't wanted to start up with his touchy wife by getting mail with Chinese stamps, so he had rented the box —

And at this very instant, and not before, a thought shook Dr. Guy Carpenter like an earthquake. *Had he not been an abysmal fool in the whole matter?* He knew perfectly well that Penny never snooped and never asked questions. Why couldn't he have been getting a very occasional airmail letter, all that time, from *any* Chinese scientist? Why had he felt the need to rent a box? Why the clumsy betraying subterfuge? As the sediment of this happy marriage swirled up in Guy Carpenter's befuddled brain, one sharp ray of truth pierced through it. Renting a post-office box signalled GUILT in blazing neon. That was Penny's case. He had stabbed a nerve forever sore and sick. If he had played around with Dolores, that flirtatious black-eyed lab assistant, and Penny had found out, there would have been hell to pay, sure. But a walkout with the baby? Hardly. It was Wen Mei Li. It was SHANGHAI.

Here she came again. "Well, we're on a nonstop that leaves LAX at nine and connects in Boston to a commuter plane. We'll get to Mom's around late dinnertime. She'll be cooking her famous Mom chowder all day long." Penny glanced at her watch. "Come to think of it, I'll sleep with Dinah. I'm not spending a night in that bedroom. Give me half an hour to pack, then it's all yours —"

"Penny, I beg of you, you've made your point, I'm desolate, I'm on my knees, don't subject our baby to this —"

"Oh, shut up." This tone of dry contempt he had not heard before in all their marriage. "You can't look after Dinah, and Mrs. Green can't either, so I have to take her. Let's not have more words, there's been too much damage already —"

"Just tell me what you think you're accomplishing, roaring off and dragging Dinah across the country —"

"I can't bear to stay under the same roof with you, okay? I don't know whether you're lying about Shanghai or not, probably you are, but what does it matter now? I've discovered that you're a *sneak*. I thought I knew you, it was inconceivable to me, but it's come out, and it can't be undone." Her eyes reddened and misted, her voice weakened. "I have trouble even talking to you." She went out, snapping off the chandelier, leaving him in the pool of light from his reading lamp, frugal housekeeper to the last.

No reason not to get drunk now. In fact, it was the only thing. Not on cognac, though. The standard remedy, much resorted to in the worst Super Collider days, was called for. Large tumbler two-thirds full of bourbon. Hot water from the kitchen. Back into the armchair to let it take hold. Great comfort, this old chair. Settle down, think about what comes next, starting with Rossiter's fast-approaching page-one *Washington Post* story. What would be the effect at the Jet Propulsion Laboratory? At NASA public relations? For that matter, at that Boson Bomb movie project? How could he handle these burgeoning problems without Penny's sharp input? Shred of hope; she still had to sleep off her anger, and in the cold morning light, whatever her momentary disgust with him, she might well reconsider hauling the poor baby all the way to upstate New York —

A furry head was bumping his free hand. "Why, hello there, old Sweeney." The cat jumped into his lap. "Poor purple-spotted little leopard." Sweeney tried to lick a purple blotch and shook his head in disgust. Guy stroked the sleek fur. "Bitter medicine, Sweeney. Such is life sometimes. Don't try to change your spots. They'll fade." The warm bourbon and water, on top of a lot of cognac, was beginning to do its work. He was maundering, he knew it, and he didn't care. "I can't change my spots, kitty. Bad daddy! I done a bad thing, Sweeney. I should never have gone with Wendy to Shanghai."

The cat listened with a searching look in those deep blue eyes, friendly blue eyes for a change. Sweeney was Penny's cat, they had all been her cats, sometimes hostile like Mehitabel, more often simply ignoring him. Sweeney was different. Guy had a relationship with this cat. Just now and then, coming to Guy by jumping up on his desk, or on a kitchen counter as he mixed instant coffee, Sweeney could seem to Guy, in such rare approaches, a pensive person reincarnated as a cat, touching Guy's face with a soft paw and looking at him out of those cat eyes with wistful resignation. That was what the eyes were telling him now, as a paw brushed his cheek. *Look, be like me, I'm trapped in here, I can't get out till I die, and she's covered me with these disgusting purple blotches, but I'm making the best of it. Prrrr . . .*

"I'll try, Sweeney, but it's hard. I've been gutted like a trout, kitty, like a goddamn trout . . ."

* * *

Automobile horn honking, loud and persistent. He sat up, startled. The picture window was bluish gray. Dawn! His mouth tasted like a sweaty sock. "Oh, you're awake." Light snapped on, hurting his eyes. "You were out cold, so I just let you sleep there. That's my limo outside. Help me with my big bag, please. I can handle the rest."

Dressed in her new suit, her hair coiffed, her face made up as for a dance, Penny was a dish, standing there holding the yawning Dinah. Even lugging a baby and a cat, she would turn heads on the airplane.

"Limo?" he said with groggy stupidity.

"Yes, limo. Geraldine said I couldn't count on cabs this time of morning —"

Miaow, mi-YEEOW. Sweeney in the case at her feet amid other luggage, cursing the day he was born, or reincarnated. "All right, where's the big bag?" There was no fight left in Guy Carpenter.

"In the bedroom, where else?"

"Give me two minutes."

Bathroom, mouthwash, more honking, voice off: "Hurry! There's all that security to go through, also I have to pay for the cat —"

Guy splashed cold water on his face and came out. "Just get into the car with Dinah. I'll bring everything —"

Penny put Dinah in his arms. "Hold on, I forgot something. I can't have him howling in there for eleven hours." She crouched on one knee by the cat case, unwrapping tinfoil from a brown cube. "This won't take a second."

"What is it?"

"Oh, Melanie calls it cat Valium, they eat it like candy and just snooze till you get where you're going." She opened one clasp enough to slip two fingers with the cube into the crack. Out pushed two ears, a brown head, a whole cat. Frantically she tried to slam the lid on him. "No, Sweeney, *no,* you miserable creature, no, NO." The cat wriggled free, scampered two full circles, and disappeared.

"Shit," said Penny, clearly vexed. "Shoot" was her usual version. "Now what?" She looked at her watch. The limo driver honked several times.

Guy handed the baby back to her. "I'll get the cat."

"Oh, sure, maybe in half an hour! And I can't leave him here, you'll let him out and he'll be gone forever. God, what a mess."

Guy had been through cat disappearances often, Penny panic and all. Under a bed was option one. He slammed the bedroom door shut to narrow the search and imprison the cat, then checked the broom closet, his shoe shelves, and the top of the refrigerator. No cat. Sliding into the bedroom, he got down on hands and knees. The twin beds were on casters, easy to move. Under his bed, nothing. Under her bed nearer the window, a furry face, ears, and gleaming eyes. He pushed the bed away, and a brown streak darted under the other bed. He shoved that one aside, and the beast shot under a heavy armchair. Sweeping an arm under the chair, he encountered fur, and Sweeney ran under Penny's bed again.

Square one. This was a sport Sweeney could play, and had occasionally played at length, like the grifter's shell game; under which of the three shells is the puss? Impatient honking outside. Pounding at the bedroom door. "Well? Well?"

Guy sat down in the armchair, watching the barely visible eyes and ears of the cat. "Sweeney, come out." Playful inching forward, nose outside the bed. "Please, kitty, I'm not going to pounce on you. You're a deep one, and you know I'm in trouble. Just come. Please come." The beast crawled halfway out from under the bed, lashing his tail. "I've got to bring you out to her. No choice. Come, cat."

Pause, then the cat approached and sat down well beyond arm's reach, tucking his tail over his paws. "Sweeney, I said I won't pounce. I won't. This is no game today. You've got to come." The cat sat there, unmoved and unmoving. "Everything is on the line, kitty. Please. *Please.*"

Carpenter held out his arms, and with a loud sad meow, Sweeney jumped into them. "Hold the case open wide, Penny," Guy called. Sweeney did not resist as Guy dumped him into the case and Penny snapped it shut.

"Thanks," she said.

"No problem."

The uniformed gray-haired driver piled the bags in the trunk.

Penny brought out the silent cat and got into the backseat, leaving Dinah with Guy to the last. He hugged and kissed the baby, who put chubby hands to his face. "Good-bye for a while, sweetheart." As he handed her over, Penny gave him a look that reminded him of Sweeney under the bed: suspicious, defiant, almost but not quite human.

"I left a letter for Mrs. Green in the kitchen."

"Okay."

"Good-bye, then."

The long black car drove away. Guy walked back into a cavernous house, quiet as death. He smelled coffee, and there it was in the kitchen, fresh and hot. He took a cup to the den and started typing an e-mail to his son in Samoa.

Hey, John Boy.

Please give me a call when you get a chance . . .

Flash on the screen:

You have new mail. Do you want to read it now?

Click. YES.

Myra Kadane again.

Hello there —

In haste, late for a committee meeting, two things. Rossiter's article will appear in Monday's Post. *Earle has read it, and from your viewpoint it's not good. Also, in the next few days you'll receive a subpoena from the Armed Services Committee. It's not the end of the world, we'll stay in touch, and Horace and I will help you as much as we can. More later.*

— MK

Numbly, Guy went on with the message to John:

. . . because you may want to fly back here for a week or two. Details when we talk.

Dad

Click.

On some godforsaken little Polynesian island where it was now dead of night, John would receive those words in seconds. If he happened to be at his computer, he might reply or even telephone at once. Guy could well remember that not so long ago contacting his son in Samoa might have taken a week, or John might have been totally incommunicado. Was the world better at all for this huge sudden change? Too heavy a question on his first cup of coffee. Anyway, Guy had more immediate things to think about; as, for instance, that his life was collapsing around his ears.

20. THE LAWYERS

Myra Kadane came down the long Rayburn Building corridor almost at a run, exclaiming as she swept into her outer office, "Pam, did Horace Wesley get my message?"

"Oh, yes, he's waiting for you in his office." The startled assistant twisted her blond ponytail with a nervous hand. "And your brother-in-law's here."

"Damn. The traffic's murderous on Independence, it's so torn up — has he been here long?"

"Well, a while. I gave him coffee, and he's reading a book."

"Tell him I'll be with him in ten minutes." Glancing in a wall mirror, the Congresswoman patted a handkerchief to the beads of sweat at her hairline. "Roasting out there, and it isn't June yet. Look at me. What was the point of getting my hair done?"

The Chairman of the Science Committee strode around his desk when she came in and gave her a fatherly, or almost fatherly, hug. "Myra, we've got the Cannon Caucus Room, and Bob Hurtle's fuming! I haven't had so much fun with my clothes on in years."

"What happened?"

"Simple, the Speaker decided that Dr. Wen Mei Li would attract the biggest mob of media and spectators, so we'd require the big chamber. Bob tried to argue that Homer Aptor would overcrowd Armed Services' hearing room, what with all the hoo-ha about his striptease lady. The Speaker said, 'Bob, will Aptor be testifying about Bambi MacFadden? If so, you can have the floor of the House.' That was when Bob walked off in a huff. I loved it."

"Have you heard from Wen Mei Li?"

"From the Chinese embassy. She's all set. So are the two Nobel laureates, one who was pro–Super Collider, one who was opposed. It should be interesting. How did you make out with Rocovsky? Your voice mail was garbled."

"He was charming, we talked on and on, but in a word, he doesn't want to testify."

Wesley made a face. "Mister Invisible Man. I could subpoena him."

"That's not advisable."

"No. Let's see how those Nobel superdomes work out. Thanks for trying with Rocovsky. I was counting on your feminine wiles."

"He's beyond them."

"No man is."

A cue to leave, with a roguish smile. In her office a small spare man in a gray suit was sunk in the couch with a fat blue book. "Hi there, Aaron, give me a minute to cool off." She hung up her jacket in her little bathroom, washed her face, fussed with her hairdo, and flung aside comb and brush. "Well, thanks for coming in, sorry I'm late. What's the book?"

"A new text on probate that I co-wrote. Dull but reliable. What can I do for you, Myra?"

"Will you take on the case of a friend of mine who's in trouble?"

"What kind of case? I'm not a trial lawyer."

"This isn't a trial exactly —"

"Would I know this person?"

"I guess you've read about him. Dr. Guy Carpenter."

"Good Lord. The *'Deep Throat Physicist'*?" Aaron Kadane

turned to peer at her, and his glasses glittered in a sunbeam slanting into the room. His features were so much like Walter's! Same mouth, same nose and brow, yet the effect was so different, a meager short placid Walter. Seeing Aaron always moved her. "Really, Myra! Dr. Carpenter, a friend of yours? How come?"

"That label is a disgusting fabrication. *Deep Throat Physicist!*" She almost snorted. "That reporter is beneath contempt. He wants horsewhipping."

"Did your friend know this Chinese lady?"

"Oh, he knew her, all right. I'll tell you about it, or he will. The thing is, he's been subpoenaed by the Armed Services Committee, and he'll be a babe in the woods at a hearing. He needs a lawyer. I mean, he advised Super Collider administrators who were on the hot seat, but he's never testified —"

"Myra, I'm just an estate-and-trusts attorney —"

"Never mind. Walter always said you were the smart brother. He was right."

"Ha! Him out there making big films and big money, then getting into Congress just like that, while the smart brother pokes along teaching law —"

"I'm thinking of how you handled Walter's messy will. The whole estate could have been wiped out by lawsuits, Aaron, you know that, yet everybody ended up pleased — Sean, your sisters, even that harpy first wife of his — and I was set for life. You're good."

"Well, thanks. A lawyer shouldn't make his own will as a rule, he has a fool for a client, we say. And don't call Sadie a harpy. She was a good mother to Sean and the girls, just not up to Walter's speed."

"Have it your way. What about Carpenter?"

"I do know wills, Myra. I don't know anything about Congressional hearings. If you ask me, the man for Dr. Carpenter is Jules Berkovits, he was in my class at Columbia Law, I can contact him —"

"Berkovits? That wild man at Yale with all the hair, who writes those books?"

"That's Jules."

"What was that last book he wrote? *Beleaguered Maiden,* or whatever?"

"*Monica Lewinsky: Besmirched Innocent.* Big bestseller, Myra. Jules teaches trial law, and he's a whiz."

"He'd cost an arm and a leg —"

"If I know Jules he'd do this gratis. Think about it! Deep Throat Physicist, Boson Bomb, Chinese female scientist, secret carrying-on . . . He'll cavort all over TV and then write another bestseller."

"That man's too flamboyant. Carpenter's a quiet obscure scientist, he's done absolutely nothing illegal, it's all vile innuendo —"

Aaron looked at her, head aslant, and seemed about to ask a delicate question, then to hesitate. "Suppose I just talk to Jules. Would Dr. Carpenter mind?"

"Carpenter doesn't know I'm looking for a lawyer for him. I doubt he's done anything about it, he must still be in shock from all the publicity. Sure, talk to Berkovits, maybe he'll give you ideas."

Putting a finger across his lips before he spoke, Aaron asked, "How do you know Dr. Carpenter, Myra?"

"I'm on the Science Committee. When this boson business mushroomed up, I asked his boss at Jet Propulsion to have him meet me, because he worked for years on the Super Collider."

"I see." Kadane slowly nodded. "Very good, I'll call Berkovits and get back to you."

"Thanks. You'll handle this, Aaron, if necessary?"

"One step at a time, Myra. It's something we teach in succession planning. That's my field, succession planning. We come to life when you die, or anyway when you face your mortality. Is Carpenter in that age group?"

"No, no, he's about the age Walter would be if he'd lived."

"Myra, I'll never stop missing Walter."

Her reply was a rueful sisterly kiss on the cheek. As he was walking out she said, "You're forgetting your book."

"So I am." He retrieved it. "Well, it's forgettable."

Guy Carpenter peeked out through the slats of a venetian blind in the front window. Nobody in sight, just Geraldine in her old red Plymouth, sunlight faintly dusting treetops across the street. Emerging cautiously, he found amid the junk in the mailbox a slim registered letter from Kadane Associates. He dropped the junk in the garbage can, slung his two valises into the backseat of the car, and slid in beside the travel agent.

"Morning, Professor, here we go, in plenty of time."

"This is very good of you, Geraldine."

"I thought I'd better see you off myself. It's a tricky business, and I know the drill."

The one-page lawyer letter was no great surprise.

Dear Dr. Carpenter:

Re: Your consultant contract of May 11 with Warshaw/Daniels Productions, LLC:

In accordance with para. VI, subhead d. ("UNFAVORABLE PUBLICITY"), be advised that the production company herewith exercises its right to cancel your contract. Please note the provision under sub-subhead d. (1): *"In the event of such cancellation prior to start of filming, all advances on consultant fee will be returnable."* Kindly remit a check to this office made out to "Shayna Daniels, Treasurer" in the amount of $25,000.

Yours truly,
Sheldon Tumulty
Assistant to Sean Kadane

Noting the drop from the enthusiastic Kadane to the dry faceless Tumulty, Guy muttered, "Wad of snotty Kleenex."

"Bad news?"

"Is there such a thing as good news? I forget."

The dumpy gray woman threw him a sympathetic glance. Geraldine had worked for years in the travel office of Paramount, then retired to Pasadena to be near her grandchildren. She served a few clients at the Jet Propulsion Laboratory.

"Dr. Carpenter, at the studio they say that a newspaper is something to wrap fish in."

"Yes, when they get bad reviews. How about the good reviews?"

"Oh, those they advertise big-time." Geraldine laughed. "That's Hollywood. I know this media problem with travel inside out. The stars want the press to follow their comings and goings unless they're in a sex scandal or a flop, then we have to throw the hounds off the track. I'm good at that. You'll have no trouble at the airport here or in Washington, I promise you." She edged the car onto a roaring freeway and remarked as she maneuvered through hazardous traffic, "I *told* you there'd be no reporters outside your house this early. They're a lazy bunch, and you don't rate a deathwatch. It'll all blow over soon anyway, I'm sure." The pallid hollow-eyed physicist only nodded, not up to small talk, and she left him to his thoughts.

Worn down by insomnia, plagued with regrets and forebodings, nerves frazzled by telephones incessantly ringing and reporters dogging him to and from the lab, Carpenter was still trying to cope with the disaster he was in. *Deep Throat Physicist!* A genie of black media smoke was now towering from that accursed post-office box, described vaguely as a "secret mail drop." Out of his refusal to talk, the journalist had concocted a snide titillating sensation. What must Penny be thinking, with her husband and Dr. Wen Mei Li linked on the TV news and in the wire services? Not a word from her, of course. On the stormy horizon ahead, there were only two bright streaks; John was on his way back from Samoa to be with Penny, and Myra Kadane had found him a lawyer.

Geraldine delivered on her promise. With her expert juggling of reservations and tickets, using false names and switching airlines, and with the check-in agents winking and cooperating, the Deep Throat Physicist passed unnoticed through the Los Angeles airport. She walked him aboard the plane with the wheelchair passengers and mothers with babies, and settled him in the empty first-class cabin. "Well, happy landings. This was fun, like in the old days. Now don't be scared of those politicians, Professor, they're just ham actors, out for publicity and money. Remember, it's darkest before the dawn. You'll do fine."

The nonstop flight was the first longish interval of peace in his recent tumultuous life. Guy passed it studying the Chinese article in

Nature, zestfully working the mathematics with pencil and paper and a hand calculator. The material called for a far more powerful computer and much checking of reference articles. Anyway, how far could he trust his harried and addled brain? Yet he thought he saw something . . .

"Dr. Carpenter?" A short girl with a black ponytail laid a hand on his arm at an exit gate in the Dulles terminal. No reporters, no cameras, Geraldine's trickery was holding up. "I recognize you from your picture in the papers. I'm Pam's sister, you know Pam, Congresswoman Kadane's assistant? She didn't want to come, too many reporters know her. I'm Suzie, I'll take you where you're going."

"Why, thank you, Suzie. I have a reservation at the Mayflower."

"Right, but that's *not* where you're going." Coy giggle. "I drove past the Mayflower. They're waiting for you there in a bunch, they even have a sound van. The media keep tabs on the main hotels."

"Where am I going?"

"To meet a lawyer, sir."

She drew up at a dilapidated red-brick building on a side street near Union Station, with an arched faded sign in gold lettering over the entrance: MILLARD FILLMORE HOTEL. "I'll be waiting, Professor."

"For me?"

"For the Congresswoman. She's here. Take your bags in, sir. This is where you're staying."

At the dingy reception desk, a little bald man with hearing aids in both ears said, "Oh, yes, Dr. Carpenter. Sign in later, sir. You're expected right now in suite 34."

Myra Kadane opened the door, laughing. "So, here you are!" Two men stood behind her in a small seedy suite. "Welcome! Good trip?"

"Uneventful."

"That's great. Your travel agent must be as clever as you said. This is my brother-in-law, Professor Aaron Kadane."

The physicist shook hands with a nondescript academic, a scrawny drab version of the worldly-wise man in the portrait. Aaron

Kadane said, "Meet Jules Berkovits, my old friend and classmate. You've heard of Jules Berkovits?"

"Who hasn't?" said Carpenter, who hadn't.

Berkovits was a wholly different and picturesque presence, a hefty man with thick locks of gray hair that came down almost to his broad shoulders. He was dressed like a 1970s undergraduate in old jeans, old sneakers, an open checkered shirt, a worn blue denim windbreaker. He looked as though he might not have worn a tie since his bar mitzvah. Jewish he surely was, Carpenter thought. Berkovits offered a large hairy manicured hand. "Hi."

"Well, gentlemen, I'm here just to make introductions," said the Congresswoman. "I didn't want Professor Carpenter to encounter total strangers. My presence is superfluous and a bit ill-advised, and now I'll be going. Aaron teaches estate planning at Georgetown Law, Guy, he's as smart as they come —"

"Objection," said Kadane.

"Overruled," Myra said with a grin. "I've asked him to help you, and he's graciously agreed. He and Mr. Berkovits will take over at this point. Any questions?"

"Yes, do you have a key to this suite? I'm told this is where I park."

"Right." She handed it to him. "Mr. Berkovits, I couldn't be more grateful. Aaron, thanks again." A brief wave to all, a quick bright look into Carpenter's eyes, and she was gone.

Aaron Kadane did not stay long, either. He described his background in trusts and estates, and assured Carpenter that Berkovits was the man to advise him on his legal predicament. "I promised Myra to help you, and I will. To begin with, I can do no better than put you together with Jules Berkovits. He's flown down from New Haven at my request. We've discussed your problem, so far as Myra and I know about it. Nobody's committed to anything. Just talk to Jules, and I'll be in touch with you again soon."

"A million thanks," said Carpenter.

Kadane left. Berkovits and Carpenter regarded each other in silence.

"You've never heard of me," Berkovits said.

Carpenter managed a lame laugh. "My wife's always telling me that I'm totally out of it. Sorry."

"No need." The lawyer raised a palm. "Sometimes it even helps. Take that old manager at the reception desk. He hasn't heard of the Deep Throat Physicist. You'll be okay here, just don't let anyone know where you are. You must be tired. We can talk in the morning."

"Let's talk now."

"Oh? I'm for that. Setting aside the media drivel, Dr. Carpenter, what's your problem, and how can I help you?"

Carpenter asked, "Are you married?"

"Not at the moment. Why?"

"My problem, first and last, concerns my wife. You have to understand about wives."

"No two wives are the same, Dr. Carpenter."

"True. On the other hand, they're all alike." At the lawyer's amused grunt, Guy added, "That's either profound or idiotic, and maybe I should take a quick shower before we talk. I've just flown cross-country —"

"By all means. Are you hungry? I am. Suppose I order up a pizza we can divvy and a bottle of wine?"

"You're on. Anchovies on my half."

"We're going to get along," said Berkovits. "Anchovies for both of us."

21. THE STRATEGY

Carpenter was stepping out of the shower when he heard a buzz at the door. He dried himself with two skimpy towels, noting that unlike the Mayflower, the Millard Fillmore did not supply bathrobes. Peering out naked, he saw on the coffee table a family-size pizza and two bottles of Chianti. "Ye gods, Mr. Berkovits!"

"Jules. It's a nuisance to run out of wine —"

"We'll never eat up that flying saucer."

"You'd be surprised." Berkovits was deftly uncorking a bottle. "Got glasses in there?" Carpenter pulled on pants and a shirt and brought out two squat tumblers. Berkovits asked, pouring the wine, "What did you think of Quentin Rossiter's article?"

"Well, he got his facts right on her life story. He even caught something of her personality. His science editor obviously helped him on the Higgs boson material, that part is sketchy, but okay. On the whole, I'd call it professional journalism."

"You're leaning over backward."

Carpenter took up a pizza slice. "Of course I am, the rotten scumbag."

"That's more like it. *'Deep Throat Physicist!'* Call that professional? Who remembers that *Deep Throat* was a porno movie about fellatio, or that reporters hung the title on a Nixon insider who squealed to them? Now it just means a stealthy betrayer of secrets, and applying it to you, from everything Aaron told me, is slanted and rancorous. What does Quentin Rossiter have against you, anyway?"

"Well, he did approach me on the story, actually flew out to California to talk to me. I guess I wasn't as cooperative as I might have been."

"In what way?"

"I told him to go fuck himself."

Jules Berkovits laid down the pizza slice he was about to eat, jumped to his feet, and held out his hand. Carpenter rose, they shook hands, and the lawyer seized him in a powerful hug, exuding a mixed effluvium of male locker room and lime cologne. "I am your slave," he said. "Tell me your story from the beginning. Why is it all about your wife, first to last?"

"It's a long yarn, Jules, and I don't come out too well."

"That I surmise. You're in deep dog poop to your nostrils. Go ahead."

Guy Carpenter started back in the Cornell days and recounted the story much as he had told it to Myra Kadane. Berkovits ate and drank with gusto as he listened, his sharp brown eyes not leaving Carpenter's face, except when he reached for another pizza slice or poured wine. At the Mehitabel incident, he burst out in a raucous bellow. "Hawr hawr, oh my precious aunt Fayga, hawr hawr! You're not making this up? That goddamned orange cat was on the shelf with those letters?"

"Are you beginning to get the idea of my problem with Penny?" Carpenter took up another pizza wedge. Between them they were making steady inroads on the flying saucer, and the wine too.

"Mehitabel! I love it. You should write a book, Guy, *Cats I Have Known.*"

"I haven't told you yet about Sweeney."

"Sweeney, hey? Also a great name. My second wife's hang-up was basset hounds, at her worst we accumulated five of those draggle-eared sad-eyed mutts. I'll tell you sometime about Fortinbras. Fortinbras broke us up, though there were other issues — sorry, go ahead."

Carpenter took up the tale, ending with a candid narrative of Penny's walkout with Dinah and Sweeney. There were two greasy cold slices of pizza left, and they were on the second bottle of wine, when Carpenter fell silent. Jules Berkovits leaned back in his chair, hooked an arm over the back, and stared at the physicist. "Well, now, what *did* happen in Shanghai?"

"I've told you."

"Right, you've told me." Berkovits turned abrasive, grating out sentences as in a cross-examination. "She got sick and puked up her toenails, so the weekend was ruined. It was all on the up-and-up, though. All very chaste and kosher. You were in different rooms on different floors. But life is full of surprises, isn't it, Guy? Just your tough luck that Rossiter's science editor was in China at the time and visited your cyclotron. And then just happened to be in that Shanghai hotel that same weekend, happened to notice the two of you merrily eating an early breakfast together, happened to recall it when this whole Wen Mei Li thing boiled up, and told Rossiter what he had seen. That's the one hook, you realize, that Rossiter can hang his hat on. He hasn't got another solid fact, except for the 'secret mail drop,' as he calls that post-office box you so stupidly rented. All the rest is Cornell background and insinuation. Your tough luck is truly pathetic. I weep for you."

"You don't believe me."

"Come on, Deep Throat," snapped the lawyer, "what happened in Shanghai?"

Guy Carpenter had drunk a lot of wine and was bone tired. He lashed back at Berkovits, "Okay, Ambulance Chaser, what happened in Shanghai is known to only two people on God's green earth, Wen Mei Li and myself, and we'll both take it with us to our graves to perfume our dust. How's that, and what's it to you?"

"Just thought I'd ask." Berkovits nodded, smiling. "A neatly crafted answer, Professor. Well done. Did the Higgs boson ever come up in those letters you and she wrote?"

"Never! When Mei puts a Chinese wall around part of her life, it doesn't exist. Mostly it was nostalgia. They're touchingly sentimental, the Chinese, once you're past those forbidding Asian features and the different eyes, or so I've found them. Infrequent warm letters, with some talk about family, and people we worked with, also current events, that sort of thing. Staying in touch, nothing more."

Berkovits unlaced his sneakers. "Nothing about a Boson Bomb?"

"Don't be silly, Jules."

"It's the silly season." The lawyer began to pace in white gym socks. "After Aaron called me, I talked to a couple of physicists at Yale. They were cautious about the *Nature* article, neither one had worked through it, but the bomb business just made them snicker."

"Of course it would."

"Doesn't matter, Guy, you're caught in a paroxysm of media imbecility. It'll soon pass, but meantime you can get badly damaged. Your own bloody fault."

"I don't deny that."

"Then let's talk strategy. For starters, I'm the worst possible man to be your counsel at a hearing."

Nonplussed, Carpenter said, "Quite all right. I haven't asked you."

"Now don't misunderstand me, I said I'm your slave, the trouble is I've won big murder trials and written books about them, and I show up a lot on TV. I was even briefly an O. J. Simpson consultant, for crying out loud, one of the regiment. With me beside you, you'd be perceived not only as the Deep Throat Physicist but also as the Unabomber and the Boston Strangler, all rolled in one. Not advisable. Aaron Kadane's just right for it. Best, of course, if you don't testify at all."

"I've already been subpoenaed."

"I'm aware of that." Padding back and forth, running his fingers through his gray locks, the lawyer talked half to himself.

"Right away I've got to see Charley Sturdevant, of course, Sturdevant's crucial, and then —"

"Who's Sturdevant? Never heard of him."

"Nobody has. He and Alan Fineman are the two most powerful movers and shakers on the Hill. How about more wine?"

"Help yourself."

"Thanks." Berkovits drank as he paced. "Now, in these hearings there's the hoopla, and then again there's what's really going on, which tends to be about money. *Cherchez l'argent.* Charley Sturdevant is Chief of Staff of the Appropriations Committee. Mean anything to you?"

"I know the Collider was killed in an Appropriations vote —"

"Quite right. Do you know that the Appropriations Committee *approved* the Super Collider?"

"I sure didn't —"

"That it was killed in a floor vote by a tricky parliamentary maneuver, which caught the committee flat-footed and couldn't be reversed?"

"Total news to me."

"Charley told me that when I phoned him today. He said, 'The Super Collider? Everybody's been calling me about it, my phone's ringing off the hook.' Charley and I got real friendly on *Columbia Law Review,* he was the editor. We double-dated a lot. Charley used to thrill the law-school girlies like crazy, giving them rides on his motorcycle. He's still a Harley-Davidson fiend, he arrives at the House every morning on his new V-Rod, so he told me. We couldn't talk much, he had two calls waiting. Alan Fineman is a different proposition, Chief Clerk of Ways and Means, a tight-assed Harvard Law man, very able. I had coffee with him once when I was looking for a job in Washington. Not my type."

Berkovits emptied the glass, pulled up a chair, and sat down face-to-face with Carpenter. "Look, Guy, you're a very, very small fish, it's just that Rossiter linked you publicly to Wen Mei Li, and she's the star of this show. The thing can go anywhere. What she says and does may well be decisive. I'll spend tomorrow in the Library of Congress, catching up on the legislative history of the

Super Collider. I'm having dinner with Sturdevant, and I may see Fineman on Monday, that's not definite yet, but I've got to talk to both —"

"Jules, Jules, back up. You're talking too fast for me. Why are Fineman and Sturdevant so powerful?"

"Sorry, thinking out loud. Okay, crude diagram, Guy — and please pay attention — the budget comes down from the President, but the House has to vote the money, right? Ways and Means handles the revenues and decides what money the government can afford to spend. Appropriations gets requests for funds from committees and subcommittees, and parcels out what money is available from Ways and Means. So in the end, where the money goes is for those two committees to thrash out between them, and that means those two Chiefs of Staff. The politicians are too busy and don't know that much. They can't, they have to get themselves reelected every two years. Follow me so far?"

"I do indeed."

"Excellent. Now, all committees have staff, and the Chief of Staff is the effective day-to-day memory and corporate brain of the committee. It's how the system works. Between them, Charley and Alan Fineman know everything about everything in this session of Congress. Their power is inconceivably great, and nobody knows about it except Congressmen and their assistants, and *they* all keep it under their collective hats. Because it's the dark secret of Congress that the politicians are out front, while smart unelected nobodies like Charley Sturdevant do the digging and make the decisions — as recommendations, of course." Berkovits pulled his sneakers on. "I'll call you tomorrow. This is Aaron Kadane's case, so basically you stay in touch with him. I will, too."

"We haven't mentioned your fee."

"Forget it."

"I will not. Isn't my money as good as O. J. Simpson's?"

Berkovits paused in lacing the sneakers. A rueful smile crossed his deeply lined face, and he hooked an arm on the back of his chair. "Why, that's right amiable of you, Guy, and deserves an answer. You said that all wives are alike. Bit of a sweeping statement, what?

Well, all guys have had a Wen Mei Li, that's my sweeping statement. My Mei was Sue Ellen Thompson, also on *Law Review,* a dark thin girl, not what you'd call beautiful, fantastically keen brain. She gave up law practice after a hot start and put in five more years in med school. She writes books on forensic medicine now, she's an authority. Your Mei was Chinese. My Sue Ellen was Christian, and I mean *Christian* Christian, Guy, Southern Baptist, absolutely unshakable in her belief in Christ, the Resurrection, and the rest. That let out her Jewish agnostic boyfriend."

He stood up and put on the denim jacket he had shed in his pacing. "We never had a weekend in Shanghai, no. We did go skiing in Aspen once — just once, for two whole weeks — during winter break, last year of law school. As you so poignantly put it, that winter break will perfume our dust. Let's say I'm doing this for Dr. Sue Ellen Thompson and our winter break in Aspen. It'll be fun, and I hope I can help."

Carpenter was finishing unpacking when the telephone rang. Dopey with weariness and wine, he thought that Penny might be calling, that somehow she had tracked him down, that she was rallying to him in his agony, that all was forgiven. He was eager to know how Dinah was, and jumped to seize the phone.

"Hi there, it's Myra. How did you get on with Berkovits?"

"Well, he's a fireball, all right. Sort of overwhelming. He'll consult with your brother-in-law, he says, but won't take a fee from me. That bothers me, Myra. You get nothing for nothing in this life. I tried in vain to insist —"

"Guy, Jules Berkovits didn't fly down here to make money. He doesn't lack for loaded clients. Aaron's another fireball, though you may not have gathered that yet. You're in good hands."

"I know it. I haven't slept for a week. I'll sleep tonight."

"Good. Have you called Penny?"

"In a word, I'm yellow."

Low chuckle by the Congresswoman. "Did you remember to go down and register?"

"It slipped my mind."

"Do it now."

"Yes, Congresswoman. I've already tired you with thanks, but —"

"Thank me when it's over and you've survived. Sleep well."

A stout gray-haired woman was dozing behind the hotel desk. She yawned and pushed the register book to him. "Yes, Dr. Carpenter. Cash or credit card?"

He gave her his Visa plastic, and she handed him a thick book. "For you, sir."

"What? Nobody knows I'm here."

She shrugged. "Box 34."

The book was the mildewed *Four Horsemen of the Apocalypse.* Tucked into it was a scrawl on Myra Kadane's gray notepaper:

Light reading to pass the time.

M.

22. THE SWITCH

At the Library of Congress, Jules Berkovits was nodding off over a thick volume of the *Congressional Quarterly Weekly Reports,* when a discreet tapping at the door roused him. "Professor Berkovits?" The head of the science section, a brisk helpful lady fascinated by the lion in her quiet domain, looked into the small office. "My, you've put in a long day. I'm leaving now. Did we give you all the material you need?"

"Lord, yes." He swept an arm at a shelf of hearings and *Quarterly* volumes, all bristling with paper inserts to mark every Super Collider passage. "You've saved me a week of digging."

She laughed with pleasure and shut the door. He turned to his laptop and wrote as fast as his fingers could fly:

CARPENTER File Memo #3

Okay, eight hours of reading, enough!

This memo follows #2 about my meeting with Carpenter in his Washington hotel hideout. Carpenter's plight traces back to his five years of work on the Superconducting Super Collider, so I've spent the day reading up on what it was and what happened to it. It's a gory horror story of a colossal abort at the interface of science and politics, and it would be utterly beyond belief, except that Congress did it. That's believable. As for the Higgs boson, I tried to puzzle it out and quit. The general public can't possibly understand it, and that gives it an aura of mystery and fear, the steak and potatoes of alarmist journalism. Carpenter's been whirled up by chance in a media tornado and dropped in the dizzying Oz called Washington. A bloodhound reporter, searching for a "gotcha!" angle on the Chinese discovery, has skewered him with a sensational hatchet job that hinted he may have passed Higgs boson secrets to China, hence the Hurtle subpoena.

Carpenter's been unlucky on several counts. There's been an odd lull in the news of late, no juicy Hollywood divorce or coupling, no bizarre murder or kidnapping, no fresh war or terrorist crisis (though I guess one could happen, God forbid, before I finish typing this memo), so the media have blown up the Higgs boson, with its preposterous extension into a Boson Bomb, as the Big Story, filling TV time and newsprint with it since there's nothing else. Meantime, Carpenter has to sweat it out. He did have a brief romance with this Dr. Wen Mei Li when they were both postdocs, decades ago. The rest is applesauce. I'm satisfied that Carpenter is quite blameless, just somewhat of a damn fool about women. (Who am I to talk?) Pulling him safely through this firestorm is a nice challenge, because as things stand now, he can be ruined for life.

The wild card is Wen Mei Li. Why is she demeaning herself to show up at a U.S. Congressional hearing? Because the Politburo sees a gain in world prestige, that has to be it. The *Nature* article created no stir in Europe. The *Economist* first carried a temperate, somewhat skeptical account of the Chinese claim, but in this week's issue the hysteria over here has become big news. Those staid Brit pundits are absolutely chortling over the American discomfiture. The lead article starts off, *"Our tabloid press is having a glorious time cocking a snook at Uncle Sam,"* and proceeds to cock a mean snook itself, ending with a tongue-in-cheek literary taunt from the chapters in *Martin Chuzzlewit* that caricature America: *"One can safely remark, as Carlyle did about Dickens, that Dr. Wen Mei Li has got all Yankeedoodledum in a fizz."*

Strategy: WAIT. *Wait* for a new happening to draw off the fickle media, and just pray it isn't another 9/11. *Wait* for her appearance. Who knows what she'll come out with? *Wait* and postpone Carpenter's testifying as long as we can. Best case: keep him out of Congressman Hurtle's gun sights altogether.

A thunder-and-lightning storm, the usual thing on a June afternoon in Washington, with earsplitting crashes and rain lashing against the windows, drowned out the buzzer on Myra Kadane's desk, or possibly she was too absorbed in the letter she was reading to hear it. Pam poked her head into the office. "Congressman Hurtle is trying to reach you. I said you'd call him back."

"Oh, yes, do that." Myra pressed a button, and Earle Carkin appeared, cool and spruce in a seersucker suit and tie. She rattled the two pages at him. "Earle, how did you get hold of this horrible stuff, and who's Jerome Wirtz?"

"Jerry was on Hurtle's staff, then he left to join a high-flying firm of lobbyists. He's doing right well, and he and Hurtle have kept in touch." Carkin's thin guileful grin appeared. "As to how I got it, let me plead the fifth. I just thought you'd be interested."

Pam on the speakerphone: "Line B for Congressman Hurtle."

The deep voice of Bob Hurtle, friendlier than usual. "Myra, are you free? I'd like to talk to you."

"Sure, I'll come to your office."

"Stay put. I'll come to you."

Carkin and Myra Kadane exchanged surprised glances. *Mountain coming to Mohammed?* Carkin shrugged, not venturing a comment.

"That's all, Earle. Thanks." She scribbled a note as he left.

Aaron,

Re Carpenter, very worrisome.

She clipped it to the Wirtz letter, and buzzed. "Pam, send this by messenger to Professor Kadane, marked *urgent, personal.*"

Conway R. Hurtle of Illinois came striding in. Full head of graying hair, red face plump but not jowly, heavy body of a onetime athlete, relaxed confident air of the Chairman of a committee controlling several hundred billion dollars, such was Bob Hurtle. Myra Kadane was not afraid of Hurtle, but wary of him. A Republican leaning to the liberal side of social issues, he had led the fight to kill the Superconducting Super Collider, and now he was out to regain the face he had lost. This visit must be to that purpose, Myra guessed.

He stopped to peer at a picture of Walter over the couch. It was a favorite of hers, a blown-up snapshot of him after a hard tennis game, perspiring, laughing, waving the racket. "Now there was a good Congressman, Myra, a real comer. Great picture. Walter to the life. He took care of himself, didn't he?" Hurtle sat down, sighing. "I don't get to the gym or the pool regularly enough. How do you stay in such beautiful shape?"

"Why, thank you, Bob. Most mornings I jog two miles on the towpath, that's all."

"Towpath?" Hurtle looked concerned. "Don't you risk being mugged or worse, attractive lady like you?"

"Oh, come on, Bob. There are forty respectable bruisers like you out jogging at that hour. My only risk is being trampled."

Hurtle laughed hard, then sobered. "I appreciated your vote on the Osprey amendment."

"Well, I didn't see canceling a multi-billion-dollar aircraft that's still being tested."

"You're dead right, and on that point my position on the Super Collider has always been misunderstood." A glance at the window. "The rain's letting up. Maybe it'll cool things off a bit." Hurtle hesitated and took a different tone. "Myra, our two committees are investigating one and the same thing, the Chinese beating us to the Higgs boson. You know, I've been thinking. Why not combine our efforts in a joint hearing? Save time, money, staff work, focus on what matters to the American people. The *facts.*"

Myra was no veteran in the House, but she was a veteran of Hollywood. Her guess was correct. Wen Mei Li would command a huge TV audience, and Hurtle was not about to be left out of the limelight if he could help it. "What about Dr. Wen Mei Li, Bob? She turned you down."

"Ah, that's just it. You've put your finger on it, Myra. You know, I don't see this process going on more than three or four days. The issue is basically about science, so it's Horace's show, isn't it? Now, my idea is to leave the gavel in Horace's hands throughout. Why not? National security is at stake. I'll not stand on seniority. Get the job done, that's what matters."

Measurable pause, Hurtle smiling at her with downright flirtatious charm. This was Hurtle the former football player, former big man on campus, working over the pretty little Congresswoman. "What do you think, Myra?"

"Well, why don't I just mention this to Horace? I have to see him now, anyway."

"Oh, do you? Fine." Hurtle stood up. Brisk change of tone. "If we go that route, there isn't much time, so let me know."

Myra had no appointment with Horace Wesley, the white lie was routine. Hurtle was avoiding the humiliation of going hat in hand to a lesser Chairman with a risk of being turned down, hence this approach through her. She hurried along the corridor to Wesley's office. Quite a turn! As for Guy Carpenter, the poor dear man immured in that shabby downtown hotel, this might be a lucky break if it came off, in view of that evil Jerome Wirtz letter.

"Well, hello, Myra." Wesley rose to greet her with a little hug, then dropped into his swivel chair. "There's a floor vote coming up on the national parks funding. I'm waiting for the bell."

"Horace, Bob Hurtle just came to my office, and we had quite a chat."

"Bob came to you?"

"He did."

"Tell me more."

At first Wesley looked puzzled as she talked, then astonished, then more and more pleased — and no wonder! Hurtle's offer to leave the gavel in his hands was an extraordinary obeisance. Grinning broadly when she finished, he put his feet up on the desk and clasped his hands behind his head. "Well, well, well. So Bob wants in, does he? That'll take some doing, and first and foremost, there's the question of Wen Mei Li."

"That's what I said at once."

"This is serious business." He buzzed his secretary. "Get me Mr. Zhang Zhui . . . He's the cultural attaché at the embassy, Myra. He's handling her itinerary. I don't think there's a chance, myself. The Chinese don't like changes, especially a major one like this. It'll have to go back up to the Beijing mandarins, and then there's the lady herself . . . Hello? Mr. Zhang Zhui? Good to talk to you. We've had an important development here. Let me tell you about it." Wesley repeated Hurtle's proposal, strongly emphasizing that as head of the Science Committee, he would chair the hearings throughout. He listened in silence to a lengthy reply, and near the end burst out laughing. "I see. Well, sir, I'll do that, and I appreciate it." He hung up. "They'll surprise you every time. He wants me to fax him the exact proposal, and he added, *'On one sheet of paper, if you please. I learned that from Mr. Winston Churchill's memoirs.'* He's all right, that Zhang Zhui."

The trees were still dripping, the slant afternoon sunlight sparkling in the falling drops, as Aaron Kadane and Jules Berkovits strolled the Georgetown campus, where myriad yellow chairs for the bygone commencement still lined the grass. Students roamed the walks, mostly paired off boy and girl, and some stared at the TV legal celebrity with the long gray hair. "Lots of Asians," Berkovits said, puffing at a big cigar.

"More and more every year," said Kadane. "And they get the top marks. Especially the Koreans, they know how to work."

Berkovits said, "In law school too?"

"Not yet, but that's coming. They've gone for the sciences first. How did your meeting work out with Sturdevant and Fineman?"

"Fineman opened my eyes about Hurtle. Knowledgeable guy, Fineman. Turns out that way back when Hurtle visited the Super

Collider, Carpenter got under his skin. They went down into the tunnel together, Hurtle insisted on it, but he's claustrophobic, and he had to beg and plead to get out of there fast. Carpenter was a witness to his discomfiture and wasn't sympathetic enough, or maybe even showed amusement. Could be it was all in Hurtle's mind —"

"This bench looks dry," said Kadane.

They sat down on a stone bench in the sun, far from the rows of damp folding seats. Berkovits went on, "Hurtle was against the Collider anyway, unlike most Republicans, and Carpenter drove the nail to the board. Hurtle's never forgotten and is out to get him. That's according to Fineman."

"Not unlikely, but marginal," said Kadane.

"How's that, marginal?"

"Hurtle is out to justify killing the SSC, Jules, that's item one on his agenda. Making a monkey of just one leading Collider scientist can do that, and the Deep Throat Physicist is a target like the side of a barn. That's Hurtle's idea."

"Very good point." Berkovits was silent for a while, smoking his cigar with relish. They had left Kadane's office to take the prohibited fumes outside. "Commencements make me melancholy," he said. "All those bright-eyed kids sailing out year after year, eager to break open life's fancy box of bonbons . . . You say you know this Jerome Wirtz?"

"Well, he took my course the second year I gave it. What I remember is that he got straight As. Seemed a quiet fellow."

"Quiet, are you kidding? That's a Roy Cohn letter."

"He was young then. He's blossomed out, I guess."

"Grown saber teeth, that is."

"Give him a break, Jules. Hurtle asked him for ways to carve up Carpenter."

"True enough." Berkovits puffed at the cigar. "And he's right on the money. Subpoena the records of the post office Carpenter used, subpoena the science editor who saw them together in Shanghai, embarrass the bejesus out of poor Carpenter on world TV about those letters, and about his wife, and Wen Mei Li, and Shanghai. Then, when he's thoroughly shaken up, move in for the kill with the aperture fiasco. That should finish him off, and with him, the SSC. Maybe wreck his marriage too, though for Hurtle that's neither here nor there."

"Jules, I haven't the foggiest what that aperture business is all about. Do you?"

"Yep, after a hard day at the Library of Congress, I do indeed."

"Tell me."

"I'll send you some stuff I got at the Library. You must inform yourself about it, Aaron. It's crucial. In a word, the heart of the Super Collider was just a pipe, a *very thin* pipe, mind you, fifty-four miles long *and less than two inches in diameter,* can you imagine? All the rest — tunnel, giant detectors, ten thousand superconducting magnets, everything — was built around that fifty-mile strand of metal spaghetti, for protons to race around in and crash into each other.

"Well, when the construction was about two years along, guess what, the physicists got cold feet! Weren't quite sure that a diameter of four centimeters — it was all metric system — would deliver the Higgs boson. Might just fall a bit short. Add one centimeter to the aperture, and detecting the Higgs, if it existed, would be a sure thing. So after much soul-searching, with a billion bucks already spent, they did change the aperture. In Hurtle's view that showed up the physicists once and for all as spendthrift ditherers, and it alone justified killing the Super Collider. Now whether Carpenter defends enlarging the aperture or admits it was a fiasco doesn't matter. By the time Hurtle's through badgering him about it, he'll be a bloody mess, a basket case."

"How do we counter that?"

"Well, Wirtz exaggerates the aperture story, but it's pretty bad." He puffed at the cigar and flipped it into a trash can. "Enough of the filthy weed. Let's go back to your office and make some notes."

"Jules, you're being generous with your time and smarts."

"Forget it, and later let's talk about my will and estate. I've got a little property, and two ex-wives, two kids, and a girlfriend I care a lot about. And these days planes do go down."

Under the door of his small book-crammed office, Professor Kadane found a message. "I'm to call Myra urgently."

"Your sister-in-law goes in for urgency."

"There's usually a reason."

On the scratchy speakerphone Myra's voice was distorted yet clearly excited. "Aaron, something's doing. You and Mr. Berkovits should know about it."

"Jules is right here."

"He is? Great. Listen, both of you." She ran through a swift account of Hurtle's visit and her meeting with Wesley. "Horace doesn't believe the Chinese will buy into the joint hearing, nor do I. What say?"

Kadane shrugged at Berkovits, who called across the desk, "They'll do it, Congresswoman."

"Is that you, Jules? Why?"

"Same reason I talk to any moronic interviewer on TV. Wen Mei Li has won the Olympic gold in brains. Beijing is all for this ticker-tape parade for her in the halls of the United States Congress, the more prestigious the committee, the better. They'll go."

"If so, Carpenter's in somewhat better shape," said Kadane.

Myra's voice: "Is he, Jules?"

The lawyer ran a hand through his gray locks without answering.

Myra: "Jules?"

"Even-stephen. Packed caucus room, banks of TV cameras, and Bob Hurtle. Unstable mixture, could detonate. Then again, Wesley would have the gavel. If it happens, should be fun."

Myra: "What about that Jerome Wirtz letter? You've read it?"

"We have," said Kadane. "Not good."

"No fun," said Berkovits, "but we'll handle it."

23. THE CRUNCH

Penny was going out of her mind in her mother's home. A lifelong devourer of novels, she was rereading mildewed copies of girlhood favorites she found in her old room, for there was little else to do. At the moment she was halfway through Thomas Wolfe's huge last book, *You Can't Go Home Again,* and thinking that Wolfe should have lived to write a sequel, *Who the Hell Wants To?*

This dreary cramped old house woke too many dormant cheerless memories. Her hometown had hardly changed, and in no way for the better. Mom doted on Dinah, but the baby was given to hostile squirming in her arms, and pushing away her hand at feeding time. Change of air and water, Mom said, but Dinah was just not the same baby since those eleven nightmarish hours of wailing and puking in airplanes. As for Penny's angry fantasy of looking into Reba Wasserman's offer of a job, with the notion of leaving the baby with Mom while she commuted to the University of Vermont, it was a popped bubble. Reba had turned vague when Penny had telephoned and pressed her for a definite proposal, and anyway Mom couldn't really care for Dinah. In a way, Penny was as trapped as Guy.

And Sweeney was gone! Gone for days, vanished the very first morning when Mom left a door open. Penny's anguished search had only started all the neighborhood dogs, fearsome mongrels every one, barking their heads off at the strange woman. What would they do to a disoriented little cat? Animal shelter, lost-and-found advertisements, posters on telephone poles — no luck. Alas, poor Sweeney! And all this was as nothing to the real gnaw at Penny's heart. Wasn't she letting Guy down, however much the son of a bitch deserved it? What was a wife for, if not for the kind of crunch he was in? Yet how could she have anticipated the impact of Quentin Rossiter's awful story? Sunk in her mother's sagging old morris chair, waiting for the evening news to come on, Penny was not enjoying her martini much.

"Penny, dear, why are you making such a face?" Mom was dragging a kitchen chair to the TV.

"This drink tastes funny."

"I have some Cherry Heering I won in a raffle, if you prefer —"

"God no! Guy and I just have a martini every night with the news, Mom, I'm used to it."

"Maybe that's why it tastes funny. He's not here." Another sly poke at her for crossing the country and moving in with a baby and a cat, no explanation. Peter Jennings came on and forestalled a prickly comeback.

> *"Tonight, Capitol Hill is abuzz,"* he began, *"over Conway Hurtle's extraordinary proposal to Horace Wesley for joint hearings into the alarming Chinese discovery of the Higgs boson and the cancellation in 1993 of America's Superconducting Super Collider. Dr. Wen Mei Li, who has been dubbed the Mother of the Bomb, refused to appear before Chairman Hurtle. Will she relent now?"* (Pictures of Hurtle and Wen Mei Li.)

"You know, dear," Penny's mother said, "I saw that Chinese lady on TV when she landed in Honolulu. Not my idea of a scientist, she's so *pretty,* sort of like Anna Mae Wong, isn't she? Though she's surely no spring chicken."

Penny swallowed her martini and her response, splashing a refill into her glass.

> *"In other news, the President today began conferring with G8 world leaders in Ulaanbaatar, Outer Mongolia, on urgent measures to save Antarctica from melting away, and whales from Japanese cuisine."* (Pictures of President and ministers amiably chatting on a balcony with a spectacular view of mountains and lakes.) *"This is the first G8 conference undisturbed so far by protest marches in the streets, because the protesters are having trouble getting to Outer Mongolia."* (Picture of streets outside the hotel, empty except for oxcarts. Picture of angry shouting activists with placards at a China Airlines counter.)

Jennings turned to interviewing stock analysts about a six-hundred-point drop that day in the market. A cheery expert was urging investors to grab the once-in-a-lifetime bargains when the broadcaster cut him off in midsentence.

> *"Sorry to interrupt, sir. Breaking news."*

Jennings put his hand to his earpiece, and after a moment spoke with a new note of drama.

> *"This just in! ABC can now confirm that Dr. Wen Mei Li . . .* WILL APPEAR *. . . at the joint hearings proposed by Congressman Hurtle! This dramatic turn of events creates a new situation —"*

The telephone rang. No doubt a neighborhood gossip of Mom's, still Penny leaped for it.

"Penny, how are you?"

God in heaven, it's him. HIM! Easy now, not too friendly. Not too mean, either, poor Deep Throat Physicist . . .

"Oh, I guess I'm okay. Where are you?"

"San Francisco airport. Great to hear your voice —"

"San Francisco? What the devil are you doing in San Francisco?"

"Mother, this is John!"

Now she could hear the different timbre. "John! For goodness sake! You're back from *Samoa?* Why?"

"You and Dad had a bit of a tiff, I gather. I've been meaning to come home anyway, I want to tell you both all about Siva — say, isn't Father in quite a jam? We talked on the phone once. Since then he doesn't answer my e-mails."

"You don't know where he is?"

"Not a clue, except that he's not at home."

"Who is this Siva, John?"

"Most beautiful girl alive, and as smart as she's lovely."

"Is, ah — is she a Samoan?"

"*Is* she? Descended from chiefs and princesses for seven generations . . . Oops, last call for my flight. See you tomorrow, Mater."

Professor Herman Rocovsky, architect of the defunct Superconducting Super Collider, was at his computer, groping for something generous to say about the Chinese accomplishment in a lecture he would soon give at the institute of technology in Delhi. In truth — though he spoke of this to no one — Rocovsky was decidedly irked that a graduate student of his had rocketed into fame by achieving the missed goal of his greatest project and greatest failure. Moreover, in the long-gone Cornell days he had twice invited Wen Mei Li to dinner, which to any other student would have been a rare accolade; and twice she had brushed him off with exquisite Chinese manners, while openly bestowing her favors (whatever they were) on Guy Carpenter.

Though he wished Carpenter no harm, Rocovsky was avidly following the hue and cry after the Deep Throat Physicist, a superb much-underrated scientist who kept making his own bad luck with maladroit moves. Now Carpenter was caught in the full glare of media attention, a bug pinned and wriggling under a microscope.

Rocovsky's own policy of shunning publicity seemed to him vindicated as seldom before, and that in fact was why he was going to India. He had been putting off the Delhi people for years, but on reading the *Nature* article he had at once contacted them. Chairman Hurtle was bound to launch a hearing, and would lean hard on him to come and testify. Being off in India at the time would forestall that neatly.

Of all things, the Rock wanted no part of a televised postmortem on the Superconducting Super Collider. Why endure a squalid public immersion in his life's worst defeat? No funding could possibly come of it for the Next Linear Collider, his abandoned dream — two accelerators, each eight miles long, pointed at each other to smash particles together at unprecedented energies — bound to produce the Higgs boson if it existed in Nature, and shoot America back into the lead in world physics. Lost cause! Those scientific illiterates in Congress would just say the Chinese had already got the boson, so why bother?

A flash across the screen:

You have new mail. Do you want to read it now?

The address for this screen was known only to a select few. Most e-mail went to his secretary.

Rock,

Imperative I talk to you. I've tried phoning, but your office says you can't be disturbed. Here's my top-secret number, and I beseech you to call me.

Desperately, Guy

How about that? The pinned bug himself . . .

Clad only in underpants, rivulets of sweat running down the curly white hairs of his naked chest, the bug was pinned to the phone in his room with a huge portable fan whirring at him full blast, for the temperature in Washington was 99 degrees, the humidity was over 90, and the hotel air-conditioning was down. Washington had once been considered a hardship diplomatic post with extra pay like the Sudan, and it was a Sudan day in the Millard Fillmore Hotel.

He snatched up the phone at the first ring.

"Hello, Guy!" Unmistakable guttural Germanic voice, intimidating yet friendly. "They're giving you a hard time, are they?"

"HELLO, old Rock. Thanks a million for calling —"

"No problem. What's that noise? Where are you?"

"I'm in a Washington hotel —" Plug pulled, the fan expired.

"That's better. You're under subpoena, I hear. What can I do for you?"

"Do you have Wendy's *Nature* article there?"

Rocovsky's voice turned cold. "What about it?"

"I must talk to you about it by page and line —"

"Just a minute." Rocovsky ordered his secretary to bring the article. "Anything else?"

"Plenty! You recall the controversy over enlarging the aperture of the Super Collider —"

"Of course, the great mistake, when only you supported me against the whole panel —"

"Right, that's exactly right! And I wrote you a long memorandum opposing the change —"

"I have it on file."

"Marvelous! Throw a lifeline to a drowning man and send me a copy. Mine's buried in my basement in Pasadena —"

"You'll have it by morning FedEx."

"Rock, live to be a hundred."

"Amen." The secretary laid *Nature* on Rocovsky's desk. "All right, here's Wendy's article. So?"

"It's flawed."

"*Flawed?* Guy, the whole world's been scrutinizing this article —"

"Professor Rocovsky, I've been in solitary confinement here for days. Nothing to do but go over and *over* that article. Remember, I was section head on the Super Collider magnets, I know a hell of a lot about all this, and if I tell you it's flawed, then by God it's *flawed!* Look at page 779 —"

"Page 779 . . . Guy, I've seen no letter challenging the results yet, not in *Physics Today,* or *Science,* or *Nature* —"

"It's early for them. Have you got the page?"

"I'm looking at it —"

"Second column, beginning seven lines down, the first paragraph —"

Rocovsky read aloud the first words of the paragraph.

"Yes, that's it. You may want to make notes —"

"I'm ready."

Unlikely though it was that Carpenter had found a real flaw — he sounded a bit crazed — Rocovsky was willing to listen. The history of science told of not a few crucial errors in important papers, and in technology even wilder oversights could occur. A recent shot to Mars had failed, for instance, because engineers had neglected to convert one step to the metric system!

In Rocovsky's opinion the Chinese had made not a breakthrough in science but a bold masterstroke in technology, by finessing the whole need to build a collider. The principle they used had been known since the 1940s, when strange particles had first been detected raining down on Earth, debris of atoms smashed by cosmic rays in the upper atmosphere. Some cosmic rays were awesomely more powerful than any beams that men could generate, and amid those billions of high-energy particles in the debris, Higgs bosons might well be falling to Earth. The trick was to capture and identify them, and that trick was known too — cover several square miles with tens of thousands of detectors, monitor them for Higgs events over several years, and collect enough evidence to claim and prove success. That was beyond Western scientists for practical reasons, and in the great surge of high-energy physics, piling up the Nobel Prizes and leading to the worldwide quest for the Higgs boson, it had not been attempted. The Chinese feat was undeniably brilliant. They had played from their national strengths — endless manpower, endless brainpower, the age-old Chinese deftness at manufacturing exact replicas in any amount — and they had pulled it off. What flaw then, Rocovsky wondered as he scrawled quick notes of Carpenter's vehement arguments, could he have discerned?

Yet after listening a full ten minutes, and shooting many sharp questions at Carpenter, Rocovsky was compelled to end the conversation on a noncommittal note. The Deep Throat Physicist might conceivably be on to something! It would not do to electrify him with hope that might dissolve into air, so he said only that he would think it over. Even that much elicited from Carpenter a wild cry. "Thank God! Thank *God!* I'm not absolutely out of my mind, am I, old Rock?"

"Let me get back to you."

Two of the longest hours in Guy Carpenter's life crawled by. The Rock had not specified the time he needed to "think it over." Did he mean minutes, days, *weeks?* He had left Carpenter hanging like a condemned man awaiting execution or a pardon.

A ring at last! "Lady visitor, sir," said the manager. "I'm putting her on the house phone —"

"No, no, don't —" Who could it be, some damned female journalist on the snoop?

"Hi, it's me, Myra. This is rude, I know, but I must talk to you at once about something terribly important —"

"Ye gods, Myra, this room's a hotbox, no air-conditioning, I'm sitting here in my birthday suit —"

"Put a towel around your middle. I'm coming up." *Click.*

He darted into the bedroom to grab clothes. A discreet tapping. "Hello? Are you decent?"

"Getting there. Come on in, door's open."

"Hi!" The Congresswoman wore a short sleeveless lemon-yellow dress, featherlight, hardly suited for Congress in session, but eye-catching. "Whew, this place sure is steamy. Well, I won't stay long. We've just had a knock-down, drag-out meeting at my house, Berkovits, Aaron, and I, all about you."

He came padding out barefoot, buttoning a loose shirt over slacks. "What have I done now?"

"Nothing yet. You have a decision to make."

"Let's hear."

"Wen Mei Li wants to see you."

Guy Carpenter fell into an armchair, staring at the Congresswoman. Hoarsely he asked, "How do you know that?"

"Verbal message from Zhang Zhui, the cultural attaché, conveyed face-to-face to Horace Wesley by an assistant attaché. Strictest secrecy, nothing on paper, nothing by phone, face-to-face only. *'Dr. Wen Mei Li requests a meeting with Dr. Guy Carpenter.'* "

"When and where? I'm utterly stunned."

"Not yet clear. Your response awaited. Aaron doesn't believe that you can do it without the media finding out, which could be fatal for you. He advises against following this up at all. Berkovits thinks the Chinese can do anything, and he's sort of for it. Upshot, I'm the one to tell you face-to-face, so I'm telling you."

With a wheeze and a groan the air-conditioning came on, and a frigid wind went whirling through the room. "Ah, there we are," said Carpenter. "This happens stochastically, and it can't be controlled. In half an hour this place will be cold as a meat locker if it stays on —"

"Let me take you to dinner. I guarantee Rossiter won't be making notes under the table —"

"I'm waiting for a call from the Rock, Myra, so no, thanks."

"Well, what do I tell Horace Wesley?" She stood up, straightening her dress. "Why not just decline, as Aaron urges? He's your lawyer."

"That's a very pretty dress."

"Why, thank you." Myra had not come straight from her house to the hotel after the lawyers left. Urgent though her visit to Carpenter was, she had taken the time to change from a blue shantung suit and white blouse to the best summery dress she owned.

"Where did you stand, Myra, in that argument at your house? For or against?"

"Oh, I mainly let the lawyers argue."

"Come on, Congresswoman. As you said to me in another context, on our flight to Waxahachie, *'You have an opinion. Let's hear it.'* "

They were alone together for the first time since Waxahachie, and the whole experience came flashing into her mind — martinis in the sunset at 35,000 feet, Verne's Club, Guy's boozy confession, the lavender-and-cinnamon shop, the Mehitabel figurine, which she had now on her office desk — and she hesitated, looking him in the eye without replying.

"Cat got your tongue, Myra?"

"Okay," she snapped. "Suppose you do this, and it gets back to Penny? Has that occurred to you? You and your wet autumn leaves, and your furtive post-office letters! Mehitabel, hell! You've never forgotten Wendy, and you never will. I don't know what she can possibly want of you, but as the poem has it, *'The heathen Chinee is peculiar.'* You'd better think about Penny first and last. That's my opinion."

He slowly nodded. "That's well said. Tell Horace Wesley I'll call him in the morning with two words: *'It's on,'* or *'It's off.'* "

"So you're considering it." She shook her head, went to his desk, and scribbled on a pad. "Here's his number. How are you coming on *The Four Horsemen?*"

"About halfway through. Rudolph Valentino is in very big trouble."

"No doubt you identify with him. Amazing how cold it's getting in here." She walked to the door. "I'm off."

What with the startling news about Wendy, and Rocovsky's encouraging reaction, Carpenter was somewhat lightheaded, and Myra Kadane was looking exceptionally nice. "No kiss, Congresswoman?"

She turned on him. "Don't you start up with me, Deep Throat Physicist!"

"Sorry, sorry."

"All right. When the Rock calls, give him my respects. The

hearing starts at ten tomorrow, so be sure to call Horace well before that."

"Don't go away mad."

"Good luck, Valentino."

When Carpenter fell asleep over *The Four Horsemen* at two in the morning, Rocovsky had still not called back.

24. THE HEARING

The Cannon House Office Building, built back in 1908, breathes old-fashioned awe of the majesty of government, and the Cannon Caucus Room, with its imposing tall red doors and its pillars rising two stories to an ornate ceiling, embodies that awe in one grand and beautiful space. Here the Wesley-Hurtle hearings were about to begin under the rubric *Restoring the American Lead in Science,* with the director of the Central Intelligence Agency as the first witness.

Very rarely does the Speaker of the House approve such usage of this noble room, and his doing so for the Wesley-Hurtle inquiry signaled its urgent and serious nature, with such eminent witnesses expected to testify as Dr. Wen Mei Li, the discoverer of the Higgs boson, and Homer Aptor, the National Security Adviser, her only rival for headlines as the accused sugar daddy of a slightly pregnant stripteaser.

When Myra Kadane arrived early in the morning at the Rayburn Building, committee members and staff were bustling about Horace Wesley's office in a general air of portentous excitement. "He wants to see you right away," the Chief Counsel greeted her. In the Congressman's wood-paneled private sanctum, decorated with craggy Vermont landscapes and a large stiff portrait of Calvin Coolidge, Wesley was at his desk leafing through papers. "Ah, sit you down, dear, we've a lot to talk about."

"You've heard from Carpenter?"

"Carpenter? Oh, you mean that Dr. Wen Mei Li business? No, not yet. Myra, I'm getting concerned about acoustics in that confounded room. It's like Union Station, you know, with that two-story ceiling and all —"

"Horace, you asked for it."

"Well, sure, it seats seven hundred, there's no committee room near that size, and at that, the requests for tickets are swamping us, but —" Wesley leaned toward her. "Myra, you're an actress, every word you say to me is always clear as a bell. Some of my staff are mumblers. Not that I need a hearing aid or anything, of course not, but in those acoustics I might miss a trick or two. I'm putting you next to me on the dais, and if I rap like this" — he lightly tapped her arm — "just repeat what's been said, will you? Casual-like, you know, sort of side of the mouth, no leaning over and whispering."

"Understood, Horace." Actually Myra had been pitching her voice higher year by year, and all of Wesley's staff were doing exactly the same thing, only she was better at it.

"Fine." He picked up a document. "Seen this? Texas delegation caucused yesterday. They mean to introduce an amendment to the Appropriations Bill —"

"So I heard, to revive the Super Collider."

"Well, that's not how they put it." He flourished the document. "They simply point out that Waxahachie is America's best shot to overtake the Chinese. Just pump out the water and you've got a third of the Collider ring all done, eighteen miles of solidly braced tunnel, so what other site can compete? Still, to regain our scientific supremacy Texas will support any site —"

"Yeah, right," said Myra.

Wesley nodded, grinning. "And Illinois is caucusing today too. What's California doing, Myra?"

"Oh, we're an anarchic bunch, not like those organized Texans. If it begins to look like there's real money in it, we'll put up a yell for the site, never fear —"

A loud click on the speakerphone. "Dr. Carpenter on line four."

Myra stage-whispered, "Tell him I'm here."

"Will do — Wesley speaking."

"Good morning, sir. Guy Carpenter here. Myra Kadane suggested that I call you —"

"She's right here in my office."

"Oh, she is? Morning, Myra."

"Hi, there."

She knew the nuances of this man's voice by now, and he was sounding decidedly nervous. "Well, it's on, sir."

Wesley glanced at Myra Kadane, raising his bushy gray eyebrows. "It's on?"

"It's on."

"Very well."

She said, "Horace, let me talk to him."

"All yours." With a smile and a wink, Wesley walked out. Little as he understood it, the old Chairman was clearly relishing this byplay of romantic intrigue in a crisis of science and politics.

"Guy, did Rocovsky call?"

"Hasn't yet."

"Tell me what that's all about."

"It can blow this whole inquiry sky-high, that's all."

"Surely you exaggerate."

"Wait and see. I'll tell you no more."

"Look, you should know that Bob Hurtle tried hard to schedule you today right after the CIA director. He's slavering to get at you. You have a friend in Horace Wesley, and you're not on until Thursday."

"That's a relief," said Carpenter in a sudden change to a cheery tone. "And I'd guess you're the friend."

"No, it's Horace, believe me."

"You don't approve of my decision, do you, Congresswoman?"

"Let's say I'm not flabbergasted. How's your air-conditioning?"

"Chilly, like this conversation."

"Easy, Valentino."

"Bye, Myra. I'll be watching you on TV."

As the select committee and the staff went streaming through the tunnel to the Cannon Building, Wesley kept the Congresswoman close to him. "Want to know something, Myra?" he muttered, almost in her ear. "I've got stage fright."

"Come on, man, you've been in a hundred hearings —"

"Nothing as big as this, and I've got the gavel."

"Now you listen to me, Horace Wesley. You're a Congressman straight out of Central Casting — leonine hair, gray mustache, shaggy gray eyebrows, and that New England twang of yours is perfection. Be yourself, that's all. In two minutes you'll forget the audience and the cameras and do just fine."

He squeezed her arm. "The actress speaks. Thanks. Anyway, my mind is clear, all I want to find out is where America goes from here in high-energy physics. It's Bob Hurtle who has the complicated agenda. He wants to justify killing the Super Collider, start a new project in Illinois, and put the Army in charge of it."

"I'm glad you've got the gavel." She added in his ear, "Have you talked to that other party about Carpenter?"

"Oh, yes. Those wheels are turning."

Jules Berkovits was a strange sight, riding down Independence Avenue on a Harley-Davidson in his faded denims, gray locks flapping below the helmet, clinging to the Chief Counsel of the Appropriations Committee. In helmet, goggles, and leather jacket, Charley Sturdevant weaved his growling machine through the heavy morning traffic to the Rayburn Building, where, in the office of the Ways and Means Committee, Alan Fineman was waiting for them. Once divested of his bike togs and properly suited up, bow tie and all, Sturdevant fitted the scene as Berkovits decidedly did not.

Fineman greeted the lawyer impassively. "I hope you won't be bored, Mr. Berkovits."

"Oh, I won't be, for sure. I'm glad I get to watch these hearings with mavens like you and Charley."

"Well, we'll have good seats."

In a crowded elevator dropping to the tunnel level, Fineman said to Sturdevant, "You've heard about the Texas caucus?"

"Inevitable," Sturdevant said.

"Yes, and futile. There isn't a dollar left for new major-budget items. The notion of bringing the Super Collider back from the dead is pure Texas. Utterly quixotic."

"They dream the impossible dream," Berkovits said.

Fineman thinly smiled. "Just so." He was a lean sour man, as befitted a penny-pincher on the scale of hundreds of billions, as Sturdevant, bestower of hundreds of billions, was an expansive hearty sort.

Sturdevant said, "Well, we'll see. Much depends on what the Chinese lady will say."

Berkovits was suitably awed by the grandiose rotunda of the Cannon Building, the marble staircase, and the lofty closed doors of the Cannon Caucus Room, where a long line of spectators waited, and TV cameras and reporters were clustering. A journalist in oversize round glasses, black hair to her shoulders, approached Berkovits with a microphone. "Well, well, who have we here? Nobody but Jules Berkovits, the celebrated and formidable defense attorney! Good morning, Jules."

"Hello, Sally."

"You're not here to defend the director of the CIA, are you, Jules?"

"He can't afford me."

She giggled. "What, then?"

"Just an interested citizen."

"Uh-huh. Jules, do you think the Chinese already have the Boson Bomb?"

"Can't comment, I may have to defend China."

"I see." Another giggle. "Well, maybe China can afford you."

When Horace Wesley rapped the gavel, the sections reserved for the TV cameras and the press on either side of the dais were jammed, but the seats in the long chamber were only half full. This relatively sparse attendance, already larger than at most hearings, was no surprise, for the director of the Central Intelligence Agency, a retired four-star admiral, was new in his post and unknown to the public. The overflow crowds were expected the next two days, when Wen Mei Li and Homer Aptor were slated to appear.

In a charcoal gray suit, the grizzled lean director, Admiral Raymond Haslett, took the oath and sat down to face the committee without counsel. He gave his background crisply, summarizing forty years in the Navy, and memberships after retirement on the boards of various banks and corporations, all resigned when he joined the Agency. Two assistants were stacking huge blowups on a display stand as he spoke.

When he finished, Conway Hurtle said with a warm smile, "Admiral, you and I go back quite a ways."

"We do, sir."

"If you were still in uniform, you'd have a bank of ribbons and battle stars halfway down your chest, wouldn't you?"

"I've seen a bit of service."

"Including command of a nuclear submarine."

"Yes."

"Now, Admiral, the American people want to know from you, as Director of the Central Intelligence Agency, why we were caught flat-footed by the Chinese discovery of the Higgs boson."

"Sir, the Central Intelligence Agency wasn't in the least surprised."

Murmurs in the audience, flashbulbs popping, TV cameras training on Admiral Haslett as he extended a long arm toward the gigantic aerial photograph on the stand. "I invite your attention, sir, to these exhibits. Our agency has the finest surveillance cameras on earth, of that the American people can rest assured. This is a view of the Chinese top-secret installation from over a hundred thousand feet. As you'll see, it's nothing like a Super Collider. Note the dark blotch, right center. That's the project." An assistant removed the blowup. "In this next view, it's considerably enlarged." The blotch was a rectangle of black dots. "Now, enlarged again." Dots like manholes covered the picture in the hundreds. "And here, sir, is a single Chinese Higgs boson detector."

Many in the audience stood up to look at an enormous picture, too big to rest on the stand, held up by the two assistants. The detector was a round metal curiosity, and beside it was a watermelon. "A watermelon is superimposed on the picture," said the admiral, "to indicate the size of the device. As you see, it's not large at all. We counted over ten thousand, and we reported our discovery to the Department of Energy well over a year ago."

"Why the Department of Energy, Admiral?"

"Sir, the CIA is equipped to detect unusual radiation anywhere in the world. It's part of our mission. These things were radiation-passive. For evaluating such exotic objects for possible advanced technology, the Department of Energy was considered the best qualified, and its evaluation was negative."

Hurtle said, "No threat to our national security, you mean."

"None at all."

"And your agency let it go at that?"

"Remember, sir, this didn't happen on my watch. I've been in office for two months, but I've reviewed the documents, and the Agency certainly was puzzled."

Horace Wesley lightly tapped Myra's arm. "Puzzled, Horace," she hissed. "The CIA was puzzled." Wesley nodded as she scrawled a note and passed it to him.

Ask him what the DOE figured the things were.

"Now, Admiral," Hurtle continued, "you've commanded an SSN, and you're in your present job because of your sound grasp of national security. In your judgment, is this Chinese discovery a threat to us?"

"Sir, China is a coming world superpower. If China has passed us in science in any way, however arcane, that's a grave development."

"And Congress should do something about it?"

"Definitely, the sooner the better."

"Admiral Haslett," Horace Wesley interjected, "about that evaluation by the Department of Energy, what was its finding?"

Admiral Haslett shifted in his chair, crossed his arms, and shrugged. "Sir, maybe the Secretary of Energy should speak to that point."

"We'll call him if necessary." The admiral glanced uneasily to Hurtle, who also shrugged. Sudden quiet descended on the spectators. No more coughing, no low chatter. "Admiral, don't you know what the DOE concluded about those detectors?"

"Oh, yes, sir. I know."

"Well, how about letting us in on it?"

"Mr. Chairman, the Department of Energy estimated that they were a very large-scale Chinese experiment for growing mushrooms."

Wesley had to hammer the gavel to still an outburst of laughter and loud talk. "*Mushrooms,* did you say?"

"Mr. Chairman, my understanding is that the Department of Energy called in some eminent agronomists for consultation on this vast array of unfamiliar objects. You'll have to ask the Secretary of Energy how that happened, but naturally those scientists took an agronomist approach, and they came up with mushrooms."

"No wonder the CIA was puzzled," said Wesley. He had to bang the gavel again to quiet the laughter. The TV crews were in a frenzy of activity, while the commentators were chattering audibly into their microphones.

In a front row, Berkovits said to Fineman, "There's your headline tomorrow: CIA: Chinese Were Growing Mushrooms."

"That's not fair," said Fineman.

"But catchy," said Sturdevant.

"In retrospect, Admiral," said Wesley, "doesn't that conclusion strike you as downright bizarre?"

"Well, that's hindsight, Mr. Chairman, isn't it? Let's give the Department of Energy a break." The admiral bleakly smiled. "After all, there are an awful lot of Chinese, and they do eat an awful lot of mushrooms."

Once again Wesley hammered down laughter. "Thank you, Admiral Haslett. Most illuminating."

"Admiral, one final question." Hurtle spoke up swiftly. "You know of course about the cancellation of the Superconducting Super Collider in 1993."

"At this point, sir, who doesn't?"

"And you're aware that Navy personnel were involved in building the Super Collider."

"My Annapolis roommate was, for one."

"Indeed! Well, speaking then as a Navy man and a nuclear-sub commander, do you have an opinion of that cancellation? Getting down to brass tacks, would the Super Collider have delivered the Higgs boson, in your view, or was it one giant incredibly costly boondoggle?"

Admiral Haslett said after a palpable pause, "Congressman Hurtle, in 1993 I was conning my submarine over the North Pole, under the ice. That sort of held my attention. I pass."

The spectators clapped as Haslett left the table, and Wesley let them applaud.

In his hotel room, Guy Carpenter uttered a loud *"Thank God."* From his worm's-eye view of the proceedings, his one worry had been that Hurtle might ask the CIA director about letters between the Deep Throat Physicist and the Mother of the Bomb.

Dr. Ira Judson, head of the Ira Judson Institute in Carmel, was a roly-poly little Nobel Prize scientist with disorderly snowy hair and rumpled clothes. He took the oath with what seemed to Myra a merry glint in his eye, and gave a rundown of his scientific credentials. Pressed by Horace Wesley about his Nobel Prize, he laughingly dismissed it as "a murky business about conservation of isotopic spin, Mr. Chairman, and I don't recommend the committee spending time on it." Dr. Judson had strongly opposed the Superconducting Super Collider, in the 1993 inquiry that had ended as its funeral service, and he was Conway Hurtle's first witness. Hurtle got right to the point.

"Dr. Judson, you were against the Super Collider, were you not?"

"Oh, absolutely."

"And you testified in favor of cutting off its funds?"

"I did indeed."

"Please tell this committee why you did."

"Quite simple. I made an idiotic mistake."

As the TV camera closed in on Hurtle's astounded face, Guy Carpenter guffawed, pumping a fist as though watching a football game. "Yes, Ira, *yes!*" he shouted. He knew Judson well, a great physicist with a streak of the pixie, and he awaited with glee what would come next.

The nonplussed Chairman of the Armed Services Committee was staring at the physicist. "Old Bob caught a crab," Wesley murmured to Myra Kadane.

"Soft-shell crab," she said.

Somewhat recovered, Hurtle said cordially, "Dr. Judson, I'm afraid you'll have to explain that."

"No problem. There's only so much money for science in the Federal budget. Back in 1993, I thought the Collider was soaking up far too much of that money for just one project. My institute, for example, was losing out on its allotment, mere chicken feed by comparison. I never anticipated, of course, that the Chinese could come up with the Higgsie."

"The *Higgsie?* Do you mean the Higgs boson?"

Dr. Judson amiably chuckled. "Sorry, around the institute we call it the Higgsie, and we regard it as rather trivial. Nevertheless there was a world race on to find the Higgsie. I was sure the Europeans couldn't hack it, and the incredible ingenuity of the Chinese never crossed my mind. That was my mistake, because the Higgsie sure was important."

"You just said it was trivial."

"Yes. Trivial, but important."

"Forgive a layman, Dr. Judson. I'm getting confused."

"I mean the Higgsie by 1993 had become a sort of Holy Grail of physics, hadn't it? So it was *politically* important. We're all here today because the Chinese have aced us, aren't we? I hope I make myself clear."

Committee members all across the dais were looking at one

another in perplexity. Horace Wesley said, "Just elaborate a bit more, Dr. Judson. Are you saying that the Superconducting Super Collider should *not* have been canceled in 1993?"

"Of course it shouldn't have been. Congress's action was fatuous."

Conway Hurtle almost snarled, "You played a part in it."

"*Mea maxima culpa,* sir, and I appreciate this chance to confess my folly in public."

In the audience, the murmuring was becoming louder, interspersed with laughter. Hurtle said, "Well, Dr. Judson, you've certainly lost me with this peculiar about-face, and I daresay the rest of the committee. Just tell us this, what should the Congress do, now that the Chinese have the Higgsie, as you choose to call it?"

"Oh, no. Last time Congress took my advice, America was much the worse for it. Permit me this time, in the vernacular, to clam up."

Having dealt with wayward scientists down the years, Hurtle evidently was not entirely unprepared for such a turnabout. Abruptly, he turned to an assistant, who handed him a paper. "Dr. Judson, I now read to you a passage from your autobiography, *Reaching for the Big Bang: A Life at High Energy.* I quote: *'Scientific knowledge has advanced to a frontier that has left most of mankind far behind. This bodes ill for the long future of the race, since between a person who knows quantum mechanics, and a person who does not, the gap is arguably as wide as the difference between man and the great apes.'* Do I quote you correctly?"

"A very crude metaphor" — Dr. Judson chuckled — "which should have been more tactfully phrased."

"Mr. Chairman," said Hurtle to Wesley, "I'll ask any member of this committee who knows quantum mechanics to raise his or her hand."

Not a hand went up.

"It would seem, Dr. Judson," said Hurtle, "by your own words, that you are testifying before a body of chimpanzees."

"I respectfully point out, Congressman," Judson replied, "that you said it, I didn't."

Horace Wesley gaveled down the laughter and loud chatter, and adjourned the hearing. Sturdevant said to Berkovits and Fineman, "The Lord delivered Hurtle into Judson's hands."

Jules Berkovits said, "This thing is only beginning."

As Wesley was gathering up his papers, an assistant behind him touched his shoulder and handed him a note. He glanced at it and turned to Myra Kadane. "Zhang Zhui is in my office, Myra, to arrange for Dr. Wen Mei Li's appearance tomorrow. Come along, and we can also talk about that other business."

25. THE ANTICIPATION

On the second day of the Wesley-Hurtle hearings, Timothy Warshaw and Shayna Daniels came to watch the broadcast at Sinclair Holloway's penthouse suite atop 1999 Avenue of the Stars, a granite-and-glass tower rising thirty-nine stories over Century City, southern California's ganglion of money and celebrity. As they entered the suite, the gargantuan Jackson Pollock stretching across an entire long wall smote them in the eye as usual, its supernally costly drips, blobs, and streaks crushing them on the instant to their proper size. So long as they needed Holloway's money to make movies, they were flunkeys who showed up when ordered to show up, even at seven in the morning.

Holloway emerged from his lair growling, "I've just been on the phone to Bob Hurtle. You're late. The thing's getting going right this minute back there in Washington, with another Nobel Prize type, then the Chinese comes on —"

"Yesterday's hearing pulled a 7.5 rating, Sinclair," Warshaw blurted. "That's almost up to the last Tiger Woods tournament."

"Yes, yes, I know. Actually, 7.43," Holloway said.

"Sinclair, this country is absolutely flipping over the Boson Bomb," Shayna Daniels said. "Fabulous for the movie."

"Let me know when the Nobel guy finishes. There's coffee in the screening room." Holloway vanished into his enormous glass-walled office with a view clear to the Pacific Ocean.

The producers settled, with coffee and Danish pastry, into plushy armchairs. "Will you look at Moira Strong sitting up there, big as life?" Shayna Daniels gestured at the TV picture, projected sharp and full size on the movie screen. "I was script girl on Moira's last movie, you know."

"No kidding, Shayna, you were?"

"Oh, yes. Right before she snagged Walter Kadane and got to be the grand Bel-Air lady. Congresswoman Myra Kadane, honestly! Back then she was a pretty hot number, Moira was."

"I never knew Kadane," said Warshaw. "By the time I graduated from UCLA, he was in Congress."

"Major movie honcho, brilliant packager. Walter Kadane's word was bankable . . . Is that the Nobel Prize physicist?"

"Has to be," said Warshaw. "He's taking the oath."

The witness had a bald dome, an oval face, a solemn expression. He was Wendell Kulka of Fermilab, and neither Warshaw nor Shayna Daniels understood anything he said about his Nobel Prize, except that the word *plasma* kept recurring.

"I thought this fellow was a physicist," said Warshaw, yawning. "Plasma is what they give you in a hospital, isn't it, when you've been run over or something? What's that got to do with the Higgs boson?"

"I think there's another kind of plasma," said Shayna Daniels.

"Oh sure, protoplasm. That's what they used to call DNA. But that's biology, not physics."

"Whatever," said his partner, rubbing her eyes. "As long as we're here, let's listen."

In the lecture room at the Jet Propulsion Lab, rows of vacant chairs awaited the expected audience for Dr. Wen Mei Li's testimony on TV, and Ottoline Porson and Peter Braunstein were already there, watching Wendell Kulka with a few other scientists. "I really don't think, Ottoline," said Braunstein, "that Wendell is about to say anything of interest to us. He'll just go on and on about the laser-plasma accelerator, given the chance, or, if not, he'll drag it in anyway. I have work to do —"

"Stay where you are, Peter."

"Yes, boss."

"Professor Kulka," Horace Wesley was saying, "you were an outspoken supporter of the Superconducting Super Collider, were you not?"

"I was indeed. To the end, to the death. Its cancellation was a grievous blow to American science. Fortunately, there is now an alternative —"

"Here we go," said Braunstein. "He's wasting no time."

"We will get to the alternative," said Wesley with a cordial smile. This was clearly his witness. "You didn't agree, I take it, with those who thought the Collider was absorbing too much of the science budget?"

"Not in the least. It was a matter of national prestige. We were in a race for the Higgs boson. We won the race to the moon, and we should have won the race for the Higgs."

"What went wrong? Do you blame Congress, like so many of your colleagues?"

"Not really. I think the Collider scientists hung themselves."

Conway Hurtle sat up, alerted. "They did? Mr. Chairman, may I ask Dr. Kulka to explain that?"

"Of course."

Kulka said, "I simply mean, sir, that in the crunch, they couldn't rally the scientific community to support them. They were too clubby and cocky. When Nixon canceled the Space Telescope, we scientists rose in a body, and the cancellation was reversed. That didn't happen, alas, with the SSC, and since then physics has quite bypassed the Collider concept —"

Hurtle nodded eager encouragement. "Bypassed it in what way?"

"New technology. The laser-plasma accelerator opens fresh vistas —"

"Laser plasma?" said Hurtle, now a hound on the scent. "Tell us all about that, Professor."

"Ottoline, that's it," said Braunstein, "I'm going to get us more coffee."

"Go ahead," said Dr. Porson. "Cream, no sugar."

Outside Waxahachie, Verne's Club was crowded for a Hearings Breakfast Special, steak and eggs with bullshots. Judge Elton Milius in his customary black suit and string tie sat at the bar near the big TV screen. "Say, Elton," a loud gravelly voice called from a rear table, "what the hell is that guy saying about bypassing the Collider?"

"Easy, Luke, this is just one professor —"

Wendell Kulka was plodding on. "You see, the Super Collider required colossal amounts of real estate and concrete, as we well know. Nowadays, the laser-plasma accelerator can produce much higher energies at a far smaller investment, so the SSC concept is out-of-date —"

Angry yells, a few catcalls. Gravel voice: "Turn off that bald son of a bitch."

Judge Milius said, "Folks, the Chinese lady will be coming on soon —"

"Turn him off until then!"

Chorus of cries in support, with some unseemly language. Elton Milius reached up and turned down the volume.

While Guy Carpenter watched Wendell Kulka expound the laser-plasma accelerator, a barber was cutting his hair. As advertised in the yellow pages, the barber had showed up at the Millard Fillmore with all equipment, and was snipping away great clumps. White though the hair was, it grew fast and plentiful, and Carpenter wanted to spruce up for his meeting with Mei. "Mister, do you understand what that scientist is saying?" the barber asked.

"Trying to."

"I wish my son Felix was here. He reads science magazines a lot. Felix says the Boson Bomb works just like sunlight or starlight, see? Same principle, and if we don't catch up with the Chinese in five years, we're finished. But Felix thinks —"

Carpenter held up a hand to quiet him. Kulka was enlightening Congressman Hurtle about plasma, and he wanted to hear it. "It's the fourth state of matter, sir, the most abundant in the universe. Here on our little earth we have solids, liquids, and gas. Not out there. The sun, the stars, the galaxies, are all plasma. Now for the laser-plasma accelerator, we generate plasma by —"

"My son Felix knows a lot about the galaxies," the barber said. "The Hawaiian natives are against those telescopes up on their mountains, where astronomers study the galaxies. The Hawaiians believe the telescopes offend the mountain gods, and there's talk of pulling them down. I think that's just superstition, don't you?"

"I think you should cut my hair," said Carpenter, "and let me listen to this."

With an offended grunt, the barber shut up and snipped away.

Penny came shuffling into the parlor in an old bathrobe that her son, John, recognized from childhood days. John was reclining in the morris chair at the TV set, a long lean fellow like his father, and like him with streaks of premature white in his hair. "Morning, Mom. This witness is about finished. Wen Mei Li will be on next." He sprang from the chair and she sank into it, coffee mug in hand.

"Happy day, that's all I need. How late did we stay up, for God's sake?"

"Half past four. It was growing light outside."

"Ah, yes, so it was." She took a sip. "This coffee's kind of tired, like me. You hit me with a lot of stuff last night, Johnny Boy."

"Well, Mom, we'd been pussyfooting around for two days. Now it's all out on the table."

"It sure is." Penny gulped the coffee and set the mug down hard. "So let's see if I have it all straight, dear. You're giving up anthropology because it's all hogwash, starting with Margaret Mead's Samoa books. You'll marry this Siva and live in Samoa. How you'll support yourself, unclear. As for me, I'm behaving like a petulant teenager about your father's correspondence with that old Chinese lady, if anything it's all my fault for being so unreasonably jealous, that's why he got that sneaky PO box, and —"

"I'm Peter Jennings."

The TV picture of the hearing switched to the broadcaster at his studio desk, all smiles.

"Dr. Wen Mei Li is about to emerge from the Chinese embassy, and our ABC cameras are on the spot to bring you live coverage of the entire —"

The doorbell rang. John opened the door to a pimply girl of thirteen or so in jeans, carrying a cat. "Oh, my God!" Penny got up and held out her arms.

"Siamese male, no collar," said the girl. "Is this him?"

"Of course it is." Penny snatched and hugged the cat. "Oh, Sweeney! You came home, bless you —"

"Ma'am, the poster said fifty dollars' reward."

"Yes, pay her, John." Penny was kissing the beast. "Poor kitty, did you miss me? Bad kitty, to run away — no, John, *wait,* wait . . . kitty, where's the spot on your nose?"

"Spot?" the girl said. "The poster didn't mention no spot."

"Nope." Penny tried to return the creature. "My cat has a black spot on his nose. This is not my cat. Sorry."

The girl backed away. "Lady, he's not my cat, either. Don't I get no reward?"

John said, "Look, here's twenty dollars." He handed the girl the money and the cat, and she left, muttering.

"Even my cat is gone," Penny moaned.

"And here she comes," Peter Jennings exclaimed. *"Dr. Wen Mei Li, discoverer of the Higgs boson, called by some the Mother of the Bomb. On the scene is ABC's Diana Caputo. Diana?"*

A wide-eyed woman with a handheld microphone, jostling amid reporters and cameramen: *"Well, this lady is something else, Peter! I've covered fashion shows in Paris, you know, and her outfit is just stunning, sheer perfection of taste —"*

Jennings, with a tolerant smile at this reporter's viewpoint: *"Tell us about it, Diana."*

"Christ on wheels, try another channel," said Penny.

"Easy, Mom," said her son. "Jennings is the best —"

> *"Okay, Peter, we're looking at a two-piece skirt suit, smartly tailored, lovely pale red blouse, minimum jewelry, just jade earrings and, a nice detail, lipstick matching the blouse. Silk scarf over the jacket, charming feminine touch. There she goes, into the limousine and off to the hearing, and it beats me, Peter, how a scientist, Chinese at that, can have such style sense. If Dr. Wen Mei Li gets bored with Higgs bosons, she can walk down any runway in Paris to model mature styles. Back to you, Peter."*

Penny jumped up. "And balls to you, Peter. I'm famished, I'm making me a cheese omelet with chives. Want some, Johnny?"

"Great, Mom. Like the old days."

Outside the Cannon Building the reporters blocking the steps divided to let the Chinese physicist pass, escorted by a stocky little diplomat with a formal mien. No microphones were shoved in her face, and she did not seem to hear the shouted queries. Cameras followed her every move across the spacious rotunda and up the marble staircase. When she entered the caucus room through the tall doors, the spectators started to stand up, peering and chattering. Soon all seven hundred in the grandiose room were on their feet, and they remained standing until she and her escort took their places at the witness table. Then, with coughing and murmuring as at an entr'acte in a theater, they sat down.

"I've been at more hearings than I can count," said Charley Sturdevant. "Never seen anything like this."

Alan Fineman said, "These people just wanted a good look at her."

"It's more than that," Jules Berkovits said. "Strange business."

So this is Wendy at last, Myra Kadane thought, trying not to stare at the physicist sitting there in the flesh before her. A perverse vivid picture flashed into her mind of Dr. Wen Mei Li dressed in the Shanghai robe, and the Congresswoman could almost understand Guy Carpenter's haunted wistfulness, and Penny's chronic jealous rage.

"Mr. Chairman, I am Dr. Zhang Zhui," the diplomat began. "Cultural attaché of the embassy of the People's Republic of China. My government regards Dr. Wen Mei Li's appearance here, at the invitation of the American Congress, as due recognition of China's progress in science. She will make a statement on the Higgs boson discovery, then answer questions, and she speaks for herself. She has not submitted her statement to official review. I myself have not read it. In my country Wen Mei Li is well known for her independence of spirit as well as her scientific brilliance. Therefore" — for the first time Zhang Zhui cracked a smile, and on television the change of the stern round face to wry humor was surprising — "she may well say undiplomatic things. I hope this will not get her into what Americans call 'hot water.' We have a similar Chinese expression, but it is much cruder, so I will leave it at 'hot water.'"

The committee members were not expecting the light touch, and they looked at one another with uncertain smiles, while amused murmurs ran through the audience.

"It is my high honor now to present to this distinguished committee a world-renowned physicist, and a patriot of whom the whole Chinese people are proud, Dr. Wen Mei Li."

26. THE STATEMENT

Wen Mei Li opened a folder and began to read her statement in a high firm slightly accented voice, glancing at the pages only now and then. Clearly she knew the text well.

"Mr. Chairman, allow me at this unique moment to begin with a personal word.

"My scientific abilities, such as they are, I owe to the training I received in the United States. I studied as an undergraduate and earned my doctorate at Cornell University in upstate New York. Before returning to China, I worked at the forefront of high-energy physics at the Stanford Linear Accelerator in California. My debt to America stretches from coast to coast, so to say, and to repay that debt just a little, I will disclose to your committee today certain facts about the Chinese discovery of the Higgs boson, which are relevant to your inquiry — how our project originated, how it was approved and funded by my government, and how, after long discouraging struggles, it succeeded.

"The basic concept was brought to me early in 1990 by Miss Huang Hairong, a graduate student in a course I was teaching at Beijing University. She is not among the authors of the *Nature* article, because when the project was begun years later, she was committed to other work; but it was her insight that the Higgs boson might be detected in the debris from atmospheric molecules, smashed by cosmic rays and falling to Earth over a very wide area. Graduate students in the past have gotten ideas leading to Nobel Prizes for their professors, not always with due credit, so at the outset I acknowledge this brilliant young physicist's contribution to our discovery. Together with her I prepared a proposal for the Ministry of Science and Technology, and the Minister thought it interesting enough to bring to Chairman Deng Xiaoping's attention. The Chairman, so I was informed, asked one question: *'Does this have any military application?'* When told it did not, he made one comment: *'Praiseworthy Chinese theoretical science, low budgetary priority.'*

"Three years later this verdict was reversed, when on October 19th, 1993, the American Congress, for budgetary reasons, canceled the Superconducting Super Collider, then under construction in the State of Texas. On October 21st, I was summoned to Chairman Deng Xiaoping, accompanied by the Minister of Science and Technology. The Chairman's first words to me were, *'How long will it take you?'*

"Although quite overawed, I plucked up courage and said, 'Seven to ten years, Mr. Chairman.'"

Dr. Wen Mei Li turned a page, paused to glance around at the committee, and read on through a somber hush that fell over the grandiose chamber.

"This was the decisive meeting in the project's history, so I will narrate in some detail my best recollections of how it proceeded. At my reply, Chairman Deng looked very disappointed. *'Seven to ten years! That is a long time. What are your chances of success?'*

"'Twenty-five percent.'

"*'So low?'*

"'Mr. Chairman, we must allow three to four years for designing and building this huge project, and three or four more for detecting, collecting, and verifying the results. The Higgs boson may not occur in nature, particle physics may be in a blind alley, so that is one big doubt. Again, an experiment on such a vast scale, at a frontier of science, can hardly have more than a 50–50 chance of success at best. So there is a second big doubt. Doubt multiplied by doubt, at a very crude optimistic guess, comes to 25 percent.'

"The Chairman, though already weakened by Parkinson's disease, was as keen as ever. He nodded and was silent, then he smiled and told a little story. He said, *'When the Soviet Union launched the Sputnik in 1957, it surprised the world. It made a big crisis for the American President Eisenhower, and Chairman Mao summoned our Politburo. "How can we call ourselves a great nation," Chairman Mao said, "when we can't even launch a potato into space?" And our budget for science was greatly increased. Now this project of yours would launch a scientific potato, and I can understand that. Very fine. But what if some other nation launches this particular potato ahead of China? Then all our effort and very costly investment will have been in vain. The prize here is chiefly face, national prestige, and it will go only to the first potato.'*

"'That will not happen, Mr. Chairman.' I spoke up with confidence, for here I was on firm ground. 'The Texas Super Collider was the only machine on earth that could have delivered the required energy, and it is dead. The Germans and Russians are working on similar accelerators, and so is the CERN consortium in Switzerland. Their funding shows no sense of national urgency, and their maximum energies are too low. If the Higgs boson exists, China will beat the world to the potato.'

"Deng Xiaoping turned to the Minister of Science and Technology. *'Is she correct in all this?'*

"The Minister replied, *'Yes.'* It was the one word he spoke during the meeting.

"The Chairman said, *'Then it must be a surprise, this potato, a world surprise like the Sputnik. Highest secrecy. Build the project well out of sight. For instance, among the fish and rice farms of Guizhou might be a good place. Tourists and diplomats are not interested in fish and rice farms. Let us call this bold venture of Chinese science the Potato Project. A quiet inconspicuous name.'*

"Such, in short, was how our project got the green light. I am now disclosing the top-secret code name, since we have launched the potato, and the secret is out."

The physicist smiled at the committee as she turned a page. Some of the members smiled too, but not Congressman Hurtle or Congresswoman Kadane.

"American science editors," she read on, "have written many lucid accounts of our project to explain the rather technical article in *Nature,* so I need not elaborate on how the project worked and what our discovery means to high-energy physics. As for the fantasies in the popular press and on television about a so-called Boson Bomb, any proficient high school student of physics can dispel such nonsense, and it is beneath discussion."

Charley Sturdevant whispered to Berkovits, "There's your ball game. The firestorm is doused."

"Not quite," the lawyer muttered.

"The Ministry of Science and Technology," she went on, "plans to publish in time a full history of the Potato Project. It was plagued for years by miscalculations and equipment failures, inevitable in any attempt to wrest profound new secrets from nature. Annual cost estimates tended to be far too low. Our project almost foundered on the rock that sank the Texas Super Collider. Unlike America, China is a very poor country, and our Budget Ministry found our overruns intolerable. In 1996 they recommended that our project be dropped. At that time only half our experimental detectors were in place, producing null results. I was summoned once more to the presence of Deng Xiaoping. The Chairman was over ninety by then, and in the three years that had passed he had greatly aged. He greeted me in a weak congested voice. *'So, you have failed to find the potato, and your project will be canceled.'*

"'It should not be, Mr. Chairman,' I replied. 'My grandmother had a good saying: "Do not show a fool half-finished work."'

"*'Are you calling my Budget Ministry fools?'*

"'They are not scientists. The theory of our project is correct. It is a long effort, and detection is difficult. China will discover the Higgs boson in the next three or four years.'

"*'So you say. What have the Americans done meantime?'*

"'Nothing. Their physicists remain in shock from the Super Collider debacle. Their space program is spectacular and their military effort is gigantic, but that is simply their advanced technology. In basic science, America has lost face worldwide. This is our chance to tell the world that though backward and poor, China is a great nation, and that if America is the superpower of the moment, China is also here on the planet.'

"*'Why did you come back from America? Why didn't you stay there like Chien-Shiung Wu, and have a fine Western scientific career?'*

"'In Wu's generation there was no physics in China to speak of. I came back to teach in the new China, and to help in the growing new field of Chinese physics.'

"*'You are a revolutionary, then.'*

"'I am Chinese.'

"*'You have no regrets? You suffered much in the Cultural Revolution.'*

"'So did you, Chairman Deng.'

"The Chairman was silent for a very long time. Then he talked about America. He said it was interesting that I had chosen a hard life in China over the good life in America. He said America was a powerful young nation and — like the young — shortsighted, overconfident, and inclined to frivolity. He said it might be a hundred years before China could equal America's science and technology, but on the other hand there were subtle signs of a decaying culture in America, and so the future was clouded. He held out a badly trembling hand and told me he would have another word with the Budget Minister about our project. A few months later he died. The project was funded each year after that until it was crowned with success. And that is the story of the Potato Project.

"Mr. Chairman, let me end as I began, on an informal personal note. When I was an undergraduate at Cornell so long, long ago, the student body was all agog over a singer named Elvis Presley, who personified what Chairman Deng said of America — *young, powerful, overconfident, frivolous.* Elvis Presley was a rebel, indeed he was rebellion incarnate, but not the sort of rebellion going on in China, to create a new society on the ruins of the old; rather, rebellion for the empty adrenaline charge of it, rebellion against nothing, for the world was at this wriggling singer's feet, naive rebellion of the young against whatever *is.* Amid this craze I felt quite alienated. It turned out to be no craze at all, of course, but an early surge of the American lifestyle that has since been sweeping the world, not excluding our Chinese youth.

"When I decided to go back to China, and came to Washington to arrange my return, I went to the Lincoln Memorial on a melancholy rainy night to see once more the heroic statue of that fallen leader, who for me represents American bedrock. I was leaving the country of Abraham Lincoln but also of Elvis Presley, the most powerful nation on earth, the light of the world, the dream place where everybody drives a car and can do what they please and maybe get rich, or in my case to acquire tenure at a world-famous university. I was saying good-bye to the road I would not take, the career I would not seek, to go home. In point of fact I had left China at the age of seven, sent by my parents to be educated far from the turmoils of civil war, and I had never been back. How then could I call it home? Because, as I said to Chairman Deng, I am Chinese.

"Chairman Deng asked me whether I had ever regretted my decision during the Cultural Revolution. It was a very, very hard time, and in the depths of my personal ordeal I clung to my best memories of America: my exalting experience at the Stanford Linear Accelerator, when I first realized that I could become a good experimental physicist, and perhaps even more, the fragrance of autumn leaves on the Cornell campus when I was so very young, walking under those flaming trees and breathing in the scent of American freedom, of youth, of unbounded ambition, and of the unfolding glory of modern physics. But at the worst of times, I never regretted going home.

"Thank you, Mr. Chairman."

Wen Mei Li closed the folder and put it aside. Horace Wesley glanced right and left at the committee. No hand was raised.

"Dr. Wen Mei Li," he said, "it is I who must thank you. With your appearance before this committee, and your frank, sober, and illuminating statement, you have performed a striking service to the country you left to go home. You have more than repaid your debt, as you choose to put it, to the United States. On behalf of the Joint Committee, I want to express our appreciation to you, and in conclusion —" Conway Hurtle raised his hand. "Well, I see Congressman Hurtle of Illinois has a question."

Hurtle said, "Madame Wen Mei Li, do you know about a major article on your discovery published recently in the *Washington Post?*"

Dead quiet in the Cannon Caucus Room. Guy Carpenter in his hotel room stiffened, on the edge of his chair. Myra Kadane, a few feet from the witness, stiffened too.

"Oh, yes, it was brought to my attention."

"Would you comment on it?"

In close-up on the TV screen, her face broke into a gentle smile that pierced Carpenter with old memories, like a scent or a song. "Not quite the best argument for your celebrated free press, was it?"

Some laughter among the spectators and even a few hand claps, to Carpenter's immense relief. Obviously she had the audience with her. Hurtle persisted. "But you are acquainted with Dr. Guy Carpenter?"

"Certainly, we were students together at Cornell. Many years later, he came to China on your country's generous program of assistance to Chinese science, among the numerous experts who have been sent to help us. Dr. Carpenter guided the start-up of a modest cyclotron project I worked on. He is one of the hundreds of thousands of unknown American scientists who, more than your Nobel laureates, are the backbone of your scientific greatness."

Charley Sturdevant nudged Berkovits. "Now *there's* your ball game."

Berkovits shook his head. "Top of the ninth."

Hurtle hesitated for a second or two. "Thank you, Madame Wen Mei Li."

Wesley brought down his gavel hard. "The hearing is adjourned."

The audience once again rose to its feet as Dr. Wen Mei Li and Zhang Zhui left the table, and scattered applause continued until they went out through the tall doors.

Alan Fineman grumbled, "Why on earth *two* standing ovations?"

Sturdevant said, "Because she is China."

Three thousand miles to the west there was applause too, Sinclair Holloway vigorously clapping his gnarled hands in the viewing room. "What a woman! If they were all like her, China would pass us in twenty years."

"But she dismissed the Boson Bomb," said Shayna Daniels nervously. "That wasn't good."

"Shayna, it won't matter," Warshaw reassured her, "it went by too fast —"

"What's wrong with you two? It was marvelous, all of it, just marvelous," said Holloway. "She's absolutely right, of course, the Boson Bomb's childishness, never been anything else. So what? Superman is childishness, and as a property it grosses billions. The movie's solid gold, just get it made fast, and give this Dr. Carpenter prominent credit as a consultant —"

On the screen, meanwhile, Conway Hurtle stood outside the Cannon Caucus Room, angrily answering questions in a circle of thrusting microphones. Warshaw said, "Hold it, Sinclair, let's listen to this."

"Of course I let her go at that," Hurtle snapped. "She's a distinguished scientist, testifying by permission of the Chinese government. It was the only courteous thing to do. She admitted knowing Carpenter, that's the main point —"

A reporter's voice: "But Congressman, didn't she vindicate Dr. Carpenter?"

"You think so? Come around tomorrow and we'll see."

Holloway pressed a button, the screen went blank, and he stood up. "That fellow's a noisy nothing. Carpenter's a national figure now. Damn good thing we've got him as a consultant. My idea, remember! Put out some publicity on him right away, and I mean this week. I'll see you here tomorrow, same time. Don't be late."

When the tycoon was gone, Shayna Daniels turned on her partner. "Tim, you fired the man."

"Listen, Shayna, I'm no lawyer. Sean Kadane freaked when that *Post* story came out, told me to axe Carpenter because he was PR poison —"

"Sean Kadane has Jell-O for a spine. Let's get Carpenter back fast. Like yesterday."

Congressman Hurtle was still fulminating about how he would skin Guy Carpenter alive once he got him under oath when Penny shut off the TV, saying, "Drop dead," and sank back in the morris chair.

John ventured to ask, "Well, what did you think?"

She gave him an annoyed look. "About what?"

"Her statement. I thought it was all right, actually."

"*All right?* For God's sake, it was wonderful. Giving credit to a graduate student for the breakthrough concept! Have you ever had a professor who would do a thing like that?"

"Mom, anthropology is all dog-eat-dog."

"Johnny Boy, *academia* is all dog-eat-dog, and so is far, far too much of science." Penny stared at the blank screen as though the hearing were still going on. "Lord, how she rocked those lunkhead Congressmen back on their heels! High time somebody told them — and in such a perfect public way on world TV — what they did to America when they canceled the Super Collider!" Penny touched a crumpled tissue to her eyes. "And when five and a half years of your father's life and mine went *poof!*"

"Hey, Mom, are you okay?"

"Oh, I'm great. I spent many an autumn at Cornell myself, you know. Many and many an autumn, Johnny, walking under those same trees with that sonofabitching father of yours. I feel sorry for that woman and also — if you want to know — for him. I love the swine like a new bride, and I wish to hell I could tell him so right now."

"Do it!" John said. "He's somewhere in Washington. I'll track him down."

"You will? How?"

"I'll find him."

27. THE TRAP

Eleven minutes to go.

At two o'clock he would be picked up and taken to the Chinese embassy; so Myra Kadane had told him in a brief breathless phone call after the hearing ended.

"Hi. Did you watch it?"

"Sure, every minute."

"Thought you would. Attaché says lobby at two. Got it?"

"Lobby at two."

"Right. Bye." Click. Bit of melodrama, that. Possibly she hadn't wanted to be overheard. Melodramatic business this was, all in all, and he knew Myra disapproved, but he was in it now, and that was that.

Last check at the half-length mirror on the bathroom door. Behold the man! Backbone of the nation's scientific greatness! Stooping white-haired sad-faced old fellow in a badly laundered shirt, threadbare tie, worn brown jacket snatched for the trip to Washington; pouched eyes and yellowish pallor from persisting insomnia, too much bourbon, sent-in meals at irregular hours. *Much* aged since their strange fleeting reunion in China, now that he sized himself up through Mei's eyes. How enchanting, by contrast, she looked in her sixties! What did she want of him? Why on earth had she asked for this risky meeting? Well, anyway, he had managed the haircut. Shabby, yes, that couldn't be helped, and the fastidious Mei would understand. Shaggy, no.

He paced and paced the hot little hotel room, still wondering about Mei, forty years since their ardent romance and agonized breakup. An everlasting enigma, Mei! The early letters, the bundle that had so infuriated Penny, had been wistfully lovely, almost poetical; hard to discard even after getting married, though it had been a damned dumb mistake not to do so. The letters since Shanghai had been altogether different; dry, chatty, just short of boring, coming at long intervals. Once, thinking that she seemed to be tiring of the whole thing, he had not responded for almost a year, and another letter had come at last, with a subtle pleading note under the usual family gossip and the comments on articles in *Science* and *Nature.* Realizing then that she must be writing under some sort of surveillance, he had resumed the desultory guarded correspondence.

Five minutes to two, time to get down to the lobby. What would the first moments of this meeting be like after all these years? A hug, a kiss? With Mei, not bloody likely — enough, *enough!* This rendezvous was her idea, so he would present himself as summoned, and she could take it from there . . .

At the reception desk the old deaf manager was busy with accounts, otherwise the lobby was empty. Carpenter settled into a threadbare purple armchair, his mind in a whirl. Who would call for him? Driver of an embassy car? Hardly prudent! What was really going on? Could her reference to autumn in Cornell have been a faint signal to him, after all? Was the spark still there? Or was he preposterously kidding himself? Mei remained inscrutable, not because like Fu Manchu she was Oriental, but because like his wife she was a woman. That difficult equation resisted solution more than Fermat's last theorem.

A skinny wrinkled man and a short-haired girl came into the

lobby, toting between them a huge wicker hamper piled with laundered towels and sheets. Both were Chinese. They got into the elevator and soon returned with the hamper full of bulging canvas laundry bags. As the old man went by he nodded, and Carpenter followed them out. They loaded the hamper into the back of a truck, the girl jumped in and closed the tailgate, and the old man got behind the wheel, beckoning to Carpenter to climb in beside him. Not a word was spoken for half an hour as they drove up Massachusetts Avenue and past Dupont Circle in heavy traffic. A few reporters and cameramen, lounging outside an old building with the yellow-starred red flag over the entrance, paid no attention to the truck driving past. Around the corner, the driver stopped at a closed rear gate and spoke half a dozen singsong words to a green-uniformed sentry, who called to Carpenter, "Mister, come please," unlocking the gate and waving the physicist through. The truck drove off, a back door of the building opened, and there stood Zhang Zhui, bowing and smiling.

"Welcome, Dr. Carpenter. This way." He led the physicist through a warren of small back rooms and up a narrow staircase. "Now, Dr. Wen Mei Li flies to New York today, and we'll be leaving for the airport at four o'clock. As it happens, our greengrocer delivers his fresh fruit and vegetables at four, so he can take you back to your hotel in his truck, if that's convenient."

I might have known! They've got this thing organized like D-day. "That'll be fine."

In a broad carpeted hallway, the attaché stopped at a half-open red lacquered door. "Well, here is the guest suite." He knocked. "Dr. Wen Mei Li, your colleague has arrived."

"Thank you, Zhang Zhui." Mei sat on a couch, dressed as she had been at the hearing. The diplomat bowed and withdrew. "So, Guy, here you are." At her inviting gesture he sat down on the couch beside her, and now he could see spidery lines around her mouth and eyes, invisible on television. She looked none the less appealing for that, perhaps more so, for the touch of pathos in this tracery of time. "Did you watch the hearing?"

"Of course. No doubt you know all about the gushing on TV over your appearance, your style —"

She said severely, "They're not serious people, your commentators. None of them! One should be properly groomed and wear pretty clothes, of course, but to take such notice of it is stupid. You look well. A bit harried, or am I wrong?"

"*Harried* will do, Mei. Still, I'm okay —"

She touched a cool hand on his. "That's why I asked you to come. I've caused you no end of trouble, Guy, and I'm truly, truly sorry. That wretched *Washington Post* article —"

"Good Lord, Mei, you squashed that story like a bug. It's gone. Don't go blaming yourself —"

"No, no, I was at fault, corresponding was my idea, and it wasn't wise. How has your wife taken all this disgusting publicity?"

"Mei, we're Americans, we're used to our media. Penny's fine."

It was the best response he could manage. Mei's shrewd skeptical glance told him it wasn't working. Awkward pause. She brought a photograph out of her purse. "My first grandchild, a boy," she said in a bright sociable tone. The bundled-up black-eyed infant looked very much like a Chinese doll.

"Handsome baby. I'm not a good father, I don't have a picture of my little girl."

"You forget, you sent me one."

"Oh, did I?"

"Of course. A real beauty. And you and your wife with a grown son, studying anthropology! You've been blessed, Guy."

"We're well aware of that. Dinah's a beguiling little miracle."

Dead end to the topic of family. They sat looking in each other's eyes. "Your statement was good," he said.

"Was it all right, really?" Her face lit up. "I slaved over it."

"You did your country proud."

"Well, thank you. I cut it in half, you know, just last night! It was very schoolmarmish stuff, Guy, my big chance to set America straight." This was the old Mei Li now, crisp and animated. "Scolding you for your self-absorption, your indifference to the rest of the planet — three hundred million people lording it over six billion — your irreversible waste of the world's resources and the resources of your own land . . . Would you believe that I had half a page about the extirpation of the buffalo?"

"No, did you?" He shook his head, smiling. "God, you and your obsession with the buffalo! That ghastly old photograph you had on the wall in your room, the grinning rifleman standing on a ten-foot pile of bison bones —"

"You remember that?" She lightly slapped his hand, a Mei gesture dating all the way back to Cornell. "Good for you! To me, that picture was and remains an ideogram of everything black in American history." She sighed and sobered. "Well, I couldn't sleep last night, I tossed and turned, and at two in the morning I said to myself, *Mei, relax, this is about the Potato Project, nothing else. Stick to that!* I got up and slashed and slashed for more than an hour. I had trouble reading from those marked-up pages at the hearing. Luckily I'd been *over* and over them, I knew the thing almost by heart —"

"It came out right, I promise you. The reaction in that caucus room was close to homage."

"You're sure? Zhang Zhui and I both took it for American courtesy to strangers and guests of Congress."

"I'm sure. In a word, Mei, you were magnificent."

She peered at him through the steel-rimmed glasses and gave him a sweet grateful smile. "Now tell me about your telescopes. I received your last letter the day before I left China. Very sad letter, Guy." Mei conveyed with glistening eyes and a resigned shrug that their correspondence was finished forever. "You wrote that your Project Scientist was in a panic about her budget because of our *Nature* article. What's happened since?"

"Well, Ottoline was right about the frenzy in Congress, but we may ride it out. You remember the Science Committee woman on the dais next to the Chairman?"

"Oh, yes. Congresswoman Myra Kadane of California. Zhang Zhui briefed me on all their backgrounds. She's a widow who took her husband's place. She used to act in the movies."

"Exactly so. She's befriended our project, and she has the ear of Chairman Wesley."

Mei said with an amused nod, "Well, well. *Guanshei!* Why has she befriended you?"

"Guanshei?"

"Influence, Guy. Connections. Protection. Pull. The lubricant that makes the world go round. In China we call it *guanshei.*"

"I see." Carpenter gladly took up her light tone. "The Higgs boson of politics, perhaps, Mei? Gives everything its mass?"

"Not bad." She laughed. "Now, why would an ex-actress support a search for terrestrial planets?"

"Well, I had something to do with that." He told the story briefly — how Ottoline had delegated him to work on Myra Kadane, how he had taken the Congresswoman to Waxahachie to give her an insight into the Super Collider fiasco, and how, in the course of that visit, she had agreed to support the telescope budget. "Myra knows no astronomy, but she has an inquiring mind. When I mentioned that oxygen in a planet's spectrum would indicate the presence of life, she wanted to know why."

Mei wrinkled her brow. "Redox reaction?"

"Sure, and the way I put it to her, oxygen is so active chemically that lifeless planets just rust out, so to say. The oxygen is absorbed, and only life-forms like our plants can reverse the process and give off free oxygen. That really intrigued her."

"I can imagine that she was intrigued," said Mei, with a narrow-eyed glance at him. "Has your wife met Congresswoman Kadane?"

"Oh, yes. Met her at a Hollywood party. In fact they sort of got tiddly together."

"That sounds like Hollywood, but not like your wife."

"Penny has her moments."

"Well, of that I have no doubt." She stood up and strode to French windows that opened onto a balcony. "This is such a nice suite, and it has quite a view. One way the Washington Cathedral, the other way the Capitol and the Monument. Come have a look."

They stepped out together into bright afternoon sunshine. Beyond the dusty green trees below the balcony, the view was hazy, and he could just discern the Capitol and the Monument above grayish murk. "We need one of your spectacular thunderstorms to clear the air," she said. A sudden hard grip on his hand startled him. She turned him around, pulling him to her. "It's all right out here, but keep your voice low. My God, how lovely, how marvelous of you to come! I didn't believe you would. I took a wild chance."

Dazed, he said, "So did I —"

"I know! But Zhang Zhui assured me, swore to me, that he could shield you from the media, and he's an old friend. Oh, Guy, that's it, just hold me, we can't stay out here long." She stood tiptoe in his arms to kiss him, and dropped her head on his chest in her unforgotten endearing shy way, murmuring, "Did you catch my words about autumn in Cornell?"

"I couldn't believe they were for me —"

"They were, they were. And the road not taken, you were that road." She glanced up, her eyes wet, and tightened her arms around him. "And now I'm a grandmother, getting a lot of loathsome publicity, and I won't be able to work anymore. They're making me Deputy Minister of Science and Technology, though I don't want it, I care only about my work, my children, my grandson. The Minister's old and sick, I'll be Minister soon, and I hate administration." Mei wept. "Oh, Guy!"

"Mei" — he groped for words — "we do what comes to hand, both of us, you're serving your country brilliantly, it's what you chose —"

"Yes, my dear." She smiled up at him through her tears. "I don't need comforting, I'm all right. It's just that I've drawn too few happy breaths in my life. These are purely happy breaths I'm breathing right now, be sure of that. No more letters, that's all finished, I know, yet we'll never truly be finished, will we? Again, again, again, a thousand thanks for coming."

Guy Carpenter choked out a reluctant truth. "I love you, Mei. That's why I came."

"And I know that. It's why I'm happy. We won't see each other ever again in this life, I wanted this moment —"

The telephone rang. She drew away from him, shocked. "Zhang

Zhui promised me an undisturbed hour. Wait here." She darted inside and came back almost at once. "He wants to talk to you."

"Ah, Dr. Carpenter, forgive the intrusion." The attaché's apology was calm and cheery. "A gentleman at the back gate says he would like to speak to you." Utterly stunned, Guy said nothing. "Ah — Dr. Carpenter?"

"It can't be. I mean, nobody knows I'm here. I've told absolutely no one."

"Of course you haven't. Well, so I went to the gate and assured the man he was under a misapprehension, but he insists he knows you're inside the embassy, and he'll wait until midnight or later if he must. Not unpleasant, but persistent. Oh, a man with him has a TV camera."

"Describe this fellow," said Carpenter, sick at heart.

"Well, I would say in his forties, mustache, eyeglasses, middle height —"

"Large mustache?"

"I would say quite large."

Then comes my fit again. "Zhang Zhui, he's Rossiter, the reporter from the *Washington Post* who wrote that wretched article."

Mei, looking on from the balcony, clutched both hands to her head.

"Really? He's good at his trade. There are no secrets here in America, though one tries to do one's best."

"Poses a problem, does it?"

"Why, not in the least." Zhang Zhui sounded positively blithe. "By all means go on enjoying your visit. Please convey my regrets to Dr. Wen Mei Li for the interruption. If you want to leave a bit early, just let me know."

Mei came into the room, closing the French windows. "That foul newspaper scribbler —"

"Mei, Rossiter just does what he does, as the wasp stings and the rat gnaws. God knows how this leaked —"

"Zhang Zhui *assured* me that you wouldn't be at risk. Did he say what you're to do now?"

"He seemed unconcerned."

"He always does. What did he *say?*"

"That I should go on enjoying the visit."

She pursed her lips, her forehead furrowed, and all at once she looked like a grandmother. "Nothing more?"

"Just to let him know if I wanted to leave a bit early."

"Ah, so you're to go immediately." She pressed a button on the phone, spoke briefly in Chinese, and hung up. "Well, let's sit down." Her voice turned crisp and cheery. "Did you admire the view?"

"Unforgettable, Mei."

She slightly shook her head at his sly warmth. "Tell me, have you worked through the *Nature* article? The peer review was gratifying, and on the whole the comments since publication have been good."

Carpenter was not about to disclose to Mei the flaw he believed he had discerned — certainly not in this room, where she was acting coolly distant again. "Not yet, it's been a hectic time for me, you know."

"Of course. Well, I hope to hear that your telescope project is approved, and moves ahead."

"If so, you'll read about it in *Nature.* One of our scientists has an in with the editorial board."

She laughed politely. "That shouldn't help, but I suppose it does."

"Guanshei," said Carpenter.

"Exactly, guanshei. You've learned something in Chinese, rather an important word."

A rap at the door. Zhang Zhui called, "If you're ready, Dr. Carpenter, we can go now."

"Ready."

Mei said as they stood up, "Well, thank you for coming. I've thoroughly enjoyed our chat. By the bye, the cyclotron we built is still in use. Graduate students train on it now."

"That's nice to know."

"Good luck with Congressman Hurtle." She held out a hand, looked deep into his eyes, and pressed his hand so hard that her nails dug painfully into the skin. "I'm not sure he's really such an ogre."

Zhang Zhui brought Carpenter down the staircase, and through a long gloomy hall smelling of Chinese cookery, to a door that he unlocked. They descended steep wooden steps to a low space lit by one dangling lightbulb, where they had to stoop under crisscrossing pipes and humming air-conditioning ducts to get past an oil burner and two water heaters. At the rough stone foundation, the attaché laboriously pulled aside a barrier of planks blocking a narrow gap. "Come, Dr. Carpenter." He shone a flashlight into the hole, and walking in behind him, Carpenter could feel dirt and small stones underfoot.

"This is interesting," the physicist said.

The attaché chuckled. "Yes, and I can't vouch for the explanation I've heard, but it seems plausible."

The title deeds of the embassy, he said as they walked, showed that this mansion, dating back to the 1920s, had been built over a massive 18th-century foundation, the original structure having been torn down, and it was said that some of the grand houses in Revolutionary times had had such covert ways of egress. This part of Connecticut Avenue was of course far outside of old Georgetown, so perhaps the original house had been a summer residence in the country. Be that as it might, a furnace repairman had come on the passage a few years ago, much to the previous ambassador's surprise.

"So it's been left this way, just boarded up," said Zhang Zhui. They crunched along in the flashlight beam for another minute or two until Zhang Zhui halted, and shifted the flashlight to offer his hand. "Well, here we are. Good-bye, Dr. Carpenter, and thank you. It was important that you came. Dr. Wen Mei Li is a national treasure of China, and she did yearn to see her old colleague once more." He pushed up a trapdoor made of rough planks, letting in daylight. Carpenter stepped out, blinking in the sunshine, and found himself on a sidewalk by a grassy slope. As the trapdoor was lowered, he could see green grass thickly sodded on top of it, so that when closed it was barely discernible. Atop the slope a raucous soccer game was in progress, and at the curb the Chinese driver of a small truck was waving to him.

❦

A telephone message lay under the door. From the Rock, no less!

I leave for India tomorrow. Imperative you call me.

Rocovsky

Carpenter dialed the unfamiliar number in New York at once. No answer. He checked his e-mail: three messages.

Professor —

I trust the rendezvous with Wen Mei Li worked out okay. I'll come for you at 7:30 A.M. Be ready. Things are heating up.

Berkovits

Another, from Braunstein:

Hi, Guy —

Ottoline and all of us are watching the hearings with fascination. We think Wendy knocked the ball out of the park. Hope I wasn't out of line, but film producer Tim Warshaw called the lab, "desperate" to get in touch with you on business, so I gave him your e-mail address. Good luck tomorrow!

Peter

And a long wordy e-mail from Warshaw seemed to retract the lawyer letter firing him. Nice, if true!

The feel of Mei's beloved slim body tingled yet in Carpenter's arm muscles, and the moment on the balcony still suffused his spirit with melancholy sweetness. Like a movie freeze-frame, it was an ending etched in the substance of his brain. There it was, there it would be while he lived.

Right now, more than time for a tot of bourbon! As he poured it he abruptly burst out laughing like a crazy man. Quentin Rossiter was still outside the embassy back gate and might really wait there until midnight or later!

"Here's to you, Deep Throat Physicist!" He lifted his glass to the bathroom mirror. "Just one more hurdle, the highest. Hurtle the hurdle. Ha ha ha! Down the hatch!"

28. THE TELESCOPES

Berkovits sounded jovial, coming in through the unlocked door. "Top of the morning, Professor! Take a look at the papers."

"Half a mo'." Carpenter was shaving a very worried face, the prospect of confronting Hurtle much on his mind. He came out, toweling off the lather. "Good news?"

"Read the headlines, then you tell me." From an armful of newspapers the lawyer laid down the *Washington Post,* then the *New York Times.*

WHEN CONGRESS KILLED COLLIDER
DENG OKAYED BOSON PROJECT

U.S. CONGRESS TRIGGERED
CHINESE BOSON TRIUMPH

"And now for the clown paper, the *New York Post* —"

MOTHER OF BOMB SAYS CONGRESS FATHERED CHINESE BOSON BOMB!

"And here's the clincher, Guy." The lawyer spread out *USA Today* like a winning poker hand.

CHINESE HIGGS BOSON PROJECT WAS KICKED OFF BY HURTLE WIN

"Wow! Rough on Hurtle, all right."

"Call that rough? See Sharon McAllister, just her first paragraph —" The lawyer yanked open the *Washington Post* to the op-ed page and handed it to Carpenter.

CONWAY HURTLE AND THE HIGGS BOSON
BY SHARON MCALLISTER

When I was a little girl, I was told that the way to housebreak a puppy was to rub its nose in its own doo-doo, though I never had the heart to find out whether it was true. Yesterday Dr. Wen Mei Li, the great Chinese physicist, rubbed the nose of the U.S. Congress in its own doo-doo, with her stunning revelation that its vote to abort the Superconducting Super Collider in 1993 convinced Deng Xiaoping to authorize China's triumphant Higgs boson project. Whether such housebreaking works, we may know soon. Will Congressman Conway "Bob" Hurtle of Illinois, Co-Chairman of the current House hearings, now publicly acknowledge the biggest flub of an able political career, his fight that brought down the Super Collider?

"How do you like them apples?" said Berkovits.

"I'm not sure," said Carpenter. "He'll be wounded and dangerous today, won't he? All the more likely to try to take my skin off."

"Listen to me, Guy. Bob Hurtle's job from here on out will be to keep his own skin shrink-wrapped on his bulky carcass. You're in good shape, and your dumb post-office box just blows away on the wind."

"God, I hope so."

"Finish dressing, we're meeting Aaron Kadane in Myra's office. I've got a car and driver downstairs."

"What does Aaron think? Any change in tactics?"

"Well, Aaron's an old sobersides, a career worrier, but even he agrees we're looking good. He's wary of Hurtle, that's all. The way he put it on the phone, *'That fellow can still pull a big white rabbit out of his hat.'* That may be so, but you won't be that rabbit. We'll see to that."

"Look here, Jules," Carpenter said, putting on his jacket, "I suppose you've had dealings with Hollywood people."

Berkovits grunted. "A bit."

"You've heard of Tim Warshaw?"

"Sure, the disaster guy. *Meltdown of the Eiffel Tower, Gaseous Aliens from Altair,* and such. What about him?"

Carpenter showed him a blurry printout of Warshaw's e-mail. "What do you make of this?"

At a glance Berkovits said, stroking his gray locks, "Sinclair Holloway, eh? Big Daddy. What's the movie?"

"It's called *Boson Bomb* —"

"No! *Boson Bomb?*" The lawyer laughed out loud. "Sounds just like Warshaw, probably another blockbuster. How on earth did you get involved with Warshaw?"

"That's quite a story —"

"Well, hold it." On a cell phone Berkovits told his driver to wait awhile, and sat down with the e-mail, reading it aloud in a monotone.

Dear Dr. Carpenter:

A letter sent to you by a low-level lawyer in Sean Kadane's firm was a glitch, just a "contingency draft" that never should have been mailed to you. Your contract remains in force, in fact Sinclair Holloway has directed full payment of advance to you now, as hearings are enormously enhancing movie potential. Looking forward to your testimony. Please acknowledge this correction.

Warshaw

"I know Sean Kadane." Berkovits nodded over the printout, his face serious and abstracted, and he lit a cigar. "Okay, Guy, now let's hear the story, and make it short."

Carpenter described how he had encountered the Congresswoman, and told of meeting Holloway and Warshaw at the party in her Bel-Air home. "I sat at Sinclair Holloway's table," he said, "and he took a shine to me —"

"Why?"

"Who knows? Maybe because of the way I explained the Super Collider. Anyway, next thing I knew, Warshaw and his partner had me out in the garden, propositioning me to be a consultant on this film. They'd just had the brainstorm after hearing a scary broadcast by Peter Jennings about a possible Boson Bomb. They named a sizable sum, and in an inebriated lapse I shook hands on it. Like a shot, a contract and an advance came FedEx. Then when the Rossiter article appeared, I got a registered letter firing me and demanding their money back." He gestured at the e-mail. "And now this!"

"I love it, love it! Pristine Hollywood. What were they paying you?" Guy told him. Berkovits pursed his lips. "Not very generous." He tossed the paper aside and began to pace, cigar smoke wreathing around him. "Now pay attention, Guy. Out there in Cloud-Cuckoo Land they all operate on one principle, fear. *Fear!* It's obvious that Holloway doesn't know they fired you. They've got to get you back fast, and Warshaw is scared out of his mind. That's what that e-mail says, and you're in the catbird seat. We can name our price, within reason, of course. We mustn't be pigs about it." He rolled the cigar in his lips with relish. "How about a hundred thousand dollars?"

Carpenter gasped and laughed. "Come off it, Jules."

"Why not? A plain shakedown, but they asked for it, the yellow bellies, running for the tall grass because of one scurrilous article. I want them to suffer for shoving a scientist around. Sit down and let's shoot a reply to Warshaw."

The physicist's fingers flicked on the keyboard as Berkovits paced and dictated.

Dear Mr. Warshaw:

Glad to know film potential is being enhanced. My lawyer will call Mr. Kadane today. His name is Jules Berkovits.

With a flourish and a grin, Guy hit SEND. "Talk about fear, Warshaw's blood should turn to Freon."

"That's the idea. I'll call Sean after the hearing, so give some thought to any other conditions you want, this is your chance. Now let's get cracking."

"I'm ready."

In the elevator Berkovits asked, "What's the book?"

Carpenter handed him *The Four Horsemen of the Apocalypse.* "I'm returning it to Myra. It's from the old house she rents in Georgetown."

"Hey, Rudy Valentino, my grandmother's girlhood crush! She sneaked out on Saturday to see *The Four Horsemen,* a big sin. The only language she knew was Yiddish, but that didn't matter with a silent picture."

"The novel's a museum piece," Carpenter said. "Still, I got hooked and finished it."

Berkovits sniffed the book and gave it back. "Smells like old Georgetown."

Heading uptown in thick traffic, the car passed a big clock on a pole outside a jewelry shop. Carpenter pointed and said dolefully, "Just two hours to go. Dead man walking."

"That's no attitude, Professor. It's Dr. Homer Aptor who should be feeling that way."

"How so?"

"For a National Security Adviser, he talks too much. He said on *Larry King Live* the other night that axing the SSC was *'a boneheaded boo-boo.'* Not very politic when he's in trouble himself. These academics who come to Washington can't resist a chance at television. And evidently in his case, at sex. Did you see that *Vanity Fair* with Bambi MacFadden on the cover in the buff?"

"What's *Vanity Fair?*"

Berkovits stared at him. "You're a true innocent, aren't you? It's *the* smarty magazine, Professor, very hot, and she wrote this article, or a ghost did, that caused a big buzz here inside the Beltway. Simon and Schuster has her expanding it to a book. Catchy title: *National Security at Bedtime.* Subtitle: *Putin Pinched Me.*"

"I miss all that clever stuff," Carpenter said, "trying to drudge through *Nature* and *Science* every week."

"Just so you're not caught unawares," said Berkovits, "Bambi will be in the caucus room today. I had dinner last night with Gerry Reilly, her lawyer. He's trying to up Simon and Schuster's bid. If she can get some real exposure today with her clothes on, that might do it."

The physicist managed a chuckle, and Berkovits said, "None of my business, but did the rendezvous with Dr. Wen Mei Li come off after all?"

"Yes."

"Myra and Aaron were against it, you know. Only I was for it."

"I know."

"Who was right?"

"You were," said Carpenter in the guillotine tone he could still summon. The lawyer nodded and smoked his cigar with no more words until they got to the Rayburn Building.

"Guy, Myra wants to talk to you right away," said Aaron Kadane, who sat in her outer office, writing on a clipboard. "So go ahead. Jules, I'm reviewing the Wirtz letter —"

The Congresswoman was at her desk in large horn-rimmed glasses, signing papers that Earle Carkin handed to her. "Oh, hi there, Guy. That'll do, Earle. Let Horace Wesley know that Dr. Carpenter's here. Not now, in about ten minutes."

Carkin gathered papers off the desk, giving the physicist an unpleasant look and a bare nod on the way out.

"Well, how are you holding up?" She took off her glasses and scrutinized him, gesturing to the chair by the desk. "Nervous about today?"

"I'll survive — bless my soul, there's Mehitabel."

Myra smiled, stroking the figurine. "I told you I'd keep her on my desk."

"Yes, to remind you that scientists are human."

"Good memory! How's your wife?"

"What's going to happen to me this morning, Myra?"

"Hard to say. Wasn't it superb, the way your Wendy handled Hurtle? Sort of declawed the old bobcat."

"Myra, those claws can regenerate overnight."

"Chin up, Guy. Coffee?" She pressed a button and gave the order. "I asked you about your wife."

"I know you did."

"Well?"

Sisters under the skin, Guy thought. Chinese physicist, American Congresswoman, both zeroing in right away on the wife. He had dodged Mei, but he had already confided in Myra Kadane about Penny, and he owed her a lot. "In a word, you called it. I was gutted like a trout."

"Oh, Lord. Let's hear."

The ponytailed Pam brought in the coffee. "Good morning, Professor Carpenter," she caroled with a knowing little grin, and she scampered out.

"Go on," Myra prompted, pouring coffee, "like a trout, you say —"

He sketched what had happened, from Rossiter's waylaying him at the lab and getting gored at the Athenaeum, to his vengeful phone call to Penny about Shanghai.

"Say no more!" Myra exclaimed. "No wonder you were gutted. *'Ask him about Shanghai'!* Gratuitous malevolence, even for Rossiter. Dirty, dirty pool."

"Well, I did provoke him."

"Have you talked to her at all since she walked out?"

"Not yet."

"Why not? Why don't you try calling her at her mother's house?"

"Two reasons, Myra. Number one, to give her space to cool off. And two, there's the slim hope that when she sees Hurtle grill me, or reads about it, she'll shift into a forgiving mode."

Myra Kadane's eyes softened, and a strange sad smile came and went on her pretty mouth. "Hm. Not bad thinking, Professor."

"Myra, in my life I've loved two women. It's a very narrow frame of reference. I do my best."

"You do all right, and they've both been lucky."

"That's a very sweet thing to say."

Horace Wesley bustled in, remarking jocosely, "Well, well, priming the witness! Kind of irregular, but I'll overlook it. Dr. Carpenter, couple of things. The French Premier comes to the White House at noon, and Dr. Aptor must be there, so he'll testify ahead of you. I've already told Professor Kadane, and he has no objection."

"Thank you, sir."

"Now as to your telescopes, I'm fascinated by all this Myra told me, about how detecting free oxygen on a planet around a star can prove there's life elsewhere in the universe. Amazing! Four space telescopes, right? Infrared, orbiting in formation halfway to the sun, or something?"

"You've got it, sir."

"Well, people like you should come down here more often to educate us. We're so busy that we can't keep up with what's important. I can't promise anything, but I'm for those telescopes. I'll see you in the caucus room. Good luck, and don't let Bob Hurtle rattle you. I'm holding the gavel."

When he was gone, Myra jumped up and closed her office door. "Well, that's reassuring. Horace is a dear, and by God, Ottoline Porson's got her telescopes! You white-headed bumbler, you've pulled it off. She sent the right man for the job after all."

"It's your doing, Myra, bless you."

"Absolutely not. You did it." She gave him a hug, and the whiff of her perfume brought back a flash of the Falcon and of her Georgetown home. "Horace was mesmerized when I quoted you about free oxygen as a clue to life out in the universe. It's grade-school science that plants take in carbon dioxide and give off oxygen, but that's the level of knowledge in this august body, and that one ray of light got to him." She sat down on the couch. "Now come tell me about your meeting with Dr. Wen Mei Li. I was against it, such a thing's damned hard to keep secret, but you got away with it, so good for you. Was it worth the risk?"

"As I live, it was worth the risk, but it wasn't kept secret. Quentin Rossiter showed up at the back gate of the embassy with a cameraman —"

"Good God, he didn't —"

"He did, and told the attaché that he knew I was inside. There were reporters staked out front, of course, so I was trapped."

"How the devil did you get out unobserved?" A bell rang. "Shoot, the hearing's about to start. I'll track down that infuriating leak, I swear to you." She picked up *The Four Horsemen of the Apocalypse* and handed it to him. "Look, come and have dinner with me at home, why don't you? Saturnina's on, she'll make you a real Guatemalan omelet, or anything else. When will you and I ever get to talk again, Guy? This craziness is almost over."

"Of course I'll come, Myra."

"Now listen, you'll do fine out there, though Homer Aptor may be in for a bit of a ride." She clasped his hand. "Breathe easy."

Dr. Homer Aptor strode to the witness table with the confident step of one who had been through such rigmaroles often. Fleshy and ruddy faced, with a handsome curly white shock all different from Carpenter's straight thinning hair, the former professor of international law had developed the horny hide of a Washington survivor in unelected posts. Horace Wesley had to gavel down the whispering and murmuring. Bambi MacFadden had been on *Barbara Walters* the night before.

"Dr. Aptor," Chairman Wesley began, "you've been reassuring the American people at press conferences and on talk shows that the Higgs boson has no military value and poses no security threat to the United States. Now, you're neither a scientist nor a military expert. How can you be so certain — and so dismissive — about this worrisome matter?"

Aptor cheerily read a prepared answer. The British Foreign Secretary was an old personal friend, he said, and had sent him secret advance word of the *Nature* article well before the news broke and alarmed the public. At once he had contacted the Joint Chiefs to request an urgent meeting with them, and with their science advisers, the Weapons Systems Evaluation Group. The upshot of an exhaustive four-hour discussion had been that there was no combat potential whatever in the Higgs boson.

Guy Carpenter, in the front row with Aaron Kadane, observed with a qualm how Conway Hurtle, who glowered steadily at Aptor, was throwing an occasional fierce glower his way. Farther back among the spectators, Jules Berkovits nudged Fineman and Sturdevant. "See that woman, gentlemen, three seats to the right of Charley, and down one row? The one in brown? That's Bambi MacFadden."

"What, that dowdy?" Fineman whispered. "She's dressed like my aunt Sophie."

"She's dressed to kill," said Berkovits. "Hold on to your hats."

Dr. Aptor moved smoothly to the subject of basic science by citing his liaison with HEPAP over many years. The Chinese discovery was in HEPAP's turf, so —

"Dr. Aptor, for the sake of country boys like me," Wesley interposed, "please state who or what *HEPAP* is."

"Of course. Sorry. It's the High Energy Physics Advisory Panel, in the DOE." With a condescending grin he added, "That's the Department of Energy, Mr. Chairman."

"Yes, thank you," said Wesley blandly.

HEPAP had taken the news with equanimity, Aptor went on, and the American people could rely, as he did, on HEPAP's view that the Higgs boson was utterly harmless. He would submit to the committee the full memorandum he had received from HEPAP.

"That will be nice," Wesley said. "Now my Co-Chairman from Illinois has a question or two for you."

Homer Aptor remarked, nodding amiably at Conway Hurtle, "Not for the first time."

"No," said Hurtle, unsmiling. "You've advised several Presidents, so we've chatted before. You were an adviser to President Reagan, I believe, when he approved the Superconducting Super Collider with his memorable remark, '*Throw deep.*' "

"I was present when he said it. Of course, that was years ago. I was in a more modest capacity."

"Naturally." Hurtle consulted a paper. "You were an assistant to the National Security Adviser, one of many. In an interview at the time, you said, I quote, '*The President has given the green light to a glorious undertaking, a reach to the stars.*' "

"I remember saying that."

"Then, under President Bush, you visited the Waxahachie site and declared that the SSC was '*A Lewis and Clark expedition into God's mind.*' "

"So I did."

"However, when it was canceled under President Clinton, you called the project '*long-haired science gone hog wild and haywire.*' "

"Well, by then it had gotten rather out of hand —"

"Thank you, Dr. Aptor, that was exactly my position, and as is well known, I acted on it. Yet the other day you called the cancellation '*a boneheaded boo-boo.*' Dr. Aptor, where do you stand on the Super Collider as of" — Hurtle glanced at his watch — "let's say, about eleven o'clock this morning?"

"Congressman Hurtle, as to that recent TV show, you're quoting me out of context. What I said was, '*When it was voted, the abort looked like a hardheaded judgment. By 20/20 hindsight it* seems *a boneheaded boo-boo.*' I said *seems.*"

"You've wavered quite a bit on the Super Collider, haven't you, Dr. Aptor?"

"Well, as the saying goes, to err is human."

"Oh, absolutely. Have you read the recent article about yourself in *Vanity Fair?*"

"Dr. Aptor," Horace Wesley hastily struck in, "that question goes far afield, and I doubt you have to answer it —"

"I'm aware of the article, Mr. Chairman," said Aptor. "It's foolishness, but if your distinguished colleague really wants to go into it —"

"Thank you, Dr. Aptor, just very briefly," said Hurtle. "You do know Mrs. Ernestine MacFadden, or *Bambi,* as she's called professionally?"

"Let me explain about that. You see, during the Korean War, when I —"

"One moment. The *Korean* War, you say?"

"Yes, sir. In the Korean War I served on a minesweeper as a reserve officer. Well, a few years ago I managed to attend the annual reunion of the squadron's crews, and that was where I met the lady. But since then —"

"Dr. Aptor, pardon me, what on earth was Mrs. Ernestine MacFadden doing at a reunion of minesweeper crews?"

The National Security Adviser hesitated. "Well, in point of fact, she jumped out of a cake. A cake baked like a mine. The lights went out, the mine sort of exploded, and there was Bambi."

"Ah, I see," said Hurtle, smiling for the first time, a mere cold baring of teeth, amid murmurs and giggles in the audience.

"She's a pleasant lady," Aptor went on obdurately, "and when she's happened to be in Washington, we've had an occasional dinner, maybe gone to the Kennedy Center. All the rest of that article is fantasy —"

"IT'S ALL TRUE, HOMER, AND YOU KNOW IT!" The lady in brown jumped up, rather as though jumping out of a cake, shaking a little fist in the air.

"Order! Order!" Wesley banged his gavel. "Mrs. MacFadden, I must ask you —"

"EVERY WORD OF IT IS TRUE, MR. CHAIRMAN. I HAVE THE PROOF RIGHT HERE UNDER MY MIDRIFF! I DARE HIM TO TAKE A DNA TEST!"

"The witness is excused," shouted Wesley, hammering the gavel. "Recess for five minutes!"

At this moment, to Guy Carpenter's utter stupefaction, Dr. Herman Rocovsky entered the Cannon Caucus Room.

29. THE SURPRISE

The sudden apparition of the Rock shook Guy Carpenter. Outside in the marble hall an impromptu press conference swirled noisily around Bambi MacFadden, reporters shouting questions, the indignant stripteaser snapping answers, the asking price of her book indubitably rising, while agitated musings raced through the physicist's mind. *Now what? What's the Rock up to? Why isn't he halfway to India by now? And why the* HELL *is he walking past me without a flicker of recognition? He's nearsighted, yes, but not that nearsighted. He must know that I'm the next witness and that I'm in big trouble . . .*

Jules Berkovits's good cheer over the headlines had obviously been premature. Conway Hurtle was on the warpath this morning, determined to reverse the media tide against him. He had bloodily scalped Dr. Aptor, and from his menacing glances Carpenter's way, he was out to collect not one white-haired scalp but two. Thoughts of the mortifying questions Hurtle was likely to throw at him plagued the physicist all during the five-minute recess, which seemed to be lasting hours.

The only daylight he could see through the anxious fog was the possibility that Rocovsky had decided he was right about the *Nature* article. Yet even if Rocovsky did concur — which would be marvelous — how could he testify at an open Congressional hearing about the serious flaw in the Chinese claim? Touching on ultra-sensitive military technology as it did, the disclosure called for a long carefully drafted letter to *Nature,* which would have to be submitted first for clearance at the highest Air Force level. That could take months or a year! Still, the Rock had listened patiently to his frantic phone harangue and had hung up with a noncommittal comment, in itself encouraging . . .

"Mr. Chairman." As Horace Wesley returned to his chair from an anteroom and took up the gavel, Conway Hurtle raised his hand. "A volunteer witness who can shed crucial light on the Chinese project has just arrived in Washington. Dr. Herman Rocovsky seldom emerges in public forums such as this, but —"

"Rocovsky? He's here?" Wesley peered at the front row. "Well, so he is. Pleasant surprise."

"He's already scheduled," Hurtle went on, "to lecture in India day after tomorrow, and he's delayed his departure so as to testify before this committee. His flight leaves Dulles Airport in a few hours, so I propose he be called on now, before Dr. Carpenter."

"By all means. The hearing continues." Wesley banged the gavel. "The Chair welcomes Dr. Herman Rocovsky, our greatest authority at the interface of science and national defense, to address the committee."

Carpenter murmured to Aaron Kadane, as Rocovsky approached the witness table, "Reprieved! Would this be Hurtle's big white rabbit?"

Kadane shrugged, his face expressionless.

"Mr. Chairman, the Chinese claim is flawed," Rocovsky began, "and the discovery of the Higgs boson remains unproven. I'm going public with this challenge because the world leadership of American science is at stake."

A tumult arose, flashbulbs began popping, and the quiescent

TV cameras swiveled to focus on the little savant. Relief and gratitude surged through Guy Carpenter's whole being. Wesley tried to gavel down the noise. "Are you saying, Dr. Rocovsky, that the Chinese have made a false claim? That the article in *Nature* is a hoax?"

"Not for the world would I say that. The science in the article is sound, as far as it goes, and I have only admiration for my former student and colleague, Dr. Wen Mei Li." Again Wesley had to pound the gavel to quiet the loud buzz in the room. "Now I must warn you, Mr. Chairman, that this matter touches on vital secrets of our national defense. There's no time for official clearance of what I'm compelled to say, so I'll undertake to explain the flaw in the Chinese project in general terms, without, I hope, going to jail for it —"

"Well, Professor," Hurtle put in with a broad smile, "I'm the one who has convinced you to speak out today as your patriotic duty, so if you get jugged, I'll go with you."

Wesley also turned waggish. "And this is happening on my watch, so I'll go to the slammer too. Proceed, Dr. Rocovsky. I'll take that risk."

"Thank you, sir. Let me bring you back for a moment to the Cold War, and to the Nuclear Test Ban Treaty of 1963, when the Air Force launched supersensitive satellites to detect Soviet treaty violations. The Soviet Union is gone, but other powers now have such weapons, and that satellite surveillance remains crucial to our national security."

So far so good, thought Carpenter, wondering tensely how Rocovsky could now edge past the third rail of closely guarded military information. He and the Rock were two of the very few civilians who were in on the secret, and if anyone could break silence publicly, Rocovsky could . . .

⚛

. . . Two FBI agents showing up uninvited at his flat when he was a young instructor at Cornell, to probe his background with steely smiles . . .

Rocovsky had recommended him to the Air Force as a reliable

physicist to study top-secret data from the satellites seeking the neutrons, X-ray flashes, and gamma rays of a banned nuclear blast. Outer space as well as Earth's skies had to be searched, because the Russians had landed instruments on the invisible side of the moon, and they might conceivably perform sneak nuclear-bomb tests there as well. The satellites could detect a blast cloud expanding beyond the shield of the moon, and the Soviet Union had never tried that dodge, but the satellites had picked up a strange space phenomenon, giant gamma-ray bursts not traceable to any solar or earthly source. The team's physicists had had a hard time getting Air Force clearance to announce their findings in a professional journal. When they did, the news electrified astronomers, and those gamma rays were now a new field of study.

The same satellites, vastly improved over the years, were recently detecting extraordinary magnetic bursts in space, invisible to scientists who lacked such high technology. Rocovsky had assigned him to write the interior Air Force memos on these cosmic events, and during his obsessive review of the *Nature* article in his hotel room — over and over — he had stumbled on a correlation between the dates of the bursts, which were fixed in his mind, and the dates of Chinese claimed detections of Higgs boson signatures. Dr. Wen Mei Li and her team, unaware of these bursts, could not have screened their Higgs boson detectors from them. Immured in the Millard Fillmore without his records, without his lab computer, Carpenter could only guess that he had really hit on something. Was the Rock about to use his discovery?

⚛

"It's a paradox of history, sir," Rocovsky was saying, "that war, which brings such great evils on mankind, can also bring great good. Penicillin, radar guidance systems, and nuclear power all came out of World War Two.

"Now, Mr. Chairman, during the Cold War, because the Soviets were capable of testing nuclear bombs on the unseen side of the moon, the Air Force had to take such possible cheating into account.

Devices of great sensitivity were created to detect nuclear-blast clouds that would expand, however faintly, beyond the moon, and as the moon went around the earth, these instruments were surveying the whole cosmos. As a result, sir, they detected hitherto unknown gamma rays which opened up a whole new field of astrophysics —"

By God, thought Carpenter in a fever, *he's leading up to my idea, he must be!*

"And more recently —" Rocovsky paused, cleared his throat, and took a new slow grave tone. "And this is the whole thrust of my appearance here this morning, sir — more recently, greatly improved Air Force satellites have been picking up rare magnetic disturbances from solar flares that simulate Higgs boson signatures. The dates of these rare magnetic storms correlate, one-on-one, with the Chinese reports of Higgs boson detections. Dr. Wen Mei Li and her colleagues could have no way of knowing this —"

Gaveling down excited noise in the audience, Horace Wesley ventured to ask, "Dr. Rocovsky, I'm puzzled, and please correct me if I'm off base, but I myself watched a total eclipse in Hawaii a few years ago, and I certainly could see flares on the sun with just the naked eye — through dark glass of course — big beautiful flares —"

"Exactly so, Mr. Chairman. Solar flares are indeed visible during an eclipse, and astronomers study them all the time through special telescopes. But these rare flares I speak of are different. They don't show up visually at all. The energy they give off in photons is primarily emitted in the ultraviolet and X-ray regions of the spectrum, which aren't visible from the earth. Even our Air Force would not have known about them, had we not developed more sensitive instruments than any other nation possesses, including China. That is the weakness in the *Nature* article, and that is why the claim must be called unproven. That's as far as I can go into the subject, Mr. Chairman."

As he fell silent, so did the talk in the Cannon Caucus Room. After a short stunned pause, Wesley said, "Quite far enough, sir."

"Incredibly reassuring," said Hurtle. "Dr. Rocovsky, please

comment on Dr. Homer Aptor's assertion that the Higgs boson has no military significance — that as he put it, it's 'harmless.'"

"Yes, Dr. Rocovsky, and let's have it straight," Wesley added. "We're cutting to the bone here."

"Mr. Chairman, Dr. Aptor aside," the Rock replied in measured somber tones, "discovery of the Higgs boson goes to the fundamental mystery of mass. Even schoolboys nowadays know that mass is only energy, compressed by an almost unimaginable factor, the square of the speed of light. If world leadership truly matters to the American people, we should at once resume the all-out quest for the Higgs boson. But as basic science, sir, not in a race for new bomb material! We have plenty of that. The Chinese have given us what I would call a good scare, and these hearings have been decidedly useful in reminding our beloved country that leaders must lead."

Hurtle persisted, "Should the Super Collider be revived?"

"I for one would advocate instead building NLC — that is, the Next Linear Collider."

Aha! The old fox breaks from cover! This was why the Rock was surfacing, thought Guy Carpenter, and why he had put off his trip to India. He was seizing a chance to grind his own axe! Rocovsky described to the committee with gusto the concept of two accelerators, each eight miles long, pointed like arrows at each other. The collision of positrons and electrons at that doubled energy, he declared, would produce the Higgs boson, if God in his wisdom had put it into Nature.

"What about the cost?" Wesley asked. "The Texas work is well along —"

"No comparison, sir. The Collider is a grandiose, still-untried concept. The linear-accelerator technology is known and proven. At Stanford it has produced Nobel Prizes. Build those two machines, turn them on, and that's it."

Horace Wesley bent his head to Hurtle, and they whispered together. "Dr. Rocovsky," Wesley said, "I'm mindful of your time pressure, so let me thank you and wish you a safe journey to India and back. Your contribution has been crucial." A bang of the gavel.

"The hearing will resume at ten A.M. tomorrow, with the testimony of Dr. Guy Carpenter."

"Interesting morning, gentlemen," Berkovits said to Fineman and Sturdevant, stretching and yawning as they stood up.

"Interesting and ominous," said Fineman. "If Rocovsky's right, we now get another two-year squabble over the site, Texas versus California, with Illinois horning in again."

Aaron Kadane was sliding folders back in his briefcase. "Well, Guy, not a bad morning. If the Chinese haven't got the Higgs boson, you obviously didn't give it to them."

"Say, Dr. Carpenter." Berkovits approached with Sturdevant and Fineman. "Charley here wants to know what you think of Rocovsky's Next Linear Collider."

Sturdevant said, "Yes, halfway through his testimony I could see the Super Collider rising again. Now I'm not sure —"

"Gentlemen, all I can say is I want no part of the Higgs boson," Carpenter returned, "ever again in my life. If I did, I'd give thought to Kulka's laser-plasma accelerator. Much cheaper, if it can work, and Fermilab's great on new technology."

"May I say something?" Berkovits put in. "I'm only a country boy — that is, the way Horace Wesley is a country boy —"

"Spill it, country boy," Sturdevant said.

"Mind you, it's just a vagrant notion —"

"Vagrant, your grandmother," said Fineman. "What's on your mind, Berkovits?"

"Well, how about a crash program, three tracks simultaneously in three states?"

The two Chief Counsels looked at each other. Sturdevant said, his face lighting up, "Hey! Manhattan Project, Alan. All three big boys get their design and development money at once, which wouldn't be all that much this year. It's a cute thought —"

"Cute and hopeless." Fineman shook his head. "They'd never get together, it's beyond them. Nice try, Berkovits —"

Aaron Kadane spoke up. "Suppose their heads were knocked

together? For instance, by Conway Hurtle? He's Illinois, he's Armed Force Services, and he's out to redeem himself."

"You don't know Bob Hurtle." Fineman uttered a dry laugh. "I was on his staff for years. Tell Hurtle to do something and the idea is dead, because he didn't think of it himself."

"He could think of it himself," said Kadane.

The others turned surprised eyes on the scrawny wills-and-estates lawyer. Berkovits said, "Come again, Aaron?"

"That is, he could believe he thought of it himself. I'll talk to Myra. That's what women do."

30. THE ROBE

Carpenter was shelving *The Four Horsemen of the Apocalypse* amid the faded bestsellers in Myra Kadane's living room when the door to the street slammed and she came rushing in. "Oh, God, you're here already, sorry —"

"I just got here, Myra. I figured seven would be about right —"

"It is, it is. I've had the most amazing day. No fiction writer could get away with what's been happening to me, just in the last twelve hours . . . Saturnina!" she called. "Hold dinner for a while."

Voice off: *"Sí, senora."*

"Guess what, Professor?" She broke out in a wild laugh. "I've just fired Earle Carkin."

"You have? That's great."

"Isn't it? Let's have a dry sherry on it."

"You bet."

"I called him on the carpet," she said, pouring the wine, "about the leak to Rossiter. Of course he tried to lie out of it, then suddenly he blurted, 'All right, Myra, I did it for you, and I know Walter would have approved. This Dr. Carpenter is no good. I can see you're attracted to him, and it's all wrong.' With that he stretches across the desk and grabs my hand in a clammy grip, like so." The Congresswoman dropped down beside Carpenter on the couch and seized his hand. "And I mean *clammy!* Slippery, slimy, you know? Sort of nervously squeezing my fingers and burbling on in that vein, his eyes all white ringed behind his glasses, wetting his lips in a disgusting way, and for all I knew he was about to propose marriage, or something even more gross. Well, I cut him short, told him flat out that he was through. I pulled my hand loose and went to wipe it off, and when I came back he was gone."

"Why did you ever keep Carkin around?" Carpenter said, sipping sherry. "He struck me as a prime creep."

"Oh, he knew the ropes, and I did need him at first. But I never could stand him. For one thing, he kept looking at my legs so damn much."

"Now, Myra, fellows will look at your legs. They're nice."

"Not the way Earle did. He always made me think my panties were slipping down. Anyway, so much for Earle, that's the least of what happened today. Right after the hearing this morning, Aaron came into my office with this bright idea about my wielding my feminine whatever on Bob Hurtle. Well, in the film business that was half the way I operated, but Congress is a new milieu for that ploy, at least for me it is. Also, I'm getting long in the tooth for it, but okay, I figured, for the good old Red, White, and Blue . . . more sherry?"

"Sure, go on."

"I can use more, I'm sort of frazzled — well, so, old Bob Hurtle had his feet up on his desk, jacket off, relaxing, when I popped into his office to tell him what a great number he'd done on Homer Aptor. Guy, he just ate it up! He preened, he turned bright pink with pleasure. We had a good laugh over Bambi and the cake, then I congratulated him on coming up with Rocovsky — *'Bob, how on earth did you do that? It was masterly, it turned the hearings completely around.'* At that he became even pinker, and said he'd phoned Rocovsky for help out of desperation, after Wen Mei Li's big impact at the hearing. And by sheer luck, Rocovsky had just had this sensational insight about the connection of the Higgs boson signatures and the solar magnetic bursts, so he talked Rocovsky into coming and testifying —"

It was on the tip of Carpenter's tongue to tell her that the insight had been his, but he spoke no word. If the Rock wanted the credit, let him have it.

"Well, that was my cue. I asked Bob which of those three ways of going for the Higgs boson he favored — Rocovsky's, or Kulka's, or Waxahachie. Bob admitted that as an Illinois project he favored Kulka's, but he had to think about it, whereupon I struck like a cobra. I said it was a pity we couldn't go on all three tracks at once, but of course that was a budget-buster and out of the question, wasn't it? At that, old Bob sits up and gives me a hard stare. 'You're talking Manhattan Project, Myra, aren't you?' *'You mean that atom-bomb business, Bob? Wasn't that all different? It was wartime.'* I'm no Marilyn Monroe, Guy, but I used to do pretty well playing dumb-bunny parts. After all, that's what *you* thought I was —"

"Not once we'd talked for five minutes —"

"Anyway, Bob Hurtle still thinks so. The cunning little ex-movie star, you know? He's never taken me seriously. 'Of course,' he said, half talking to himself, 'you're right, this isn't World War Two, it's different, the urgency isn't there. On the other hand, knocking the Chinese out of the box on the Higgs boson is one hell of a national priority now . . . excuse me a second —' He took a pad and started to scrawl. I said I'd be off, I'd just looked in to compliment him on what he'd done today. He walked me out of his office, holding my elbow friendlylike, and lo and behold, right after lunch comes this urgent caucus call for the California delegation! And our Chairman tells us that Illinois and Texas are caucusing, too, on a Hurtle proposal for the three Chairmen to co-sponsor an amendment to the Appropriations Bill, authorizing development money for all three tracks —"

"Good going, Myra! Let's hear it for the dumb bunnies —"

"Not so fast. Of course Texas will be for it, and Hurtle can bring along Illinois, but our unruly California delegation is all over the place, from flaming liberals to hard-shell conservatives, and nobody much likes Texas. The idea that the misbegotten Super Collider might get the water pumped out, and billions more dollars pumped in, had the place in an uproar, so the Chairman didn't dare take a vote. We're caucusing again in the morning, and it'll go down to the wire. Say, are you getting hungry? I am. I'm suddenly famished. Let's eat, yes?"

"I'm all for it."

"Good. I'll change out of this suit later. Lord, I'm getting tired of suits, Guy. I've *become* a suit, you know? A suit with hips and a bust. Revolting."

In a dim dining alcove off the living room, on a small round table set for two, tall candles were burning, champagne cooled in a bucket, and at the settings there were oysters on the half shell. "Wow, Myra!" said Carpenter. "The works! Bless your heart."

"Why not? Farewell dinner," said Myra. "Open the champagne, Professor."

The cork came out with a loud festive pop. "I should be throwing a dinner for you," he said, helping her into her chair and pouring wine. "You've been my good angel in a very bad time."

"My pleasure. What do we drink to?"

"To dumb bunnies in Congress," he suggested.

"Nothing doing." She laughed and lifted her glass. "To the Higgs boson, the reason we met."

"Right, the Higgs boson, by all means," said Carpenter, remembering Penny's toast to the boson at the Athenaeum. They clinked glasses and drank.

"Now then," she said as they ate. "You've left me hanging all day. How the devil did you get out of the Chinese embassy, really? Come to think of it, with the media dogging Wen Mei Li's every move, how did you get *in* there?"

"Well, it's a story. To start with, there was this Chinese laundryman who —"

"No, no, don't tell me, let me guess!" She chortled. "You were smuggled in and out in a laundry basket, like Falstaff!"

"Not even close." He described how he was picked up and

driven past the reporters at the entrance, to the rear gate where Zhang Zhui brought him in. "He had it all planned, that Zhang Zhui, he's a shifty one —"

"Guy, he couldn't have planned for Rossiter's showing up at the back gate —"

"Ah, but he had, even for that."

When he told her about the tunnel escape, and Rossiter left camped at the back gate until midnight, Myra Kadane clapped her hands and cried, "Bravo! Gorgeous! I fear the Chinese will inherit the earth."

"Zhang Zhui didn't dig the tunnel, Myra. It was just there."

"He had it up his sleeve all the time. Damn clever, the Chinese."

"This is terrific champagne," said Carpenter.

"Walter's private stock, and there's more on ice. Drink hearty, Professor."

They both drank hearty.

Afterward, feeling jollier than he would have thought conceivable a day or two before, the physicist sat in the living room, finishing his champagne while Myra changed out of the suit. Walter Kadane seemed to be beaming at him from the wall, a good host glad to see the guest enjoying his choice wine. He heard her gaily humming as she came tripping down the stairs. "Jesus Christ, Myra!" he exclaimed when she walked in. Then he burst out laughing. "Okay, you got me."

With a slightly abashed smile, she did a pirouette in the Shanghai robe. "Did I? I kind of thought I would. Anything for a laugh, you know. Actually, it's tight." She patted her middle. "I haven't jogged for a week, and I feel the difference."

"Myra, you're thin as a rail." *Why,* WHY *did I blow the moment with that stupid laugh? She looks so enchanting . . .*

"Ho! But I do keep trying. When I was acting I had to live on cottage cheese and Ry-Krisp. I'm a natural roly-poly. Walter always said he liked me that way, not that I believed him, but it was wonderful to let myself go for a while. Back in Bel-Air I still have a closetful of fat dresses. How do you stay so thin?"

"Genes. Tennis. Indifference to food. I like Penny's cooking, but at work I just drink coffee all day —"

"Have you called her yet?"

"Nope."

"Why not? Aaron thinks you're home free, and he's Old Man Caution."

"I didn't consult him about calling my angry wife, and I'm not consulting you, Madame Congresswoman." Slight silence. "Sorry."

"No offense. Not my business."

Shouldn't have snapped at her like that, what's wrong with me? "The thing is, Myra, it's a cinch that Penny watched Mei testify yesterday and got riled up again. That's all."

"I quite understand, Guy. Tell me about your meeting with Mei." At his startled reaction she added hastily, "Oh, never mind, never mind. I get pushy sometimes —"

"No, I'll tell you about it." He hesitated. "Something about it, anyway. We met in the guest suite of the embassy, and she was pleasant enough, but stiff and formal, not at all herself — actually distant, almost chatty . . ."

The maid walked in dressed to leave, purse under arm, bringing champagne and glasses in an ice bucket. "Cold now, senora. *Buenas noches.*" She left it on the coffee table and went out.

"Nice thought, Myra."

"Well, just if we feel like it. She was being distant, you say —"

"Yes, clearly she figured — or she knew — we were being overheard. We talked politely about this and that, then she invited me out on the balcony to see the view of Washington, so she said." He fell silent. Myra looked at him inquiringly. It was a minute or so before he spoke again, in a strained shaken tone. "Well, it was all different out there, I'll tell you that much. As Mei put it, the last time in this life . . . We couldn't have been out there five minutes, though, when the goddamned telephone rang inside, Zhang Zhui calling, to tell me about the reporter at the back gate."

They were both quiet, so quiet that Carpenter could hear the ticking of an antique clock on the mantelpiece.

"I've never known requited love," Myra said.

Carpenter stared at her, then at the portrait.

"Oh, Guy, you know perfectly well what I mean. You had Wen Mei Li, and you have Penny. In Waxahachie I made stupid fun of your chaste Chinese first love because I envied you so much. As for the men in my life, Walter always excepted, what can I say? Bad cards in a losing hand. Walter saved a drowning cat, I love and cherish his memory, always will —" Her voice trailed off.

A long silence. The Congresswoman's eyes were brimming. His emotions roiled, Carpenter wanted to take her in his arms but could not, and he blurted, "Look, Myra, I'm thinking I have to face old Bob Hurtle tomorrow, and one never knows —"

"Right, right. You're welcome to stay for a while, Guy, of course, but one never knows indeed —"

"Why don't we open this bottle," he said, "before we call for a cab? The way those drivers dawdle, we might polish it off before he gets here."

"Excellent idea. I'm all for the bottle. And much as I hate to see you go, for the taxi."

He opened the wine and poured it while she telephoned. "Well," she said, picking up a glass, "to the autumn leaves at Cornell."

"Oh, you caught that, did you?"

"I did indeed. Very moving, if one knew."

Carpenter raised his glass. "And, Congresswoman, to the lavender and cinnamon in Waxahachie."

Her eyes spilled over. She brushed them with the back of her hand. "God love you, Dr. Carpenter."

A horn honked outside when they had drunk only one glass apiece. "Wouldn't you know?" she said. "Just this one time, it had to come fast." She took his hand and walked with him toward the door. "Well, it's been lovely. See you tomorrow in the Cannon Caucus Room."

"Thanks, Myra, thanks for everything —" All at once they were embracing and kissing at the door, again and again and yet again, despairing passionate kisses, and she managed to murmur between kisses, "The last time in this life."

"Who can say, Myra?" He could hardly get out the words. "If the driver can't find the hotel, I'll be back."

"If so, the latch will be off. Bye, Professor."

When he was gone she turned out the lights, except for one pencil-thin ray, illuminating the portrait from a hole in the ceiling. She sat on the couch facing the portrait. "Well, Walter, so that's that." She poured and drank. "Waste not, want not, eh, dear? It's a fine champagne."

"He won't be back," Walter said.

"Oh, who asked you? Shut up."

"And what were you thinking, putting on that dumb robe? He laughed at you."

"Shut up, I say, or I'll turn you to the wall."

"Anyway, what would have been the point, Myra? You're getting long in the tooth for one-night stands."

She jumped up and snapped off the ceiling light, leaving the room black dark except for flickers from the candles burning down in the alcove. By that weak light she finished the wine.

31. THE TURNING

We all have good days, however infrequent. Guy Carpenter was aroused next morning by a blaze of sunshine full on his face, ricocheted from a glittering window across the alley into his gloomy dingy hotel bedroom. The golden light faded before he was fully awake, but the sunny theme of the day was set. Two e-mails on his laptop sustained the theme with variations, one from his son, one from Rocovsky. With a twinge of concern he called up John's message first.

> I give up, Dad. Where are you? All's well here at Grandma's house. Dinah now loves Granny, but she thinks I'm a fake because I'm not you, so I get the cold shoulder. Mom's in good shape and she wants to talk to you. Better call her. Will I see you before I return to Samoa?
>
> Love,
> John

Fine, nothing too worrisome there. *"She wants to talk to you"!* A cheering note, after words stormed at him a week ago: *"I have trouble even talking to you —"* Next, what could the Rock want?

Carpenter —

I'm sure you realize why I ignored you at the hearing. Any indication that I was there on your behalf would have been contrary to your interest, and to my purpose.

Your discernment of the flaw in the *Nature* article was a grand stroke. I suggest that you and I collaborate on a letter to the *Astrophysical Journal.* I've already talked in very guarded terms to the editor, an old friend, and he's eager for it. That 1973 disclosure about the gamma rays remains a star in the journal's crown, so we may even be featured on the cover. We'll have to clear it with the Air Force, of course, which could take months. I'll be making notes on these long flights to and from India, and when I get back let's work up the letter together. My name will be under yours in the signature. It's your achievement, I merely confirm it.

Well, Carpenter, it's a long lane that knows no turning, and you've been down a long mucky lane. Welcome to the public life, and good luck with your testimony today. My best to Penny — and of course to the charming widow Kadane, if you happen to talk to her.

Rocovsky

Charming widow Kadane, indeed. Just like the all-seeing old Rock to pick up those vibrations.

Well, well, a letter in the *Astrophysical Journal* authored by himself and Rocovsky, with his own name first! It was more peer recognition than he had yet achieved in his career. It would raise his stature and brighten his earnings future. Call Penny with this news? Not a bad icebreaker, but on second thought such a phone conversation might be touch and go, perhaps still shadowed by the autumn leaves of Cornell. The smart thing was to fly straight to Binghamton after the morning's hearing, which was bound to be short, and give her the good word face-to-face. One look into Penny's eyes should tell him how he really stood. Hold off on the phone call, just pack up and get ready to leave once and for all this godforsaken fleabag called the Millard Fillmore.

So, first order of business was to check on flight schedules. He called one airline and another, getting busy signals, or "Eine Kleine Nachtmusik," or the "William Tell Overture." Shaving and dressing, he composed in his mind sharp astute sentences and whole paragraphs for the letter to the *Astrophysical Journal.* He hurried to the computer to bat off these gems before he forgot them. Written out they seemed remarkably flat and dull, but anyway, there they were. He called the airlines again: more busy signals, also "Humoresque" and "Clair de Lune," with assurances that his call was important.

He threw together his meager belongings and was about to try the airlines once more when the phone rang. Jules Berkovits said, "Professor, I have to leave Washington pronto. I can't stay for the hearing. I'm calling from Charley Sturdevant's office, and I don't want to whistle off without saying good-bye. What are your plans? You'll be through with this nonsense this morning."

"I want to rejoin Penny, she's staying with her mother in upstate New York, but I'm having hell's own time trying to get a flight —"

"No problem, let me handle that. I'll send my car and driver to fetch you. Just check out and come along. Room H-218, Capitol Building."

As Chief Counsel, Sturdevant rated a private chamber in the commodious Appropriations offices. There Carpenter found Berkovits talking on the phone and puffing on a cigar. "Right, Clancy, I should be in Roanoke at two o'clock. Have the lady meet me at your office if possible. Otherwise I'll call on her at home." He hung up and handed Carpenter an envelope. "Morning, Guy. This came FedEx, I had Warshaw send it to my hotel."

Dear Professor Carpenter:

As per my e-mail, our contract is still in force. You have received $25,000, and on start of filming another $25,000 is due. Cy Finkle is rushing the screenplay, we roll in October. Meantime, recognizing your special scientific eminence in the boson field as recently testified by Dr. Wen Mei Li, I've agreed with your counsel, Jules Berkovits, that at this time you are to receive a bonus of $50,000. Check herewith.

Cordial regards,
Timothy Warshaw

The scrawled signature was *Tim.* The check was on orange paper, with a detachable white section full of legal jargon. Carpenter passed the letter and check without a word to the lawyer, who gave them a glance, nodded, and handed them back. "That's right. Total, a hundred thousand. Now as to that other thing you asked about, the airplane, I'm sorry —"

Carpenter interrupted him, contemplating the check in his hand with a bemused expression. "A fifty-thousand-dollar bonus! They really paid it! For what? It's lunacy, Jules."

"Relax and cash it. Think about athletes' salaries," said Berkovits, rubbing both hands over his eyes, "or the fees I get. For a beautiful brief moment an unworldly scientist had a film producer over a barrel. Enjoy." He took a last puff at the cigar and ground it out. "Aaron Kadane's got your situation in hand, and I hate to miss the last inning, but down in Roanoke there's this tobacco billionaire's fourth wife, a singer. She seems to have done in her aged hubby, murdered him in his bed, except she denies everything and wants to talk to me . . . Hello, would this be your flier friend?"

"Morning, Dr. Carpenter." The grizzled sunburned pilot, in his usual Hawaiian shirt and chinos, gave Carpenter a familiar grin.

"Ray!"

"Yes, sir, Jerry's gassing up the Falcon at Reagan North Terminal, ready to go in an hour —"

Utterly staggered, the physicist turned on Berkovits. "For God's sake, Jules, I was just fantasizing —"

"I knew you were, but I thought, well, no harm in trying. I'm sorry they couldn't let you have the plane for two weeks, just for ten days. They had a scheduling problem. I couldn't bear down too hard on Warshaw, he was already weeping about the bonus —"

"Well, I'll be a son of a bitch," said Carpenter.

"Nah, sons of bitches are my specialty. You're a living doll. I'll be going." Berkovits stood up and shook hands. "I'm glad Aaron called me in on this flap of yours, Professor. Something different, no money or gore, just science and politics. As my practice goes, a breath of fresh air."

Carpenter was an undemonstrative sort, and he surprised himself by grabbing the lawyer in a hug. Berkovits said, returning the hug, "Good-bye, Deep Throat Physicist. Don't rent any more post-office boxes."

Without the buzz of crowded spectators and their collective body warmth, the Cannon Caucus Room seemed desolate and chilly. Many rows of empty chairs conveyed a bleak picture of waned interest.

When the committee filed in to the dais, Hurtle's pleased demeanor at once told Carpenter that the deal had been struck. Wesley called on the Co-Chairman, and Hurtle spoke about the agreement at some length. He cited the Manhattan Project as a precedent, heaped praise on the Chairmen of Texas and California, and wound up with an orotund rhetoric flourish. "So, as a son of the great state of Illinois, I say may the best project win out! May the industries of all fifty states take part in these historic endeavors, with multitudinous subcontracts! Above all, may the United States of America demonstrate once and for all its preeminence in world science by finding the Higgs boson!"

"I thank my distinguished colleague," Horace Wesley said, "for the pragmatic outcome of these hearings, reflecting credit on the Congress, on American science, and on our free press. I've served on many House hearings down the busy years, none more satisfying and productive than this inquiry. For Dr. Guy Carpenter, our last scheduled witness, I turn over the gavel to my Co-Chairman."

"Oh, Lord," Carpenter muttered.

Aaron Kadane, sotto voce: "Not a problem."

"Dr. Carpenter, no need for you to be sworn in," Hurtle said, smiling pleasantly. "This committee is well aware that it was you who discovered the flaw in the Chinese project, for in a memorandum Dr. Herman Rocovsky submitted for the record, he gives you full credit. He told me you probably preferred to be kept out of his testimony, and I'm sure he was right. You've had enough media attention, I daresay, to last you a lifetime. We're used to that glare here, but a dedicated scientist like yourself doesn't expect it to penetrate his laboratory. I remember with pleasure the guided tour you gave me on the Superconducting Super Collider. If I've been a bit abrasive here now and then, well, that's our style. The work you scientists do is important and lasting, what we do is noisy and transient. You're discharged as a witness, with thanks for your patience. I invite you to comment at any length you wish."

Carpenter got to his feet. "Thank you, Mr. Co-Chairman, I just want to go home." As he sat down, the few spectators laughed and applauded. Hurtle laughed too and banged the gavel. "These hearings are adjourned sine die."

Carpenter asked Kadane, "Was that okay?"

"Spot-on. Look, Myra's waving."

Carpenter's eyes stung, seeing her smile as she went out with a gesture of good-bye. "Quite a lady, your sister-in-law," he said. "Thanks, Aaron, for pulling me through this."

"She did it all," said Kadane, "getting you shifted from the top to the bottom of the witness list, out of Hurtle's line of fire while it mattered. Only she could have done it."

The Falcon was smaller than Guy Carpenter remembered, not all that luxurious, and not all that silent, either. When it took off in a steep climb, thrusting him back in his seat, the motors seemed to bellow. He had the aircraft fixed in his memory as little less marvelous and quiet than Air Force One. It was hardly that, but having it at his disposal for ten days was marvel enough, and the armchair was just as soft as he remembered.

Ray Luntz came into the cabin when they leveled off, removing his sunglasses, and told the physicist they were flying to a small airport twenty minutes by car from Binghamton. Beyond that, what did Dr. Carpenter have in mind? Carpenter told him his plans, and the pilot made notes. "Is all that feasible, Ray?"

"No problem, sir. As it happens, I've just come back from Samoa. So — Alaska first, you say, then Samoa? I'll make up a flight plan. How long will you be here in Binghamton?"

"Just overnight. How did you happen to go to Samoa?"

"Scouting locations for a *Mutiny on the Bounty* film, sir, with the producer and director."

"What, not *Mutiny on the Bounty* AGAIN?"

"Well, I heard them talk a lot about it, of course. They have a fresh angle. Fletcher Christian is African American, and Captain Bligh is gay."

"It's an inspiration. Will my cell phone connect to a phone in Binghamton?"

"Why, sure."

It was John who answered. Penny was in the garden with the baby, enjoying the sunshine after three straight days of rain. "No, no, don't call her," Carpenter said, much relieved. "There's this small airport not far from Binghamton. We'll be landing there about four o'clock. Now here's what's happening, Johnny Boy, so you'll know what to tell her. Be there to meet me, okay?" He gave his son the name and location of the field, and ran rapidly through the events of the past days, explaining about the airplane but not mentioning the bonus or the Rocovsky letter. John became more and more amused and excited as Guy talked.

"It all sounds terrific, Dad. How did I know you'd come out smelling like a rose? Hard work and clean living, that's you. I'm delighted, and proud of you —"

"How's Mom, really?"

"Oh, fine. She'll be thrilled by all this. I still have no idea what really went on between you two, you know Mom, next to her the Sphinx was a gossip, but whatever it was, she's pretty well over it, so don't worry. We'll meet you at the airport."

"Perfect," said Carpenter, though not entirely reassured by *pretty well* and *don't worry.*

As the Falcon swooped in over the trees, he could see Dinah waving in Penny's arms. Penny handed the baby to John when Guy descended from the plane, rushed to him, and threw herself in his embrace. "Hi. You're something else, aren't you? Getting off scot-free, arriving in a private plane —"

"I just stumble along, Penny, trying my miserable best —"

She brushed his cheek with kisses. "The first time you were ever in real trouble, I didn't stand by you."

"All's well that ends well." Dinah was stretching out her arms and babbling at him. John looked stouter and older, and the premature white streaks surprised his father. He gave over his little sister. She put her hands to Carpenter's face, her eyes alight in a glorious smile. "Hello, sweetheart. Yes, I'm back. So, John, you're marrying a Samoan princess, or queen? I'm not quite clear on that yet."

"Tell you all about her. Wait till you see her pictures. They're at Grandma's house."

While John drove, Carpenter told Penny at greater length what he had summarized for his son on the phone. "Well, now I sort of understand," she said, "but it's still confounding, especially about the plane. I've seen this man Berkovits on TV often. He looks weird, with that long lanky gray hair and the blue-jeans outfit, but he must be mighty smart. Was he your lawyer at the hearing?"

"Not exactly. Sort of an adviser. Congresswoman Kadane has this brother-in-law who handled it, a friend of Berkovits, a Georgetown Law professor —"

"How fortunate," said Penny, and perhaps it was Carpenter's imagination, but he heard flash-red undertones. He hastened on to the Rock's proposal for a joint letter to the *Astrophysical Journal,* which led into the large topic of the magnetic bursts from the solar flares. So they were off the Myra Kadane ground, and Carpenter was careful to stay off it.

"Well, Dad," said John, "I congratulate you! That's astrophysics, where there are hard facts. What you did was cut through to a hard fact that made a difference. In anthropology there's only soft palaver that makes no difference."

"I've been hearing such talk for days," said Penny. "You'll get an earful tonight, no doubt."

So Carpenter did, that evening when Penny was bathing Dinah and putting her to bed. John showed him the pictures of Siva, a lissome olive-skinned girl, and his father resolutely suppressed a notion that she resembled the young Mei Li. She was Polynesian, not Chinese, he told himself, and there was no connection except in his still-overheated mind.

"It's terrific that you're planning to visit us," John said. "You'll see for yourself how bright and sophisticated her family is. In their way, that is. Like the aborigines in Australia, these Samoans revere Nature and believe in their gods. Siva does herself, though she's been to college in Melbourne. We Westerners are destroying Nature, and we have no gods."

"I try to understand Nature," said his father mildly, "and I have a God. I'm not about to argue about God, Johnny, we'll kick Him around in Samoa."

"Absolutely, Dad. Can't wait."

Carpenter and Penny talked far into the night about the week's events and about his travel plans, which raised the immediate urgent question of Dinah. "Look," he said, "I promised you we would eat wild salmon in Alaska. We're going to eat wild salmon in Alaska."

"I hear and I obey, mighty hunter, mighty warrior," said Penny. "Samoa's the problem. I know Mrs. Atkinson can look after Dinah for two or three days." Mrs. Atkinson was a motherly parent of five children, who had taken Dinah under her wing when Penny had been laid up with the flu. "Ten days pose a money problem. She charges like fury. We can't afford ten days."

"Well there, Penny, we now have elbow room." He told her about the bonus from the Warshaw production.

When Penny got over gasping and laughing, which took a while, she said soberly, "What are you paying this Berkovits? He'd be entitled to ask for half, it's all his doing."

"Well —" In that slight pause, Carpenter's brain neurons fired a series of instantaneous connections: Berkovits and his hopeless love for Sue Ellen Thompson, their winter break in Aspen, the lawyer's equating it with Mei Li and himself in Shanghai, and for that sentimental reason refusing a fee. "Aaron Kadane is a very old friend of his, you see, and Berkovits wouldn't take money from me, though I tried to pay him."

"How generous," Penny said and let it go at that. Her husband's opaque look was recognizable and impenetrable. Something was behind it, but fifty thousand was fifty thousand, a gift horse if ever there was one.

"In short, Penny, we can pay Atkinson whatever she asks. Start working on it in the morning."

"Believe me, I will."

That night, when they retired to Penny's room, declining Grandma's offer of her double bed, it was an awkward business, after the brief sharp freeze, getting into her rather narrow bed together. Carpenter was not sure about making a pass at his wife, and whatever she was thinking, she did not make it easy. After a while, however, there they were in each other's arms, starting to make love in the old familiar delicious way, and it was going along hotly when they were both startled by a tremendous walloping BANG at the screen outside the window, followed by a loud *Meow! Meow! MEOW!!!*

"God in heaven," exclaimed Penny, leaping out of bed. "It's Sweeney. He's on the screen! He's come back! Oh, *Sweeney!*" She opened the window, loosened the screen, and in jumped the cat. She pounced on him. "Sweeney! Sweetheart, welcome back! Where have you been? Oh, Guy, feel him, he's just skin and bones!"

"So he is," said Guy, not wholly enchanted by his return just then. But he had been hearing a lot of moaning this evening about the beast's disappearance, and he was glad for Penny.

"Guy, darling," Penny said, "you know I love you to tiny little pieces, but do you mind if I just go down first and feed this poor little kitty? He's barely alive."

The animal was clawing at her with more than a semblance of

life, but how could he argue? Penny left, and was a long time coming back.

A very long time. Time enough for Guy Carpenter to lie there and think over everything that had happened since the bad day when the animal had gotten out, the same day he had learned that the Chinese had the Higgs boson. Time enough to recall the Bel-Air party, the trip to Waxahachie, the explosion over the post-office box, the Cannon Caucus Room hearings, Mei on the balcony, Myra in the robe; time enough for him to drowse, for this had been a long complicated day, and he was beginning to sink into sleep when he felt her slip in beside him.

"Hi," he muttered.

"Oh? You're awake?"

"Barely."

"Good enough." She wrapped her arms powerfully around him, and the Deep Throat Physicist was home.

ABOUT THE AUTHOR

Herman Wouk's acclaimed novels include the Pulitzer Prize–winning *The Caine Mutiny; Marjorie Morningstar; Don't Stop the Carnival; Youngblood Hawke; The Winds of War; War and Remembrance; Inside, Outside; The Hope;* and *The Glory.* Earlier works are *City Boy* and *Aurora Dawn.*

Look for these other novels by Herman Wouk

The Winds of War

"Hypnotically readable. . . . Wouk is a matchless storyteller with a gift for characterization, an ear for convincing dialogue, and a masterful grasp of what was at stake in World War II."

— *San Francisco Chronicle*

War and Remembrance

"The genius of *The Winds of War* and *War and Remembrance* is that they not only tell the story of the Holocaust, but tell it within the context of World War II, without which there is no understanding it."

— *Washington Post*

Inside, Outside

"Absorbing . . . uproariously funny. . . . Throughout these pages one can see Wouk's mastery of the novelist's supreme art, the ability to relate social history to individual destiny." — *National Review*

The Hope

"*The Hope* is moving, informative, ultimately a glorification of man's possibilities. It is in this new country of Israel — where the values of the citizen are the values of the family, where the soldier is also a scholar — that modern man has the most hope. The title is apt, the book is magnificent." — Anthony Burgess

The Glory

"A sprawling, action-packed novel. . . . *The Glory* is gripping historical fiction. Wouk's portraits of historical figures are altogether convincing." — *Philadelphia Inquirer*

BACK BAY BOOKS

Available wherever paperbacks are sold